CATEGORY 5

CATEGORY 5

Paul Mark Tag

To Jess,

Best wishes!

Paul Mark Tag

December 2013

iUniverse, Inc.

New York Lincoln Shanghai

Category 5

Copyright © 2005 by Paul Mark Tag

iUniverse books may be ordered through booksellers or by contacting:

iUniverse
2021 Pine Lake Road, Suite 100
Lincoln, NE 68512
www.iuniverse.com
1-800-Authors (1-800-288-4677)

Cover image courtesy of MODIS Rapid Response Project at NASA/GSFC: Hurricane Isabel, September 14, 2003, 1445 UTC.

ISBN: 0-595-34075-X (pbk)
ISBN: 0-595-67058-X (cloth)

Printed in the United States of America

CONTENTS

▼

Acknowledgments

Many people contributed to the research and proofing that went into the completion of this novel. Foremost among them is my wife, Becky, who offered patience, encouragement, insightful readings, and constructive criticism. Beyond her, my overwhelming thanks go to my primary reader, Robin Brody, who kept my plot lines consistent and my meteorological references accurate. I need to acknowledge a host of secondary readers. In alphabetical order: Doug Basham, Myra Golphenee, Jeff Hawkins, Ward Hindman, Kris Hoffman, Fran Morris, Ann Schrader, and Alan Weinstein.

Tara and Cihan Ağaçayak graciously agreed to additional scouting for my Istanbul location and provided the Turkish translations. Tina Hay, Editor of *The Penn Stater* magazine, provided reference material concerning black enrollment and experiences at Pennsylvania State University during the 1970s. Brian Kolts gave me a tour of, and much information regarding, the Bermuda Weather Service. In addition to proofing the manuscript, Alan Weinstein proved to be a valuable tour guide for my Washington, DC locations.

I would be remiss if I did not include my writing instructor and mentor, author Arline Chase, who taught me the essence of good storytelling and provided critical reviews early in the writing.

Two books provided important reference material:

Evans, Eli N., 1997: *The Provincials: A Personal History of Jews in the South*. Free Press Paperbacks, 1230 Avenue of the Americas, New York, NY, 391 pp.

O'Balance, Edgar, 1997: *No Victor, No Vanquished*. Presidio Press, 505B San Marin Drive, Suite 300, Novato, CA 94945-1340, 370 pp.

All persons and materials listed above provided invaluable, accurate advice and data. Any errors that remain in the manuscript are mine.

Author's Note

My novel, *Category 5*, is a work of fiction. That said, I have attempted to create an interesting story set within realistic scientific, theoretical, and geographical boundaries.

The science behind my book is believable. While it is currently impossible to produce a laser beam powerful enough to heat ocean water to any significant degree, the concept is reasonable and the resulting effects on a hurricane plausible. The meteorology discussed in the novel is real.

Except for the Suez Canal, Christmas Island, and the CIA, the geographic locations chosen for scenes in my book come from my personal travels; I have scouted the locations for realism and have imagined the action occurring there. Although the locations are real, the Mountain High Inn in Fort Collins, Colorado and the Asylum Tavern in Washington, DC are imaginary.

The time given at the beginning of a chapter is valid for the location in which the action occurs. When that location is ambiguous (as in an airplane) and the time is important, I state the time zone (e.g., Eastern Daylight Time).

Please note the Glossary and Cast of Characters at the end of the book. Information there will assist the reader as the action unfolds. The mission statements and information for the various organizations come from their Web sites.

PROLOGUE

▼

Getting Started

Kantara East, East Bank of the Suez Canal: 30° 51'N Latitude,
32° 19'E Longitude
Saturday, 1435 hours, October 6, 1973

Back then, he went by the name of Ahmed Abu Hamasay. He scanned left, then right, to appraise his troops. As part of a wave of twelve thousand assault craft, they had successfully forded the Suez Canal. Battle had begun for soldiers of Egypt's Second Army.

Hamasay's superiors had honed his wits and skills to a blade's edge, more so than back in 1967. Hamasay ran his fingers along the indentation, a facial scar that would be a lifelong reminder of Egypt's earlier war with Israel. He and his fellow citizens had waited six years for this moment. To demonstrate to the world that Egypt could fight and that their soldiers were not the cowards the Israelis believed.

In 1967, Israel had surprise-attacked Egypt and destroyed nearly their entire air force. Their forces had also routed Egypt's ninety thousand man army and taken much of their Soviet weaponry. Further, the loss of the Gaza Strip and the Sinai Desert created an Egyptian embarrassment of the highest order. After much planning and preparation, the Egyptian military intended to restore their wounded pride.

Having survived the canal crossing, Hamasay, now a Captain, surged forward with confidence. Using wooden and rope ladders, his company climbed the sand embankments the Israelis had built as a buffer. Thus began the War of Ramadan. The Israelis would call it the Yom Kippur War. To everyone else, fourteen hundred hours on October 6 signaled, simply, the start of the Arab-Israeli War of 1973.

Atop the sand ramparts, Hamasay surveyed the scene and watched as his men set their flag. His eyes burned from the smoke the Egyptians had created as a screen. Deafening concussions from their artillery affected him less so and reminded him of 1967. Hamasay had proven himself in battle then, one of the few who had. He recalled, painfully, the exploding ordnance in their midst. Pain from the shrapnel wound to his face still bothered him late at night; hearing was absent from his right ear. Minutes later, he and his men forced an Israeli retreat. For his bravery, Hamasay received the highest level of the *nuut al-shaga'a al-askarii*, the Military Medal of Courage, and the privilege to attend the Nasser Higher Military Academy. But beyond that fulfillment, a sensitive memory clouded his thoughts. The same mortar that erased half of his hearing had also snuffed out the life of his brother, Mohammed.

Hamasay's focus returned to his men and he charged forward. Initially, their campaign went well, with Egypt overrunning fourteen Israeli forts on the East Bank by the end of the first day. Captain Hamasay watched as Egypt's air defense above the canal brought down many planes and forced back the Israeli Air Force. As combat progressed, the Egyptian offensive necessarily switched to a defensive posture. After two weeks of heavy fighting, the American and Russian superpowers arranged ceasefires—although Israel ignored these truces and continued their skirmishes. But following the last round of fire, Egyptian armed forces stood tall. They had proved their mettle. The world now saw that the mighty Israeli war machine was less than invincible.

As Captain Hamasay witnessed battles surge back and forth, the dominant edge that modern technology gave in combat, sometimes to Israel, sometimes to Egypt, became clear. Technology often overcame the stupidity of a general or the ruthlessness of the enemy. In 1967, Israeli Phantom jet fighters, developed by the Americans, dominated the skies and came highly respected. Nonetheless, the first days of the 1973 war devastated them because they fell victim not to other aircraft, but to the surface to air missile. In terms of reconnaissance from space, compared to the Americans, the Soviets held the advantage in flexibility and provided vital information to the Egyptians. But it was the superior American-provided TOW anti-tank missiles that destroyed many Egyptian tanks.

Long before the War of Ramadan stalemated into years of back and forth conflict, Captain Hamasay accepted as fact his observation that technology still undiscovered held the key to success in any future conflict. He looked to the skies and mused over his epiphany. He would dedicate his life to make a difference, not only to his country and beliefs, but also to the memory of his brother Mohammed. Advanced technology was paramount—no matter where it came from.

CHAPTER 1

▼

CRITICAL COMPONENT

South Point, Christmas Island, Indian Ocean: 10° 5'S Latitude, 105° 42'E Longitude
Friday, 0700 hours, October 6, 2006

"Speaking on behalf of my people, I thank you for your contribution to our cause. You can be assured that you will be praised not only here on earth, but in the afterlife as well."

The man most people called Ghali, who would soon speak these words, recalled too well that he had used them before. Several situations had dictated it. Tonight he would fight the demons of recrimination as he always had. There would be no sleep for him. Ghosts from the past, some friendly and others not, would make sure of that. For now, he would force himself to ignore the consequences of his upcoming actions.

Ghali looked to the east for propitious signs. The orange sphere burned bright, not far above the eastern horizon. Easterly trade winds barely ruffled the Australian flag at the entrance to the Asian Pacific Space Centre, or APSC as the locals called it. No clouds spoiled the milky translucent sky. Perfect conditions for a space launch. Only thirty minutes until liftoff.

Just to the west of the launch area, Ghali's body cut an imposing figure against the background of sky: lean, straight-backed, hands crossed behind his back, face stern and determined. Perspiration stained the baseball cap covering graying strands of black wavy hair, inherited from his mother's side of the family. He still felt uncomfortable wearing such strange head-gear, part of the price of fitting in. Tense facial features and pulsating temples revealed anxiety.

Ghali blinked into the bright sun. He reassured himself that commercial space flights were reliable these days. But until his payload launched safely into orbit, he would worry. His job description demanded it. *What was it the Americans say? Don't count your chickens before they're hatched?* The Americans had a saying for everything.

Ghali scanned the horizon and puffed out his chest. *Why should he not be proud?* After today, his superiors would praise his name. He alone had coordinated the acquisition of the primary payload, its transport to Christmas Island, and now its launch into space. He had recognized the value of technology and taken the initiative.

Ghali reflected on his recent journey. Truth be told, he would be sad to leave Christmas Island and its inhabitants. He remembered his faux pas, when he had called the local residents natives. No natives lived here. Some sixty percent of the population descended from Chinese lineage. And they, as well as smaller proportions of Malays and Caucasians, had emigrated from Australia, twelve hundred miles to the southeast.

Measuring scarcely four by fifteen miles, Christmas Island hadn't been settled until the United Kingdom annexed it in 1888. A phosphate mine provided income for most of the following century. In 1958, the UK transferred sovereignty to Australia. Recently, tourism supplanted mining as the primary source of revenue.

But Ghali hadn't traveled here for phosphate or tourism. He required the capabilities of its new satellite launch facility, now one of the foremost in the world. He had given the selection much thought.

Reliability proved foremost. Commercial insurance companies wanted to know what their money underwrote, and that wouldn't do just now. Ghali could count on one hand those who knew the contents of his payload. He smiled inwardly. As western capitalists would term it, his project was self-insured. So, there had to be a high probability of success on the first try.

The APSC facility, an Australian company, staked its future on the trusted AURORA rocket, an updated version of the reliable Russian Soyuz. The Soyuz design had weathered the test of time, for years delivering supplies to the International Space Station. The technical skills needed to operate these systems proved equally important. Ghali's superiors told him they slept better once they learned that Russian technicians dominated the launch crew.

Beyond reliability, proximity to the equator placed second in importance—the closer the better, in terms of both cost and odds for a successful liftoff. At ten degrees south, Christmas Island fit the bill. Ghali remembered cursing Mr. Fitzby's requirement that his payload launch into a geosynchronous orbit, some 22,300 miles above the earth's equator. How much easier and cheaper it would have been to field a polar-orbiting satellite. Dr. Warner, Ghali's American associate, had patiently explained that for its intended purpose, their instrument had to remain stationed above one geographic location—which meant a geosynchronous orbit.

A wisp of motion in the distance caught Ghali's squinting eyes. The promontory on which he stood afforded a good view of the launch site and the surrounding base. This location afforded privacy, important to him just now. Long before he could identify the vehicle rushing toward him, he saw the rooster tail of dust. During most of the year, the usual supply of rain would squelch this signal. Because climatology pointed to October as the driest time of the year, Ghali had chosen this month to maximize chances for a successful launch.

Ghali had expected his Russian contact, Alekseyev Gulyanov, would come to share the spectacle of the liftoff. The exuberant Gulyanov would want to communicate the good news in person, that all was in order; that the payload Gulyanov had smuggled out of Russia would soon be in orbit and would perform according to specification. Gulyanov had great faith in his comrade scientists from the fatherland.

Gulyanov leaped from the Toyota pickup and ran, in the way a fat man runs, a broad smile covering his weathered, wrinkled face.

"Ghali, my good friend, you can stop your ceaseless worrying. My technicians tell me all is proceeding normally. Electronics from your payload show it is well within calibration. The launch countdown is proceeding. Even the weather, Ghali. Look around you! Could you ask for more?"

Ghali looked down resolutely at the overweight, former Soviet Colonel. Even the physical strain evident from his exertion failed to diminish the smile. *How could this man be so cheerful after what he had experienced?*

The fractured Soviet state that followed the cold war made many Russian military officers long for the good old days of pre-glasnost. Gulyanov had held a prominent position in the Soviet Air Force, head of a secret research facility. From this lofty position, he had fallen far. Military pay fell nearly a year behind. Colonel Alekseyev Gulyanov, once a man of prestige and power, barely fed his family.

When Ghali had first approached him regarding the purchase of some of their new, top-secret technology, Gulyanov demurred. The hungrier he and his research colleagues became, the better Ghali's offer sounded. Gulyanov capitulated and the two consummated a deal acceptable to both. A win-win, as the Americans would say.

"Colonel Gulyanov, I will smile only when my payload is in orbit and functioning properly."

Gulyanov, bending over with his hands on his knees, tried to regain his wind. Between breaths, he continued. "My technicians are the best in the world. We have tested this module repeatedly. This prototype performs at one hundred times the power of anything the Americans have yet to develop. Now, you alone have this state-of-the-art instrument at your command. You should be very happy."

Soon, they watched the distant plume of exhaust gases billowing from beneath the rocket. Seconds later, the rocket's blast resonated for the entire island to hear. The white cylinder rose slowly, picked up speed, and streaked skyward. Once it evaporated beyond sight of the naked eye, both men trained their binoculars on the glinting metal. They watched until there was nothing more to see.

Minutes passed. The electronic chirp of Gulyanov's cell phone punctuated the morning stillness. Ghali studied his facial expressions as Gulyanov listened quietly. Nothing to indicate alarm. The conversation ended. Gulyanov turned to Ghali, his face beaming.

"My technicians tell me all rocket functions performed within normal limits. Liftoff was uneventful. Problems, if any, would have revealed themselves by now. Following insertion into a temporary polar orbit, a second stage rocket will maneuver the payload into its permanent geostationary position. I foresee no problems."

Ghali turned to Gulyanov. He spoke slowly, in Gulyanov's native tongue. He wanted to make the sentences meaningful because they would be the last words Gulyanov would ever hear.

"Speaking on behalf of my people, I thank you for your contribution to our cause. You can be assured that you will be praised not only here on earth, but in the afterlife as well."

Gulyanov bowed his head in acknowledgment. In the following split second, Ghali's hand snaked from behind his back. The stiletto took an upward trajectory and pierced Gulyanov's cotton shirt and flesh just below the rib cage. The eight-inch blade continued upward and entered the lower left ventricle. The strength of the upward sweep lifted the heavy man briefly off the ground.

Unconsciousness, then death, came in seconds. The smile was gone.

Ghali walked slowly down the promontory and reflected on his actions. It hadn't been his decision. He had orders and no choice but to obey them.

Just a minute ago, five individuals knew the contents of the launch capsule. Now only four people in the world knew that the world's most powerful laser, which three weeks earlier had sat in a clean room within a secret Russian laboratory, would soon attain geosynchronous orbit—thirty-five degrees longitude east of Miami, Florida, United States of America.

CHAPTER 2

▼

BETRAYAL

Halcyon Heights home subdivision, Monterey, California, USA:
36° 33′30″N Latitude, 121° 46′29″W Longitude
Sunday morning, 0220, October 22, 2006

Silverstein gasped for air, mummified in cotton sheets, and struggled to free himself. In the distance, he could visualize his bedroom and bed, but they seemed so far away. A distant form beckoned. This must be a dream, he thought. But, maybe not.

A stranger approached. He took the form of a Jewish rabbi.

"What is it that concerns you so, my child?" The rabbi looked the part of a concerned parent, his facial features displaying compassion. "Tell me your troubles and maybe I can help. But we must all remember that God works his wonders in mysterious ways."

This time it would be different, thought Silverstein. He needed to confide in someone. Otherwise, the pain would tear him apart.

"Someone in my past, long ago, did something terrible. The memory still eats at my soul."

"Tell me about it."

"My college roommate, Cameron Fitzby, raped my girlfriend. After I discovered the truth and returned to campus to confront him, he not only dismissed the incident, but contradicted another horrible episode six months earlier."

"What did he say? I want to hear it all."

State College, Pennsylvania, USA: 40°48'N Latitude, 77°52'W Longitude
Wednesday afternoon, 1350 hours, July 7, 1982

"You've got to turn yourself in, Cameron. That's the right thing to do." Silverstein cringed internally at his own words, but kept his outward emotions in check. "I'll do nothing of the sort. Leave me alone. Just go on to your fancy new job with the navy." Fitzby waved in dismissal and turned to leave.

Silverstein seized Fitzby's shoulder and held tight. "You raped Sylvia. That's why she left campus. She couldn't deal with the shame."

Fitzby swiveled his head, stared at the hand, and turned to face Silverstein. Silverstein mentally flinched at Fitzby's expression. He had never witnessed such an outward show of hate firsthand. Even in his street fights back in Atlanta, he had never seen such a look.

Fitzby glared at Silverstein for a moment before he spoke. "Like I said, get out of here. I'm not going to admit anything, and you can be sure no one will believe *you*...a person with your background."

Silverstein gaped in amazement. "What background are you talking about?"

The evil evaporated from Fitzby's face. In its place came a cocky gaze. "Victor, how soon you've forgotten your troubles with the law."

Silverstein recoiled at the comment. "That was self-defense and you know it!"

Fitzby smiled. "I do, do I? That's not the way I saw it."

"What the hell are you talking about? You told me you ran home."

"I was *there*. I *saw* what happened. Both of you lied. You needlessly killed that poor bastard on the street that night. The spic couldn't possibly have had as clear a view as I did."

Silverstein scowled, not believing what he had just heard.

Fitzby cocked his head to the left, lips curling up at the edges. "The way I see it, you owe me. I kept my mouth shut."

Silverstein reeled from Fitzby's devastating words. Not only had he raped an innocent co-ed, Fitzby now contradicted the events of that horrid night.

Silverstein stood in place, legs limp, and head faint, not knowing what to say.

Fitzby peered downward, then raised his eyes to meet Silverstein's. "Just in case you get any bright ideas about pursuing your misguided idea of justice, you should know one more thing."

He paused and shifted his weight from one foot to the other. "With regard to your little brawl that night, I was so shocked by what I saw that I confided that information to a friend."

Fitzby raised his head and looked hard into Silverstein's eyes, his expression emotionless. "As you can tell, I've covered my bases."

As Fitzby turned and sauntered away, Silverstein took one final bearing. He looked to the sky, to the ground, and to Fitzby's retreating form. This was no dream!

Silverstein clenched his fists and shook with rage. With all the strength he could muster, he turned and walked away.

The rabbi continued. "This Fitzby, you must hate him considerably, to remember such detail from so long ago."

Silverstein looked up, groping for a measure of consolation, an escape from the pain that had stalked him for so long. "If only there had been justice, if only he had shown some remorse…if only I could sleep."

The rabbi cocked his head to the left, lips curling up at the edges.

"Here," said the rabbi, "hold my hand. I will take you to your precious Sylvia. I will take you straight to hell!"

Silverstein gasped audibly as the rabbi ripped the mask from his face to reveal Cameron Fitzby. Fitzby howled in laughter.

Again, Silverstein had been tricked.

He screamed aloud.

*   *   *   *

Silverstein leaped out of bed and slumped to his haunches, his face awash with tears and hurt. Again and again this nightmare returned, sometimes with Fitzby disguised, and sometimes not—but always with a similar conclusion.

Each time after he awoke from his dream, he would recall the crushing reality of all that had transpired back in 1982—and its sinister implications—when he, Dr. Victor Mark Silverstein, a newly-minted PhD from Pennsylvania State University, had departed State College for his new job in California.

Back then, in a period of less than five hours, Silverstein had twice experienced emotions so raw he could hardly control himself. Vengeful thoughts had saturated his brain. There was no doubt his college roommate of two years, Cameron Fitzby, represented evil in the flesh. To make it worse, Fitzby had played him for a fool. Silverstein had been the sounding board for Fitzby's PhD dissertation and had quietly interceded with the department's faculty on Fitzby's behalf.

On his way out of town that terrible day, Silverstein considered returning to campus, killing Fitzby outright, and letting the future be damned. The alternative had been to tread his way into the future as if nothing had happened—and let God take care of past infractions. His parents would choose the latter, he knew. And because he owed them more than he could ever repay, he abided by their unknowing wish.

Aside from this tragedy, at twenty-three years of age he had had much to be thankful for: caring, loving parents, three college degrees under his belt, an enviable appointment waiting for him—and a bright future.

Looking back, Silverstein had taken the high road in that abominable situation. He proceeded to California and started a life that, in theory, held much promise. He forgot, as best he could, the future that might have been. And, he decided he would avoid Cameron Fitzby until the day he died.

On judgment day, Silverstein would testify that Cameron Fitzby had destroyed one life for sure. God himself would tally the devastation attributable to collateral damage.

CHAPTER 3

▼

SUPPORT

Pandeli Restaurant, Istanbul, Turkey: 41°01'03"N Latitude,
28°58'17"E Longitude
Wednesday, Noon, November 15, 2006

As he had been told to do, Cameron Fitzby stood in front of the restaurant and waited. He was out of his league and knew it. But he wasn't about to let anyone sense this potential weakness. *Never let anyone suspect you have an Achilles' heel.* Fitzby's beloved, gypsy mother had drilled that dictate into him at an early age. His English-born father had tried to ameliorate the feral qualities inherited from his mother, but with little success. Fitzby's mother made it clear to her husband that her methods and manners would be the ones her son would learn. When Fitzby turned twelve, his father left them both. Shortly thereafter, his mother expected her son to fill his father's shoes. Fitzby learned the ways of the world quickly enough.

Fitzby had traveled halfway around the world to confer with a moneyed Arab. Why? His research project needed funding, a lot of it, and he didn't much care where the money came from. He had already given his American contact, Dr. Clement Warner, his initial requirements.

Warner had told Fitzby that his Egyptian associate would find *him*, and not the other way around. Warner held a prominent position within the

Department of Defense, wore a western business suit, and spoke perfect English. That he referred Fitzby to a Middle Easterner, who Warner said he had known for some forty years and trusted implicitly, spoke volumes. To Fitzby it was remarkable that Warner had trusted him. But then, thought Fitzby, he had been born with chameleon-like acting skills.

The Delta flight from JFK two days earlier had been uneventful. Although forty-seven years old, Fitzby had ventured out of the country only twice, both times to meteorological conferences—to Clermont-Ferrand, France in 1980 (while in college) and Tallinn, Estonia in 1984. He had devoted his life to science; nothing else mattered. Some would consider certain aspects of his life immoral. Fitzby considered the term *amoral* a more accurate description.

The Grand Haliç Hotel, a harrowing half hour's taxi ride from Istanbul's airport, fell short of a five-star rating but proved comfortable enough. The location, a short stroll from the British Consulate, offered some reassurance. A connoisseur of mystery novels, Fitzby made a point of visiting the Tokatlian Hotel, also nearby. Fitzby considered it eerily coincidental that Agatha Christie's Inspector Hercule Poirot had begun his mysterious journey here, in *Murder on the Orient Express.*

Warner had provided instructions, handwritten on heavy notepaper, obviously of foreign manufacture:

> *From your hotel, proceed on foot toward the Golden Horn and cross the Galata Bridge. On the other side, you will see a large mosque to the left. Cross the street and bear to your right. In five minutes time you will see the Spice Market. Just inside the market, to the left, sits the Pandeli Restaurant. Wait outside the restaurant. Be there at noon Wednesday.*

Fitzby gave himself plenty of time and studied his surroundings as he crossed the bridge. He pulled up the zipper on his jacket against the crisp fall air. Although he had few preconceived notions about Istanbul, Fitzby conceded that the city proved far different from what he imagined. A bus tour the day before had given him perspective. The guide insisted that, although ninety-nine percent of Turkey's population claimed Islam as their religion, theirs was not a Muslim country. The Turkish language had nothing in common with the Arabic tongue. Further, democracy ruled and had done so since a revolutionary called Kemal Atatürk had brought modern thinking to this crossroads of ancient civilization in the 1920s.

As he crossed the bridge, Fitzby felt neither out of place nor unsafe. His complexion differed from most pedestrians, but otherwise he didn't stand out. Dress ranged widely, from the occasionally outrageous to the traditional covered garb for Islamic women.

Fitzby had never seen anything like the Spice Market. A covered bazaar devoted to cooking and medicinal spices; one shop after another with dozens of mounds of fresh spices on display, much like fruit at a produce stand, and just as colorful. After being solicited for the third time to come inside to drink apple tea, and the second time to consider Turkish Viagra, Fitzby returned to the restaurant entrance.

Next door to the restaurant sat a jewelry store and Fitzby made the mistake of window-shopping. Only seconds passed before a shop clerk solicited him, in English, promising a special price as the *first sale of the day*.

As Fitzby checked his watch and turned back, a deeper, more authoritative voice caught his attention.

"You are interested in jewelry, Mr. Fitzby, perhaps for your girlfriend? My sources tell me you are unmarried."

Fitzby spun around to the sound of his name. The body behind the voice stood large and tall, well over six feet, dwarfing Fitzby's diminutive five-foot-six stature. The brown suit and pinstriped shirt were obviously expensive. Black hair revealed minor graying around the temples. He guessed the man was in his mid to late fifties. Fitzby avoided looking at the facial scar that extended from the nose to his right ear.

"If your sources tell you I'm not married, they no doubt have informed you I have no girlfriend as well. I'm what is known in my country as a loner."

Fitzby forced himself to maintain eye contact. He would show no weakness. Besides, Fitzby reminded himself, he held the upper hand. Certain parties on this planet had expressed interest in the impressive claims he had made in scientific circles.

"Loneliness is a terrible thing, Mr. Fitzby. I speak from experience. Shall we do lunch, as you Americans say?"

"You obviously know a lot about me. What should I call you?"

"You can call me Ghali."

"Pardon my naiveté, but is Ghali your first or last name?"

Ghali smiled and gestured to the stairs that led to the restaurant. "I have long ago abandoned both."

Just one name, huh? The epitome of success, Fitzby had always believed, was a one-name moniker. Tank and Split came to mind from childhood days. Madonna and Sting claimed such a distinction in Fitzby's mature years. True to his obsessive nature, Fitzby couldn't help but count the well-worn steps as they climbed upward: thirty-three. They seemed to moan, as if complaining of their age, as did much of this ancient city. The beleaguered stairs reminded him of his own life not that long ago. He had progressed into a world of despair and considered chucking it all. All those years of being an outcast to his science, and working boring menial jobs to support himself, had taken their toll. His resurrection came earlier in the year when a stranger proposed a solution, support from certain foreign parties—investors who had the foresight to see the potential in Fitzby's work.

That stranger had approached him following his presentation at the American Meteorological Society's annual conference in Atlanta, Georgia, the previous January. Fitzby's address extolling his theory on hurricane modification had not gone well, to say the least! Ridicule by Dr. George Blackbeard, a noted tropical expert, stung particularly hard.

With an annoying Southern drawl, Dr. Blackbeard leaned forward on his cane and addressed the podium. "Would you be so kind as to tell the audience, *Mr.* Fitzby, how long you plan to subject me and my colleagues to your ceaseless drivel? Though I am well along in years, I hold out the hope to attend just one more national conference without hearing your senseless modification theory. How your paper passed screening is beyond me. You have no credibility here, *Mr.* Fitzby."

Dr. Blackbeard's emphasis on the word *Mr.* was intentional. Everyone in the room knew that the Department of Meteorology at Pennsylvania State University had booted Fitzby from its graduate program more than two decades earlier—even though Fitzby, with an IQ over one hundred and eighty (and the audience knew this as well), represented the most gifted meteorologist to come along in half a century, at least to Fitzby's way of thinking. Remarkably, there had been one other near genius in his class, not at Fitzby's level, but one who could stand toe to toe with him intellectually.

Fitzby's advisor had done her best to support him against an increasingly hostile faculty, one that couldn't understand how the relatively new field of Artificial Intelligence (AI) could apply to numerical weather modeling, the root basis for modern weather prediction.

The Department of Meteorology did acknowledge Fitzby's accomplishments. He had single-handedly developed a global spectral model, a new form of weather forecast model, to test his hypothesis for hurricane modification. It took him only ten months! No one in the department could recall anyone who could write computer code as quickly and accurately as Fitzby.

During his second year, he developed a form of AI to apply to the large data sets produced by a global forecast model. In his third year, he discovered a method to reduce significantly the computer power necessary to operate these AI algorithms, normally a crippling constraint to such applications. *Weak minds in the proverbial rut*, he used to remind himself.

The audience turned silent. No one offered support. Fitzby held his head high, descended from the podium, and left the conference room. *It's a damn shame none of my colleagues has the mental capacity to understand what I'm saying. I can only hope that son of a bitch Blackbeard lives to eat his words.*

Fitzby based his weather modification proposal on documented, empirical evidence: with all else being the same, the underlying sea surface temperature (SST) determined the degree to which a tropical cyclone developed. The Joint Typhoon Warning Center in Guam had conducted a two-year study in 1966 that supported that concept. For years, other scientists had written papers dissecting this topic.

In fact, no one questioned the basis for his postulate; they could not understand the technical details behind the application. Fitzby received further ridicule when he proposed that the government fund his research for the benefit of all humanity.

At Penn State, Fitzby had proven to himself, with both mathematics and computer simulation, that his design had merit. The complex logic that involved new applications of AI befuddled his professors. His arrogance, impatience, and belligerent behavior hardly helped matters. The department had no idea how to handle Fitzby and discretely forced him from the university.

It was the last day of the Atlanta conference, then, when the stranger appeared. Fitzby meandered along the length of the vendor pavilion at the Atlanta Convention Center, making one final examination of the displays, soon to be boxed up and shipped out.

Vendors ranged from the behemoths of the industry to the smallest of companies, all peddling their technological wares to the conference attendees. The latest in satellite remote sensing, computer visualization, and physical measurement dominated the displays. The exhibit from EUMET-SAT, the European agency responsible for meteorological satellites, was particularly impressive: a description of Meteosat Second Generation, Europe's weather satellite.

As Fitzby turned to leave, a man stepped directly into his path. Contrary to the vendors in the room, this stranger made his point quickly.

"How is it that a person of your brilliance and foresight can be treated so unjustly? I know I would be ready to take revenge if I were ever talked to that way in a public forum. Has that ever crossed your mind, Mr. Fitzby?"

How uncanny, thought Fitzby, that words from a complete stranger could mirror his own thoughts so closely.

*   *   *   *

"*Sakin bir köşe istiyorum.*" Ghali uttered what sounded like Turkish words to the maître d'. Although they meant nothing to Fitzby, *the table in the corner will suit nicely* seemed as good a translation as any. Fitzby's linguistic capabilities extended only to German and Latin. He still regretted his coerced decision to take Latin in high school. "It will do you good in the long run, Cameron," his English teacher, Mrs. Wilson, had reasoned. *Fat chance! I should have trusted my gut. I never liked that woman anyway.*

With no verbal or facial response, the maître d' led the way to a table by the window and departed hurriedly. Ceramic wall tiles, turquoise hexagonal shapes interspersed with vertical lines of blue diamonds, reminded Fitzby he wasn't in the states any more. Out the window, the bridge across the Golden Horn, framed against Istanbul in the background, provided a chamber of commerce photograph.

"Please take a seat, Mr. Fitzby. You are aware, are you not, that Turkish food is considered one of three world cuisines, after French and Chinese? You know how it is said, it is impossible to eat a bad meal in France? That is true here as well. Turkish cooks use only the freshest vegetables and meat, and the seasonings are superb."

Food was obviously a fundamental interest to Ghali, thought Fitzby. For the first time, Ghali's face became animated, and so did his hands.

"You have visited the Spice Market? Yes? Take a look around you! There is an added benefit to this diet. Fat Turks are rare." Ghali smiled, as if to reinforce the fact he had made a joke.

Fitzby deadpanned and fidgeted. He feigned some interest in the words, but knew it was no use. He leaned across the table and spoke in a subdued voice. As Fitzby had noted earlier, Ghali instinctively turned his head to the right while listening—even while keeping his eyes locked to the speaker. Contrarily, when Ghali spoke, he faced straight ahead.

"Excuse me, Mr. Ghali, or whatever your name is. While I appreciate your efforts to make me feel at ease and provide idle chitchat, you must know that little excites me except my work. I have come here because your colleagues are willing to fund my research. But I need to know more. Tell me who you represent, and not least importantly, the depth of your client's pockets."

Ghali's face and hands returned to rest. He spoke slowly, as if to a child. "Slow down, Mr. Fitzby. Everything in its own time."

Ghali snapped his fingers. The ensuing conversation with the waiter seemed to take longer than it should, but when it was over, Ghali seemed satisfied. He unbuttoned his jacket, removed a cigarette from a metal case, lit it, and stated the obvious. "I have taken the liberty to order for both of us."

Fitzby accepted the fact that Ghali worked according to his own timetable. The next few minutes passed with nothing said. Pita bread, olive oil, and a plate full of raw vegetables served as the appetizer. Fitzby dug in while Ghali finished his cigarette. Fitzby sensed the dark penetrating eyes sizing him up and imagined the thoughts behind them. *Can this pipsqueak of an American possibly pull off what he's proposed? Worse, can he be trusted?*

Ghali ground out the half-smoked cigarette and folded his hands in front of him. He looked at the ceiling and sighed, as if drawing a conclusion.

"I know little about you, Mr. Fitzby, and that causes me great concern. That said, I have known your American contact for many years. If he says you can be trusted, it is so. He also says you are a crazed fanatic, but a brilliant one."

Warner was batting one for two, thought Fitzby.

Ghali's words faded as the main courses arrived. The small table barely contained the assortment of foods: lentil soup, tomato halves covered with slices of fresh mozzarella cheese and fresh pepper, lamb kabobs on wood skewers, and grilled sea bass. And beer, Tuborg. Neither of them would go hungry today.

Ghali's assessment of Turkish food proved correct, thought Fitzby. While he continued eating, Ghali finished early and lit another cigarette.

Fitzby placed his fork and knife on his plate and looked around the restaurant. All the adjacent tables sat empty, even though the rest of the restaurant was packed. *Strange.* He scanned the other patrons. At least half of them were smoking.

"It would seem that news travels slowly to this part of the world, Mr. Ghali. Are you not aware that the Surgeon General of the United States of America himself has determined that cigarette smoking can be hazardous to your health?"

Ghali turned his head, this time before speaking, and smiled, at the same time blowing a long stream of smoke toward the floor. "It pleases me to know that a sense of humor lies behind that façade of yours. My grandfather used to say that a man without humor has no soul."

Fitzby knew how to play his hand. *Always relinquish to your opponent some sense of meaningless conciliation,* his mother had coached knowingly.

The waiter removed their plates and replaced them with small cups filled with Turkish coffee. Espresso to the extreme, thought Fitzby, complete with coffee grounds to chew on if the liquid caffeine proved insufficient. Any soothing influence from the beer would soon vanish. Just as well. Fitzby wanted a clear head to absorb the words he expected to hear.

Ghali stubbed out his cigarette and, at last, seemed ready to talk shop. He spoke clearly and deliberately, but in a voice low enough to make eavesdropping impossible.

"I represent an organization called Blade of the Sinai. Few outside of our group know of our existence. Many members are Palestinian, but not all. I am Egyptian, although I have lived most of my life in Turkey. We have affiliates from Saudi Arabia, Iran, and Syria.

"Do not confuse us with Hamas, Hezbollah, or other Middle East terrorist organizations, Mr. Fitzby. We don't go around with plastic explosives coiled around our bodies and blow ourselves up. Our methods are more sophisticated, but motivated for a common good."

Fitzby listened carefully. He had no political philosophy and cared less about foreign affairs. If religious extremists wanted to blow themselves up, who was he to stand in their way? Nonetheless, he found it interesting to hear the Arab point of view. "And what would that common good be, Mr. Ghali?"

Ghali laughed. "That is the easiest question of all to address, Mr. Fitzby, and the answer will please you. We have several goals, but one is the same as that of your government, to achieve peace in the Middle East. Despite our wealth in oil, our area of the world has been a source of instability for the past half century."

Fitzby responded with a pokerfaced expression. He understood full well the potential leverage his technology could give someone who possessed the will to use it. Fitzby considered it better to feign ignorance.

"I fail to understand how my expertise could possibly relate to peace, Mr. Ghali. You must forgive me. I am a scientist, not a politician." *Meaningless conciliation.* His mother had wisdom far exceeding any human being he had ever known. No one could match her understanding of human psychological weakness.

Ghali shifted in his chair and folded his legs. "That is a good point and one I'm not sure I can address to your satisfaction. Our organization is little known; we work in the shadows. We support several researchers like you, with the long-term expectation that new technologies might influence a common good. It is possible your work will come to nothing. But based on your credentials and assessment by our advisors, we are willing to take that chance.

"And, to answer your earlier question, our pockets are deep indeed. You have a blank check, Mr. Fitzby."

Ghali leaned back, obviously waiting for Fitzby's reaction.

Fitzby maintained his game face. *Common good.* An interesting way to put it. On the other hand, the term *blank check* held no ambiguity. For the first time since graduate school, Fitzby could see himself moving ahead full throttle with his research.

"I am impressed, Mr. Ghali. But I'm sure you are aware that an important component of my project is completely beyond my control."

Ghali reached inside his coat, removed an envelope, and handed it to Fitzby. "Here are the precise specifications. A little over a month ago, we launched a satellite into geosynchronous orbit. All components you requested are aboard. As we speak, it sits thirty degrees west of equatorial Africa and awaits your commands."

With these words, Fitzby snapped to attention. He could scarcely contain his excitement.

"This is good news indeed, Mr. Ghali! My discussions with Dr. Warner told me nothing about you or your organization. I'm sure you understand that I doubted your commitment. I see now I needn't have worried."

Ghali smiled and replied quickly. "Commitment is not a quality we are lacking, Mr. Fitzby. You can be assured of that."

Ghali removed his wallet from his inside coat pocket and prepared to settle the bill. Simultaneously, Fitzby reached inside his jacket and withdrew an envelope.

Ghali glanced up. "Lunch is on me, Mr. Fitzby. Put your lira away."

Fitzby handed the envelope to Ghali. "An hour ago, you said you were unsure of whether I could be trusted. You can be assured, Mr. Ghali, that my commitment is more than equal to yours. I have one more requirement, one I trust you have the resources to carry out. This request may convince you of *my* sincerity and commitment."

Ghali opened the envelope and stared at the contents. For the first time since their initial meeting, Fitzby sensed he had dealt a surprise.

Ghali's eyes registered disbelief. "Are you sure, Mr. Fitzby? Why?"

"Don't for a second underestimate me, Mr. Ghali. I will do *anything* to ensure this project succeeds. You ask why? Suffice it to say there is only one person on this planet who has the intellect and wherewithal to stop me."

Ghali lingered by the entrance to the Spice Market and watched as Fitzby headed back to his hotel.

Ghali replayed the conversation with Fitzby in his mind, concerned he had used the proper words. *Herkesin yararına.* A common good—yes, that was the correct translation. Of course, depending on which side of the fence one stood did influence one's perception. Having witnessed first-hand in 1967 the swift destruction of his military and consequent loss of Egypt's territory, Ghali's own perception of common good was clear. Nevertheless, in all the years Ghali had aided the Blade's objectives, their actions had been mostly honorable. What he had told Fitzby was true; his organization did not conduct or condone outright terrorist acts.

But, minutes earlier, Cameron Fitzby had given *him* a shock, one that erased any doubt as to Fitzby's dedication. The last thing Ghali had expected from Fitzby was a request for a hit man.

C H A P T E R 4

▼

TROUBLE

Naval Research Laboratory (NRL), Monterey, California, USA:
36°35'N Latitude, 121°51'W Longitude
Friday, 1300, August 3, 2007

"Bauer, you're out of your mind! You're blaming *me* for your marginal ability at writing code for your data assimilation. Get the hell out of my office!"

Dr. Victor Mark Silverstein was upset, a condition that beset him frequently. He slammed the door behind his colleague and returned to his desk.

"Goddamn modelers," he swore under his breath. "How am I supposed to prove it's not my problem? How do you prove the negative?"

Silverstein opened the left drawer of the desk, removed one of his treasured Marlboro cigarettes from its pack, and stared at it longingly. Although he had finally broken the filthy habit two months earlier, the stress of the day made him consider a temporary relapse. The thought of lighting it up—*right here in my government office, in direct violation of the dictates of the almighty federal government*—proved tempting. But he had tried that once before and gotten a severe reprimand.

"There will be no smoking in any government office. *I* know that and *you* know that!" he had been warned by the Associate Superintendent, Dr. Mary Kenworth.

Silverstein threw the weed into the drawer, slammed it shut, and turned back to his computer. Even considering his fame and clout, he had to pick his battles carefully.

Dr. Victor Silverstein laid claim to being one of the navy's preeminent civilian scientists. Forty-eight years old, Silverstein had worked for the navy his entire career, some twenty-five years.

Silverstein had been one of several student prodigies who attended Pennsylvania State University in the late 1970s. In 1975, he had enrolled there in the field of meteorology at the age of sixteen. Three and a half years later, he received his BS diploma, in another year his MS and two and a half years later, his PhD.

Silverstein shared departmental distinction by being one of only two meteorology students who had *never* received a grade lower than an A—on *any* course, either inside or outside the department. The required physical education classes with their share of pitfalls made this distinction no small feat. But having been an accomplished high school athlete who could have attended any number of colleges on a sports scholarship—which his parents strongly discouraged—made athletics no challenge at all. To persuade his parents he could make wise decisions on his own, and much to the consternation of his mother, he made a good showing in the heavyweight division at the state level for the Golden Gloves championship in Pennsylvania in 1978.

As word of Silverstein's brilliance spread beyond Happy Valley (colloquial name for Penn State surrounds), numerous commercial and government laboratories competed for his talents. Silverstein ended up choosing a small research facility in Monterey, California, far removed from Pennsylvania and his native Atlanta.

During his career, Silverstein had made his reputation as a *can do* scientist, dabbling in nearly all aspects of research at the Monterey facility. Although his job description tagged him as a *meteorologist*, his considerable skills suggested another title, a forensic meteorologist, a meteorological detective. If a phenomenon or problem required explanation, interpretation, or elucidation, everyone turned to Dr. Victor Mark Silverstein when other avenues had failed.

Silverstein was good at what he did and he enjoyed it. Anecdotes abounded, some true, some not. One story that became legend concerned a newcomer who casually asked Silverstein for the time of day. Silverstein proceeded to explain how a watch functions and, as the befuddled new scientist tried to escape, how to make a better watch.

Although Silverstein had attained the highest pay grade of any scientist at NRL Monterey (only the division superintendent earned more), every other researcher there envied him—not because of his pay, which no one begrudged him—but because he had *made it* without ever doing a shred of management. Silverstein despised bureaucracy and even eschewed the minimal administrative paperwork required of him. An unholy alliance had evolved between Silverstein and his bosses, to the benefit of both.

The Monterey division (numerically known as Code 7500) lay organizationally within the larger Naval Research Laboratory in Washington, DC. The politically motivated division title, Marine Meteorology, belittled the scope of work conducted at this relatively small organization of one hundred or so researchers and staff. Research ranged from developing sophisticated computer models that predict the weather on both regional and global scales, to producing scores of satellite-derived weather products, to applying AI techniques to weather problems—with a variety of projects in between, some classified.

Silverstein swiveled around in his Steelcase Leap chair (his prized, and only, office luxury) and focused across Sparks Park, named after a previous facility manager, Bob Sparks. The flag on the mast flapped vigorously in the stiff westerly wind. Fog and low stratus, common for this time of year, almost obscured sight of the Fleet Numerical Meteorology and Oceanography Center, (FNMOC).

Co-located with NRL Monterey, and voiced as "FINMOC," FNMOC had the operational responsibility for producing the navy's numerical weather products. What the National Weather Service did for the geographic United States, FNMOC did for the US Navy worldwide.

The meteorological foursome: NRL Monterey, FNMOC, the Meteorology Department at the local Naval Postgraduate School, and the local office of the National Weather Service (situated adjacent to NRL and FNMOC) gave the Monterey Peninsula the dubious honor of having more meteorologists per capita than nearly anywhere.

About the time Silverstein regretted his caustic words to his colleague, he heard a soft knock on the door.

"Come." Silverstein had a reputation for efficiency in language as well as science.

The door opened slowly and an attractive blonde head peered around the corner. "Is it safe to enter or is the storm still breeching the outer wall?" Dr. Linda Kipling, affectionately known as Silverstein's right-hand man, smiled appealingly and pushed the door fully open.

"Oh, come on in. You've been around me long enough to know my bark is worse than my bite." Silverstein leaned back in his swivel and placed his hands behind his head. The color in Silverstein's face had returned to a more normal hue—although few would notice the difference. Silverstein knew he could hide facial emotions easier than could white folk.

Kipling closed the door behind her. Silverstein knew she understood the usual sequence would soon play out; major eruption followed an hour later by lava that would soon be cool enough to touch. That scene had repeated itself numerous times in the eight years they had worked together.

"What did Bauer want? Is he still blaming your cloud classification for their problems in the tropics? That can't be it!"

"I know. It's impossible. Our routines were running for months before shit started hitting the fan. I think he knows that; he's picked me out of frustration. To tell you the truth, I'm not so sure it's his data initialization either. He claims he's made no significant changes since the beginning of summer."

Kipling pulled up a chair and sat in it backward. Seven years his junior, Linda never wore dresses, rode a powerful BMW motorcycle, and acted more like a man than many of the biologically defined specimens in the division. "That's what they always say. I only changed one line of code."

Silverstein laughed at Kipling's verbal mockery of the numerical modelers who, truth be told, had been responsible for much of NRL Monterey's success over the years. In the early 1980s, they had developed the first version of the navy's global forecast model. Upgraded continuously over the years, that model represented the bread and butter of FNMOC's operations.

Silverstein smiled back affectionately. *She always knows what to say, and how to place things into perspective.*

No doubt spawned by folklore that black men preferred blonde white women, rumors surfaced periodically that he and Linda had something going. In fact, it was never so. Not that he hadn't thought about it! Silverstein's own wife, Sheila, had divorced his ass seven years earlier, stating in court, "There was no future in being married to someone who prefers sleeping in his office than in his own bed."

Silverstein had to agree; he hadn't been much of a husband. It hadn't helped that he had sought out a woman who reminded him of his first love in college—hardly a sound basis for a long-term relationship. Remarkably, it wasn't until late in his marriage that he recognized this self-inflicted deceit. He maintained a modicum of personal dignity by never admitting to anyone, and especially Sheila, that she had been a stand-in. Fortunately, there were no children to be hurt from the dissolution of their twelve-year union.

Silverstein sat straight in his chair and turned serious. "You know, Linda, I find it interesting that Bauer's problem with his tropical wind statistics is coinciding with a very unusual start for the hurricane season. What do you think?"

Silverstein understood full well what concerned Bauer. He himself had developed computer code for forecast models.

A modern computer weather model, whether theirs or anyone else's, was predictable—meaning that its error rates were usually consistent—a point, Silverstein knew, that would make no sense to a layperson. Also, in contrast to the middle latitudes (where most people live), tropical weather proved notoriously difficult to predict. As a result, the usual mid-latitude statistical measures (for judging model reliability) proved useless. Instead, meteorologists preferred wind error rates to judge model consistency in the tropics. What had agitated Bauer were wind errors in the tropical Atlantic, and *only* in the tropical Atlantic, that far exceeded the normal range—meaning something was wrong, very wrong.

Kipling stood and began pacing, her usual modus operandi when she gave serious thought to anything. "We've already had six named storms in the Atlantic, four that have pushed to hurricane strength. If this pace continues, heaven help the east coast and the Caribbean."

The electronic chirp of the telephone broke their concentration. Silverstein turned to the phone, but not before smiling up at Kipling. "Uh, oh! You don't think my little outburst has upset the delicate psyche of my learned colleague, Dr. Bauer?"

"Yes, sir; Silverstein here." The *caller ID* eliminated surprises. Before Silverstein lifted the receiver, he knew the superintendent's voice would be at the other end.

"That's right, sir…no, sir…are you sure, sir?" Silverstein listened to further details and responded. "Tonight? Not a problem, sir."

Silverstein set the receiver back into its cradle and slowly swiveled back toward Kipling. Seconds transpired, with Silverstein deep in thought.

"Well? What? Do you need to apply for unemployment compensation? Talk to me!" Kipling's face registered concern.

Silverstein looked at Kipling and rose from his chair. "Did you make any plans for the weekend?"

"No. Why?"

"Go home and get packed. You and I are flying to New Orleans tonight."

CHAPTER 5

▼

REMEMBRANCE

United Airlines flight, somewhere over Oklahoma
Friday evening, 2345, August 3, 2007

Linda Kipling sat in the first row of the Airbus 320, adjacent to the window, her first-class seat partially reclined. Silverstein sat alongside on the aisle, seemingly in deep thought. She had chosen the filet mignon, which together with two glasses of fine French Bordeaux, soon softened the harshness of reality and turned the vivid colors of the long day into more mellow tones. The male flight attendant removed plates and cloth tablecloths and offered an after-dinner drink. Kipling watched dreamily as the Courvoisier in her glass undulated gently in response to the aircraft's motion.

Silverstein had generously upgraded Kipling's seat as well as his own. The travel section at NRL had worked overtime to process the superintendent's hurried request. Analogous to the unusual alliance Silverstein had with his bosses, Travel had learned years earlier to tolerate the idiosyncrasies of their star scientist and make do with the minimal cooperation they received. He rarely filed the required travel claims, proclaiming the process too much trouble and a waste of everyone's time. Travel did its best to estimate his comings and goings and at least give him the required per diem allowance. Money was not one of Silverstein's concerns.

"No, thank you; I'm fine." The attendant offered headsets for the seat-mounted flat-screen monitor. Normally, Kipling would have jumped at the chance to see *Ray*, a movie she had missed not only the first go-round, but the second as well. The night would be short—only four hours flight time to New Orleans.

Kipling's thoughts returned to Silverstein—and not for the first time. Theirs was a professional relationship and had been so since she arrived at NRL nine years earlier. Coming off a sad divorce, she welcomed the move to California from Boulder, Colorado, where she had worked at the National Center for Atmospheric Research (NCAR), another of the country's foremost meteorological research facilities.

Kipling smiled at the thought of *sunny* California, which a lot of the time Monterey was *not*. A local joke made fun of that peculiarity. The best seller in gift shops being the sweatshirt, sold to hapless tourists who realized too late that coastal California was darn cool during the summer. Mark Twain said it best: *the coldest winter he ever experienced was a summer in San Francisco.*

During Kipling's first year at NRL Monterey, she worked with the numerical modelers, the group from which Dr. Bauer came and who now suspected Silverstein lay behind their equatorial forecasting problems. Theirs was a curious lot, with their noses always stuck to the front of a computer screen, analyzing and correcting complex lines of computer code critical to tomorrow's forecast in some offbeat segment of the globe. Numerical modeling had been her specialty at NCAR as well, where she had worked for three years following graduation with a PhD from Colorado State in 1995.

As it happened, after one year at NRL (when she had become bored with numerical modeling), an opportunity arose across the street, in Building 704—a chance to work with the legendary Silverstein. Of course, Kipling had known of him long before she moved to California. Who hadn't? Kipling thought long and hard before making the transition. He needed a modeler who could help him in the area of artificial intelligence. Silverstein's accomplishments were well known, but so were his incendiary moods and exacting standards. More than one scientist over the years had politely requested a move into another section to work on something *different*.

When Kipling volunteered to work with Silverstein, it took many by surprise. She would be the first female. To management's surprise, their professional alliance worked well. Known for her straight arrow, Virgo-like (some said anal-retentive) nature, she turned out to be a perfect match for the demanding Silverstein. From a professional standpoint, her scientific reputation soon bolted upward. Every journal article and conference presentation carried either a Silverstein-Kipling or a Kipling-Silverstein byline. Management recognized the benefit of this newfound scientific collaboration and did nothing to interfere.

But what of something more? Kipling had considered, more than once, making a move on Silverstein. God knew he was good-looking—tall, a face that reminded her of Denzel Washington, and a body to die for. But, Kipling had joined Silverstein's team just prior to his divorce and knew better than to move in on someone so emotionally fragile. She might have had him, but for how long? And so, she had waited—and waited, and waited. In the back of her mind, she hoped he would make the first move. To her, the fact that he had not, provided implicit proof that he lacked interest.

Most of NRL probably figured that race was a showstopper: Silverstein being black and Kipling white. But to Kipling, Silverstein's skin radiated perfection, with that alluring shade of brown that more than a few white women today would trade for—imagine Halle Berry. Beyond that, anyone who knew Kipling's background would understand she was about as color-blind as they come. Her parents had been 60s' hippies who raised their daughter in a Colorado commune where love ran free and liberalism prevailed. In fact, Kipling's babysitter for most of her preteen years had been a black boy seven years her senior. To her, the issue of race neither dented nor scratched the proverbial surface of acceptability.

All these thoughts roamed Kipling's mind until they made no sense at all, just a blurry mass that retreated into the distance. She dozed peacefully, with only an unpleasant interruption an hour later when someone coughed and became sick. As she had trained herself to do in prior dreams when a repulsive or scary situation arose, Kipling left that window in her mind—and moved to another.

Silverstein wanted some shuteye, but knew it wouldn't come. Kipling slept quietly. Silverstein allowed himself a brief glance at the sleeping form beside him. The airplane blanket did little to hide her shapely hips and breasts. Her breaths came slow and shallow, her delicate skin visible well below the open button of her blouse. He wondered if she had ever caught him looking at her that way. *Damn!* Thank God, her eyes were closed. They were bedroom eyes to be sure and lent credence to the old saying that sexual attraction originates between the nose and the forehead. Silverstein had had to teach himself to avert his gaze after the usual interval of conversational eye contact. It would be much too easy to lose himself there.

Silverstein reclined his seat, turned toward the aisle, and forced his thoughts elsewhere.

Silverstein reviewed the few facts he knew already. Earlier, at the office, following his short discussion with the superintendent, he made one call to get further explanation for their short-notice trip.

"Victor, the Atlantic temperature maps are crazy," exclaimed Mercer. Silverstein had known his oceanographic contact, Dr. Anthony Mercer, since he had joined NRL.

NRL Monterey's division superintendent had asked Silverstein and Kipling to participate in a hastily arranged weekend session that Mercer would chair. Dr. Mercer worked at NRL Stennis, another division of NRL, located at the Stennis Space Center (named after Louisiana's legendary senator) in Mississippi, about an hour's drive from New Orleans.

What NRL Monterey was to meteorology, NRL Stennis was to oceanography. Among other things, scientists at Stennis modeled ocean "weather" much the same way meteorologists did for the atmosphere. The only difference was the medium, water versus air. The same physical principles applied.

"Go on; I'm listening." Silverstein replayed the conversation in his head.

"We're seeing day to day sea surface temperature changes in the equatorial Atlantic…Victor, the equator for Christ's sake…that are unheard of. Increases mostly."

Silverstein reviewed what he knew about the ocean. In terms of the earth's heat budget, the tropical oceans represented the most stable masses on the face of the earth. To keep an eye on SSTs worldwide, important for a variety of meteorological and other reasons (not the least of which, submarine operations), the navy used satellites to sense water's infrared emission, from which one could calculate temperature.

Compared to the atmosphere where temperatures (and weather) can vary markedly (on an hour-by-hour basis), ocean features change more slowly. Therein lay the rub. Mercer told Silverstein that automated temperature maps, overseen by human analysts, were changing more frequently than had ever been observed before. Stennis scientists considered numerous reasons: atmospheric contamination, satellite instrument error, plotting algorithm error, even underwater volcanic eruptions. They contacted the US Geological Survey on the last one.

Silverstein and Kipling had discussed all this at length on the first leg of their trip, a one-hour commuter flight to Los Angeles. Silverstein had purposely refrained from mentioning one further possibility. *No, it's not possible! There's no way he could have pulled this off.* Silverstein could scarcely forget his old roommate's struggle to sell his dissertation to his doctoral committee. The irony of Fitzby's failed attempts at completing his PhD was that Silverstein represented one of the few who understood the mathematics behind his theory.

Silverstein grasped the sides of his seat, palms and body now sweating—even though all those around him snuggled in blankets. Raw memories he had struggled all these years to forget still plagued him. Far worse than the possibility that Fitzby might be involved in the SST mystery was Fitzby's crime at Penn State—and its consequence—just before Silverstein headed to California.

Silverstein brought his seat to the vertical position, lifted himself quietly to avoid waking Kipling, plodded the short distance to the forward lavatory, shut the door, crouched to his knees—and threw up. Silverstein hoped the dull roar of the jet engines masked the sound of his sickening pain.

CHAPTER 6

▼

ODD GOINGS-ON

Bermuda Weather Service, Bermuda International Airport,
Bermuda: 32° 22'02"N Latitude, 64° 40'39"W Longitude
Saturday afternoon, 1745, August 4, 2007

The Delta flight from Atlanta had just taxied to the terminal. Wind and rain buffeted the runway. Plane maintenance personnel labored in full rain gear. But the worst would be over by nightfall.

Jim Avery stood by one of two large-paned windows and peered out at the long northwest/southeast runway, Bermuda's air link to the outside world. In contrast to other weather stations where he had worked, the large forecast room (previously part of the Radar Approach Control before the US Navy left in 1995) had ample accommodations and good working space.

Avery turned to the large-numbered digital clock on the wall to check the time. He had just gotten off the phone with his wife, reassuring her for the second time that the worst of the weather would subside before this evening's dinner party.

"No, dear, we won't have to cancel. What time are our guests arriving? Seven thirty? I'll be home on time. Don't worry! The satellite shows clearing forty miles to the east and this storm is moving fast."

Jennifer, or Jennie as her friends called her, had never fully appreciated her husband's work. This fact didn't bother Avery because her understanding of the science behind meteorology mirrored that of most laypersons. To nearly everyone, he represented a "weather-guesser," not the skilled scientist who examined daily the complex hydrodynamic and thermodynamic interactions that produce what mere mortals refer to as weather.

Jim Avery carried the distinction of being the senior of five weather forecasters at the Bermuda Weather Service (BWS). Although the British claimed Bermuda as one of their territories, Avery held an American passport. He and Jennie moved here fourteen years earlier after Avery had worked a five-year stint with the National Weather Service in Buffalo, New York. Before their marriage in 1988, Avery had spent ten years in the US Air Force, which afforded him a Masters in Meteorology from Pennsylvania State University. Although Buffalo had most of the makings of a permanent home, the temperature extremes of upper New York State combined with the occasional winter inundations from lake-effect snowstorms suited neither of them. Bermuda's moderate, year-round climate proved more to their liking. They never regretted their move.

Avery sat at his computer examining the daily weather products. Because Bermuda lay only six hundred miles east of the continental United States, Avery relied principally on forecast products from the National Weather Service in Camp Springs, Maryland. To the chagrin of American forecasters, their computer-generated weather forecasts beyond a couple of days' duration were *not* the best in the world—if only marginally so. The European Centre for Medium-Range Weather Forecasts (ECMWF) in Reading, England, had that distinction. There was no secret why they were the best. With resources culled from twenty-five different European states, they had significant financial backing to draw upon—which meant bigger, faster computers and as many top-notch scientists as needed.

Even so, Avery preferred American weather products tailored for the continental US and the eastern Atlantic seaboard—which included Bermuda.

Particularly at this time of year, from June through November, the only abnormal weather of concern came from hurricanes or their weaker cousins, all of which could be termed tropical cyclones. Although most tropical cyclones had the good sense to remain south of the island, Bermuda got its share, as history could attest.

Hurricane Fabian in 2003 had left its share of destruction and death. (Interestingly, for centuries, the looting of ships—scurrying for shelter from passing hurricanes that had run aground on Bermuda's shallow coral reefs—provided a portion of the island's economy.) For this reason, forecast products from Miami's National Hurricane Center (NHC), one of three branches of the Tropical Prediction Center, proved crucial to the BWS. Avery knew many of the forecasters there by name and called them frequently when a situation demanded it.

This afternoon, for the fifth time in as many weeks, Avery had reason to talk to Dr. Alfred Davis. The situation had demanded it. Tropical storm Felix had struck Bermuda head-on. Fortunately, Felix's maximum winds never exceeded forty-five knots, well shy of hurricane force. NHC predicted a westerly track for this storm, followed by recurvature to the north, likely avoiding the Carolinas. If Felix didn't reach hurricane strength soon, it likely wouldn't as it headed north into cooler waters.

The sharp-sounding click of the retinal scan-activated door latch reminded Avery his twelve-hour shift was nearly complete. Their new junior forecaster, Marsha Kendall, who had arrived just six months earlier, would take over.

"Thanks for your input, Alfred. I'll be in touch." Avery lowered the wireless handset to its cradle.

Avery craned his neck in time to watch Kendall exhale the final puff of cigarette smoke she had gulped just before entering the room. Management had installed the wall-mounted ashtray outside the station at her request. "Afternoon, Marsha."

The accompanying silence on a Saturday afternoon likely meant one thing: Kendall and her new boyfriend had had another altercation. As far as Avery could tell, their quarrels never included fists or other objects thrown in anger, but the war of words nonetheless left its marks. It didn't help that Kendall usually instigated the fights. Kendall possessed a curious physical condition. Avery had adapted to this peculiarity, but doubted her boyfriend had. Importantly, Kendall required an adequate supply of food. Once hungry, she became mean. Avery had experienced this phenomenon first hand on two different occasions. For that reason, Avery always kept a supply of Snickers bars handy for the occasional emergency.

"How bad was it this time, Marsha?"

"It was something trivial, as usual. I won't bother you with the details. But it revolved around Barry's new job. Barry works at this new company, Anselina Corporation. Remember?"

"Yeah, I remember. They set up operations this past spring in the old Winston building, down in Hamilton. By the way, in case you don't know, Winston is *Sam Winston*. He's a recluse now, but back in the eighties, he was quite the industrialist and local socialite. That building's been sitting vacant for a decade. No one ever understood his thinking. I'm told it has enough rebar and concrete to survive a nuclear blast. The *Gazette* sent a reporter down to do an interview with the new owner and couldn't get past the guard at the gate."

Kendall shook her head. "*No one* knows what they do. Barry says everything there is hush-hush, that he's sworn to secrecy and can't tell me anything."

Avery turned toward Kendall. "It must have something to do with computers if Barry is working there. From what you've told me, he's the best when it comes to UNIX operating systems."

Kendall sighed. "Yeah, he's the best all right. Sometimes I'm not sure I can handle the best."

Avery returned to his computer display. He still marveled to himself how computer technology and modern satellites had revolutionized the way meteorologists displayed and analyzed their data. When he had started his air force career in the late seventies, paper weather charts were the norm, even for satellite pictures. Hand analysis, using acetate overlays, proved common. *I wonder if they still teach hand analysis at Penn State?* A weather station earned credits by how well forecasters organized their charts on the wall. Avery mused that was probably why older weather stations had few windows—a throwback to the days when wall space commanded a premium.

"Come take a look at the Meteosat, Marsha."

Kendall poured coffee grounds into the hopper of the Bunn-O-Matic and pressed the button. "Is it happening again?"

"I'm afraid so. I just got off the phone with Dr. Davis. I've never seen anything like this and neither has the NHC. This hurricane season is going to go down in history. Mark my word! Felix is the second tropical storm to nail us this summer. Four more have passed just to our south. *And*, we're only two months into the hurricane season!"

Avery pointed to a cloudy area to the west of northern equatorial Africa. This region of the globe sat too far east of the North American continent for the geosynchronous American satellite (GOES East) to provide a good view. Instead, the corresponding European satellite (labeled Meteosat-8 by the European Space Agency) filled the geographic void where GOES East left off, providing a good view of Europe, Africa and the eastern half of the Atlantic Ocean.

"Take a look at this new tropical wave, just west of the Cape Verde Islands. Look at the strength of the convection. Thunderstorms are popping off right and left! Once it left the African landmass, it started amplifying like Felix did. Then, look across the ocean here to the west. There are five altogether. Stacked up all the way to Cuba for God's sake!"

Kendall came close and focused on the area where Avery pointed. "You're the one with years of tropical experience, Jim. You know I'm a mid-latitude forecaster who's spent her entire career forecasting in Scotland. For weeks now, you've repeated over and over that what we're seeing is unusual."

Avery pushed himself back from the terminal. "Unusual is too weak a word, Marsha. We know most hurricanes have their roots in the easterly waves that slough off northwest equatorial Africa. As you remember from Scotland, the prevailing winds in the mid-latitudes are from west to east."

Kendall interrupted. "Jim, I know all that. I also know that in the tropics, the situation is reversed, east to west, and that air over the Atlantic Ocean west of central Africa started out over the landmass of Africa. I also learned from my tropical class—thank you very much—that for a variety of reasons, primarily the fact that part of Africa is damn hot come summer, small ripples form in those winds. Those perturbations are what we call easterly waves."

Avery smiled. "Very good, Marsha. You could fool me that you've only forecast in the middle latitudes. What else?"

"You've got to give me some credit, Jim. I wasn't second in my class at the University of Reading for nothing, I want you to know. I learned about these waves in the Tropical Weather Systems course. They move westward across the Atlantic in the prevailing easterlies. Some pick up steam, turning first into tropical depressions, then tropical storms, and eventually hurricanes…assuming conditions are just right."

Kendall leaned back and took a sideways glance toward the Bunn-O-Matic. Too soon. She refocused her attention.

Avery hesitated before speaking, running his finger down the statistics he had printed from the Web. On the average each year, he saw, about sixty easterly waves slough off Africa and, of those, as many as five reach the hurricane threshold of seventy-four miles per hour. Since 1995, however, it said that hurricane seasons have been unusually active, with over sixty hurricanes and half again as many named storms.

"I'm at a loss here, Marsha. I may have more tropical experience, but your schooling is more recent than mine. What's the latest scientific thinking about why an easterly wave intensifies or disintegrates? Can we tell in advance?"

Kendall sighed. "I doubt that what I learned five years ago is much different from what they taught you. Here's what I remember. Ocean temperature is one. You need at least eighty-degree water. That's where tropical cyclones get their energy, from the warm water, and why they lose their winds so quickly once they turn onto land. There is one thing I can tell you though. Researchers do think the ocean between Africa and the Caribbean is warming and that's at the root of the increased activity."

Avery smiled to himself. Kendall was no dummy. Time to give her a quiz. "Those are generalities that are useful to climatologists, Marsha, but don't help us much. You're obviously up to date on this stuff. Why does one easterly wave take off and the next one not?"

Kendall seemed to take her assignment in stride. "All the usual stuff you've read in the textbooks. First, tropical cyclones won't form too close to the equator. You need a certain amount of Coriolis Force. Second, there can't be too much wind in the middle atmosphere. Otherwise, the fledgling storm gets torn apart. There are other factors, but the only other one I remember is that you need some sort of weather disturbance to kick things off."

Kendall turned her head. The coffee pot had stopped dripping. She rose and headed in that direction. "There must be something unusual about this year. What do your friends in Miami say?"

"Nothing…nothing unusual that I've heard. You can bet, though, that more than one Masters thesis or PhD dissertation will come from this year's data."

Kendall filled her cup and returned to her monitor. Avery gathered his lunchbox and raincoat, took a last look around the office, and headed to the door.

"I'll see you tomorrow. Oh, by the way, don't forget about the sixth graders from Saltus Cavendish coming for their tour at seven. I can't believe they scheduled an evening visit. They called and told me it would take more wind and rain than this to stop them." Avery paused, turned, and looked back toward Kendall. "Go easy on 'em, Marsha. If you get in trouble, there're some candy bars in my drawer."

Kendall looked up, her face scrunched into a sneer. "Cute, Jim, real cute."

CHAPTER 7

▼

HISTORY

Westbound on Interstate 10, Mississippi, toward New Orleans Monday morning, 1045, August 6, 2007

Nothing much had come from the all-day sessions at NRL Stennis on Saturday and Sunday. Silverstein and Kipling listened to hours of discussion and examined scores of sea surface temperature (SST) charts. No one in the room doubted that something odd was occurring in the equatorial Atlantic.

The oceanographers at Stennis responsible for the dynamic models that forecast currents and waves complained that their models had become unstable from the constantly changing SST fields. Remote sensing experts considered the unlikely prospect that instruments on the weather satellites had gone out of calibration, maybe the result of an electromagnetic storm or an accidental *blinding* caused by sunlight that had somehow violated the pre-programmed solar Keep-out Zones. Biological, chemical, and geological oceanographers from Scripps and Woods Hole offered advice from their perspectives. Biologists could think of no explanation from a marine organism point of view. Chemists knew of no usual maritime chemical reaction that could cause such temperature changes.

Only the geologists, with their underwater volcanic theories, held any sway. Underwater eruptions, too small to show up on seismic detectors, could be substantiated using drifting buoys that allowed subsurface measurements. More useful would be ship-or air-released bathythermographs targeted to the oceanic areas in question. These radio instruments, designed to transmit their information as they fell through the water, could provide temperature/depth plots. Such measurements could substantiate underwater heating that might correlate with the elevated surface temperatures.

The meeting adjourned with the understanding that all available oceanographic research vessels should steam to the areas in question and release their bathythermographs as soon as possible. If navy, air force, or NOAA aircraft became available sooner to provide initial data from airborne drops, so much the better.

Silverstein's attention returned to the highway. He glanced over at Linda Kipling, riding shotgun in the rented Dodge Viper on the fifty-minute drive to the New Orleans airport. The quiet rumble of the ten-cylinder engine communicated the latent power that lay under the hood. Silverstein smiled to himself, knowing that Kipling had long since stopped questioning his irrational behavior when it came to automobiles. The economy rental authorized by the government would hardly do.

Kipling expressed concern. "You've been awfully quiet, Victor, ever since we arrived in New Orleans. Even in the meetings. This isn't like you. Is something wrong?"

Silverstein shifted in his seat and delayed his reply; he didn't want to talk about it but knew that his silent demeanor stood out like a blinking light on the dashboard. He loosened his tie further as the sweat from his neck started to dry. The air conditioner had only begun making headway on the eighty-five degree outside temperature and the hot Louisiana sun— and it wasn't even noon yet!

"Linda, can I confide in you…tell you something about my past that I've never told anyone…about someone who may be at the root of our environmental dilemma?"

Kipling turned and faced the driver's seat. "Someone or something in *your* past that's related to the SST anomalies? You're kidding me?" Linda's mouth hung open in disbelief.

"Do I look like I'm joking?" Silverstein turned his head and stared blank-faced at Kipling.

"No, you don't. I'm sorry." Kipling briefly hung her head but then rebounded. "Of course you can confide in me; I'm your friend! But I already know most of your extraordinary background. Your personal history is common knowledge. It's not very often you come across a black Jew. Sammy Davis, Jr., and Whoopi Goldberg come to mind, but they converted. I know that your single mother served as a housekeeper for a Jewish family in Atlanta, that she was hit and killed by a city bus. The childless Silversteins then adopted you as their own. Is there more?"

"You know that I got all three of my meteorology degrees at Penn State." Silverstein stared straight ahead down the highway.

"Of course! You were, and are, one of the most brilliant meteorologists to ever graduate from that school."

"What you may not know is that there was another student who attended graduate school when I did, and who was smarter than I was."

Kipling laughed. "You're teasing me, right? I've obviously entered the Twilight Zone. There is no way in hell the Dr. Silverstein I know would ever admit to that."

Silverstein ignored her comment and continued. "His name was Cameron Fitzby. He was a certifiable genius. Unfortunately, his mental command of abstract concepts exceeded the intellects of our professors...and almost beyond me." He chuckled.

"You've got me going now. What happened?"

"I graduated and moved to California in 1982. Fitzby left shortly after that. He never could convince his dissertation committee that his weather modification theory held water. Ironically, that period in time followed several decades when both the Departments of Defense and Commerce funded numerous weather modification projects. Artificial fog dissipation, cloud seeding for precipitation augmentation, and hail suppression. If he hadn't been so short-tempered and impatient, on top of being unbelievably arrogant, I think he would have prevailed. I read his thesis, looked at his mathematics, and all his data. From what I could tell, everything he proposed was correct."

"What theory, Victor?"

"Fitzby claimed he could control tropical cyclones by altering their surrounding SSTs. In the first part of his dissertation he showed how you would go about strengthening tropical cyclones."

Kipling jumped in. "There's nothing new there! We've know for decades that SST can alter the intensity of a tropical cyclone."

"You're absolutely right, Linda. Where Fitzby's dissertation took a leap of faith was in the second part, his contention that tropical cyclones could be steered by selective heating around the cyclone. In that way, a threatening storm could be maneuvered, away from land for example." Silverstein glanced over to gauge Kipling's reaction.

"Wow, that's hot stuff. That would be radical thinking if proposed today, let alone back in the eighties. So how did he propose to do that?"

Silverstein wiped his right thumb across his forehead. "First, he demonstrated it using a sophisticated numerical model together with software to link cyclone dynamics interactively with the SST. His model was way ahead of its time."

Linda furrowed her brow. "I remember how NOAA tried to modify hurricanes back in the sixties. Project Stormfury, wasn't it? I don't remember any talk of steering, though."

"That's right. The concept behind Stormfury was to seed the rain bands just outside the eye wall with silver iodide, to expand the eye outward. The idea was that if you made the storm larger and less wound up, it would have lower wind speeds. Everyone knows that most hurricane damage comes from wind and storm surge induced flooding, not the rain itself. Unfortunately, results from the few hurricanes they seeded were ambiguous at best."

Kipling folded her hands in front of her. "Okay. Assuming you had some way to heat the ocean, how would you know when and where to do the heating?"

Silverstein looked ahead as the column of cars slowed to a stop. "Damn! There's an accident. We may end up missing our flight. What'd you say? Heat the ocean? Right. What was unique about Fitzby's theory and what made it so difficult to understand was that he said you couldn't just go out, in a ship say, heat the ocean, steer the storm, heat it again, and so on. The dynamics of the tropical cyclone would change too quickly and you would never know if you were heating the right spots. Fitzby proposed that the only way his method could work was to update a computer hurricane model in real time as sea temperatures changed."

Kipling responded impatiently. "We're doing that today, at NRL! Our regional model uses actual SSTs, as does the global model."

"Correct! But Fitzby's theory went way beyond that. Fitzby proposed that SSTs in the model change every hour. We adjust our SSTs *daily*, if that. And under normal conditions, that's fine because SSTs change slowly. But remember, Fitzby proposed to modify the temperatures artificially. The heart of Fitzby's dissertation was the mathematics that allowed him to perturb the hurricane/ocean synergism in his model and experiment numerically with different heating patterns to direct the storm in the direction he wanted, all on the fly, in real time. Based on what happened in the hurricane model, you would then heat the water to make it happen in reality."

"This is getting complicated, Victor. For the sake of argument, let's say I subscribe to Fitzby's hypothesis, his mathematics and all the theory, which you say you are convinced of. How the hell could you possibly heat the ocean ahead of a cyclone?"

Silverstein repositioned his hands on the steering wheel. "The only way Fitzby said his technique could work in practice, meaning that the temperatures could be controlled fast enough, would be to change the SSTs from the air or space."

Kipling whistled. "Are you suggesting a laser beam? In space? That's new technology even today. I can imagine how his professors reacted back then.

"Still, I see two huge problems. The obvious one is that it would take a humongous laser to produce a temperature change, and then, in only a tiny area of water. A second problem, even more serious, is that even this huge laser could heat the water only if there were no clouds in the way."

Silverstein blew out a breath of air and raised his left hand to adjust his collar. The air conditioning had finally gotten the upper hand. "Believe it or not, Fitzby addressed and, in his mind, solved both of those problems. He recognized that it would be years before a powerful enough laser could be hoisted into orbit. However, the beauty of his hypothesis, and he proved it numerically, was that only small temperature changes were needed to alter the direction of a cyclone. With regard to clouds, he figured that one out too. He proposed a cloud detection algorithm, to reside on the satellite, much like the one you and I developed for the modelers."

Linda paused a moment. "What are you saying? That the satellite would look for clear areas between clouds and only fire the laser when it could see to the ocean? Is that what you're saying?"

"You got it, Kimo Sabe! The cloud detection and laser firing circuitry on the satellite would link telemetrically to the hurricane model running on a supercomputer on the ground. With the power of computers these days, a high-powered workstation would suffice. Software would control the interaction." Silverstein faced Kipling. "Do you see the complexity of the system Fitzby proposed...back in the early eighties?"

Kipling shook her head. "Damn! Unbelievable."

Traffic crawled to a stop. Soon, a traffic patrol car and an ambulance raced by on the shoulder. Silverstein shifted into Park.

Kipling released her seatbelt. "Surely you aren't suggesting that Fitzby has put all of this together...that he is now sitting at his desk somewhere sliding his mouse across the Atlantic, double clicking on any tropical cyclone that strikes his fancy? All the components you described would cost *millions* to set up. That presupposes there is a powerful enough laser. And further, that he got it launched into space." She lingered on her last words. "You have a security clearance higher than mine. Are there lasers that powerful?"

Traffic began to move again. Silverstein shifted the Viper into gear. He avoided her direct question. In fact, although details had been skimpy, recent intelligence coming out of Russia suggested that scientists there had made some breakthroughs in laser technology.

"I don't know, Linda. I wish there were some other explanation. I'm positive the geologists aren't going to find any underwater volcanoes. First, there would have to be a lot of spread-out volcanic activity to produce so many areas of anomalous temperature increases. You saw the temperature maps! Second, there is no way any random volcano activity could correlate with this year's increase in tropical cyclone activity."

It wasn't long before traffic proceeded again at speed and they crossed the border into Louisiana.

Kipling gestured toward Silverstein. "So why didn't you bring this up at the meetings?"

"I need to give it some more thought. It's obviously pretty far-fetched." Silverstein hesitated. "But there is another reason."

Kipling turned, her face registering concern. "I'm listening."

"What I haven't told you is that Cameron Fitzby was my roommate my last two years at Penn State. We shared an apartment downtown. That's why I know so much about his work; he often used me as a sounding board. When he started having troubles with his PhD committee, I privately interceded on his behalf, trying to lend support. I never told him that. But there was only so much I could do.

"A year before I finished, I started to date a black social science undergraduate, a junior. Back then there weren't many black coeds to choose from and I considered myself lucky to find one who could tolerate me." Silverstein smiled. "Sylvia Brown was her name. We got along like you wouldn't believe. She came from a strict Baptist background. I spent several weekends at her home near Pittsburgh and even took her once to meet Mom and Dad in Atlanta. They liked her. Everybody liked Sylvia."

"What happened, Victor?"

Silverstein started to fidget in his seat. "We had been dating just five months when Sylvia informed me she no longer saw any future to our relationship and that we were finished. A week later, when I had recovered from the shock of her pronouncement and had decided to make a fight of it, I went to see her at her dormitory. I discovered that she had left the university. I called her parents. Mr. Brown informed me that Sylvia said she wanted nothing more to do with me and that I shouldn't call again."

Kipling placed her left hand on Silverstein's shoulder and squeezed. "Oh Victor, I'm so sorry."

"I graduated six months later. I packed all my belongings into my car, left Penn State, and headed for California. Even though I had pretty much gotten over Sylvia, I still thought about her and hoped she was doing well. Out of the blue, I decided to stop at her house in Pittsburgh. As I walked to the door, I remember feeling my heart hammering. I think I still held out hope for our relationship.

"I knocked and Mr. Brown came to the door. He seemed shocked to see me and I remember preparing to run if need be. But, he invited me in. Meanwhile, Mrs. Brown entered the room. Her demeanor was equally strange. I stood for a moment and finally broke the silence. 'I don't mean to intrude,' I said. 'I'm heading to California to my first job and just wanted to see how Sylvia's doing. I cared about her a great deal, you know.'

"By the look on their faces, I knew something terrible had happened. 'What's happened? Where's Sylvia?' I asked.

"Mr. Brown motioned me to a chair. In a calm voice, Mr. Brown explained that Sylvia had left campus because she had been raped and became pregnant." Silverstein smiled weakly. "Because of Sylvia's strict Baptist upbringing, I had been called out on several occasions, well shy of second base...so I knew I couldn't have been the father." "'She should have told me,' I pleaded. 'I would have understood; it wouldn't have made any difference! She should have known that. Where is she? I'll talk to her.'

"I became momentarily ecstatic, thinking I hadn't lost her after all. I knew there was something seriously wrong when Mr. and Mrs. Brown turned to face each other. I can remember what he said, word for word, to this day."

Kipling recognized something was wrong. "Victor, what's going on? You're hyperventilating. Pull off the road. Now!"

Silverstein angled his vehicle to the berm and pulled into the high weeds beyond the pavement. Kipling reached across and moved the gearshift into Park. Silverstein laid his head against the top of the steering wheel.

"Mr. Brown said to me, 'Victor, I don't know how to tell you this. Margie and I were hoping that we would never see you again, that you could be spared this news.' Mr. Brown paused and looked again at Mrs. Brown. 'Sylvia swallowed a bottle of pills and died here at our house two months after she returned. She couldn't take the shame of what had happened.'

"I felt faint. I tried to stand but couldn't. My legs were like rubber. Mr. Brown grabbed me and set me down. I said, 'Did Sylvia notify the university or file a complaint with the police? Did they catch the guy? Did she know him?'

"For the third time, Mr. Brown glanced toward Mrs. Brown. He said, 'Yes, she knew him. He told her if she ever formally accused him, he would deny it, that it would be his word against hers, and that no one would believe a cheap black bitch over him. Those were his exact words. It happened in your apartment, Victor. It was your roommate. It was Cameron Fitzby.'"

With the name Cameron Fitzby, Silverstein's voice trailed to a whisper. By now, tears ran freely down his face. He opened the door, got out, stumbled to the front of the car, and stared ahead.

Kipling sat momentarily stunned. She regained her composure and joined him, reading his behavior over her left shoulder.

Silverstein didn't move. "For twenty-five years now I've avoided Fitzby, making sure he wouldn't be at any meetings or conferences I attended. Once in Miami, I didn't find out he'd be attending until I got there. I returned home that very night. That was a hard one to explain to Travel."

Kipling turned away from Silverstein.

"The worst of it, Linda, is that I'm afraid if I were to meet Fitzby face to face today, I would kill him. I've been fighting that urge for a quarter of a century. It hasn't gone away."

The two of them stood quietly for minutes, looking into the distance.

Finally, Kipling broke the silence. "It's not right that you carry that entire burden, Victor. If I'm there when you confront Fitzby, I'll pull the trigger myself."

CHAPTER 8

▼

NUTS AND BOLTS

Anselina Corporation, Hamilton, Bermuda: 32° 18'20"N Latitude, 64° 47'20"W Longitude
Tuesday morning, 0730, August 7, 2007

Fitzby sprang from his seat at the computer terminal.

"Shit! Can't anyone around here write computer code without any fucking errors in it? Do I have to do it all myself?" Fitzby paced back and forth, eyes darting about the room.

Barry Emerson, Fitzby's UNIX whiz kid programmer provided some moderating feedback. "Cameron, we've been working eighteen-hour days for four straight months now. You've hired the best there is, but you can't expect perfection under this kind of schedule. Give us a break for God's sake."

Fitzby knew he had been pushing hard, maybe too hard, but wasn't about to admit it. He had waited for this opportunity since graduate school. Whatever effort or sacrifice it took, they *would* be ready on time. He would show everyone, particularly the disgusting Blackbeards of the world, that what he proposed would perform as advertised.

Cameron Fitzby had wasted no time once Ghali told him his laser had launched into orbit the previous October. First, he had to find a base from which to operate, preferably in as remote a location as possible, but also within the transmission arc required to maintain continuous satellite contact. Bermuda fit the second criteria exactly. Several desirable remote locations in the Caribbean lacked the technical infrastructure needed to assemble the operation.

Second, Fitzby required technical assistance. His status as a genius notwithstanding, he couldn't do everything himself. Beyond the AI software that Fitzby needed and Ghali promised, there remained the considerable task of setting up the system, including the electronics, antennas, and such needed to communicate with the satellite. All of this required specialists: electricians, electronic technicians, computer technicians, UNIX operating system specialists, and computer programmers. Ghali's offer of a blank check proved crucial. Skilled personnel didn't come cheap.

To add to the pressure, Ghali had made it clear he wanted Fitzby's system operational in time for the 2007 hurricane season, starting in June. That had given him only six months.

The final assembled team featured a combination of local and imported talent. Ghali himself provided Russian technicians to handle the satellite communications and equipment.

It didn't take much imagination to figure that Ghali did not intend to use Fitzby's technology for the benefit of all humanity. But what of it? Wasn't there a greater morality here, well beyond the cloak and dagger saber rattling of the Blade? Wouldn't any brief, deleterious effect instigated by the Blade be more than offset by Fitzby's contribution to science at large? With this opportunity, Fitzby could demonstrate to the world the soundness of his science. It would be foolish of him—selfish, in fact—to ignore the bigger picture, or the *greater good* as Ghali had articulated.

Considering that certain episodes in his own life had no more positive effect than his own personal gratification, Fitzby considered his actions here to be nothing short of heroic. Once he demonstrated his method and vindicated his science, he could only imagine the respect and glory his life would achieve.

Of course, much of his fame would come from those who would praise his contribution to humanity, to life and to property spared by the disastrous effects of future hurricanes. But to Fitzby, such practical results seemed irrelevant. It was his scientific accomplishment that would stand the test of time. Wouldn't his contribution rank up there with, say, those scientists who developed the atom bomb? It wasn't much of a stretch, thought Fitzby, to suggest they resided in the same league.

Fitzby reconsidered. "You're right, Barry. I'm sorry, everybody. You all are doing a fantastic job under great pressure." Fitzby knew there was a time to back down and be gracious—even though it stuck in his craw to utter the words.

In fact, Fitzby's team had produced a quasi-operational system by June 1, the official start for the summer's hurricane season. Unfortunately, not everything ran smoothly and additional work remained. Fitzby's greatest relief had come back in April when the Russians had transmitted their first commands to the spacecraft. Onboard diagnostic procedures communicated that all systems performed nominally.

Fitzby could sense a question coming; Emerson had that look. "I've patched together your hurricane model with the global wind, temperature, and moisture fields. I still don't understand how that model will tell you where to fire the laser."

Fitzby mused to himself that the whole process was surprisingly simple—when viewed from a layperson's point of view. "It's actually quite straightforward, Barry. As you know, there are two components to my system: the computer hurricane model and the space-based laser. As in all things simple, though, the devil is in the details."

"You've got that right. I'm no scientist, but humor me a little."

Fitzby sat down and leaned back, hands folded in his lap. "Back when I was in graduate school, I proved two things. With a powerful enough laser, I could increase the strength of a tropical cyclone and, more importantly, steer it in the direction I wanted. The key to both is in knowing where and when to heat the water surrounding the cyclone. That's where the hurricane model comes in."

Emerson, still standing, squirmed, his mind seemingly backtracking. "How does a hurricane model work in the first place? The wind and temperature fields...what purpose do they serve?"

Fitzby remained patient. He knew most civilians had little appreciation for the scientific side of weather forecasting. "My hurricane model is not that much different from other computer weather forecast models that form the basis for modern weather forecasting. There are two kinds of models: global and regional. In a global model, we divide the geographic surface of the earth into subsections that we then represent mathematically on a computer. Everything else being the same, the more subsections you have, the better weather forecast you'll get. Make sense?"

Emerson squinted. "I think so. I wish I had paid more attention in my elective physics class."

Fitzby continued playing the part of a doting professor, a role he had more than once wished for. "Come on, Barry! What makes up the weather? Nothing more than wind, temperature, and moisture. Right? So, there are wind equations, temperature equations, and moisture equations. Computer modeling means nothing more than stepping these equations forward in time to produce a multi-day forecast. Because weather moves continuously around the globe, you need a global model to produce a forecast longer than a couple of days. Right now, weather forecasts are accurate to about a week to ten days, depending on the season. But there is a limit to how many subsections you can divide the surface of the globe into, because the more subsections, the more computer power you need. Meteorologists always want bigger and faster computers."

"Is that why you have regional models, so you can have more subsections and therefore better forecasts?"

"That's very *good*, Barry. You catch on fast. A regional model runs the same wind, temperature, and moisture equations, but on a limited geographic area or *box* that covers, for example, the United States or Europe. The global wind, temperature, and moisture data you asked about we use first to initialize the box, and second, to provide changing conditions on the sides of the box. As we move forward in time, we supplement that data with satellite-measured data. For us, though, we supplement the data in our box with data from our own satellite. We have twelve channels of data that we receive via x-band transmissions, including visible, infrared, and microwave imagery."

Fitzby reveled in his realm. "The downside of a regional model is that its forecast won't be valid beyond more than two or three days because it's not easy to handle the changing conditions on the sides of the box. The upside, as you point out, is that you can afford much higher resolution, which translates into finer scale and better weather forecasts."

As if the light bulb had just illuminated in his head, Emerson appeared to understand. "So, your hurricane model is a regional model?"

"Yes. But one developed specifically for hurricanes, with better equations for moisture. My model isn't that different from what the National Hurricane Center runs. What is unique is my method to determine where to heat the ocean surface to produce the effect we want."

"And how do you do that?"

"First, I have special software that makes an educated estimate, or in scientific lingo a *first guess*, of a heating pattern that will accomplish what we want, either strengthening the cyclone or moving it in a certain direction. Using this blueprint, we step the hurricane model forward in time one hour, over the projected water temperatures, to see if the predicted result is correct. If the prediction duplicates the effect we're shooting for, there's nothing more to do except instruct the satellite to heat the ocean in those locations. More likely, things won't progress quite the way we want and we have to repeat the process.

"That's where the AI software comes into play. This software summarizes the hurricane mathematical output into a form that allows us to provide a more refined estimate of where to position the heating. Using this new heating pattern, we run the hurricane model again. We repeat this process until we get what we want. *Only then* do we fire the laser.

"After the model predicts ahead another hour, the entire process is repeated based on the new location of the cyclone and the new surrounding water temperatures. These water temperatures, by the way, are being measured and transmitted to us continually by instruments on our laser satellite. One satellite does it all."

Emerson nodded. "Why not go forward further in time, say out twelve or twenty-four hours? Wouldn't that save time?"

Emerson's no dummy. "Good question! There's a good reason we don't go out more than an hour. Even if we suppose the model simulation is perfect, which it isn't, the satellite won't be able to duplicate the desired heating pattern exactly because the onboard satellite cloud detection algorithm ultimately determines whether the laser will fire. Because hurricanes have a lot of clouds around them, portions of the ocean's heating pattern may not occur. The laser can't work through thick clouds. Therefore, the hurricane's reaction will differ from what we expect. We repeat the process over a relatively short time period to refine our ultimate goal."

"That's fantastic, Cameron. It seems to me it won't be long before you're in line for the Nobel Prize."

Fitzby resisted the urge to puff out his chest. "You've got a good head on your shoulders, Barry. You're going to go far."

CHAPTER 9

▼

SOFTWARE

*Naval Research Laboratory, Washington, DC: 38° 49'N Latitude,
77° 1'W Longitude*
Wednesday afternoon, 1500, August 8, 2007

A thunderstorm seethed outside. Lightning split the skies, thunder rocked
the urban landscape, and wind-blown rain streamed across the window.
The few meteorologists she knew would all stand mesmerized by these
visual displays, but Barbara Lopez didn't much care for this form of
nature's power. She reached for the seclusion of her sweater even though
the office thermostat registered seventy-two degrees. The sickening recollection from her childhood surged through her mind: the thunderstorm
had come up so quickly, the tree their only shelter. Her baby brother,
Jimmy, never had a chance. *It could just as well have been me*, she reminisced. Violent weather of any kind—especially lightning—should be
feared, avoided. Lopez reached for the louvered blinds to shut out the
storm, and her memory.

According to her weather radio, extrapolations from Doppler radar said
the weather front wouldn't pass Washington, DC for another two hours.
Should be gone by quitting time, Lopez hoped.

Lopez blanked out the storm in her mind and stared at the wall above
the flickering computer monitor. She had other concerns, real ones, ones

not based on imprinted memories, but on the here and now. Something had to be done. She was unhappy and her earlier lack of social graces toward her colleagues made others acutely aware of this fact. She hated when she acted that way. *PMS* she heard one remark as she turned the corner from the copy machine. No! That wouldn't be for another five days. If nothing else, Barbara Lopez was regular.

Lopez smiled, recognizing that this weather complemented her mood precisely. One of the gifts she possessed was her ability to identify links and associations, or to devise strategies to determine those links. This talent explained why her earlier graduate work in artificial intelligence had been so easy for her, why she had garnered awards for that research, and why she now faced a pressing deadline—a deadline with no justification, no support, no one to talk to, no nothing.

Not that there was much else to make her unhappy. Not when you viewed the facts objectively. She had a solid marriage. She and her husband made a reasonable amount of money, enabling them to do just about anything they wanted. They had a comfortable, unpretentious, two-story home in Alexandria. They had no children, but that was okay too because they hadn't planned on any just yet. And central to Dr. Lopez's image of herself was her role as an important scientist at a leading research institution. What could possibly be wrong?

What *was* wrong related directly to the professional role she so cherished. Following an undergraduate degree at the University of Pennsylvania, Lopez had completed graduate school at Stanford thirteen years earlier, with a newly acquired PhD in computer science. Upon graduation, she decided to move closer to her Pennsylvania roots and accepted a position at the prestigious Naval Research Laboratory in Washington, DC. She had been there ever since. Nothing wrong with that!

But, she hadn't published one solitary journal article in the past three years. Formerly, she had averaged three a year. *That's what scientists do, for God's sake—publish their research so others can build upon their efforts to expand human knowledge.*

Not that her opportunities for promotion had been adversely affected, which they normally would have been with a lack of publishing credits.

Upon joining NRL, she had learned rather quickly that publishing credits meant everything, at least for those involved in basic research. No published journal articles meant no promotions and, after enough time, maybe no job. But things had proved different for Dr. Barbara Ann Lopez. She had progressed quite nicely, thank you. Much faster than a few envious fellow scientists who undoubtedly questioned her sexual habits. She was, after all, a beautiful woman.

Suspicious colleagues notwithstanding, Lopez hadn't slept with anyone except her husband, nor had she been tricked into accepting her current lot. She had voluntarily agreed to the conditions that accompanied her research funding. Her sponsor at the Office of Naval Research, Dr. Clement Warner, made clear when they met that his money paid for research classified as Top Secret—and unpublishable. She had accepted that stipulation, satisfied in the knowledge that her work benefited her country in some small way. Obviously, no one complained about her work performance. Why else would she continue to receive yearly bonuses?

But on top of the frustration of working in a vacuum, she now had a deadline, and one she wasn't sure she could meet. Of course, Lopez acknowledged to herself that it was the sudden imposition of that deadline that upset her. As Lopez stared at the lines of code on her computer screen, her thoughts strayed. She recalled that morning's surprise meeting with Dr. Warner. She hadn't been concentrating on work then either.

It had been ten o'clock when Warner's soft voice penetrated the quiet of her office.

"Dr. Lopez, may I interrupt? I knocked, but you were obviously deep in thought. The mark of a practiced scientist I always say."

As usual, the voice came across as respectful and conciliatory.

Lopez rotated in her swivel chair to face the smiling bearded face. Although there was little to dislike in Dr. Warner's mannerisms or his looks, Lopez felt less at ease in his presence. She wondered why.

"Oh, Dr. Warner. Hi! Sorry about that."

Should she tell a lie or manufacture a statement to preserve her integrity? A lie felt more in tune with her mood. "I was thinking about the final phase of our software. I've run into somewhat of a hitch."

"Oh?"

Warner pulled up a chair and listened to an update on their project, now nine months in the making. Lopez had been taken aback the previous November when Warner had strolled into her office, in much the same way he did just now, and told her to discontinue all current work. The project he had championed eight months earlier had to take back burner. Something new and urgent needed precedence.

"As I explained when we started, there are three components to the software you requested. Each is up and running and I've tested them thoroughly. They're bulletproof. But without system integration to allow them to work together, they're useless. That's what's giving me grief right now."

Warner shifted in his chair, his eyes registering concern, but other visible facial features revealing little else. *Visible*, because the thick salt and pepper beard covered most of what the matching mop-top hair did not. Lopez had decided early on that he'd make one hell of a poker player. On top of that, as much as Lopez tried to purge the comparison from her mind, the piebald pattern of white and black reminded her of a skunk.

Warner sighed. "I would be lying if I said you could take your time, that there is no urgency here. This project is different from any before. My bosses tell me we have just one more month."

Lopez tried to hide her surprise at this new deadline, but failed. Never before had Warner specified a schedule, let alone a deadline—and so near the end of a project! Always before, she had the luxury of working to her own calendar. Lopez had that unusual combination of skills not usually packaged together in one scientist: the talent to solve complex procedural problems and, at the same time, visualize that solution in computer code—no doubt the reason Warner had selected her. What had changed that required a deadline? Then again, what was she thinking? She had no right to question his motives or authority.

"One month. That doesn't give me much time, does it?" Lopez frowned, but her facial expression proved wasted.

Before she could expect a few words of sympathy in return, Warner rose to his feet and walked to the door. He turned and, again with an expressionless face, caught her eyes directly. "I know I can count on you, Barbara."

A distant bolt of thunder made Lopez jump, but also returned her mind to the present, and reality. Lopez looked up at the wall clock, surprised to see it was almost five o'clock, her normal time to go home. Lopez peeked through the blinds, through the glass, and across the Potomac. Although a thunderstorm still raged to the south, brightening skies appeared to the northwest. Score one for the Doppler radar.

The electronic chirp of her digital phone broke the temporary silence.

"Lopez here."

"Lopez here too. I've been worried about you! Are the blinds closed?"

"Hector! It's good to hear your voice. Yes…I'm all right."

"You don't sound like it. What's wrong, baby?"

"I've had one hell of a day. How about dinner out? Meet me at home at six and I'll treat dinner at Chadwicks. You can drive. I need wine and lots of it. This may be the last time you see me for the next month."

"What?"

"I'll tell you all about it later."

"You got it, babe. See ya."

Lopez returned the phone to its cradle and acknowledged that, contrary to her earlier thoughts, her husband—not her job—was the most important component in her life. Ironically, as little as she could tell her husband about her scientific endeavors, she knew less about Hector's work activities. His employer was the CIA, the Central Intelligence Agency, and he worked at the George Bush Center for Intelligence, their headquarters in McLean and named after President Bush the elder. Those two facts represented the extent of her knowledge about his occupation.

Just for one evening, thought Lopez, it would be interesting for them to compare notes. What fun that would be. Well, maybe not—at least not for Hector. Who could possibly be interested in software that converted numerical data from a computerized hurricane model into empirical orthogonal functions from which were selected certain summary variables to which one applied data mining tools and genetic algorithms to optimize search strategies for assessing the reaction of a hurricane to surrounding warm pools of water—all within an expert system based on fuzzy logic?

Who could possibly be interested in something as boring as that? Another scientist, maybe, but not Hector. He was interested in people, not science.

CHAPTER 10

▼

PERSUASION

Pandeli Restaurant, Istanbul, Turkey: 41°01'03"N Latitude, 28°58'17"E Longitude
Tuesday, Noon, August 14, 2007

Ghali obviously sensed Fitzby's agitation. "You look nervous." Ghali's cigarette had burned halfway. He never seemed to smoke more than half before starting a new one. And this was his third.

"You should be too. Unless I have the targeting software soon, you can kiss this hurricane season goodbye."

Since the previous November, Fitzby had traveled to Istanbul three times. Conversation never extended beyond their professional relationship. He wanted to know more about Ghali and his organization, but hesitated to ask. From what he had surmised regarding the Blade's varied and sinister interests, Fitzby concluded that Ghali was best kept at arm's length.

Only twice had Ghali visited Bermuda, to ensure the Russian scientists were doing their jobs. Other than that exception, Fitzby did the traveling, always to Istanbul and the restaurant Pandeli. Fitzby suspected Ghali worked out of Istanbul and even mused that he lived within walking distance of the restaurant.

"You will have it soon enough. Be patient." Ghali snapped his fingers and performed the requisite ordering of the midday meal.

Food arrived and they ate slowly. Conversation proved minimal and one-sided. Most of the words came from Fitzby. As in their previous meetings, Ghali insisted on knowing all details regarding Fitzby's operation. Ghali soaked up the minutiae and seemed to remember them all. Although Fitzby recognized that few minds on this planet matched his, he accepted Ghali as a formidable intellect and one who Fitzby could respect on the cerebral level.

Ghali finished eating and lit a cigarette, probably his sixth. Fitzby had lost count. "Mr. Fitzby, I want more frequent updates on your progress." Ghali removed a pad of paper from his breast pocket, wrote a few words, tore off the top sheet, and handed it to Fitzby.

Fitzby chuckled. "You have an e-mail address; I'm impressed. Get much spam?"

Fitzby memorized the address, folded the sheet in eighths, and placed it in Ghali's ashtray. Ghali touched his cigarette to the paper, which soon flashed to life.

Ghali continued speaking, ignoring Fitzby's attempt at humor. "From this day forward, I wish to receive a daily report. I want details on everything: software and hardware reliability, personnel problems, and any local issues of concern. If you encounter any difficulties, I want to know immediately. Also, I want your scientific analysis of your efforts to manipulate hurricanes manually."

Fitzby interjected. "My manual testing with the laser has confirmed what my mathematics have said all along."

Ghali looked up quickly, as if he just remembered something. "That's good. But I think it may be time to back off. Warner told me the navy sponsored a meeting to discuss the anomalous SSTs you've been creating. I don't have to tell you that the last thing we want is to draw attention to ourselves."

Fitzby placed both hands flat on the table. "Speaking of which..." He stared across the table to make sure he had Ghali's attention. "I've been patiently checking newspaper obituary columns in Monterey, California, waiting for a certain Jewish name to surface. I've seen nothing. Why *is* that? What are you waiting for? And don't tell me to be patient anymore!" Fitzby's voice rose in pitch.

"Be careful, Mr. Fitzby. I'm not the kind of person you can make demands of."

Fitzby's face flushed, but he concentrated on keeping his voice low. "Why not, Mr. Ghali? Do you think I'm worried about what you might do to me? Right now, I think you need me just as much as I need you."

"Do you recall what I said at the end of our first meeting? I remember my words verbatim. I will repeat them. *There is only one person on this planet who has the intellect and wherewithal to stop me.* Did you think I was *joking*, Mr. Ghali?"

If Fitzby's rebuttal to Ghali's brief display of emotion upset him further, he did not show it. He snuffed out his latest cigarette and, for the first time since sitting, made no motion to start another.

"I've checked out your Dr. Silverstein. He is not your usual laid-back government scientist. He is quite famous, you know. There is some danger in killing him. Now is not the time to generate any suspicion. I thought I made that point quite clear."

Fitzby hyperventilated and nervously shifted back and forth in his chair. "Let me redefine our circumstance in mathematical terms that might give you a clearer sense of the threat you have chosen to ignore. If you kill Silverstein, there is a minimal, acceptable risk his bosses will go looking for the perpetrator. But if you do *not* eliminate him, there is a near one hundred percent probability he will find us out. Do I make myself clear?"

Fitzby knew the temporary respite from smoke-laden air couldn't last. Ghali pulled another from the pack lying on the table. But after putting it to his lips, he removed it unlit and rested both hands on the table. "How is it you are so sure, Mr. Fitzby? Why is it I sense there is more here than meets the eye, as you Americans say?"

Fitzby had had enough. He pushed his chair back sharply, rose from the table, shaking with anger. "Just do it, goddamn it!"

Fitzby turned and stomped toward the door and the stairway to the street. Within two steps Fitzby heard the signature snap of Ghali's fingers.

Two men who had been sitting at a table near the doorway stood immediately and blocked departure from the room.

From behind, Fitzby heard words, completely calm, but now raised to a level where all in the restaurant could hear. "Mr. Fitzby! It is in your best interest to return to this table."

Fitzby stopped, twisted his body, and peered back toward Ghali. What brought a shiver that moved slowly through his spinal column wasn't that Ghali had raised his voice inside a public facility, or that he kept his own personal entourage. Something else proved much more disconcerting. Except for Fitzby, not one other patron or staff member in the restaurant turned toward the forceful voice at the corner table. It was as if Ghali had spoken in mime.

CHAPTER 11

▼

COMING CLEAN

Naval Research Laboratory, Monterey, California, USA:
36°35'N Latitude, 121°51'W Longitude
Friday morning, 0945, August 17, 2007

A week and a half had passed since their return from Stennis. Silverstein's body and brain had woven themselves into metaphoric knots. Following dozens of mental games searching for an alternate explanation that would free his mind of Fitzby, Silverstein concluded that nothing other than his theory in action could account for this summer's strange events in the ocean and atmosphere.

Silverstein's efforts at locating Fitzby turned up cold. The only supporting information of some interest came from Silverstein's CIA contact who had discovered the launch of an unknown satellite from Christmas Island the previous October. The launch coordinator, a Russian, was found murdered after the rocket left the pad. From what the CIA could piece together, the payload had come from Russia. But when government officials made some informal inquiries, the Russians turned mute, offering nothing.

Silverstein and Kipling spent the week analyzing oceanographic charts provided by Stennis. Close examination of the abnormal heating patterns indicated that there was nothing random about them—which Silverstein had suspected all along. They always appeared ahead of a hurricane, whether fully grown or in one of its formative stages. Coincident satellite imagery of hurricanes, for which NRL Monterey was a widely known repository, made the comparisons straightforward.

"You've called it, Victor." Kipling had just finished one more SST overlay for Tropical Storm Humberto. "There's no doubt. Someone's pretending to be Mother Nature. It's interesting that no one else has picked up on this yet." Kipling looked across at the closed office door. "Do you think it's time we tell someone?"

Silverstein arched back in his office chair as far as it would go, feet on the desk, staring at the ceiling. Without moving a muscle, Silverstein replied. "You know, we're in a unique position, Linda. Besides Fitzby's team and us, there's likely no one else on the planet who knows what's going on. We're the only ones who both know what Fitzby proposed years ago and have easy access to hurricane and SST data. I'm sure the National Hurricane Center thinks we're just experiencing an unusual hurricane year. Our friends at Stennis obviously haven't put two and two together or we'd have heard."

The wrinkles in Kipling's forehead scrunched together. "What are you saying, Victor?"

Silverstein pulled himself upright and faced Kipling. His eyes twitched and burned from lack of sleep. This was going to be uncomfortable, he thought. "What I'm saying is that I think we should keep this to ourselves, at least for the time being. We have no proof it's Fitzby and we could damn well make fools of ourselves."

Kipling's mouth dropped open. She started to say something, stopped, and then began again. "What's going on, Victor? You've sure convinced *me* about this being his work. We've proved to ourselves that the warm pools of water aren't natural. And they always show up around developing hurricanes. What more do we need?"

Silverstein stood, turned, and faced Sparks Park. The sun had finally shown its face through the low clouds. Although long fingers of fog still clung to the pine trees, the lack of higher-level clouds beyond the breaking stratus gave promise of a beautiful afternoon for the Monterey Peninsula.

"Remember the story I told you in the car on Monday?"

"How could I forget?" Kipling asked.

Silverstein continued to stare out the window. "I didn't quite finish. I told you only part of it. After I left Sylvia's parents' house, I didn't drive straight to California. Instead, I returned to Penn State to find Fitzby."

"Uh-oh. Shit!" Kipling paused to reflect. "Well, I know you didn't kill him since you've made some effort in trying to find him this past week."

"No I didn't, although I probably should have."

"What happened? Don't leave anything out this time. Okay?"

Silverstein sat back down and gathered his thoughts.

"For you to appreciate my confrontation with Fitzby, you have to know what happened six months earlier on campus, long after Fitzby and I became roommates. And, to understand *that*, you need to know a little about my growing up in Atlanta." He smiled. "You're going to get more than you bargained for."

"I can handle it. Go on." Kipling turned the chair around, sat in it backward, and rested her chin on her thumbs, seemingly ready for the long haul.

"I grew up in Atlanta during one of the most turbulent times in interracial history. My perspective, though, is far different from any other you'll hear. I lived within a city where blacks represented a significant fraction of the population and, at the same time, within a smaller community where blacks were all but nonexistent. I'm fortunate I'm not more schizophrenic than I am." Silverstein chuckled. "My parents did their best, though, to make me appreciate my black heritage. They knew they owed that to my birth mother and they couldn't have done more.

"On the flip side, they sent me to a private school where there were only three black children. If I had been in their position, I don't know that I would have done differently. They recognized early that I had potential and worked to get the most out of me. At the same time that they needed to protect me, they also wanted to prepare me for the real world."

Kipling listened intently, obviously interested in this historical account of someone she had known for eight years and knew must have had an interesting childhood. "Did you get hassled by the white students?"

"In class, not at all! We black kids were vastly outnumbered and hardly posed a threat. Plus, since I was smarter than everybody else, I soon gained respect. Outside of class, though, *that* was another story. I had my share of fistfights, but learned to take care of myself pretty well. My worst recollection comes from one day when I was walking home and got called Jew-lover and nigger all in the same trip. Talk about the ultimate dichotomy. On the positive side, by the time I was sixteen, I knew more about anti-Semitism, racism, and human personality than most sociology professors. I well understood the cruelties man can inflict upon man."

Kipling interrupted. "You should write a book! But I'm not stupid; I see where this is leading. Let me have it. What happened at Penn State?"

"Although Fitzby and I had been roommates for some time, I didn't really know him that well. It was like I could never warm up to him, but I figured that was just his nature. We obviously had a lot in common, being in the same department and being the smartest students in our class. We could speak together on intellectual and scientific levels far above our classmates. So, our being roommates was a natural fit.

"The incident that gave me a clearer insight into my roommate's morality occurred one night when we were returning to our apartment in downtown State College. It was late. Ahead of us down the street was another student, not a meteorologist, but one whom I had seen frequently, since he walked the same sidewalks we did. He was Hispanic, another of a tiny minority at the university. And crippled! I know the politically correct word now is disabled, but back in 1982, he was crippled. His one leg was shorter than the other and misshapen, causing him to walk with a sideways gait. He got around okay. He was just awkward and slow.

"Suddenly, two men jumped out in front of him and, as I found out later, demanded money. When he said he didn't have any, they threw him to the sidewalk and started kicking and yelling racial slurs. I immediately took off running and shouting to try to scare them away. Unfortunately, they didn't budge and when I arrived, they saw I was black. I won't repeat to you what they said, but it was something to the effect that, in their words, a nigger held a significantly lower position on the human evolutionary chain than even a spic."

Kipling leaned forward in rapt attention, mouth open, eyes transfixed. "Unbelievable!"

"When it became clear to them I wasn't about to run from their threats, one of them pulled a knife. What they didn't know was that, besides my skill at boxing, my parents had insisted on me taking self-defense classes as a teenager." Silverstein stopped to laugh aloud. "What *I* didn't know was that the one with the knife was just as tough as I thought I was. We ended up in hand-to-hand combat over the knife.

"It was a nasty fight and it quickly became clear to me this guy wasn't about to take any prisoners. Then, how it happened, I'm not sure, it was so fast. The guy lunged at me with his knife. As I had learned in self-defense class, I sidestepped him and turned the knife around on him. He was bleeding heavily when I finally struggled free and stood up. His partner ran away. About this time, the neighbors heard all the commotion and called the cops. It took another twenty minutes before an ambulance came and we were taken to the hos—"

"Where was Fitzby during all of this?" Kipling interjected. "Didn't he come to help?"

Silverstein gestured with his hands. "He disappeared. The last I saw him was when I started to run down the sidewalk."

Kipling's mouth still hung open. "So, what happened? You were a hero, right?"

After sitting for all this time, Silverstein got up and stood next to the desk, his hands in his pockets. "My wounds were all superficial and required nothing more than stitches." Silverstein pointed to the scar next to his right ear. "This one took seven."

"You were lucky, that's for sure. What about the other guy?"

Silverstein looked down and frowned. "I'm afraid he didn't fare so well. He lost so much blood that by the time they got him to the hospital it was too late. I was told later that the knife clipped a major artery."

Kipling stood up herself, and looked beyond Silverstein, seemingly trying to make sense of this incredible story. "It was self-defense. No one could blame you for the outcome."

Silverstein shifted his weight back and forth from one foot to the other. "That's the way it came out, although that didn't make me feel any better, having just killed a man. My parents flew up immediately, got me an attorney, and the incident blew over rather quickly. The other assailant never came forward and, unfortunately, none of the neighbors saw anything. Fitzby claimed that as soon as the fight started, he ran off. The His-panic student testified in my behalf and was my only witness. The university did everything it could to play down the incident. The last thing they wanted was bad publicity for one of their prize minority students. And so, it all blew over."

Silverstein paused and looked across, thoughtfully, at Kipling. It had been many years since he had shared this much personal information with one person. It felt strange, but at the same time consoling. He had to acknowledge that Linda Kipling represented the sole person in the world to whom he felt comfortable enough to share this painful past.

Kipling looked back quizzically. "I know this story has to come back to Fitzby one way or the other. Keep going. I want to hear it all."

Silverstein returned to his seat, folded his hands on the desk, and con-tinued. "Believe it or not, once I returned to our apartment, it was as if nothing had happened. When I asked him about it, he admitted running away. I concluded that he was so embarrassed about not coming to my aid he wanted to forget about it. I understood that. I remembered times in Atlanta, on the street, when I felt that kind of fear. I figured Fitzby had never encountered such a situation. When Fitzby later recounted precise details from that night, it amounted to the second biggest shock of my life."

Kipling's breathing quickened. "Later? When later?"

"When I arrived back in State College, after my visit with Sylvia's par-ents. By then I had calmed down enough to know I couldn't take the law into my own hands. And although I blamed Fitzby for Sylvia's death, I realized no court of law would see it that way. At the least, I wanted justice for him having raped Sylvia. But as I approached him on campus, my emotions took hold one more time.

"I told him I knew he had raped Sylvia. I told him I wanted him to go to the police and turn himself in, confess, and accept whatever justice society deemed appropriate. It was then he threatened me."

"Threatened you? Threatened you with what?" Kipling became agitated and began to fidget.

"Fitzby told me that when I ran up the sidewalk that night, he stayed behind and witnessed the entire episode. He said what the Hispanic testified to wasn't true at all, that even though the young man had initially brandished the knife, I easily disarmed and then needlessly murdered him. He said that from his position on the sidewalk, the Hispanic couldn't possibly have seen the details of the fight. He also said he confided to another student what had happened. To help me out, Fitzby said he kept quiet and never again brought up the incident in my presence.

"I'll never forget standing there, looking into his eyes, with him looking back, realizing I was looking at evil itself, a practiced liar who could look straight at me and not blink. Twice in one day, I had experienced unimaginable feelings. First, immense grief, followed by utter sadness. And then...I did what I have regretted now for some twenty-five years."

Kipling stood quickly, seemingly not wanting to breathe.

The phone rang, but Silverstein chose to ignore it. He had to complete this testimonial, as if there were some catharsis in doing so. "I did nothing; I just walked away. I was a coward. I should have stood up for Sylvia's honor, but didn't. I bowed under the slightest pressure and I regret it to this day."

Kipling breathed again. "You did the right thing, Victor. You knew the truth and so did the Hispanic student. And that's all that matters. If Fitzby dredged that all up again, it could have ruined both you and the other guy. Even if you didn't care about yourself, you wouldn't have wanted to hurt him. You did the right thing."

Silverstein appreciated Kipling's empathy and stared back into her eyes. "I know that, Linda, but it doesn't make me feel any better. But this time I'm not going to back down. That's why I want us to find Fitzby before anyone else. Will you help me?"

"Of course, Victor." Linda smiled. "But before I agree to that, please tell me that's the end of this story. I can't take any more excitement."

Silverstein nodded in agreement, his lips pursed together.

Kipling let out a huge sigh of relief. "So, where do we go from here? How do we find Fitzby?"

Silverstein turned, noting the blinking light that indicated a message from the previous call. "I've inquired in all of the obvious places. It's now time to move up the food chain and use some governmental resources that the average citizen can't draw upon."

"You mean your friends at the CIA? Why would they want to help you on the sly?"

"Oh, I don't know." Silverstein whistled and, at the same time, looked at the ceiling. "It's just that there's one particular high-level spic there who I've come to know fairly well. We go back a long way."

Kipling turned her head and smiled in unbelieving amazement.

CHAPTER 12

▼

CRIMINAL INTENT

Halcyon Heights home subdivision, Monterey, California, USA:
36° 33'30"N Latitude, 121° 46'29"W Longitude
Friday evening, 1800, August 17, 2007

Silverstein eased back on the gas as his Porsche 911 Turbo weaved its way up the steep hill to his home overlooking Monterey Bay. He reflected briefly on the road's name, Whip Road. Whoever had named the roads in these parts, he or she had been one serious horse fancier: Bit Road, Saddle Road, Spur Road, and so on.

For the first time in a while, there seemed no reason to hurry. Silverstein felt oddly at peace with himself following his cathartic confession to Kipling. Besides, despite how smart he thought himself to be, another explanation might explain this summer's oceanographic and meteorological oddities.

Silverstein likened his feelings now to the early days of his marriage when mutual trust allowed him a degree of contentment to his hurried life. Those same sensations had surfaced this afternoon when he opened himself to Kipling. Maybe it was time to rethink his attitude toward her. It had been seven years since his divorce; a man should grieve for only so long.

But before he diverted his energy down that path, an environmental abnormality, likely involving Fitzby, required attention. And if one judged Fitzby's morality from Silverstein's experience, Fitzby had dubious intentions at best. It was too much to hope that he had sided with the good guys and now worked for the salvation of humankind. The scientific community would know about it if he had. Silverstein concluded it was time to call his friend, Lopez, at the CIA. He would do so first thing Monday morning before leaving the house. The spooks at Foggy Bottom would be bright-eyed and bushy-tailed by 0600, west coast time.

Silverstein lived outside of town, but not far. Although several smaller towns laid claim to the geographic distinction, five primary communities made up the Monterey Peninsula. Monterey itself, settled in the 1700s, had the largest population and most noteworthy history; Steinbeck immortalized the town's early twentieth century sardine factories in *Cannery Row*. Adjacent Pacific Grove boasted a small-town atmosphere, whose main street once made the list of top streets in the country. Cozy Carmel remained the quaint tourist attraction, stimulated partly because Clint Eastwood had been its mayor in the 90s. Those interested in golf would recognize Pebble Beach, an unincorporated gated enclave noted for its world-renowned golf courses and famous Pro-Am golf tournament. Finally, there was Seaside, the second largest of the Peninsula communities and mostly a lower-cost bedroom community. These towns together brought the peninsula population to a little over one hundred thousand.

Silverstein's house lay outside Monterey proper, technically in Monterey County, in Halcyon Heights, one of several upscale housing developments in an area called Hidden Hills. Hidden Hills lay alongside Highway 68, the crowded two-lane corridor connecting Monterey to the larger agricultural town of Salinas, eight miles to the east. Traffic withstanding, he could drive to work in fifteen minutes.

Silverstein preferred the quiet solitude of life outside of town where the only distractions at night were coyotes howling, owls hooting, and the occasional barking dog. The previous year, a great horned owl had chosen Silverstein's chimney as a resting spot for its nightly courting of a nearby female. The first time the owl let loose, Silverstein all but leaped out of bed when the owl's normally loud hoot amplified as it cascaded down the metal walls of the prefabricated chimney directly into the bedroom. He soon identified his new tenant as the male of its species, once he learned that the male hoots in a higher-pitched voice than does the female—musical thirds, according to his wildlife book.

As Silverstein gunned the Porsche up the two hundred foot curved driveway that led to his house, all seemed peaceful. Nothing much ever happened in this gated community, more than a mile from the main highway. Gardeners, the previous week, had trimmed the Myoporum trees that lined the drive. Oblong shadows to the east complemented their perfectly sculpted spheres. Unexpectedly, Silverstein's mind snapped to attention.

Silverstein had been plagued since birth with qualities attributed to the astrological sign of Virgo. Although he didn't believe in such celestial mumbo-jumbo, Silverstein had to admit he fit the type: organized to a fault, neat, perceptive to miniscule details. Thus, after rounding the last bend, and seventy feet from the house and his four-car garage, Silverstein leaned heavily on the brakes, stopped, and peered ahead.

With the Porsche's throaty exhaust resonating through the lowered windows, Silverstein scanned the sides of the drive and his house ahead. The shrubs and trees looked normal; the windows and garage doors were closed, as they should be; the driveway, as it should be. But no! Ahead and to the right, Silverstein noticed turnaround marks from a vehicle that had driven up the drive, backed up, and turned around, obviously forgetting to make sure the car was moving before turning the wheel—a particular pet peeve of Silverstein's. Silverstein had long ago taught his regular guests the proper method for turning around without leaving tire marks. Other than his housecleaner, Martha, there should have been no daytime visitors this week—and today was Friday, not Martha's day. Someone had driven into the driveway since this morning.

Nothing to get worked up over, thought Silverstein. On the other hand, why not play it safe? Silverstein decided to call his home answering machine. There might be a message saying who had been by. The cell phone's voice recognition system accepted his command of *Home One*. The phone rang four, five, six times, but the machine did not pick up. If no messages sat waiting, the machine should have answered on the fourth ring.

Silverstein chose to play out the implied logic. This meant one of two things: either the house had no power or the phone line was out. To ensure that his treasured Buick still sat safe, he reached to his visor and pressed the last button to open the right most of the four garage doors. The hinged, cherry-stained panels rose slowly to reveal the maroon, 1956 Roadmaster hardtop, a car his late father had meticulously maintained and Silverstein had washed hundreds of times as a kid. Obviously, the house had electricity.

Silverstein next triggered the left-most door where he would normally park the Porsche. Nothing! *That's strange.* Why would the right-hand door open and not the other? Still, the fact that one door opened meant the house had power. *Therefore*, the phones had to be out. He considered two further branches to this decision tree: either the telephone company had line difficulties outside of his house *or*, someone had purposely cut the phone line to his house, an unlikely scenario—you had to go to burglar school to know that, and nonprofessional burglars never took the time to learn their trade properly.

He remembered the logic he had used in designing the security for his house. What anyone breaking into his house would not know was that Silverstein had a backup telephone line that also serviced the security system. A burglar wouldn't anticipate that possibility and, even if he had, would never locate the underground wiring that bypassed the visible telephone box. So, by cutting the normal telephone line to the house, they would not have disabled the automatic dial feature of the alarm system that called the security company when a window or door break occurred.

But, he had received no telephone call. The alarm company would have notified him on his cell phone before calling the police; standard procedure. (That had happened only once before, when a houseguest had inadvertently triggered the alarm.) If someone had broken into his house, they had bypassed the alarm system and disabled the door and window sensors, including the five infrared motion sensors that scanned the interior rooms.

Silverstein lifted his cell phone and spoke deliberately, *Home Two.*

He listened intently. This phone number accessed an answering machine and phone hidden in an office desk drawer. Silverstein's heart skipped a beat when the machine played its message—it was an unlikely scenario that one phone line would be out and the other functional. He immediately punched "6" to activate the room monitoring feature of the PhoneMate. If someone had cut the house's primary line, he or she would not be expecting a phone to ring.

Silverstein killed the engine and listened warily as he jacked up the volume on the small cell-phone speaker. Seconds passed. Something in the background, *maybe*—probably my imagination, he thought. But then, a smooth rolling sound—that of the drawer in the desk. Damn!

Silverstein's pulse quickened. Someone was in his house! A burglar? What to do? Should he call the police? There had never been a break-in in the neighborhood in the thirteen years since his move.

He thought quickly. If someone had been casing his place, wouldn't they know his normal work schedule, know he would be home by now, and have been long gone? Of course! But if someone possessed the sophistication to disable the security system and alarm, which had the ear-shattering power to awaken the entire county, this wasn't a garden-variety burglar. Silverstein chose to ignore the small voice in the back of his mind suggesting a different motive. That thought proved too frightening.

Silverstein gripped the steering wheel tighter and knew it was time to become scared. If someone had broken into his house, by now they knew he knew. He had tossed the ball back into their court. He looked at the house, waiting for signs. They weren't long in coming.

He heard the sound of a starting engine. The left-most garage door opened slowly, the one behind where his Porsche normally sat. Had he inadvertently triggered the button? No, it hadn't worked a minute ago. There was trouble to be had—and soon!

Silverstein's hand leaped to the key. The 911's engine and twin turbochargers spooled to life. Before the garage door rose more than halfway, he jammed the transmission into reverse, took one last look through the windshield, turned to look out the back window, let out the clutch, and floored the throttle.

All four tires squealed as Silverstein flew down the driveway at more than forty miles per hour, backward. Just prior to exiting onto the street, he glanced up and saw a black Mercedes rushing to meet him head-on. For an instant, he caught the eyes of the driver. In the subsequent microsecond, his vision caught the face of a surprisingly similar-looking passenger, his hand now extending from the window. *It can't be!*

A fraction of a second after he made his decision Silverstein heard the gunshot. He jammed on the brakes, initiating a backward slide. Simultaneously, he turned the wheel sharply to the right. After skidding for the last twenty feet, the car now pointed down Whip Road, away from the driveway. Silverstein marveled to himself that he actually remembered how to perform this driving stunt, a move he had practiced numerous times at various racing schools held at the local Laguna Seca raceway, visible from his property. *So much for a driveway free of black tire marks.*

He had to make an immediate decision—only a hundred feet to the stop sign. Should he go left, back down Whip Road to Highway 68, or go right onto Spur Road? Either way, he'd run into a gated exit that would take time to open. If his pursuer caught him at the gate, there'd be nowhere to go.

Silverstein chose to turn right. Going left would be suicide. There was no way he could outrun his pursuer going downhill, toward the Whip Road gate. Going right, he could count on two miles of curvy, uphill road. Assuming he could gain a few seconds—he drove a 911 Turbo with four-wheel drive, more than a match for the larger Mercedes—he would have time to exit the gate before his pursuer arrived. Once on public roads, he could blend in with traffic and escape.

Silverstein stayed in first gear and took the hard right onto Spur Road easily. As the tachometer spun quickly past 6000 RPM, he shifted smoothly into second. The speedometer shot past sixty all too quickly and Silverstein forced himself to slow down—fear too quickly overrode common sense. Tight turns loomed ahead and he could easily lose control. If that happened and he ended up in the ditch, he would be a sitting duck. In the rearview mirror, he watched the Mercedes fishtail around the stop sign.

At once, Silverstein's concentration lay solely on getting to the back gate as fast as possible through the neighboring development of Bay Ridge. He had to arrive there with enough time to allow the gate to open. Although the gate opened automatically on the way out, it was a slow process. Silverstein figured he should have plenty of time. His four hundred and fifteen horsepower Porsche should prove more than a match for the less powerful Mercedes. Nevertheless, with a skilled driver behind the wheel, Silverstein's advantage would be erased. Worse, he was driving scared. He had faced sticks and knives before, but never guns.

Stay calm; stay focused. I have the advantage here. No way can he catch me. I have the faster car. Sweat formed on Silverstein's forehead and dripped downward. He reached up to clear his right eye, then his left. *For Christ's sake, keep both hands on the wheel!*

The Porsche hugged the asphalt the way only a four-wheel drive car can. The normal thirty-five mile per hour back roads yielded to Silverstein's sixty mile per hour pace, except on the hard turns. He braked fast and then accelerated, the way race drivers do. A quick look in the rearview mirror revealed nothing. But that didn't mean much because the turns came ever so quickly. A sharp one hundred and ten degree bend appeared, preceding an especially steep half-mile hill. *Steep is good! No way can the Mercedes accelerate like I can.*

The eighteen-inch Pirelli radials strained sideways through the hard right turn as Silverstein fought to keep the car out of the concrete drainage channel that lined the road. The fifty mile per hour speed brought into the turn was lost to sideways friction as he forced the transmission back into first gear. He needed high RPM coming out of the turn before engaging the steep hill to maximize his acceleration upward. The engine screamed as the engine revolutions hit the fuel cutoff just beyond the sixty-six hundred RPM red line. He jerked the transmission into second.

Before flying over the top of the grade, for only the second time since the stop sign, Silverstein permitted himself a look into the rearview mirror. He saw the Mercedes sliding sideways around the tight turn, a quarter mile to the rear.

Silverstein crested the top of the hill at more than eighty miles per hour, pleased with himself that he may have gained enough time to exit the Bay Ridge gate. But he was going *much* too fast. He was terrified and that led to careless driving. The next second brought that fear clearly into focus.

Three hundred feet ahead, a large road grader moved across the narrow road from left to right. At the instant that image registered in his mind, all four wheels of the Porsche lost contact with the road's surface as the cusp of the hill launched the car skyward.

Horror filled Silverstein's mind as he realized he headed straight toward the large-wheeled steel construction vehicle. When the tires once again made contact with the pavement—all four stopped in midair when he slammed the brakes while airborne—the antilock braking system immediately took charge and started to pulse at the requisite fifteen times per second. One-half of the available distance had disappeared and he stared directly ahead at the yellow vehicle. Silverstein reacted intuitively, knowing his only hope was to steer hard toward the graded wall of dirt to the right. The construction vehicle continued moving, oblivious to the impending disaster unfolding—until the driver heard the Porsche's screaming tires.

With the antilock braking system pulsing relentlessly, Silverstein whipped the wheel savagely to the right. *Turn, goddamn it!* He looked up to see the surprise on the face of the driver. The Pirellis now had full contact with the pavement. The mechanics of the car fought to obey the disparate instructions telegraphed from the automobile's sophisticated electronics and the driver's commands through the steering wheel and brakes. The force on the brakes and tires told the machine to stop as fast as possible. At the same time, the antilock braking system pulsed at speed to allow the driver to steer and remain in control of the vehicle. That miracle of electronics allowed the hard right turn to stand a chance, to keep the car from skidding straight ahead.

After no more than a fraction of a second, the Pirellis responded to the instructions transmitted through their controllers, fighting to overcome the straight-ahead momentum. Simultaneously, the Porsche's electronic stability control system accepted a myriad of inputs describing the vehicle's movement in a heroic attempt to keep the vehicle under driver control.

In the seconds before the impending collision, Silverstein noted that the world seemed to slow, the detail in his senses exquisitely clear. He peered down and saw his hands gripped tightly around the wheel, the muscles in his arms straining to the right, the speedometer rapidly descending. He glanced up, saw the horror on the face of the grader's driver and the decision telegraphed through his eyes to leap from the large vehicle to escape the looming collision. *Did these sorts of details face Sylvia in the moments before she went unconscious from the pills? Was Fitzby a part of those moments? Was Silverstein?*

The instant that preceded the impending collision culminated in his vivid realization that death was not at all a certainty. Time and reality returned to normal.

The Porsche reacted, screamed to the right, and cleared the grader. Suddenly a new concern: the steep embankment to the right would flip the car onto its roof if he did not now force the steering wheel hard to the left. Again, with the antilock braking system grinding hard, the stability system now recognized that the vehicle had transitioned to an over-steer condition and applied breaking action to the outside front wheel. Flying rocks and scraping metal punctuated Silverstein's visual and audible senses as the right door slammed hard against the embankment. He was *past* the grader. He would live! The Porsche continued another hundred feet. The speedometer needle finally rested on zero.

Silverstein looked up from the steering wheel, mouth agape, heart racing from near-fibrillation speed, and realized he had escaped death. He forced himself to take a breath, to reflect that his brush with eternity had passed, that he should command his heart to slow down.

A split second later, the comprehension that all was not over gripped him a second time. He released one hand from the wheel, twisted in the seat and, simultaneously, heard the scream of rubber tires. He turned in time to see the Mercedes slide sideways directly into the side of the grader—both passengers with their hands raised and shielding their faces.

The Mercedes split the difference on either side of the grader's low earth-moving blade. The accompanying explosion of sound forced Silverstein instinctively to turn and duck—as metal, glass, rubber, plastic, and human body parts from the large automobile became as one with the metallic monster.

CHAPTER 13

▼

MAN IN PLACE

*George Bush Center for Intelligence, McLean, Virginia: 38°56'N
Latitude, 77°8'W Longitude*
Saturday morning, 0500, August 18, 2007

Lopez eyed his desk with contempt. A clue lay buried, but damned if he
could find it. All the field reports, all of the signal intelligence, all the Intel
from foreign spies on the payroll. Why didn't they lead to a common
denominator? Although his intuitive proof would be laughed out of a
courtroom, he knew that a mole had infiltrated the Department of the
Navy. But Hector Rodriguez Lopez, Jr., senior counterintelligence agent
for the CIA, could not find him. Worse, he had been on the trail for more
than two years and now questioned his right to cash his paycheck.

Lopez's job at the CIA involved counterintelligence. He smiled to himself as he pondered his job description: To thwart the efforts of an enemy's
intelligence agents to gather information or commit sabotage—sort of like
an anti-missile missile. On days like this when nothing made sense, he
often fantasized a discussion with his counterpart on the other side.
Except, he reminded himself, no classic *other side* existed anymore.

Lopez reflected warmly on earlier days from the cold war when adver-
saries, no matter how clever, convoluted, or cold-blooded, could be
counted upon to act rationally, to abide by de facto standards accepted

implicitly by both sides. The day when the life of a sole terrorist intent on blowing himself up became mainstream was the day when rationality skipped town. The world had changed dramatically since 9/11 and Iraq, and Lopez bemoaned that logic proved less useful than in the past. Worse, this sorry situation complemented the fact that today's wars seemed to be neither won nor lost. America had discovered this new maxim the hard way.

And to top it off, last evening a call from Silverstein. Someone had tried to kill him! He sounded scared and Lopez felt sorry for his old friend. Lopez immediately dispatched two agents from the San Francisco office to attempt a body identification of the two corpses—although Silverstein made it clear the resulting barbecue following the explosion left only charred remnants. Further, the chances of finding a DNA match were remote at best. The agency's stratagem to build a DNA database for all known terrorists remained behind schedule and underfunded.

"Two of our agents from San Francisco were on the scene by twenty-two hundred, Hector. They're in control." Marc Miller had the annoying habit of rushing into Lopez's office without knocking. Still, Lopez could excuse his annoying quirks. Miller had one of the best minds on his staff.

"Thanks. We can hope for an ID, but from what Silverstein said, it doesn't look good."

Miller threw himself into the guest chair, brows furrowed and eyes closed tight, another of Miller's odd characteristics, meaning he was in deep thought. "I assume you didn't let on, that Silverstein's still in the dark."

"Of course. Just because he has a security clearance close to that of God himself doesn't give him a need to know here. He'll find out soon enough. I now understand why he asked for that information on satellites some weeks ago. He wouldn't say then why he was asking."

"How did you handle yourself when he mentioned the name Fitzby?"

Lopez tapped his pencil on the desk. "I implied I barely remembered Fitzby, although I doubt my words were convincing. I'll *never* forget that son of a bitch. I'd give you ten to one Fitzby saw what happened that night on campus. His story that he ran home at the first sign of trouble never rang true with me." He stopped tapping. "On the other hand, I can tell you I never again expected to run across the name of Cameron Fitzby in this lifetime."

Miller finally opened his eyes and chuckled. "I know. I'll never forget the look on your face when I told you we had fingered Fitzby as the research scientist Sidki approached at the conference. Your story of how you met Silverstein is classic."

"Yea, déjà vu, and a lot more. I've got to hand it to Silverstein, though. He's done us a big favor by giving us more pieces to the puzzle. If I didn't respect Silverstein so much, I could easily dismiss his hurricane theory as the exaggeration from a conspiracist. But that's hardly possible. If he's jumped to the conclusion there's fire, it's time to start looking for smoke signals."

"You said Fitzby needed—"

Lopez interrupted and wagged his finger at Miller. "It's time to start paying attention to the TV meteorologists' grumblings that this hurricane year is like no other. Silverstein said he could be wrong, but it's all fitting together now."

Miller's eyes closed again. "You said Silverstein insisted that Fitzby's proposal at Penn State required big financing. Once we ID'd Fitzby, it didn't take Research long to learn that Fitzby's been looking for support since graduate school. Although the meteorological community has written him off as a nut case, he's been hitting the national meteorology conferences for the past twenty years. It was a stroke of luck when Baxter spotted him with Sidki. So, what do we do now?"

Lopez reflected on the totality of what they knew. Fitzby had indeed found funding for his research, but that source was still unknown. Lopez and his team had been tailing Ali Sidki, a Saudi national, for years and knew that he freelanced for several worldwide terrorist organizations, mostly coordinating arms deals. The agency had proof he had ties to the first World Trade Center bombing, the *USS Cole*, and al-Qaeda in Iraq. Adding complexity to the issue, he had recently visited Russia.

The state of the globe being as it was, Lopez ruled out the former Soviet empire as a sponsor; they had no money. A government that accepted cash from private millionaires for rides on the shuttle was hardly awash with reserves ready to fund oddball foreign scientists.

Sidki represented the first of the agency's success stories using the Delta Chip, developed by the CIA's Mensa team. Mensa had come up with the idea just two years earlier: that it was technically feasible to track an individual worldwide, at least while he or she remained outdoors, using National Assets—an ambiguous reference to the nation's global satellite network used for spying. It was simply a matter of implanting the Delta Chip, a microchip powered by a similarly micro lithium battery (good for ten years), on the body of the intended.

The chip's innovation lay in its unique transmission pattern involving thousands of broadcast frequencies. Any single frequency transmission lasted no more than a fraction of a second and took place microseconds before the subsequent, alternate-frequency broadcast of electromagnetic energy. Unless you knew the sequential order of the firing frequencies, the microchip proved undetectable.

The Mensa team concluded that the ideal location for the chip lay beneath the skin directly on top of the head. *For two reasons.* First, when outdoors, this location permitted unfettered transmission to a satellite, with no intervening body mass to weaken the faint signal.

The chip had to be inserted surgically—and therein lay the second advantage. Assuming that the victim had no knowledge of the surgery, the tiny incision would produce only minimal soreness for a day or two afterward. The top of the head is one of several places on the human body that cannot be examined (by oneself) without a mirror. Because of the brief duration of any discomfort, and the fact that the chip lay beneath hair (hopefully), by the time the victim got around to thinking about it a second time, any pain would have disappeared. The dissolving sutures would leave no trace.

Of course, as in all things ostensibly simple, the difficulty lay in the execution—implanting the chip without the victim's knowledge. The geniuses in Mensa claimed they had a drug that would reliably bring about memory loss. They were also convinced that the sedated victim would remember nothing, including the immediate seconds preceding the administration of the drug. Their in-house tests confirmed this result, or so their reports suggested. Even so, it would still be tricky to administer since the victim *would* remember what happened prior to those few seconds. No one in the agency had yet exploited the drug in the field, for fear the technology behind the chip would be lost if the drug failed to perform as advertised.

In the case of Sidki, pure serendipity intervened and there was no need for the drug. While being tailed by an agent, Sidki suddenly fell victim to appendicitis and required surgery.

The speed with which the agency responded to this fortuitous occurrence became an in-house legend. An agency surgeon arrived on the scene within eight hours. That the hospital happened to be located in a less than affluent country, where corruption and payoffs proved routine, facilitated matters. Money changed hands. The agent required only fifteen minutes alone in the operating room. It was this chip that pinpointed Sidki at the American Meteorological Society's conference the previous year and led Baxter to Fitzby.

Miller grew impatient. His boss had sat motionless for a full five minutes, obviously in deep thought. "Talk to me. What's your thinking?"

Lopez stirred, turned, and acknowledged the fact he wasn't alone in the room. "For now, we just sit back and wait. Fitzby is only the tip of the iceberg. We've got bigger fish to fry. If we rush in and bust him...even if everything Silverstein says is true...we'll lose our link to the top. We've got to find out where the money's coming from."

What Lopez didn't say, but both of them knew, was that the CIA had known for some time that a secret organization, probably Middle Eastern (because it took oil money to produce the sums of cash being handed out), funded its own research projects. While such a discovery wouldn't be newsworthy, the research being sponsored hardly benefited humankind. Words like chemical, biological, and nuclear normally surfaced with these projects. A vaccine for the prevention of AIDS was not among them.

Moreover, whoever set things up had done a fine job of hiding both the organization's, and the money's, trail.

Miller nodded in agreement, but then countered. "You're taking a big chance, aren't you? You're assuming Fitzby's project relates to what we've been chasing. Maybe it is, maybe it isn't. This kind of research isn't typical for them, you know. Either way, if someone's fiddling around with hurricanes in the Atlantic, it's not something we can keep under our hats for very long."

Lopez threw his hands into the air and gave Miller an exasperated look. "I know that! But this is the only thing resembling a lead we've had. We can't risk it by rushing in on Fitzby."

Lopez paused and continued. "At the same time, we can't risk any of this information with Silverstein."

The muffled electronic twitter of Lopez's telephone interrupted his thoughts.

"Yeah, what is it? You're kidding me?" Lopez scratched the side of his head above his left ear.

"What?" Miller had immediately recognized Lopez's personal, telltale gesture that meant he was surprised, an unusual occurrence.

Lopez hung up the phone and continued to scratch. "Guess where our electronics people told me Ali Sidki just showed up?"

"Where?"

"Monterey, California."

The room turned silent, as both men pondered the meaning this new information contributed to the evolving puzzle.

Miller stood and faced the window. "Son of a bitch. First, we find Sidki talking to Fitzby, and now he shows up at the site where two henchmen tried to whack your friend. Do you think he's been sent in to finish off the job?"

Lopez drew in a big breath of air and let it out slowly, at the same time leaning back in his chair. "No, we've never had any evidence Sidki does that line of work. He's a negotiator. My guess is he was sent to find out what went wrong and report back."

"Should we tail him?"

"Yeah; good idea. It wouldn't hurt to approach our problem from multiple angles."

Miller cupped his face in his hands and then looked up. "There's something else, though. When Sidki reports back, don't you think they'll try to hit him again? Shouldn't we assign someone to Silverstein?"

"Not yet. It'll take them a while to regroup after this setback."

"Okay, if that's what you think. Anything else?"

"No, not right now. I'm still counting on our ace in the hole. We'll just sit back and let Tom O'Toole earn his pay. Thank God we had a UNIX expert standing by for a field assignment."

CHAPTER 14

▼

APPEAL TO GOD

Naval Research Laboratory, Monterey, California, USA: 36°35'N Latitude, 121°51'W Longitude
Monday morning, 0800, August 20, 2007

"You fool! You could have been killed. Did it never occur to you to just back away quietly and call the police? Noooo! Instead, you decide to outrun these guys in your testosterone-fueled toy car." The veins in Linda Kipling's forehead stood out visibly. Her face flushed and her nostrils flared. She paced back and forth and continued ranting.

Silverstein kicked back in his Leap chair and tried to maintain a straight face. He loved to see Kipling angry. Something particularly sexy revealed itself through all that fury. He wanted to laugh aloud but stifled himself so as not to hurt her feelings.

Instead, he decided the smart thing to do was match her emotions one on one. Otherwise, she would think less of him. Silverstein bolstered himself for his upcoming outrage.

Silverstein leaped to his feet and feigned anger. "Jesus Christ, Linda. When was I supposed to *do* all this calling? Oh, forgive me." Silverstein paused and slapped his forehead for effect. "I'd forgotten about the two milliseconds of time I had between seeing the garage door open and shifting into reverse. Somehow, I never considered that at the time. What was I thinking? How stupid of me!"

Silverstein turned quickly to face the window. He had to hide the smile that had crept across his face. He hoped he hadn't overacted. He listened for some sign of diminishing emotion behind him. It came soon.

"I'm sorry, Victor. I don't know how you stayed so calm and reacted so quickly. I'm sure I wouldn't have had that sort of composure."

Silverstein knew it was time to capitulate.

He turned and revealed a face that truly reflected his feelings. He looked Kipling in the eye. "I don't deserve any special credit, I can assure you. My reaction was pure reflex. You would have done the same. Believe me, I was scared to death."

Kipling took a seat and Silverstein followed suit. He looked down and, for the hundredth time, scanned Sunday's issue of *The Herald*. The accident and a photograph of the charred wreckage made the front page. The driver of the grader had suffered a broken arm but otherwise escaped unharmed.

He had made headline news—but not quite the way he remembered it. He came across as an innocent observer of a terrible accident. He had just finished explaining to Kipling what really happened.

Lopez's team had arrived late Friday evening and took immediate charge of the investigation; making a veiled suggestion to the county sheriff that they had been trailing these two for some time. They asked the authorities to downplay the incident—and ignore the fact that half of Silverstein's Porsche now looked like it had been through a meat grinder. A week and a half was the quickest any body shop would promise its repair.

"There's no doubt they were out to kill you? Isn't there some other explanation?" Kipling looked up hopefully.

"I'm afraid not. As I backed from the driveway and the first shot ricocheted off the roof of my car, I realized these guys were more than annoyed salespeople."

Kipling jumped to her feet. "You didn't tell me that! They shot at you too?"

"Just once…they never got another chance. I was too fast." Silverstein pretended to take a puff from an imaginary cigarette. "Bond, James Bond. Shaken, not stirred, thank you."

Kipling twisted her face into a disbelieving stare and sat down. The veins in her forehead began to pulse again. "You're crazy! You *know* that."

"Afterward, Lopez's guys checked out my house. The thugs were professionals all right. They had not only gained entry through a door that was wired to my alarm system, which wasn't that hard to do, but they also bypassed my infrared sensors, found the control box, and disabled it. That's getting pretty damn sophisticated."

"Did they leave anything incriminating? Fingerprints? They weren't expecting to leave your house when they did."

"That's good thinking, Linda. But no, nothing. No obvious prints. Must have been wearing gloves the whole time."

Kipling's thought brought something to mind that he had not considered, but now made perfect sense. His pursuers had obviously planned to do away with him in the house and make it look like a burglary. In preparing for that eventuality and a quick departure, they would have been careful to leave no clues.

"*What?*" Kipling had long ago learned to read Silverstein's facial contortions.

"Oh, nothing. Just going over some things in my mind." He had decided earlier, for Kipling's sake, to minimize the gruesome nature of what had transpired, and the real possibility of what could have occurred. Kipling's next statement made him realize she had done more thinking than he gave her credit for.

"It's Fitzby, isn't it?"

"Huh?" Silverstein tried to play dumb.

"Don't play coy. I know you're convinced he's behind what's happening with the hurricanes. And from what you've told me, he knows you're the only one on the face of the earth who could put two and two together."

"Probably."

Kipling was on a roll. She stood and started pacing again. "And another thing! The fact that he or his sponsors would stoop to murder means two things. First, his benefactors have the resources to pull it off. And second, and more important..." Kipling paused for effect. "It means that whoever hired Fitzby wants to keep his operation secret." Kipling maintained a look on her face as serious as Silverstein had ever seen.

Silverstein marveled that Kipling's thought process mirrored his own. There was no sense in trying to keep anything from her anymore. Besides, he needed someone to confide in.

Silverstein looked up and replied with a soft, accepting voice. "I couldn't have said it any better myself."

Kipling, facing the door, whirled back. "How much did you tell your friend, Lopez?"

"I told him everything...well, almost everything. Told him I thought Fitzby was behind this year's hurricane anomalies. He acted surprised at my mention of the name Fitzby, but I think that was an act. He would never have forgotten that Fitzby was the sole witness who could have testified to what happened on the street that night."

"Did you ever tell him about Sylvia?"

"No! And I purposely neglected to tell him about Fitzby's threat after I confronted him about Sylvia. Lopez doesn't know Fitzby witnessed the attack from beginning to end. He still thinks he ran home. If I had brought that up, I would have had to go into all of that. I didn't have the strength." Silverstein looked down solemnly.

Kipling spun her chair around, sat down, and faced Silverstein, resting her hands and head on the seatback. "If you believe what you say and you sensed Lopez was faking surprise, that means he's holding something back."

Silverstein leaned back and returned his feet to the middle of his desk, hands folded in his lap. He had to give Kipling credit. He hadn't considered that possibility.

"Makes sense, but why would Lopez know, or care about, Fitzby. Hell, it's been twenty-five years since that incident at Penn State."

"I don't know, but something sounds fishy..."

Silverstein blanked out the rest of Kipling's words. All of this talk about Fitzby and Lopez brought back painful memories of Sylvia. He had never felt more alive in his life than during those months with her. When she had suddenly dumped him and inexplicably left campus, his life had been shattered.

Of course, now with age and wisdom on his side, he realized that he had been young and in love, and those things happen. But back then, he remembered proudly, he did his best to get her back. He recalled his father's favorite saying, words that had inspired him to this day: *The most you can achieve from inactivity is a little rest.*

In an attempt to get Sylvia back, Silverstein wrote letter after letter, addressed to her parents' house. No response.

And then, to leave no solution unchecked, he turned to his faith for salvation. Although religion had not been a high priority to his parents, they had fully indoctrinated him into the Jewish faith. He became a card-carrying Jew, albeit with the watered-down Judaism sect known as Reform, in contrast to the stricter Conservative, and even more fundamental Orthodox sects.

As if he recognized the Reform movement had taken Judaism too far in the direction of the Gentile faiths, during high school he became devoted to studying Judaism and, on his own, mastered the intricacies of the written Hebrew. Word soon spread across Atlanta about this black, converted Gentile, who read the Torah more fluently than most rabbis. His parents admitted to friends that their adopted Gentile son had transitioned into a far better Jew than they had ever been. They put their foot down, finally, when he suggested they keep a kosher kitchen.

As a last resort, Silverstein approached the lone rabbi available to students at Penn State and asked that he help Silverstein pray for Sylvia's return. Silverstein suggested that he would pray to God until Sylvia returned. He fondly recalled the old rabbi's kind disposition and sound advice: "We mortals never know God's intentions. If I were you, I'd set a time limit on your prayers. If God hears you, he will respond soon enough."

At that suggestion, Silverstein chose a period of three months. He prayed in the all-faith Helen Eakin Eisenhower Chapel on campus morning and night—and in between as much as possible. If prayer to the almighty should prove to be Silverstein's last avenue of hope, he would give it everything he had.

Three months passed and Sylvia hadn't returned; neither had any replies to his letters. Silverstein gave up. He decided then and there that God did not answer prayers. When her parents later told him what had happened to Sylvia, he decided that God not only had snubbed his prayers, but had kicked him in the ass as well. Silverstein decided never to set foot in a temple or church again.

"Wake up! Earth to Victor, earth to Victor." Kipling snapped her fingers.

Silverstein raised his head. He instinctively wiped at his face, sensing moisture beneath his eyes. He turned away in embarrassment.

"I'm sorry. I was remembering the words to a plea I made a long time ago, to someone very senior in my religion. But I was rejected, Linda, and I walked away."

CHAPTER 15

▼

AVOWAL

The Asylum Tavern, Washington, DC: 38° 55'02"N Latitude, 77° 01'51"W Longitude
Tuesday evening, 2330, August 21, 2007

The seedy looking bar on U Street, the Asylum, had the requisite atmosphere for secreted meetings—a dark, smoke-filled, back-alley sort of establishment where everyone spoke in hushed tones. No one socialized or looked strangers in the eye because it wasn't that sort of place. Often, meetings ended with simple handshakes. On other occasions, envelopes of various sizes changed hands. Ghali felt uncomfortable with the handshake, but completely accepting of envelopes.

He arrived early and chose a booth hidden in the corner. Used by him previously, that booth provided two benefits, one of which was a discrete location away from curious eyes and ears. The second advantage, of somewhat more importance to Ghali's cultivated nature, stemmed from its position as far away as possible from the grubby bathroom, the slightly less grubby counter of a bar and, most grubby of all, the small closet-size space called the kitchen. It was safe to order liquor in this establishment but nothing else.

It took less than a second for him to catch Warner's shifty eyes as Warner turned the corner toward the booth. He slid into the booth opposite Ghali. They exchanged unemotional glances that substituted for official acknowledgment of each other's presence.

"Two beers, German." Ghali ordered for both of them.

The obviously gay waiter accepted the order with no eye contact. Although Ghali technically represented a trespasser on Warner's turf, his senior position within the Blade gave him immutable authority, even in a decision as minor as ordering drinks.

Warner pushed himself back into the seat, hands clasped lightly to the table in front of him. "Do you bring news?"

Ghali bemoaned that Warner's facial hair hid all outward appearance of emotion. Although they had known each other for most of their lifetimes, Ghali accepted the fact that Warner had created a façade that would always separate the two of them. Then again, Ghali acknowledged that pretense served its purpose within the community where Warner lived his secrets. Warner had survived unscathed for more than fifteen years in lesser jobs within the US government, and within the upper reaches of the Department of the Navy for the past thirteen years.

Warner's current assignment within the Office of Naval Research had been a stroke of luck, and brilliance, which had served the Blade well. The position provided Warner access to various sources of intelligence, as well as his private, US taxpayer-funded, research facility.

Ghali recalled his initial impression of Warner, in Egyptian basic training in 1965. A skinny, self-righteous runt of a man who possessed self-confidence well beyond his physical appearance. When Ghali had questioned his background, Warner shamelessly explained he was a half-breed.

Warner's Egyptian mother had married an American who worked for a US firm in Cairo. Conceived in Cairo and later born in Boston after his father had transferred stateside, Warner held both US and Egyptian citizenships. Following the breakup of his parents, he spent time and felt at home on both sides of the Atlantic. When Warner turned twelve and his father remarried, he transferred semi-permanently to Egypt—and had the misfortune of being drafted and fighting in the '67 war with the Israelis.

It was then he met Ghali, and not much later when the Blade recruited them both. While Ghali continued to advance within the Egyptian military, Warner attended college in the US, culminating with a PhD in physics from MIT. Warner's brilliance in all things technical made his career ascent within the US government a steady process, all within the covert control of the Blade.

Ghali stared into the dark eyes across the table. "I have news, but it is not what you wish to hear. The Ishmael twins are dead."

Two beers arrived, dispensed on the table with nonchalant abandon, as if the waiter recognized that any association with the clientele here was ill advised.

Warner reached for his beer, fingers steady, emotions contained after years of practice. "And Silverstein?"

"Scared shitless, I'm sure, but still very much alive. When the twins failed to report, I asked Sidki to check on them. He didn't have to go far. The incident was front-page news in the local paper. I read about it myself over the Web. The twins were careless. But, at the least, they had the good sense to burn themselves to ashes in their failure."

Warner maintained eye contact and took a second sip. "Well then, the news is not all bad, is it?"

Ghali reflected to himself that neither of their remarks communicated any obvious respect for their two fallen comrades. Years of doing business in the shadows, of justifying ends through any number of means, had hardened them both. Life meant far less to Ghali than it had before that fateful day in 1967, when he held the limp body of his brother Mohammed and simultaneously cursed the Supreme Being above—which Ghali had long since concluded never existed.

Ghali himself gave the order to the twins. At the time of their first meeting in Istanbul, Fitzby's request seemed inconsequential and Ghali set it aside. When Fitzby later asked why Ghali had not acted, Ghali's questioning made clear why Fitzby considered Silverstein so much of a threat. One week ago today, Ghali issued the command.

"You have grown to be as cold a man as I. From what I read, little remained from which to make identification. You can be sure, though, that Silverstein's friends in the upper reaches of the government have their speculations."

Warner fidgeted, but in a manner only Ghali would recognize. "I've sensed nothing through my channels that would suggest Silverstein has alerted anyone that this summer's hurricanes are anything more than a natural occurrence. He did attend a navy-sponsored meeting on anomalous SSTs, but nothing much came of it. I saw the report myself. Perhaps Fitzby gives too much credit to this Silverstein."

Ghali glanced around the room and lowered his voice. "Fitzby is certain Silverstein has made the connection."

"Then why haven't I heard anything? I keep my ear pretty close to the ground."

Ghali folded his hands in front of him. "I don't know. It doesn't make sense."

"What was their relationship? Were they friends?"

"They were roommates in college. That's all I know. Fitzby's quite close-mouthed about it. The fact he wants Silverstein killed hardly means they're friends."

Warner sighed. "I'm afraid my news isn't a whole lot better. It's going to take another month before Dr. Lopez can complete and check out Fitzby's software."

Ghali felt his stomach tighten. "*Kahretsin!*" Warner had no reaction to Ghali's Turkish profanity. "We've got to get that program to Fitzby while we're still within the hurricane season, while we still have something to work with."

"I know you're anxious but, if we have to, why not wait until next year's hurricane season? That would give us plenty of time to get things right."

Ghali's voice rose in pitch, but then quickly descended when he recognized he was on the edge of losing control. "We *can't*, we don't have that luxury. What you don't know, and I haven't told Fitzby, is that the laser has a one-year half-life. For technical reasons, the Russians tell me its strength will decline markedly by next year. It's either this fall or we start from scratch."

Ghali observed Warner's reaction. He wished he had such nerves.

Warner reacted calmly to the statement and coolly took a sip of beer as if to prove it. "I've given Lopez a thirty-day deadline. I'm confident she'll come through. I can't push her any harder."

Ghali locked eyes with Warner and then laughed aloud. "I know! Of all the scientists available to you, you had the incredible wisdom to pick someone whose husband works in counterintelligence. That's hardly a situation that makes me sleep well at night."

Warner smiled back. "It's worked for three years now, hasn't it? I haven't heard any complaints. I can trust her. Don't worry. In another month you'll have your precious software."

"I'm counting on it."

Warner signed deeply. "Now that you know my situation, what about yours? From my point of view, I'd much rather be sitting on this side of the table than yours. If Silverstein puts two and two together and opens his mouth, you're going to have a lot more to worry about than unfinished software."

Ghali smirked in reply. "Did you bring it?"

Warner reached into his leather satchel and removed a nine by twelve manila envelope. He handed it across the table. "It's lucky I didn't destroy my copy after I faxed it to the twins. I wondered why you wanted the file. Now I know."

Ghali folded back the metal clasp, ripped open the flap along its seal, and withdrew the paper clipped packet of papers. A black and white photograph lay on top.

Warner closed his satchel and looked across at Ghali. "The photograph is five years old, but it's the best I could find from his records. I doubt whoever you assign next will have any trouble identifying him. He *does* stand out."

Ghali glanced up at once, eyes squinting and cheeks raised in disbelief. "He's a *black* man?"

"You didn't know? I would have thought Fitzby told you."

From Fitzby's description of the intellectual capacity of his nemesis, together with the name Silverstein, Ghali had pictured a white man with conspicuous Jewish facial characteristics. That Fitzby had purposely chosen not to mention this otherwise significant detail meant more than a simple oversight. Fitzby was hiding something.

Warner interrupted Ghali's train of thought. "Who are you going to send, now that the Ishmaels are communing with Allah?"

Ghali gulped the last of his beer, threw several bills from his wallet onto the table, buttoned his jacket, and slid from the booth. Before departing, he leaned down close to Warner, steadied himself, and replied in a whisper. "We've worked too long to get this far. I'll do it myself."

Ghali hurried from the bar into the street and sucked in deeply the hot humid air, feeling sweat form on his body almost immediately. In many respects, the miserableness quotient in Washington, DC exceeded that of Cairo during the summer. Not quite the blowtorch hot air, but humidity you could cut with a saber.

A black man? Fitzby was afraid of a black man? Ghali could count on one hand the number of blacks he had known personally over the years. None of them came close to his intellectual equal, although they had all served his purposes loyally when needed. From his photograph, this Silverstein represented one of African descent, far beneath even the intellectual match of a West Indies black such as Colin Powell, America's former Secretary of State. That the African black had achieved parity with the white in the United States was a mistake, thought Ghali.

Ghali hailed a taxi and headed back to the hotel. It would be a short night—the wake-up call for his six o'clock flight out of Reagan National would come soon enough. He would make Monterey by late Wednesday morning.

Ghali smiled to himself as the taxi sped off into the night, content with a new perspective to his mission. He had never killed a black man before. This assignment should prove to be more satisfying that he had originally thought.

CHAPTER 16

▼

INSTANT RECALL

United Airlines Flight, San Francisco, CA to Denver, CO
Wednesday afternoon, 1510 (MDT), August 22, 2007

Silverstein possessed multiple talents that made him the exceptional scientist he had become. Beyond his analytic ability, which had given Silverstein an edge throughout high school and college, lay his gift to recall, on demand, not only everything he had ever read, but voices, faces, and conversations as well. Sometimes he wished he had been spared this faculty. Inconsistencies that jarred his mind—and not always when they occurred—bugged him until he figured them out. And so it happened, that one of those contradictions revealed itself somewhere over western Utah.

Silverstein and Kipling sat in first class and had just finished lunch. Silverstein peered out the tiny window and scanned the undulating structure of the wave clouds that spread across the Rocky Mountains. One of his early meteorology professors had explained that this type of cloud exposed nothing more than waves in the ocean, an ocean of air. How poetic he had thought at the time.

Thinking back to still earlier days, Silverstein reminisced in the warm sensation of his mother's love. That he happened not to be her natural-born child—or, to anyone else, could ever be suspected of being her child—hadn't mattered a whit. Victor Mark Silverstein *was* the son of Sara and Ivan Silverstein. His parents would tactfully admonish anyone foolish enough to question that fact.

Both of his parents had passed away within months of each other ten years earlier. He had taken it hard. But, he reminded himself, because of his natural ability at recall, an overflowing cache of memories endured, available for review whenever he felt low—and that was now.

Silverstein smiled at the clouds outside his window. His mom had reminded him, repeatedly, why he kept running into things—he always had his eyes focused on the sky and not on the ground in front of him. He pursed his lips and held back the tears for the memory that followed. He recalled her profound mortification when she once started to say, in jest: *One of these days you're going to get yourself run over by....* He was twelve-years-old at the time. He had known the truth about his birth mother as soon as his parents thought he would understand. How her life had ended one summer day in downtown Atlanta when she inexplicably stepped in front of a transit bus. His mom never again questioned his studying the clouds.

By the time Silverstein turned eight, his curiosity toward weather overshadowed all other interests. He knew then that his life's work would revolve around meteorology. He built his own weather station by age nine and, for seven years, before heading off to college, became a recognized *official observer* for a local radio station. He recorded the daily maximum and minimum temperatures, precipitation total, and average daily amount and type of cloud cover.

The Boeing 777 rocked mildly during their descent into the Denver airport, some sixteen miles northeast of Denver proper. The voice next to him reminded Silverstein he was not alone.

"Do you think they're interested more in the theoretical or practical aspects of our cloud classification scheme?" Kipling thumbed through her PowerPoint presentation on her laptop.

Silverstein turned away from his clouds and faced Kipling. "Sorry. What did you say?"

"Pay attention! I know this whole hurricane thing has you tied in knots, but you've got to spend a little time working on what the navy pays you to do. Besides, Stennis hasn't called lately. The Atlantic SSTs seem to be behaving themselves for a change."

Silverstein sighed. "Yeah, I know, and that's got me worried too. What's Fitzby up to now? Why the sudden back off?"

"Forget about that now. We've got to earn our keep. How should I structure my talk at NCAR?"

NCAR, the National Center for Atmospheric Research, had earned its status as one of the country's primo civilian research facilities for meteorology. Located just a short drive north of Denver, the central facility commanded some of the area's choice real estate, situated on a bluff overlooking the town of Boulder. Administered by a consortium of universities, and funded by the National Science Foundation, NCAR represented one of the country's finest institutions in which to conduct meteorological research. Silverstein remembered fondly a summer he had spent there while in graduate school.

After Silverstein finished his PhD, scientists from NCAR had courted him zealously. Nevertheless, he chose to work for the navy. Silverstein knew his decision pleased his father who had served as a young navy physician during World War II.

"I'd split the difference. Your presentation will be electronic. You can deviate if you sense the audience wants more of something than another."

Silverstein had no concerns with Kipling's presentation. Her briefing technique was probably superior to his own. A colleague had once commented that Silverstein's style emitted a sense of arrogance. Silverstein concluded long ago that a few of his fellow scientists confused confidence with arrogance, an easy mistake in Silverstein's case.

Although Silverstein had avoided managerial and administrative responsibilities, his duties still included frequent scientific presentations. Recently, he had encouraged Kipling to give more talks—to increase her exposure, and thus her standing in the meteorological community. His own scientific stature had been assured long ago. Kipling was still establishing her credentials.

The plane landed smoothly and taxied to the gate. Fellow passengers rose from their seats in response to the electronic tone. Kipling stood and stretched to retrieve her bag from the overhead compartment.

"Linda, do me a favor? We're in no rush. Do you mind if we sit here and wait until everyone gets off the plane?"

Kipling sat down and turned, concerned. "Are you feeling okay?"

"No, it's not that. I need to check something."

Silverstein rotated to scrutinize the passengers.

Kipling turned too. "Can I help? Tell me what you're looking for?"

"Later." Silverstein focused his concentration on the faces passing by.

Men, women, and children plodded by. Silverstein's seat next to the window on the left side of the two-aisle aircraft forced him to strain to check both pathways. The two hundred and fifty passengers of the chock-full 777 would take some time to disembark. Silverstein studied each of them, as best he could, given his position. He was determined to crack one mystery before he left this airplane.

First class had emptied; only he and Kipling remained. Strictly coach passengers going by now. In particular, Silverstein searched for one face he had seen before—and not that long ago. Why he would be on this plane made absolutely no sense.

The frequency of departing passengers became less, primarily families who had chosen to wait. Silverstein worried. No, he couldn't be mistaken!

And then, there he was, the tall, disheveled man in the left aisle next to their seats! He sauntered by, seemingly paying no attention.

"What is it, Victor? Tell me."

"Soon, Linda." Silverstein stared hard at the back of the dark-headed man about to exit the aircraft to the left.

And then it happened! Just before disappearing from view, the man whirled, glanced back, and caught Silverstein's eye. The communication that transcended the short distance took Silverstein by surprise.

Silverstein caught his breath and turned briefly toward the window, contemplating certain facts that made no logical sense. Silverstein recalled the old axiom that controlled much of scientific discovery: When you eliminate all logical explanations, one's only recourse is to accept the illog-ical.

Silverstein faced Kipling. "Why would someone I saw just this morning at the airport in Monterey, who had just arrived from San Francisco, then buy a ticket and follow us back to San Francisco and on to Denver?"

Kipling stared at Silverstein, seemingly in thought, and her mouth dropped open. "Oh, my God," she stammered.

Silverstein watched the color drain slowly from Kipling's face. He was sure she had observed his own blood sucked dry just seconds before. The significance of the solution to Silverstein's puzzle was not lost on her.

CHAPTER 17

▼

CALM BEFORE THE STORM

Bermuda Weather Service, Bermuda International Airport,
Bermuda: 32° 22'02"N Latitude, 64° 40'39"W Longitude
Wednesday evening, 1815, August 22, 2007

"What do you think Barry meant by that? Has he taken an interest in meteorology?" Jim Avery turned to face Marsha Kendall, busy typing up the local forecast. Her shift would soon be over and his beginning. Avery had replied on autopilot—the Meteosat image on the monitor held more sway. Kendall's rants about her boyfriend were practically daily fare.

"I don't know, but I thought it was strange. He said he's been reading about the unusual hurricane season and wants to know more." Kendall kept typing.

The last two weeks had seen Bermuda facing further brushes with tropical cyclone activity. But for the first time in months, the atmosphere west of Africa showed signs of settling down. During previous weeks, two more tropical systems had come streaming across Bermuda. The winds and rain hadn't been enough to trigger any significant damage, but they did cause concern among local hoteliers who noticed increased cancellations for the summer tourist season. Kendall's five-day forecast, for the first time in weeks, lent some optimism to local officials. Although convective disturbances still skirted off western Africa, typical for this time of year, they remained benign.

Avery turned away from his monitor. "You know my contact at NHC, Alfred Davis?"

Kendall smiled. "Of course! I hope our salaries aren't affected by your long distance bills."

Avery ignored the sarcasm. "Well, yesterday I was on the phone with him. He told me there's something strange going on with the SSTs in the Atlantic."

Kendall stopped typing. "What do you mean, strange?"

"Davis says that more than a month ago, they started noticing anomalous SSTs showing up across the Atlantic. The navy even sponsored a workshop to get ideas on what's going on."

Kendall returned to her typing, becoming impatient. "Give me details. First, you say strange. Then, you say anomalous. What are you talking about?"

Before Avery could reply, Kendall turned, scrunched up her face and made circular motions with her hands in the air. "Don't tell me there *is* something to this whole Bermuda Triangle thing. If I'd known that, I would never have asked for this job."

Avery laughed. "Good point! I hadn't considered that possibility. No, what they're seeing are patterns of warming, usually near tropical storms."

"That doesn't make any sense. Everybody knows that as hurricanes move, they stir things up and bring *cooler* water to the surface. Not warmer."

"We know that and their scientists know it too. They've been trying to find an explanation. They've considered satellite instrument measuring error, computer algorithm error, and underwater volcanic activity. You name it. So far, they've turned up zip."

"Do they think—?"

Avery interrupted. "And listen to this! They're seeing these changes *only* in the tropical Atlantic. Nowhere else."

Kendall paused to consider this new information. "Well, that pretty much rules out instrument error. Does he think there's a connection between the warming and this year's hurricane activity?" Kendall stood.

Avery nodded. Her thinking already paralleled his. He spoke deliberately. "If Davis thought it, he didn't say. He mentioned the workshop and their theories, with the condition that nothing we discussed go beyond this office. The last thing Davis wants to see is a quotation from the National Hurricane Center showing up in the Bermuda *Royal Gazette*, citing curious phenomena in the waters around Bermuda."

Kendall snickered. "I don't think he needs to worry about a leak from this office. We all know on which side our bread is buttered. Tourism would take a definite hit."

"You've got that right. I sure hope the room's not bugged."

Kendall smiled. "On the other hand, you've got me convinced. Sounds like the Bermuda Triangle!"

"Don't go batty on me, okay?"

"But, seriously, in this day and age, no one would fall for that, would they?"

Avery sighed. "Don't you believe it, Marsha? I can't tell you how many times I've been cornered at parties and asked my opinion about the Triangle. By seemingly intelligent people. You stay here long enough you'll see what I mean. Superstition can run deep in these parts."

Kendall traipsed to the Bunn-O-Matic, filled two cups, hers halfway, returned to Avery, handed him the other, and looked him in the eye. "No offense, Jim, but how come you didn't notice what's going on? You spend more time than anybody here staring at the satellite images. Don't the SSTs show up in the infrared?"

Avery took the cup and set it aside. "The changes they've spotted are too subtle, Marsha. You'd never see them by looking at the raw infrared images. The Naval Oceanographic Office computes them, with the infrared being the primary input. The only reason the navy discovered that something was wrong was because of the computerized algorithms that calculate the temperature."

Avery stopped to take a sip of coffee. He then grabbed two fingers from his left hand with his right. "There are several inputs to those equations, Marsha. One of those is the previously computed temperature at that same spot. As you know, ocean temperatures change slowly and the algorithms operate on that premise. Davis said the new temperature being computed was so far different from the previous one that the algorithm failed."

Kendall finished typing the forecast and handed it to Avery. "You know, Jim, everything you've told me now makes me wonder more about Barry."

"Why?"

"I told you about Barry asking about hurricanes, about what makes them tick."

Avery chuckled. "Yeah. He's obviously trying to impress you, thinking the quickest way to a woman's heart is through her profession. Not a bad strategy."

"You're forgetting what I told you earlier, what Barry asked me exactly."

"Sorry. Hit me again."

"Last night, Barry quizzed me about ocean temperatures and how they relate to the growth of a hurricane."

Avery pondered Kendall's comment for only a split second before he exclaimed. "There hasn't been anything in the papers about the SSTs! I just found that out myself from Davis."

Kendall stared back, her facial features tightening. "I know."

CHAPTER 18

▼

FOOLED

***United Gate B47, Denver International Airport: 39° 51'34"N
Latitude, 104° 40'14"W Longitude
Wednesday afternoon, 1700, August 22, 2007***

"If you're continuing on this flight, we won't be leaving for more than an hour. You might want to get off and stretch your legs." The male flight attendant sensed concern and confusion between the two passengers seated in seats 4A and 4B.

"No, we're fine. Can you give us a minute, please?" The flight attendant retreated. Silverstein turned back toward Kipling.

The color in Kipling's face had only partially returned. "What do we do now, Victor? Do you think he's out there waiting for us?"

Silverstein slumped back in his seat. "I'm thinking."

If there had been any question in Silverstein's mind that what had transpired was anything more than happenstance, that thought rendered itself null and void the instant he and the stranger locked eyes. This man had recognized Silverstein in the Monterey airport and followed him to Denver!

Silverstein removed his cell phone from his jacket pocket and dialed.

"Who are you calling?" He heard the words but they didn't register. Too many thoughts raced through his mind.

"Lopez, please. Tell him it's Victor Silverstein and it's sort of an emergency."

Silverstein's eyes squeezed tight. "I see. Can you page him, please? Ask him to call me on my cell."

Silverstein gave the number, pressed the off key, thought for a moment, and turned to Kipling. "The first thing we do is split up and get you out of this mess. I doubt he'll remember your face. You get off the plane, rent a car, drive to the hotel in Boulder, and I'll call when I know what's going on."

The color returned to Kipling's face—and then some. "Two words, Silverstein, and listen carefully. *Like hell!*"

Silverstein flinched. "What's wrong with you? I'm the one he's after, not you. I can look after myself."

"Sure you can, double-oh-seven! Where's your Walther PPK? Or did they take that away from you in security? And your little toy car? It's still in the shop, isn't it? Or has Q pulled some strings? Forgive me for saying it, but you need someone with a little more experience in this line of work." After the initial shock from his revelation, Kipling had returned to her normal spunky self.

"What the hell are you talking about? Experience in what?" Silverstein couldn't believe the direction the conversation had taken.

"Experience in dealing with bad guys. Although you had a few run-ins with malcontents over the years, as you've told me, you grew up with a silver spoon in your mouth. You may be a good boxer and know how to drive a car, but you know diddly about the criminal element."

"And I suppose you do, Sherlock?" He noticed his rising voice had drawn the attention of the remaining flight attendants. He lowered his tone to a whisper. "For your information, I think our friend who just got off this plane is way beyond criminal. This guy isn't interested in my Rolex!"

Kipling looked sheepishly toward Silverstein. "I guess I never told you what I did after that year in the Soviet Union learning Russian…after I got my Bachelor's in biology but before I returned to graduate school to study meteorology."

"Evidently not!" Silverstein half chuckled. "You never did say why you went to Russia." He hesitated. "Please don't tell me you worked for Lopez at the CIA."

"No, but afterward I did work in law enforcement for three years. That's where I learned the martial arts and how to ride a motorcycle, for your information. It took me that long to decide I wanted to return to science. With regard to my supplemental linguistic capability, I'm still waiting to make use of that." She smirked. "We do foolish things when we're young."

"No, you never did mention that tiny detail in your life. What sort of law enforcement?" Silverstein looked sideways at Kipling, confounded by this new bit of information tossed in his direction. He thought he had known most of Kipling's life history.

Kipling's eyes veered from Silverstein's, some embarrassment evident on her face. "I was a state game warden in Colorado. My degree in biology played a role in that decision."

Silverstein felt the strain in his face abruptly vanish. He threw back his head and laughed loudly. The flight attendants looked back yet again, apparently confused over the range of emotions emanating from their two remaining passengers.

Silverstein's face suddenly turned serious. "Now, tell me. I know it must have been rough duty, but you can confide in me." He lowered his voice to a whisper. "Did Bambi look at you cross-eyed one day? Did you lock him up for sinister intent?" Silverstein paused. "Or, did you just blow him away on the spot?" Silverstein howled again, laughing at his own joke.

Kipling folded her arms and looked straight ahead, her eyes blinking rapidly to overcome the barbs thrown her way. "Go ahead and laugh. You have no idea what went on in those woods. Drug transport, assault, and even murder. I'd like to tell you I never had to draw my weapon, but that would be a lie."

As happened yet again, Silverstein recognized he had stepped over the line and immediately backpedaled. It was one thing to dissect, chew up, and spit out a fellow scientist over a technical issue, but quite another to poke fun at someone who so obviously wanted to help him. He placed his right hand on Kipling's shoulder, turned her head toward him with his left forefinger, and looked her in the eye. He could feel a tear forming. He wondered how many friends of his would have the guts to stay and confront this potentially dangerous situation.

"I'm sorry, Linda. I had no right to talk to you that way. Please forgive me." As had happened numerous times before, Silverstein maintained his gaze for only seconds before he had to look away.

The electronic tone of Silverstein's cell phone punctuated the otherwise quiet of the deserted forward section of the aircraft. Silverstein removed his right arm and pressed the receive button.

"Silverstein here…Lopez? Hold on. I'm putting you on speakerphone. My colleague, Linda Kipling, is here with me. As I speak, we're sitting on an airplane at the terminal in Denver."

Silverstein pressed the speakerphone button and held the tiny phone between them.

"Victor, what's up? My secretary said it was an emergency. By the way, a colleague of mine, Marc Miller, is on the line too."

Silverstein explained in detail their itinerary, what had transpired earlier, and his suspicions. A long pause ensued at the other end. Silverstein suspected Lopez had muted their conversation at his end.

"What did he look like, Victor?"

"Dark, olive skin, pockmarked face; black, graying hair; tall, well over six feet. I'd say middle fifties. But, here you go. He had one distinguishing characteristic that set him apart, a long scar that ran from his right ear to the corner of his mouth."

Again, a pause at the other end. Seconds ticked by.

"Hector, does that description mean anything to you? Talk to me."

Still more seconds, with total silence on the line. Silverstein and Kipling looked up at each other.

"I can't talk over this unsecured line. I'd like to help, but we have no assets in Denver right now. You and Kipling have to figure a way to elude him. Do you think you can do that?"

"We'll do it, Hector. I'll get back to you."

Before pressing the off button, he heard Lopez's final admonition. "Be careful, my friend."

Kipling spoke first. "Lopez knows who he is."

Silverstein pocketed the cell phone and replied glumly. "Yup."

Kipling turned in her seat, bringing her left leg up to cross over the right, revealing the cowboy boots he always kidded her about. "Okay, here's what we do. He's obviously out there in the terminal somewhere, waiting to tail you. He wouldn't be stupid enough to try to make a hit in a crowded airport. So, he'll wait until you've gone somewhere less crowded. On the other hand, if he knows you've ID'd him, he knows that won't be easy either. He'll try to make you think you've lost him."

Silverstein sat, intrigued with Kipling's quick logic. "Go on."

"Our ace in the hole is that he doesn't know me."

Silverstein nodded. "That's right."

"All we have to do is get away from the airport. We could easily lose him then, even if he followed us, which he won't be able to do with my plan. Remember, he has no idea why we're on this flight or where we're headed."

Silverstein sat transfixed and understood. "I see where you're going. You go on ahead, rent a car, and then come back to pick me up."

Kipling nodded. "That's right, but I've got to pick you up in a busy location, in a crowd of people."

Silverstein snapped his fingers. "I know where. It'd be unexpected and crowded too. Most people get picked up at Arrivals, right? Pick me up at Departures. It's usually a zoo there, more congested. But I need to know what kind of car to look for." Silverstein paused and snapped his fingers again. "You can call me on my cell."

Kipling winced. "I've got a better idea. If you're busy trying to avoid someone, the last thing you need is to worry about receiving a call. Besides, we'd be screwed if I caught you in a dead zone."

Silverstein looked back, confused. "Good thinking! So how will I know it's you?"

Kipling smiled. "One of the advantages of my folks living here is that I know this airport." She stood, stepped into the aisle, reached for her bag overhead, and prepared to leave.

Silverstein remained seated, looking up, hopeful for the last part of Kipling's plan.

Kipling looked at her watch. "Give me an hour and ten minutes. Stand on the street by the United Departures. Don't bother calling me; just be there." She scrambled up the aisle.

"You've got to give me more information, damn it! What kind of car will you have?"

Just before turning toward the Jetway and out of view, Kipling turned, peered back, and smiled provocatively. "Oh! I think you know I'm not a car kind of person. Look for a good-looking, forty-one-year-old on a motorcycle."

"Wait!" Silverstein jolted from his seat. Kipling stopped and looked back, feigning exasperation. "I'll need a helmet."

Kipling laughed and then replied before disappearing from view. "That's *so* California, Victor. Colorado is much more progressive. Helmets are optional here."

Silverstein waited twenty minutes before exiting the aircraft. Kipling's plan made sense. It was now his job to make his way across the terminal. He worried that his adversary might be waiting right outside the Jetway. Probably not. Kipling would have called on her cell if she had seen him. She said she would remember his face.

Silverstein exited the Jetway, proceeded into the pedestrian area, and took a quick look up and down the corridor. Putting aside his narrow escape from death just days earlier, he tried to remember any comparable situation when he had been as fearful. Even when he had fought off Lopez's mugger back in college, it wasn't the same. Back then, he spotted the danger ahead and confronted it. Now, that same threat magnified itself in two ways. First, he didn't know where the menace lay. Second, the stakes had risen—there was no doubt this stranger wanted him dead.

Silverstein looked at his watch. He still had forty-five minutes to burn. No point in rushing. Besides, he needed to use the head. He timed his entry into the bathroom with a group of men just getting off another flight. Back in the open, he made his way down the escalator to the train. Hiding among a throng of people proved comforting and he exited the forward car without incident, heading toward the terminal and baggage claim. He tried to use peripheral vision exclusively, but every so often would stop, turn, and scan the crowd walking toward him. So far, so good.

Silverstein continued past baggage claim. In a quick decision, he chose the elevator to go up to the airline ticket counters. From there, he walked deliberately toward the street and the arriving passengers. Fortunately, at this time of day passengers scurried everywhere and Silverstein felt safety among the numbers. Unfortunately, he also knew he didn't blend in as well as he would have liked—this was Denver, not Atlanta.

Silverstein angled his watch to the light. He had noted the time when Kipling left the plane. Sixty-seven minutes and counting! Silverstein moved along the front of the terminal, scanned the sea of people, and backed himself into a corner. He reached into his bag for his sunglasses—as if that would make a difference.

Silverstein searched the oncoming lines of cars, trucks, and SUVs. No motorcycles! Picking out Kipling would be a piece of cake. He began to wonder where she could possibly rent a motorcycle, and so quickly.

Sixty-nine, seventy, seventy-one. Silverstein glanced at his watch every thirty seconds. A minute late is no big deal, he thought. How could she possibly time it so precisely anyway? He wouldn't be surprised if she were five or ten minutes late. Silverstein knew he could rationalize with the best of them. Denver was a busy airport; there could have been others ahead in line, whatever line it was she used to rent a motorcycle. Seventy-three, seventy-four. Silverstein was getting worried, now not for himself but for Kipling. She had ordered him not to call, but Silverstein decided he couldn't wait much longer.

Realizing he had only been searching upstream, Silverstein stepped away from the building and looked at the departing taillights. *Nothing!* He checked his watch again. Eighty minutes! Again, he scanned approaching vehicles. Not one motorcycle.

Reacting to every movement in sight, he heard the muffled sound of someone's cell phone. *Why didn't they answer it?* It took ten seconds time before Silverstein realized it was his own. His hand dived into his jacket pocket and he scanned the screen. It wasn't Kipling. Caller ID would have identified her cell number. He didn't recognize the number, one with a Virginia area code.

Silverstein punched the button. "Who is this?"

A pause. "Victor, it's me." It was Kipling, but she didn't sound right.

"Linda!" Silverstein hyperventilated. Why would she have avoided using her own cell phone? "Where are you?"

Another pause. A male voice replaced Kipling's. "You didn't think I would be so stupid to overlook your lovely traveling companion, did you? If so, you have underestimated me, Dr. Silverstein."

Silverstein felt faint. He turned and buried his face in the glassed-in corner. "Who are you? What do you want?"

"I am someone who very much wants to meet you in person, Dr. Silverstein, to get to know you better. But for the time being, your attractive escort will do. I ask only that you contact no one. If I sense in any way you have betrayed me, Dr. Kipling will die. Do I make myself clear, Dr. Silverstein?"

"I will do what you say."

"Good. For now, I want you to proceed to your meeting in Fort Collins as if nothing has happened, except for the sudden illness of your assistant who couldn't make the trip. I will call you there. Keep your cell phone by you at all times."

It didn't take long for anger to replace concern. "Now you listen to me, you bastard! If you hurt her in any way, I will find you and I will kill you! Do you understand?"

"My, my. You have a temper, don't you? You must learn to control such feelings. As I said, do as I say and your friend will live. Contact no one!"

The line went dead. Silverstein turned back to the street, and collapsed to his haunches. *How stupid! I should have known he would remember Linda. I couldn't have done a better job of setting her up.*

Silverstein reconstructed in his mind what had happened. Kipling's kidnapper had obviously ambushed her, threatening her convincingly enough that she thought her life was in danger. She sounded drugged.

Two signs, however, suggested that Kipling wasn't completely under her abductor's control. First, she hadn't volunteered to use her own cell phone to call. Second, she had lied to her captor about their destination. Silverstein wondered in what other ways Kipling might be manipulating the situation to her advantage. Pragmatism overshadowed that positive thought: Kipling's life had value only as a hostage. If Ghali got the better of Silverstein, Kipling's fate would be sealed.

With the weight of the world now seemingly on his shoulders, Silverstein rose slowly to his feet and walked back inside the terminal. He was about to go down one level and back to baggage claim to look for the Hertz counter, when his cell phone rang again.

This time, the caller ID read *Incoming Call Private.*

"Hello."

"Victor? Lopez here. Talk to me."

Silverstein paused and thought. He had no choice. "You have the wrong number. Please don't call me anymore."

With his bag gripped firmly in his right hand, Silverstein ran down the escalator, breaking first into a jog and then a quicker stride. If it had been the 1970s, other passengers could have been forgiven for thinking that a certain athlete and movie star—later acquitted for the murder of his wife—was rehearsing a role for a television commercial.

CHAPTER 19

▼

CLUES

Alexandria, Virginia: 38° 48'N Latitude, 77° 3'W Longitude
Wednesday evening/Thursday morning, August 22/23, 2007

Barbara Lopez lay in bed, unable to sleep, the evening's details swimming in her head. The bedside clock read one o'clock and Hector had left the house more than four hours earlier. He hadn't called, and wouldn't—not for a day or two anyway. Had she been too impetuous in her earlier decision? Had she betrayed Hector's trust? No, of course not! *Well, what's done is done.* But nothing could undo the fact that she now possessed information that was, at best, confusing and, at worst, troubling.

The evening had started out innocuously enough. She had prepared beef stroganoff for Hector, in preparation for a quiet evening together. No matter that this dish possessed enough saturated fat to choke the arteries of a horse. Because Barbara had introduced this very non-Hispanic dish as the first meal she had ever cooked for him made it a sentimental favorite. *There should be moderation in all things—including moderation itself, which means there should be an occasional excess.* Never mind his circular reasoning, Barbara's college philosophy professor's bizarre logic seemed rational just now.

"Can I help? What're you making? No, don't tell me! I bet I can guess." Hector's voice from beyond the swinging kitchen doors teased, one of the qualities Barbara Lopez had fallen for on their first date. That, together with honesty and respect for all things living, human or otherwise, completed the package she agreed to marry one year later. The reason no one else had snatched him up was his physical deformity, no doubt. Young women too often eschewed men who didn't meet the physical standards set by Hollywood and the media. Fools! *Finders keepers, losers weepers.*

"Just hold your horses. Make yourself useful by uncorking the wine." Barbara glanced up at the clock in time to see the minute hand creep past six.

As of late, dinners alone with her husband came too infrequently, Barbara lamented. All the more reason to make this one special. The nature of Hector's job made his schedule problematical, and with Dr. Warner's new deadline for her software two weeks away, Barbara felt the pressure. She had been working fourteen-hour days since their meeting and wasn't much closer to solving the integration problem. She began to question her ability to get the job done. Maybe a quiet evening with her husband would rejuvenate the creative juices.

"Outstanding!" proclaimed Hector, as he mopped up the last of the stroganoff gravy with one remaining flour tortilla, the meal's sole concession to his culinary heritage. "If you ever lose your job as one of NRL's genius scientists, you can always open a restaurant."

Barbara laughed. "Thanks! But, it wouldn't be right, putting so many restaurants out of business, what with the economy and all."

Barbara reached across the table with her left hand. Hector stretched back, the tips of their fingers touching. *Yes, the magic was still there.* Their eight-year marriage hadn't diminished the chemistry.

Hector sighed. "This has been nice, Barbara. I had hoped to forget what life was like before I married you, but it's all been coming back. What's so damn important that you have to work so much? I've a mind to call your boss and give him what-for. What's his name again?" Hector withdrew his hand and pretended to be angry, his eyes beading together. "Speaking of which, where'd I leave my gun?" Hector grinned widely and looked back and forth around the room.

"Two glasses of wine and you're already two sheets to the wind." Barbara cocked her head to the side and grinned. Barbara had used Hector's minimal tolerance for liquor to her advantage on previous occasions—or at least she thought she had. But it all could be an act. Barbara recalled one party when colleagues informed her privately that Hector was sloshed and that she should drive him home. Because of an antibiotic he had taken late in the afternoon, what they didn't know was that he hadn't had a single drink all evening.

"Even if I explained it to you, you wouldn't understand. Suffice it to say, national security hinges on the very computer code that I write." Though her Top Secret research precluded her from dishing out specific details, that didn't prevent her from exaggerating the importance of her work.

"I'm not as dumb as I look, Dr. Lopez. Try me."

"Okay." Barbara waved her hands in the air as a gesture of frustration. "I'm using genetic algorithms to search through a series of empirical orthogonal functions to define control rules for use in a fuzzy logic expert system."

Hector stared straight at Barbara and squinted. "You're right. That makes absolutely no sense. But that's nuts and bolts kind of stuff. I want the lowdown. Why are you doing all of this, and for whom?"

"Nice try, super spy. But, you know that if I told you, I'd have to kill you. And I'd hate to lose a good husband." Barbara mimicked Hector's earlier head motions. "Where'd you say you left your gun?"

"Darn! My interrogation skills need some honing. I swear I just about had you." Hector removed the napkin from his lap, folded it, and reset it neatly on the table.

Barbara duplicated Hector's motions. "But, fair is fair, and I am curious too. My work involves nothing more than developing boring computer code for some secret system that no one will ever hear of, and probably will never become operational. But you! You deal with bad guys and all that spy sort of stuff. You've said yourself that only a part of what you do is actually classified."

Barbara sensed she had caught Hector off guard. A moment's hesitation suggested that he was battling his weakened condition to formulate a diplomatic reply. She also knew that classified or no, he would tell her very little.

Hector gathered his wits and initiated a reply. Barbara smiled in reaction, sensing his dilemma.

Then, his words surprised her. "You want to know what I do? I'll tell you what I do. For the past two years I've been chasing down a goddamn mole who's infiltrated the Department of Defense. A mole I know is out there, and a mole I'm irritated as hell over because I can't find him. *That's* what I do." The frustration evident in Hector's facial features matched precisely what he just said.

Barbara strained hard to keep from smiling, not to gloat over the fact that Hector had just told her more in one sitting than she had heard *en todo* since they married.

Conversely, Barbara empathized with Hector's disappointment. "Couldn't you be wrong?"

Hector thrust his right index finger toward the ceiling. "It's possible, but—" Before he could finish his thought, Barbara cursed the interruption, the soft electronic tone she had heard too often before, the one she knew came from the agency.

Hector wrinkled his face, signaling his displeasure and, simultaneously, the fact that he could do nothing about it. He flipped open his cell phone and placed it to his ear, resting his right elbow on the table and moving his left hand fingertips to his forehead, seemingly for stability, thought Barbara.

"Yea, Sheila, what is it?...when?"

Barbara recognized the name. Sheila was one of several agents who staffed the switchboard in Hector's division.

He listened for a moment, withdrew a pen from his shirt pocket, left the table to retrieve a notebook he kept in his jacket, and returned. "Okay, go ahead. I got it…thanks." Hector refolded the phone and seemed to be in deep thought.

Barbara did her best to keep the conversation light. "Good news, right? They've cornered that goddamn mole and are waiting for you to put on the handcuffs. The director wants you to call him so he can express his appreciation directly."

Hector looked up slowly, obviously deciphering the information he had just gotten, and smiled weakly. "I wish! No. An old friend of mine, who happens to be a noted NRL scientist by the way, called my office and said it was an emergency. I've never told you about Victor." Hector paused. "In earlier days, I'd have been too embarrassed…Victor once saved my butt. At this stage of my life I'm no longer ashamed."

Barbara's mouth dropped open. "Damn! *I'd say* you owe me that story. I'd like to meet him and give him my own personal thank you."

"Victor wants me to call him immediately. I think I need to get Miller on the line for this one."

"Go ahead and I'll clean up." Barbara caught Hector's eyes. "I'm warning you, though. If you have to leave the house, I'll be very disappointed. If you know what I mean."

"I *do* and I will be too. Hopefully, it won't come to that."

Barbara stacked the plates and walked to the kitchen. Hector called Miller, brought him up to speed, and told him to hold on while he placed the call. As she moved back and forth, she knew she shouldn't eavesdrop but couldn't resist. In the past, he had always left the room. *Had the wine had that much of an effect?* Doubtful. Hector would go into the bedroom if he didn't want her to hear something.

"Victor, what's up? My secretary said it was an emergency. A colleague of mine, Marc Miller, is on the line with me."

Hector opened his notebook and made an entry.

"Marc, I don't like the sound of this. I could have sworn it would have taken them longer to regroup after last Friday." Barbara noticed Hector manipulate a button on the telephone, probably muting his conversation with Marc from Victor. Hector pushed the button again. "What did he look like, Victor?"

Barbara had cleared the table. As she carried teacups to the table in preparation for dessert, she slowed her movement. Hector pushed the button again.

"Damn! Are you thinking what I'm thinking?...I agree, but there's nothing we can do." Hector jotted some notes in his book.

Barbara walked outside of Hector's field of vision. This obviously was a situation of some consequence, judging by Hector's tone of voice. He pushed the button once more.

"We know who he is, Victor, but I can't talk over this unsecured line. I'd like to help, but we have no assets in Denver right now. You and Kipling have to figure a way to elude him. Do you think you can do that?...Be careful, my friend."

To ensure Hector didn't think she eavesdropped, Barbara headed for the kitchen. She had gotten the gist of the call. She also knew that Hector's comment about the unsecured line wasn't for *her* benefit. Barbara knew Hector's conversation with Marc over agency phones used voice encryption. Any connection to an outside telephone would not be secure.

Hector spoke some more and then the house turned silent.

"Want some tea? The water's boiling." Barbara peeked through the swinging doors into the dining room. Hector was scratching the side of his head. Barbara meandered over, took his hands into hers, squeezed onto his lap, pulled his head to her chest, and gave him some needed reassurance that at least all was well in this tiny corner of the world.

"Is Victor in trouble?" Barbara intoned empathetically.

"Yeah, and I'm worried. If anything happens, it's my fault. Marc and I had evidence that something was in the wind and I downplayed it."

Standing and leading Hector to the sofa, Barbara then coaxed Hector to tell the complete, unabridged story of how he met Victor at Penn State twenty-some years earlier. The chronicle stretched through two cups of tea.

Barbara snapped her fingers together on her left hand. "Don't tell me! The last name of your friend Victor isn't by chance Silverstein, is it?"

Hector nodded.

"*You* know Dr. Victor Mark Silverstein, the most famous scientist in the navy community! *And*, he saved your life! Damn." Barbara shook her head.

Suddenly, Hector jumped to his feet. "I've got to call Victor back to see how it's going." Hector retrieved his phone and notebook, sat down on the sofa, placed the notebook in front of him, and punched numbers.

Moments passed. "Victor? Lopez here. Talk to me." Hector listened, but did not reply. He slowly refolded the cell phone and stared down at the floor. In the dim light of the fireplace, Barbara swore she could see his darker complexion lightening. In the following instant, Hector reopened the phone and punched one button. "Marc, there's trouble. Call Andrews and get a plane. I'll pick you up in twenty minutes."

Without hesitation, Hector ran for the closet at the base of the staircase. He opened the door and removed the packed suitcase he kept at the ready. Barbara knew their evening had ended.

"I'm sorry, Barbara." Hector walked over, grabbed her in his arms, and squeezed tightly. This sequence had played itself out many times before, but this was the first time she could recall that she saw fear in his eyes. "Something's wrong, very wrong," Hector whispered in her ear. "Victor's in trouble."

"Be careful, my love," Barbara whispered back. "Go find him."

With those words, Hector flew out the door to the street, his limp noticeable but far less so than when she first met him—or maybe it just seemed that way. She walked outside and waved goodbye to the car driving up the hill, as she always did when he was the first to leave the house. She continued her short vigil as he made the turn against the backdrop of the George Washington Masonic National Memorial, one of Washington's historical landmarks.

Barbara returned to the living room to retrieve the teacups, the last physical vestige of Hector's presence. Barbara was sentimental that way. She could still feel the warmth from his cup.

"Uh-oh," Barbara said aloud. Hector forgot his notebook. There it lay, open on the table. Never before had he left it on display, let alone forgotten it. Such an oversight provided an indication of how worried he was.

Barbara knew she shouldn't look, but there it sat, and open to the page where Hector had just written. The penmanship—or lack thereof—was obviously his. No one could mistake Hector's pathetic scribbling and cryptic note-taking style that included circles and lines going every which way. He had jokingly told her early in their marriage that the CIA taught all its agents to write that way, that such encryption proved superior to many modern methods.

Barbara hesitated but couldn't resist. She knelt, took off her glasses to examine the print closer, and scanned the two visible pages, being careful not to touch or move the book lest Hector return to retrieve it. The open pages contained notes for two days: Today, the twenty-second, and back on Saturday, the eighteenth. *Interesting.* There was a reference to a conversation Hector had with Victor the previous Friday, the seventeenth. That must have been the earlier *evidence* he mentioned.

From what Barbara could discern, there had been an attempt on Silverstein's life, possibly related to an automobile accident. Hector had requested assistance from the San Francisco office.

One word in particular drew Barbara's attention. She rose to her feet and hurried into their second bedroom that served as the office. She activated the laptop, always connected to the Internet through their DSL line. She paged to the secure section of the NRL Web page, entered her password, scanned for *Personnel*, typed S-I-L-V-E-R-S-T-E-I-N, and pressed return. Of the four thousand plus researchers, there were eight with that last name. She clicked on one in particular. Although she had heard offbeat stories about this famous NRL scientist, the information had always been in passing and she knew no details. She scanned the position and background of the man Hector said had once saved his life.

Barbara completed her reading and switched the laptop to standby. She ambled back to the coffee table, grabbed the notebook, shut it without looking further, and carried it to the office safe.

Barbara felt as if she had just violated Hector's trust. But she had looked only at the open pages, hadn't she? And they had merely corroborated what Hector had told her earlier, that an attempt had been made on Silverstein's life. She shouldn't feel bad. She hadn't paged through the notebook; that would have been wrong. It was only natural, wasn't it, that she would want to know something more about the man who had saved her husband's life?

Still, Barbara did notice—how could she not?—other curious details among Hector's scrawl. Details not tied together in sentences, but posited more like discussion points. Two of them were proper names: *Cameron Fitzby* lay next to *Silverstein* and the two enclosed in a circle. Farther down the page, at the end of his notes, came the single name *Hamasay*, with a question mark to its right. Most interesting of all, and what caught Barbara's eye immediately, was a reference to this summer's hurricanes. Everyone knew of this year's unusual hurricane activity, hardly up-to-the-minute news, thought Barbara. Of what relevance was that? What could that possibly have to do with Silverstein?

For that reason, Barbara had scanned Silverstein's background, to confirm his title as a meteorologist. A coincidence? Probably.

Barbara fought the covers, pitching back and forth. She crawled from the bed, padded to the bathroom, and downed an Ambien, a sleeping pill she kept for situations like these. She had to get some sleep. The six o'clock alarm would ring soon enough. So much for a relaxing evening to revive her creative juices.

Back in bed, Barbara tossed for a good twenty minutes, whereupon the effects of the drug overpowered her concern over the deeper meaning inherent in Hector's chaotic notes. That worry stemmed from one simple pen stroke.

Why did an arrow connect the circle to two other words on that page? It was of some interest to Dr. Barbara Ann Lopez that those two other words were *hurricane modification*.

CHAPTER 20

▼

INCAPACITATED

Super 8 Motel, 18600 E. 63rd Avenue, Denver, Colorado:
39° 48'37"N Latitude, 104° 46'12"W Longitude
Wednesday evening, 1930, August 22, 2007

"I'm over *here*...please help! The hospital's on fire and I'm soaked and freezing. I need to get this IV unhooked. Move the ladder to the right. I'll crawl over from my bed. Please don't leave me here!"

Kipling's words seemed as real to her as if she had spoken them directly. In fact, she had not voiced them—the duct tape covering her mouth would have prevented it. The words resided inside a nightmare. She had just returned to consciousness, enough to realize that the water that drenched her body was nothing more than her own cold sweat. The building she imagined herself in wasn't a hospital at all—just a room, seemingly a small hotel room. The IV that held her in place proved to a strange looking pair of handcuffs attached to her right wrist and the bed frame. She lay on her stomach. The voices she heard didn't come from firefighters trying to rescue her, but from someone next door.

The chemical fog lifted from Kipling's brain, if only to the point she would call it a stupor. She raised her left hand to glance at her watch. Seven-thirty! It had been over two hours since she left Silverstein at the airport.

The tall man who grabbed Kipling had been unexpected indeed. She had stepped off the airplane, walked down the Jetway, and entered the pedestrian traffic making its way to the main terminal. It seemed like rush hour. Kipling focused her mind on what she needed to do. Never in her imagination had she expected to be in danger. He approached her from the right rear and pulled her firmly toward himself with his left hand on her left shoulder. They then walked as a couple.

The voice that accompanied the body conveyed authority, quiet but firm. "If you wish to live, you will not cry out or make any sudden moves. Attached to my right hand is a syringe that contains poison. If I squeeze you much harder than I am squeezing you now, you will feel a slight prick and be dead within five to ten seconds. My own personal record is twelve seconds, but that individual weighed considerably more than you."

Kipling called upon the experience she had gained from two previous situations involving extreme danger. They had both occurred during her stint as a game warden—once when she had been held hostage by an escaped felon, deep within the Colorado Mountains, and a second time when a crazed mountain lion caught her by surprise and attacked.

"What do you want me to do?"

"Just keep walking. We'll make our way to the terminal and find a taxi."

Kipling had no way of telling if the hand-mounted syringe was real or merely a bluff. She halfway wanted to spin away and risk it. Should she take the chance? No! Police training had taught her to remain calm, evaluate the situation, and make a move when the odds tilted in her favor.

A casual glance to the right, allowing her peripheral vision to do the rest, confirmed what she already knew.

Although trapped in a dangerous situation, Kipling couldn't help but push the envelope. Giving the mountain lion a fighting chance by not firing until the rabid male was in a midair leap had earned her the nickname *Ice*—which represented the frozen version of what her forest service colleagues assumed surged through her veins. She had almost forgotten that handle, it had been so long ago.

"Syringe? What happened? Didn't want to take a chance with your plastic handgun getting by security? I thought you spies were cleverer than that."

Kipling sensed the head to her right rotate sharply in her direction while at the same time the grip on her shoulder tightened. The voice remained controlled. She looked and caught sight of the scar.

"First of all, I am sorry to disappoint you. I am not a spy. Second, you don't think a syringe that uses a specially designed rounded needle, and that has two bladders from which to draw different chemicals, isn't clever? You hurt my feelings, Ms...by the way, what shall I call you?"

"My name is Kipling, Dr. Linda Kipling." She turned her head completely to take in the face to her right. Her eyes met his. She saw day-old whiskers that covered weathered skin. The dominant nose barely edged out the full lips as the most noticeable feature on his face. The eyes quickly averted her gaze and stared ahead. "Now that you explain it that way, I'd say yes, that is damn clever. I can assure you the last thing on my mind is to hurt your feelings. But fair is fair. What do I call you?"

"Call me Joe."

Kipling laughed aloud. "You've got to be kidding me. Joe? I'll give you ten points for the syringe idea, but zero for the name."

Moving through the airport, on and off the train, getting in and out of the taxicab, as well as their performance for the desk clerk at the Super 8 Motel, had been awkward. Nonetheless, because his detailed explanation of the syringe had been so convincing, Kipling forced herself to conform to the charade. *Joe* continued to milk her for information. Where were she and Silverstein headed, and why?

Once in the hotel room, Joe edged her to the bed and they sat down together, his arm still firmly attached to her shoulder.

"If I had known you wanted to be affectionate, I would have worn something more inviting." Kipling faced the stranger.

Her captor pursed his lips, squinted his eyes, and again turned away from Kipling's look. "Are all American women like you?"

Before Kipling could come up with a clever reply, she felt the jab. "Ouch! Oh my God!"

The stranger released his grip. "Don't worry, Dr. Kipling. Remember, I told you there are two vials that feed the needle. You will have a pleasant sleep."

Kipling's words into the telephone were the last she could remember: "Victor, it's me."

Now, here she lay; mouth duct taped, arm shackled to the bed, and a fog that saturated her brain. The horrendous dream returned.

"Don't leave me here. I don't want to die."

CHAPTER 21

▼

ON THE TRAIL

Denver, Colorado, on ramp to Interstate 270 from 70:
39°46'41"N Latitude, 104°53'26"W Longitude
Wednesday evening, 2230, August 22, 2007

Silverstein sat alone in his rental car, off the highway, engine idling quietly. The gas gauge of the Ford Taurus registered half-empty—not half-full, but half-empty. *What point was there in making this dismal situation appear better than it was?* His natural tendency to be less than optimistic revealed itself, he knew.

Numb from the conversation at the airport, he had rented this innocuous-looking automobile and driven around the area for hours. *Looking for what?* He now questioned himself. Did he think he might stumble across Kipling and her abductor by chance?

But shortly after he had departed the Hertz parking lot, for the first time since his communiqué decades earlier after Sylvia had left him, Silverstein had seen fit to reestablish communication with his creator. If something happened to Kipling, it would be the third time in his life when destiny had inflicted an early, unexpected death on someone he cared about. *Help me, dear God; don't let Kipling die. Give me the wisdom to save her.*

As the shock of what had transpired lifted from his brain, logical thinking returned. *For now, I want you to proceed to your meeting in Fort Collins as if nothing has happened*, Kipling's kidnapper had said. Since she had been the source of this fabrication, would it not be best to follow through with this order? And, if Silverstein wanted to rescue Kipling, didn't he need to find her? *Damn!* Silverstein stepped hard on the accelerator and screeched onto Interstate 270.

Silverstein merged onto Interstate 25 and headed north. He looked to his left, toward Boulder, and imagined that by now his colleagues were wondering what had kept them from the scheduled icebreaker. He made a mental note to call the office and have them phone his contacts at NCAR, explaining that an emergency had intervened and they couldn't make the meeting. He had to concoct a story that the office staff would believe. Explaining that a colleague of his old college roommate had kidnapped Kipling—and that Silverstein had to go and save her from near-certain death—hardly seemed the proper message to deliver to Judy, his boss's secretary. Nonetheless, that mental note stimulated a degree of optimism that Silverstein had prayed for earlier, that lent some hope to carry forward.

"Contact no one!" her captor had said. *He has no way of verifying that threat!* With that important detail now clearly understood, Silverstein needed a pay phone. He found one at Exit 235. The Phillips 66 service station and a connecting restaurant had a bank of four on the wall. Silverstein got out of his car, laid his cell phone on the ledge beneath the pay phone, and dialed.

"This is Silverstein."

Before he could continue, the agent replied. "Please hold. I will transfer you."

"Victor, where are you?"

"Hector! He's kidnapped Kipling. I'm on I-25, headed for Fort Collins."

Silverstein explained all that had happened, from the time Kipling left him in the aircraft until he received the cell phone call.

"I was beside myself when you called. He told me to contact no one, that he would kill Linda."

After Silverstein heard some discussion in the background, Lopez replied. "Victor, my skill at making predictions has not been very good lately. But I'd say Kipling is safe, at least until he has access to you. I'd like to say more, but you're still on an unsecured line."

Unsecured line, hell! I wouldn't be calling if I thought the kidnapper could monitor this line. In violation of this mental show of confidence, Silverstein turned and glanced around the parking lot, as if the captor had his rifle sights set this instant.

Silverstein took a deep breath to calm himself. "I understand. What do you suggest?"

The electronic tone of Silverstein's cell phone pierced the silence of the late night air. Silverstein jumped and again scanned his surrounds, feeling as if he had just been caught robbing the cookie jar. "Hector, that's him. I've got to answer it."

"Victor, quickly! Is his number registering on caller ID?"

Silverstein hurriedly raised the cell phone to his eyes. "Yes." He read off the number.

"Victor! Remember, he has no way of knowing where you are. Set this phone down so I can listen to your end of the conversation."

Silverstein lowered the headset below the pay phone and let it hang. He licked his lips, took a deep breath, and pressed the receive button. "Silverstein here."

"What took so long? In the future, I recommend you answer on the second ring. Otherwise, I might think you're up to no good. Do you understand me, Dr. Silverstein?"

"Yes sir, I do. When I heard the phone ring, I pulled off the road. I'm standing outside my car. I'm sure you know it's unsafe to drive an automobile while speaking on a phone."

A long pause followed Silverstein's remark. "If you are where you say, return to your vehicle and blow the horn twice."

"Why the hell would you want me to do that?" Silverstein knew the answer, but also wanted Lopez to understand why he would move from the pay phone. Silverstein walked quickly toward the car.

"Dr. Silverstein! First of all, my sources tell me you are an intelligent man, unusually so for someone of your race. If I don't hear the sound of a horn within the next ten seconds, your memories of Kipling will be complete. And second, don't *ever* question my motives!"

Silverstein opened the door and reached in to sound the horn.

"Very good, Dr. Silverstein. I presume you understand that a certain amount of trust is required between us."

Silverstein stepped quietly back to the pay phone. "I do understand that, and the same is true from you. If Kipling is already dead, there's little need for me to listen to you. Let me talk to her."

"As you wish."

Kipling's voice came over the phone. "Victor, the building's burning and I can't..." In the background, Silverstein heard the words, "that's enough." Kipling's voice echoed the drug-like state Silverstein had sensed previously.

"Your friend is alive and well, just a little sleepy. Where are you?"

"I'm on my way to Fort Collins. I got a late start." Silverstein had already thought of a ready excuse for his delay. "I had a problem with the rental car just outside the airport. It took me forever to get a replacement." Silverstein had made up this fabrication earlier to cover his delay.

"I find that hard to believe, but will trust it is so. I want you to continue to your usual Fort Collins hotel and book yourself under the name, Francis Potter. I will contact you later."

The line went dead. Silverstein looked down at the cell phone's LCD to confirm that the call had ended. He pushed the line disconnect button to make sure.

Silverstein reached down and picked up the dangling pay phone. "Hector? He wants me to book into a hotel in Fort Collins. That would be the Mountain High Inn, where Kipling and I stay when we visit Colorado State. Hector! Linda purposely gave him the wrong information. We were planning to go to Boulder, not Fort Collins."

Seconds passed. "Victor, listen carefully. Do as he says and get there as soon as possible. Check in, lock the door, and don't open it for anyone. Do you understand me, Victor?"

"What do I do then?"

"Hang tight! I'm on a plane right now and we're headed for Fort Collins."

Silverstein's eyes widened at the thought of his old friend on his horse, galloping to his rescue. Déjà vu in reverse.

"And one more thing, Victor. The guy who's after you is called Hamasay, H-A-M-A-S-A-Y. He's a professional. Don't try to be a hero." Lopez hung up.

Silverstein reset the pay phone on its hook, turned and looked across the desolate parking lot into the deepness of the night. The moon shone full and the stars bright.

Silverstein arched back his head and looked skyward. *Please God—take me, but not Kipling.*

Lear Jet, two hundred miles east southeast of Fort Collins, CO Late Wednesday evening, 2330 MDT, August 22, 2007

Lopez reclined in his seat mulling over emerging details. Minutes earlier, Marc Miller stuck his head into the cockpit, telling the pilot to change course, to head for Fort Collins, vice Denver as originally planned. Lopez watched Miller as he lingered at the fax machine. The printed facsimiles would be near perfect, the result of their high bandwidth via satellite.

Miller handed Lopez a cup of coffee from the forward galley. "Good news! We'll land in about thirty minutes."

They had been in the air for three hours when Silverstein's call came in. Stiff westerly winds at altitude had added thirty minutes to the normal three-hour flight time.

Lopez hated flying. On the other hand, this plane almost made the act bearable. While most agency planes had minimal appointments compared to those in the private sector, this Lear, a Model 60 built in 1994, had numerous conveniences. Confiscated from a drug deal that went south (for the dealers), this aircraft had more than the requisite two wings and two engines. A cherry wood-finished forward refreshment bar with wine rack, a ten-disc CD player, a VHS/DVD player, and microwave made comfortable human amenities. There would be no time to enjoy such niceties, thought Lopez; better that he make use of the lavatory with its hot and cold running water while he had the chance.

Lopez set his coffee to the side, switched off the electric heater in his beige leather seat, and walked aft. He would not have to wait in line. Although the plane comfortably flew seven passengers over and above the two pilots, Lopez and Miller completed the human manifest.

Lopez sensed Miller's eyes on him as he walked, though Lopez knew it was probably his imagination. His limp, from a birth defect, was barely noticeable, much less so than back in his younger days. Two bouts of corrective surgery during his mid-twenties, with the liberal insertion of titanium hardware, had repaired ninety percent (according to his surgeon) of the misshapenness in his thighbones. Lopez had learned to accept his setting off alarms in airport security lines. What was important was that he could run fast enough to pass the agency's physical fitness guidelines. Nonetheless, he knew that his memory of childhood taunts over his physical deformity would never completely leave him.

Lopez returned to his seat, steadying himself as the Lear hit a few pockets of clear air turbulence.

"God, I hate to fly! And in a Lear Jet for Christ's sake. Wasn't that a Lear that golfer died in? Did they ever figure out why everyone became incapacitated? Goddamn thing just flew on autopilot until it ran out of gas."

Miller looked up, his face cold and professional, seemingly ignoring Lopez's commentary on their mode of transportation. "It's too late for the bureau to get us a car. We'll have to wing it. The pilot tells me there's an airport outside of town and the Mountain High Inn's only a twenty-minute drive from there. Assuming we can find transportation, we should arrive ahead of Silverstein…but not by much."

Lopez fastened his seat belt only seconds before an unusually sharp bump lifted him toward the ceiling, coffee now dripping down the sides of the cup holder.

"Anything on Hamasay?"

"These just came through on the fax." Miller held four black and white photographs and pointed to the facial scar. "The most recent was taken fifteen years ago, but the wizards in image restoration digitally aged the face. The four versions represent various guises. Note that no matter what the facial hair, the scar is still visible, which is why it was so noticeable to Silverstein." Miller studied the images for another moment and handed them to Lopez. "Hamasay would have done himself a service by having plastic surgery."

Lopez examined and, simultaneously, committed the images to memory. He prided himself on his ability to remember facial patterns, an important talent in his line of work. Irrespective of the scar, unless Hamasay had had a complete facial reconstruction, Lopez could pick him out. In many respects, Lopez thought, his abilities mirrored those of his wife, although he had made a point to never draw that fact to her attention.

Lopez handed back the photographs, swallowed what was left of the coffee, and dabbed up the rest. "Let's just hope Hamasay thinks it's only Silverstein he's up against. He won't know us."

Miller scrutinized the images further. "Silverstein's probably worried we're sending him into an ambush."

Lopez nodded. "No doubt! I didn't want to tell him he was safe for now. I'd rather him be too edgy than careless."

Miller smiled, with a look that indicated appreciation. "Thank God they've adapted 911 technology to cell phones!"

The reason Lopez wasn't concerned about Silverstein was because of new cellular technology, Enhanced 911 (E911), which had only recently come on line. Lopez had asked Silverstein for Hamasay's cell phone number because of E911. While Lopez stayed on the line with Silverstein, Miller had called the Denver office of the FBI, requesting a location ID (LID) for that cell number, as well as Silverstein's. From an active cell phone signal transmitted to the nearest cell towers, software operated by local 911 personnel could triangulate its location to within a mile or so. That was Phase I of E911.

In the Denver area, however, Phase II had been enacted. This advanced system, using GPS technology, could narrow down a phone's location to within three hundred and thirty feet—assuming that the user's phone included the corresponding technology. As it turned out, Silverstein's phone had the advanced system, but Hamasay's didn't. Nonetheless, the FBI crew had determined that Hamasay had phoned from a location forty-five minutes south of Fort Collins—and at least fifteen minutes behind Silverstein.

Miller raised his hand, as if to make a point. "By the way, as soon as possible, we've got to get these pictures of Hamasay to O'Toole in Bermuda. O'Toole's too new to have ever heard of him."

Lopez looked up hastily, at once both surprised and irritated that he hadn't been the first to comprehend this. Although it had been only hours since the name Hamasay had surfaced, Lopez cursed himself for being so concerned with Silverstein's safety that he missed this possibly significant connection. Was Hamasay connected to Fitzby's operations in Bermuda? If so, was he part of the clandestine organization they had been searching for all these years?

"Do it, Marc. Now."

Miller rose and made the request back to the office through the plane's secure communications channels.

The pilot's voice came over the cabin speakers. "We're on final. Touch down in a few minutes."

Miller returned to his seat and both men peered out their windows during the descent. The sudden electronic whine of the fax machine caught their attention. Miller, ignoring the pilot's recent admonition about turbulence during their descent, unbuckled his belt, rose, and stood by the fax machine until its latest reception had been discharged. As the wheels touched the runway, his legs bent slightly in response to the impact. Miller reached into the machine to remove the paper and scanned the one-page transmission.

Lopez knew in an instant that something was wrong—Miller's eyes squeezed tight shut. "What's wrong, Marc?"

As the aircraft braked down the runway, Miller raised his hand to the ceiling to steady himself and, at the same time, slowly turned his head back toward Lopez. "The LID folks screwed up! The locations they gave us on the phone were reversed."

Miller handed the machine-drawn plot of their relative positions on I-25 to Lopez. Lopez studied the printout and confirmed Miller's assessment. He then bowed his head and felt the same sensation he had experienced days earlier when Silverstein had called, after his brush with death—a shiver that started at the neck and moved slowly downward.

Lopez unbuckled his seat belt and jolted from his seat. Miller jumped to the side. Lopez grabbed the headset at the communications console, dialed the number on his notepad, and waited. "Answer the phone, goddamn it!" Lopez turned hastily toward Miller. "I got his voice mail. That means one of two things. Hopefully, he's in a dead zone. I pray to God it's not the second."

As the plane rolled to a stop, Lopez couldn't contain his anger any longer. "Those fucking assholes! Hamasay will arrive at the hotel *before* Silverstein! We've just sent Silverstein into a death trap."

CHAPTER 22

▼

DEATH'S DOOR

*Mountain High Inn, Fort Collins, Colorado: 40° 35'00"N
Latitude, 105° 02'08"W Longitude
Thursday morning, 0010, August 23, 2007*

Kipling forcibly lifted her head from her chest. She had a killer headache. To compound her physical discomfort, what felt like needles radiated from her wrists and hands, handcuffed to the vertical mounts that supported the front passenger side headrest. Blood had drained from her arms and they felt lifeless. Worse, she had to go to the bathroom.

A second injection when they had departed the hotel room earlier had transported her again to the hospital nightmare, a repetition of one she had experienced during her recovery from appendicitis at the age of twenty-one. Probably not by coincidence, her father had undergone identical surgery at that age. In Linda's case, she had almost died when the doctor misdiagnosed her initial complaints. Her appendix had burst. She still had evidence on her abdomen from the two tubes the surgeon had inserted to drain away the poison. Whatever drug Joe had injected mimicked her morphine-induced trance from that fifteen-day hospital stay.

Kipling fought the haze that made her want to go back to sleep. She shook her head side to side. *That didn't work.* If anything, her head throbbed worse. The mental fog undulated through her brain in waves.

Nonetheless, her eyes could now focus and she scanned the parking lot bathed in shadows from the occasional light standard. She was alone inside a car that faced a large building.

Kipling's head snapped to her right. At once, she recalled her earlier words to her abductor and recognized the rear parking lot to the Mountain High Inn in Fort Collins. What had prompted her to give him this false information was beyond her grasp. Probably just a measure of defiance, but at the same time, a signal to Silverstein that she had maintained some control of the circumstances. *Yup, no doubt about it. She had this situation well in hand!*

Although the process progressed in slow motion in Kipling's mind, the significance of the past eight hours returned. *I've got to warn Victor!* In the weak light that penetrated the car's windows, she examined the ceiling, seats, and dashboard. Judging from the OnStar button, it was a General Motors product, maybe a Cadillac. Joe obviously traveled first class. Although she would never own such a vehicle, Kipling had seen enough television commercials to know that if she pushed the OnStar button, help would be on the way. Kipling dismissed that thought. Victor was in danger *now*; there was no time.

Kipling pushed with all her might on the headrest above her head. The physical exertion made her head throb worse, until the pain became excruciating—approaching eight on a scale of ten, thought Kipling. She let her hands hang free. She had to be careful. Memories of teenage migraines reminded her that if this degree of pain continued, she would throw up. On the flip side, from those same experiences, Kipling remembered that vomiting also provided relief. As things stood now, the hammer-like throbbing rendered her useless—and now was not the time to be ineffective.

Kipling leaned over as far as she could into the driver's seat, started coughing to initiate the process, and soon had covered the leather seat in putrid vomit. This act in itself made her throw up more. Moments later, she spit out the last of the foul-tasting stench in her mouth. Although the thoughts in her brain remained murky, the pain had disappeared. Once again, she stretched her forearms with all her strength against the mounts to the headrest. A pitiful, but increasingly angry, cry escaped her lips.

Silverstein knew he should do exactly as Kipling's abductor—and later Lopez—had instructed. Go to the hotel, check in, and wait. The more Silverstein thought about it, the more he realized this course of action made sense only for the man who wanted Silverstein dead. Besides, there was more to consider here than his own safety. Unless Kipling came out of this escapade unharmed, his own fate mattered little. At a minimum, he knew that Kipling had been drugged. What other physical assaults her abductor may have considered, Silverstein forced himself to ignore.

Lopez identified their assailant with the name Hamasay. The physical description Silverstein and Kipling had earlier dictated to Lopez must have keyed the identification. *It was probably the scar.* Silverstein knew it wasn't too much of a stretch to assume this mayhem originated with Fitzby. *Who else would go to this trouble to kill me?* Further, this man Hamasay held some distinction if Lopez could identify him so quickly. Silverstein wondered if Hamasay had sent the two in the Mercedes. *They had failed and so Hamasay decided to take on the job personally. Makes sense.*

Silverstein had taken Exit 269B from I-25, maneuvered his way to CO-14, and proceeded west. *I want you to continue to your usual Fort Collins hotel and book yourself under the name, Francis Potter.*

What if I don't do that? Lopez did make the point that Kipling would be safe until Hamasay had Silverstein in his sights. Noticing a pay phone, Silverstein pulled off into a service station several blocks before the hotel.

"I'd like to make a reservation for tonight; the name's Francis Potter…thanks." Silverstein quickly realized he couldn't reserve the room with a credit card that had a different name. "I'll be paying cash and, by the way, I'm meeting a colleague and I've no idea when he's arriving. Would you mind checking with the front desk to see if anyone has asked for me?" A pause. "No?"

Silverstein parked on a side street west of the hotel and walked east, as much as possible hiding in shadows formed from the streetlights. *Thank God I at least know what this guy looks like.*

*   *   *   *

Fort Collins-Loveland Airport: 40°26'58"N, 105°00'29"W
Thursday morning, 0015, August 23, 2007

Because Lopez had changed their flight destination at the last moment, there had been no time for the Denver bureau to send a car to Fort Collins.

While still in the air, Miller had called for a taxi. As it rolled up, Lopez leaped out in front of it, startling the cabbie. Lopez grabbed the passenger side front door while Miller jumped into the rear. The driver's appearance as well as the name listed on the license pasted between the two visors caused Lopez to recognize him as Pakistani.

Lopez dangled paper currency between his index finger and thumb as he turned to the driver. "Pervez…this one hundred dollar bill tells me you will drive to the Mountain High Inn in record time. Would you agree?"

Pervez snatched the bill and verified its denomination. While shifting into gear, and without facing Lopez, the driver took on an unusual air of responsibility, thought Lopez. "Sir, I will match or exceed my own personal record."

The large Ford Crown Victoria squealed away from the curb and entered traffic.

Having stayed at this hotel numerous times, Silverstein knew all entrances and purposely walked to the rear, approaching a service access that, at this time of night—morning actually—proved deserted. Silverstein turned the doorknob and pulled, relieved to feel the heavy metal entry give way. Although hotel proprietors in this day and age underscored security to their clientele, this establishment had less concern about local riffraff, or worries about terrorism. Fort Collins was a university town. Unpleasant events didn't happen here.

Silverstein walked silently down the hall and turned left into the hotel's laundry. Lights blazed, but otherwise the room stood unoccupied. It was time to think things through.

Silverstein reviewed in his mind his earlier conversation with Lopez and deduced the significance of his asking for Hamasay's cell phone number. He remembered a *USA Today* article on Enhanced 911 for wireless phones. Did Lopez have access to that technology? That would explain why Lopez insisted he proceed directly to the hotel. Plus, the desk clerk had verified, ten minutes earlier, that no one had asked for him. These two facts made clear to Silverstein that he would arrive before Hamasay. With that conclusion well substantiated, Silverstein decided to do as he was told, to register, and lie in wait. Silverstein breathed easier.

Silverstein returned to the corridor, exited into the hotel proper, and turned right toward the multi-sided walled courtyard that dominated the left side of the large lobby.

Silverstein walked down the ramp into the courtyard, stopped, and took in what he saw. Water from the fountain to his right made it hard to hear. Straight ahead stood the formal entrance to the hotel, several cars visible outside. Ahead and to the left was the registration desk, behind which a single young man stared at a computer screen. Beyond the courtyard to the right, a young couple strolled across the lobby. To the left in front of him, two men lounged on one of the multiple sofas arranged within the courtyard, obviously engaged in a vigorous discussion. Their voices, although controlled, were loud enough that anyone who wanted to could listen in. No other competing sounds. The coast appeared clear.

Silverstein walked directly across the courtyard toward the registration desk. He approached within ten feet of the steps that exited the courtyard when he realized that entering the lobby had been a bad idea.

It took a mighty final shove, but the headrest suddenly exploded from its permanent mounts within the backrest of Kipling's front seat. The headrest hit the ceiling and the sharp ends of the two vertical bars then retraced their paths downward and struck Kipling's skull. Kipling grimaced from the jolt and felt immediately the warm sensation of blood flowing somewhere on her scalp.

Nonetheless, she was free! In the process of this action, both arms came loose. The *handcuffs* that had kept her hands in place were nothing more than heavy-duty nylon ties, nothing that would now interfere with her movement.

Kipling reached for the door lock but then vacillated. Having adapted to its monotony, she had nearly forgotten the blinking red light on the dashboard.

Kipling looked first at her door, then the driver's side door, and then the back seat. All doors were locked, which meant if she opened any door, the car's burglar alarm would sound. Under normal conditions, she could outrun and hide from her abductor. But right now, with her dubious physical condition, she had no idea how fast she could run—or even if she could walk—once she exited the car. If her abductor lay in wait anywhere within earshot, the reward for her effort would be another injection to the shoulder, or worse.

As Kipling withstood another wave of confusion that assaulted her consciousness, she struggled to concentrate. She couldn't open any of the doors. Even if she managed to tunnel her way into the trunk, that opening would be wired as well. That left only one alternative.

Kipling twisted herself in the passenger seat so that she lay crosswise toward the passenger door, head facing the ceiling. She reached with her right hand behind the seat. *Good!* She grabbed tightly the leather that surrounded the magazine pouch formed against the rear seat. At the same time, Kipling opened the glove compartment, reached in, and found a suitable handhold.

Kipling took three deep breaths to both clear her head and collect her strength. She then drew her legs as close to her chest as possible and swiftly extended her body with all the force she could muster. The cowboy boots that Silverstein made a point of disparaging proved to be the perfect extension to the power she generated through her thigh muscles. They burst through the window in one try. She then kicked out the remaining shards of safety glass.

Kipling righted herself, turned around, stretched her arms through the window, placing them flat on the roof, and then lifted her head and chest backward through the window's opening. At the same time, she slid her butt onto the window ledge. Fortunately, it was now obvious that the car had no motion or sound sensors to trigger the alarm. Afraid to take a breath, Kipling looked across the roof of the car and scanned the area. *So far so good!*

Kipling drew a breath of outside air, warm but fresh compared to the now fetid interior environment of the vehicle. Kipling trained her ears to the nighttime sounds, terrified she would hear steps running toward her. Nothing.

Kipling slowly pulled her legs through the window, dropped to the ground to a squatting position, and remained still, carefully controlling her breathing. She stood slowly, cautiously testing her stability, and looked around the parking lot.

All was quiet—except for a sudden unexpected popping sound!

Kipling walked at first, but soon realized she indeed had the strength to run. She saw the rear entrance to the hotel some fifty feet away.

That Silverstein had seen movement out of the corner of his eye is what saved his life—a minute change to the visual pattern at the limit of his peripheral vision. He turned instinctively and dove to the floor behind one of the sofas. The bullet narrowly missed his head and struck the marble facing that lined the registration desk, five feet to the left of the startled desk clerk. A second couple who had just entered the lobby quickly reversed direction and headed back outside. Silverstein looked over his head and saw the two men who had seconds earlier been engaged in conversation now cowering together on the floor, looking in his direction.

Silverstein crawled along the base of the sofa and glanced around the edge. He had to determine from what direction his attacker had come. His effort was rewarded with another gunshot that shattered the wooden leg of the stand adjacent to the sofa.

Silverstein had nowhere to go. Repeated gunshots now penetrated the front of the sofa. He lay as low as possible, hoping the wood or metal frame would absorb the bullets.

Unless a miracle occurred soon, he was a goner. Silverstein prayed once more to the Supreme Being above—and hoped it would not be his last opportunity.

*   *   *   *

Kipling entered a door at the rear of the hotel and found herself in a service hallway. She looked to her right and saw what appeared to be the kitchen. To her left the hallway continued. Shots became louder and seemed to be coming from straight ahead. She opened the door in front of her and found herself in a conference room. Ahead, and to the right, she could see lights from the lobby through open doors on the other side of the large room.

Kipling ran across to the opposite wall and inched her way toward the open door. She peeked around the corner. Straight ahead stood her abductor, facing away, and firing into a blue sofa. *He must have hidden and waited. He obviously has someone trapped. It has to be Victor!*

Kipling had no weapon and there was no time to lose. Silverstein could be killed or maimed at any instant. Only one option made any sense or held out any hope.

Kipling backed up quietly, took three slow breaths as she had been trained to do, and then stopped. She recognized the voices of both Silverstein and her abductor, listened briefly, and then tensed her muscles for action. Silverstein spoke again—a fleeting camouflage to cover her movements. It was now or never.

Nausea, mental fog, and pain be dammed! Kipling sucked in another three breaths and took note of four stair steps that she would have to hurdle. It was time.

The last bullet made its way through the sofa, ricocheting off internal parts, striking Silverstein's leg in the thigh, and penetrating the flesh. Only a minor flesh wound, Silverstein reminded himself.

Silverstein decided this was the time to buy a delay. "Don't come any closer; I've got a gun." Silverstein thought quickly. In case the reference to a firearm didn't have the desired effect, Silverstein added some insurance. "By the way, Mr. Hamasay, what is it you want? That is your name, isn't it?"

Silverstein's comment elicited a multi-second pause.

"I don't believe you have a gun, Dr. Silverstein…but I am curious. How is it you know my name?"

Surely, the hotel staff had called the cops, Silverstein reassured himself; they would be here soon. He boasted, "Oh, I know a lot more than that about you, Mr. Hamasay. I know you work for Cameron Fitzby and he will use you to his advantage, not yours."

Silverstein stopped to draw out more seconds. "I must warn you, sir, and you should listen carefully…I wouldn't trust him if I were you."

"Before I kill you, Dr. Silverstein, let me make two things absolutely clear. First, I do not work *for* Mr. Fitzby. And second, Mr. Fitzby has made similar comments concerning you. Who do *you* think I should believe?"

Silverstein quickly reversed position on the floor in an attempt to catch a view from the opposite end of the sofa—but not before he made one final remark so his voice sounded like it had not changed location. "His character is severely flawed, Mr. Hamasay. Has he explained to you why he wants me dead? I suspect he has not."

In the ever-shortened pauses that followed Silverstein's words, Silverstein sneaked a peek around the left side of the sofa. His eyes fully bulged from his face at what he saw transpire in the forty-foot distance directly behind Hamasay—Kipling running full speed toward Hamasay.

From the sudden change in demeanor on Hamasay's face, Silverstein saw that he sensed something. But it was too late.

At once, Kipling's body became horizontal with the floor, her legs compressed, and feet aimed like a battering ram at what would have been Hamasay's back, but now was his side. In the split second before impact, Kipling's legs pulsed forward. Hamasay tried to turn to face head-on this unexpected threat, but had too little time.

Silverstein watched as the force from the human projectile struck Hamasay below his right shoulder, driving his right arm vertically upward. The strength required to hold onto his firearm during this violent movement caused Hamasay's weapon to discharge high into the atrium. The impact of Kipling's blow propelled Hamasay to the floor, and toward Silverstein. Hamasay's eyes blinked first in surprise, and then in pain.

Silverstein leaped from behind the sofa and sprinted the fifteen-foot distance to Hamasay. Adrenaline pulsing through his body overwhelmed any sensation of the wound in his thigh. Hamasay, thrown to his stomach with his arms stretched outward along the floor, still held his weapon.

Kipling lay in a crumpled mess on the floor, writhing in pain after she fell obliquely onto her left shoulder.

Silverstein arrived just as Hamasay flipped himself over to face Silverstein, his weapon rising instantly to confront Silverstein as he drew down. Silverstein looked down and realized he had not been quick enough. Hamasay had him dead in his sights.

Silverstein flew through the air into the face of the pistol, unconsciously turning sideways in an attempt to minimize his cross-section. Silverstein heard the click—but there was no explosion! Hamasay managed to pull the trigger a second time, to no avail. The shot that Kipling had forced had been the last in his clip. Hamasay instinctively reached down to his pocket for a replacement clip, but there was no time. Silverstein slammed down on Hamasay.

Instead, Hamasay took the side of his weapon and slammed it against Silverstein's head. But not before Silverstein's fist connected to the right side of Hamasay's head in a glancing blow, as Silverstein simultaneously tried, unsuccessfully, to knee Hamasay in the groin. Silverstein briefly caught Hamasay's eyes. They looked little different from what he had faced back in the airplane.

Having less than the desired effect from his first blow to Silverstein's head, Hamasay tried a second time. This time, however, Silverstein was ready and grasped Hamasay's right wrist with both hands, twisting and pumping until the gun let loose and skidded across the floor. Unfortunately, at the same time, Hamasay's left hand shot upward and caught Silverstein on the jaw, stunning him, and throwing him backward to the floor.

Silverstein lay dazed for a moment. Realizing that his and Kipling's lives were still very much in danger, he jumped to his feet, ready to continue the fight. But, his opponent was temporarily out of sight. Silverstein heard footsteps and stepped to the side in time to see Hamasay in retreat, gun in hand, down the hall to a nearby door to the outside.

Why had he run away? Silverstein did a mental audio rewind that replayed the sound of screeching tires outside the lobby moments earlier.

Doors flew open and two men burst into the lobby, guns held horizontally in a two-handed stance. Silverstein immediately recognized the shorter one as his old friend.

Silverstein yelled loudly. "Hector, over here!" At the same time, he pointed down the hallway. "Hamasay ran out that door."

Silverstein turned again to look, just in time to see Hamasay disappear from view.

Lopez's assistant took off down the hall while Lopez scanned the lobby for alternate threats. Once Lopez decided there were none, he also took off running. "Stay here!"

It wasn't long before increasingly loud sirens betrayed the nighttime quiet outside the hotel.

With the crisis seemingly over, Silverstein took stock of himself. Except for the now sharpening pain in his thigh, he was none the worse for wear. Ahead of him on the floor, however, lay someone who *was* worse for wear, someone who had just saved his life, and someone who had performed the bravest act he had ever witnessed in his life, bar none. Kipling tried to get to her feet.

"Don't get up, Linda." Silverstein ran over to Kipling, who fell back into Silverstein's arms. She looked a fright: her blouse sweaty and torn, her face drawn, eyes puffy, a trickle of blood evident below her left temple. Kipling held her left shoulder and whimpered in pain.

"Joe drugged me, Victor."

"Who's Joe?"

"That's what he told me to call him." Kipling took a deep breath before speaking again. "I told him that was a poor excuse for a made-up name and I didn't believe him." She smiled halfheartedly.

"His name is Hamasay. Fitzby is working for him, Linda."

As Silverstein held Kipling and provided comfort the best he could, uniformed officers entered the lobby and fanned out.

Silverstein yelled over. "We have an injury here!"

Minutes later, Lopez came walking back up the hallway to join Silverstein. Ambulance personnel entered the lobby and ran toward Kipling.

Silverstein made the introductions. "Linda, this is Hector Lopez, my friend I've been telling you about. Hector, this is my associate Linda Kipling, who just saved my life."

Lopez and Kipling looked at each other in mutual appreciation and then back at Silverstein. Silverstein knew that Lopez wished he had been the one to repay the favor once granted to him.

Lopez looked seriously at Silverstein, grabbed him, and hugged him closely. "How are you, my friend?" He then drew back and stared sheepishly at the ceiling. "I got bad information, Victor, and sent you into a trap." He looked over at Kipling. "Now I'm beholden to both of you." Lopez paused briefly, but then looked down at Silverstein's leg. "You've been shot!"

At those words, Kipling lifted herself with her good arm up from the stretcher. "You're shot?"

Silverstein grimaced, the sting of his wound coming back in spades now that his adrenaline had ebbed. He gave a time-out signal with his two hands. "It's not all that bad. I'll go with Linda to the hospital."

The medic attending to Kipling heard the words and stepped around the stretcher to inspect the damage.

Silverstein suddenly realized a more immediate concern. "Did you catch Hamasay?"

Lopez shook his head. "By the time Marc got to the back of the building, he was already in his car. He did get a vehicle description and is calling in an APB as we speak. Hamasay shouldn't get far; his car is easily identifiable. Marc said the right front passenger window has been blown out."

Lopez turned to Kipling. "Did you do that?"

Kipling, now positioned comfortably on the stretcher, addressed Lopez. "I may have." Her initially serious look evolved into a sly smile. "But, you should mention one more thing in your APB that might be of use in his identification."

Lopez took out his notepad. "Right! What's that?"

"Your Mr. Hamasay now smells like, and is covered by, puke."

To Silverstein, Kipling seemed serious. Her eyes shone clear and focused.

Silverstein glanced over at Lopez. While Lopez scratched the side of his head, Silverstein turned back to Kipling and did his best to keep a straight face. Probably hit her head when she fell, he thought.

CHAPTER 23

▼

INKING SUSPICIONS

*Bermuda Weather Service, Bermuda International Airport,
Bermuda:32° 22'02"N Latitude, 64° 40'39"W Longitude
Tuesday morning, 0900, August 28, 2007*

"Darn it! It's starting all over again."

Jim Avery leaped from his swivel seat and headed to the coffee machine. He poured two cups, turned, placed one on the desk next to Marsha Kendall, and continued back to his desk. His twenty-inch, high-resolution monitor allowed him as good a look at satellite imagery as the BWS's budget could afford.

"Is something wrong, Jim?" Kendall's voice permeated the otherwise quiet of the weather station. Only occasionally did Avery and Kendall share the day shift.

"No, why?" Avery flipped back and forth between the GOES East and Meteosat visuals.

"Because you just gave me a cup of hot water, not coffee. What's in your cup?"

Avery looked down to see the same clear liquid. He laughed. "Sorry about that." He retrieved Kendall's cup and traipsed back to the coffee machine to try again.

Owing to the British traditions of this island, several of the staff drank tea. Kendall's geographic birthplace notwithstanding, both she and Avery preferred coffee. Avery replaced the unflavored, but excellent tasting Bermuda water, with the more appropriate dark Columbian beverage. He retraced his earlier steps.

"It's starting all over again, Marsha. Look at the development in these waves here. There's three of them and they're all gaining steam. We've had two weeks of calm and now this." He pointed to the screen as Kendall approached. "Just like back in July. If I were a person who bet on long shots, I'd say there's some kind of hanky-panky going on here."

Kendall took a closer look. "What about the SSTs this time?"

Avery snapped his fingers. "Good point, Marsha." He turned to check the clock. "It's just past eight in Miami. Davis should be in by now."

Avery rotated back to his desk and hit the speed dial.

Anselina Corporation, Hamilton, Bermuda: 32° 18'20"N Latitude, 64° 47'20"W Longitude Tuesday morning, 1000, August 28, 2007

It had been more than a week since Fitzby had last heard from Ghali—unusual compared to the early days of the summer, when Ghali sometimes contacted (bothered was more like it) him several times a day. Fitzby continued to e-mail his reports daily, as requested by Ghali. But for the past several days, these summaries had omitted one important development: Fitzby had once again begun to fire the laser at the tropical waves sloughing off Africa. Ghali had made it clear that Fitzby should wait. *Fuck Ghali. Bastard!*

The reason for Fitzby's decision to restart his earlier testing emanated from one tiny detail that Ghali had neglected to pass on to Fitzby.

Being in charge of the Bermuda operations, in the absence of Ghali, gave Fitzby access to all personnel. Of particular interest were the Russian technicians, those responsible for the satellite laser and its operation. Fitzby had never let on to Ghali (or to the Russian technicians) that he understood and spoke fluent Russian. *Unless there is an obvious reason to reveal them, you should always hold your strengths in reserve*, another of Fitzby's mother's admonitions.

What Fitzby had learned from the Russians' conversations proved devastating to his plans. The power of their laser would deteriorate markedly in the months following this hurricane season. That Ghali had withheld this crucial piece of information infuriated Fitzby, who now concluded Ghali could not be trusted. Armed with this new information, Fitzby intended to milk the satellite for all it was worth. His actions now could determine his status in future history books. As the hurricane season petered out, Fitzby's opportunities for proving and documenting his research theories would fizzle as well. He might never get another chance.

As it stood, Fitzby still lacked the hurricane-targeting program Ghali had promised. Without that software, he could not reliably steer a storm. Fitzby had tried, manually, to do what the software would do automatically. But it soon became clear that he could not duplicate in his head the complicated hydrodynamic and thermodynamic interactions that occur inside a mature (or even a fledgling) hurricane as the result of the laser's heating.

The best Fitzby had been able to do was influence the cyclone's movement somewhat, but with no reliability. To his chagrin, he had directed two minor tropical cyclones directly over Bermuda. Not that this had caused any local problems. The native limestone used to build most island houses proved sturdy indeed. Moreover, the building Fitzby had leased had even stronger walls. It hadn't even been necessary to switch to backup generator power, although Ghali insisted they practice that exercise daily.

Despite this limitation, he had proven the first part of his thesis: that he could strengthen a hurricane using the laser. To steer a storm would be the *coup de grâce*.

Ghali obviously had his own ideas of what he wanted done using Fitzby's technology, but he had yet to voice them—another reason to be suspicious of Ghali. Ghali trusted Fitzby with only what he wanted him to know. Fitzby's mind reverberated with that thought. It was happening yet again. *I'm being used, just like Dad used Mom before he abandoned her, leaving her to face the world alone.*

*   *   *   *

"Are you sure?" Avery held the phone tight to his ear, although the speakerphone amplified Davis' voice for both to hear. Kendall sat on the edge of Avery's desk.

"Yes," came back the reply. "Same kind of anomalous temperature changes we saw earlier, and again only in the Atlantic." Avery raised his eyes and nodded at Kendall.

Avery started tapping the end of his pen on the desk. "Remind me, didn't you tell me a couple of weeks ago you had a workshop to address this?"

"That's right, but nothing came of it. We did send out a plane to drop some bathythermographs in spots where we noticed the heating. Interestingly, the anomalies we observed from our satellites turned out to be quite shallow. Only the first measurement from the BT reflected any resemblance to the surface temperature. Which meant the maximum depth was no more than tens of centimeters. And get this! Later, when our ship arrived at the same spot, even the surface anomalies had disappeared."

Avery leaned back in his chair and turned to face Kendall. "You don't say? Thanks. I'll be back in touch."

Kendall stood and returned to her desk. "It all makes sense, doesn't it? The anomalies didn't last because they were shallow and got mixed away."

Avery rose from his seat and followed Kendall, who glanced back, surprised to find him tailing her. "Marsha, none of what's going on makes any sense. I've been looking at satellite photos of wave development in the eastern Atlantic for over ten years. What's going on is far beyond unusual. As much as I've forced myself to ignore it, I think that someone or something, somewhere, is causing this. I don't know; maybe space aliens are fiddling with our planet. More likely, though, it's homegrown."

Kendall nodded. "I'm with you, but how could anyone possibly do something like that, Jim? And especially, without anyone in the scientific community knowing about it."

"I don't know, Marsha, but that leads me to the following question."

"Yeah?"

"How would you and Barry like to come over and have dinner on Sunday?"

Kendall nodded. "I see where you're going with this. I'll ask tonight."

Fitzby looked up from his desk, annoyed that someone had entered his office without knocking. Upon seeing who it was, he leaned back in his chair, planted his feet on the desk and placed his arms behind his head.

"You've been making yourself scarce as of late. Where the *fuck* have you been?" Fitzby took a closer look at the man standing in front of him. "And what happened to your face?"

Ghali pulled up a chair and sat down. His demeanor, as usual, was reserved and even. "I'd like to remind you that I'm the one who asks the questions, Mr. Fitzby."

Fitzby stood, walked to the window, and looked out. He couldn't contain his anger any longer. He had been reminded many times in the past that he would be much better off if he followed the count to ten dictum, but that just wasn't in his nature.

"What would you say if I went against your last order, and started experimenting with a few waves coming off Africa?"

"I'd say you were a fool, Mr. Fitzby."

Ghali stood and walked slowly toward him. As he got closer, Fitzby saw the veins in Ghali's neck pulsing. He had never before noticed any overt sign of anger.

Ghali closed the last of the distance between them and stood mere inches away. Fitzby's diminutive five foot six frame felt fiercely inadequate compared to the giant of a man in front of him. Fitzby vaguely heard his telephone ringing on the desk but mustered all his attention to hold his ground. It didn't matter anymore, thought Fitzby. If he failed to prove the second half of his hurricane hypotheses before the satellite lost its strength, he didn't see much reason for carrying on anyway.

"You can kill me if you want; I don't care. But it's your own fault, you know." Fitzby paused, his gaze fixed on the disgust evident in Ghali's eyes.

Fitzby saw no reason to hold back on his primary complaint.

"Why didn't you tell me the laser would be good for only one hurricane season?"

To Fitzby's relief, Ghali backed away, the pulsating veins lessening as he did so. "Because it was none of your business, Mr. Fitzby. That is my concern, not yours."

His fury now culminating, Fitzby couldn't contain himself. He threw his hands into the air and shouted across the few feet separating him from Ghali.

"Not my concern? Goddamn you! I've made it clear to you this work is my life."

"I am aware of that, Mr. Fitzby."

Fitzby watched as the throbbing in Ghali's neck returned.

"With your huge intellect, Mr. Fitzby, I would think you would have figured out that this project is just as important to me. For your information, my sponsors recently reminded me they have spent more than two hundred million dollars on you."

Ghali turned animated, and livid. *"İki yüz milyon dolar."* He now roared at Fitzby. "Two hundred million dollars! Two hundred million, Mr. Fitzby! Do you have any idea the pressure I am under to make sure I show some result from such an expenditure?"

Ghali walked sharply toward Fitzby. "As I stated when I came into this room, *I* am the one who makes the decisions and asks the questions."

With his right hand, Ghali grabbed Fitzby's shirt above the sternum and threw him backward into his office chair. Fitzby struck the chair squarely, but the momentum of his movement caused the chair to flip onto the floor. Fitzby landed on his back, his head striking the tiled floor, his legs pointed upward over the top of the chair. He lay momentarily stunned.

Fitzby slowly slid his legs to the side and struggled to his feet. Nothing seemed broken. In the meantime, Ghali had returned to his seat facing the desk.

Ghali's voice returned to a reasonable level. "Sit down, Mr. Fitzby, and listen carefully. If I want a response from you, I will so indicate. Do you understand?"

Fitzby stared across at his adversary, shaken but unbowed. *When faced with an immediate threat, feign weakness and humility. You will get your revenge on your own terms.* Mother's advice seemed important just now.

Fitzby nodded respectfully, righted his chair, and sat down.

Ghali crossed his legs. "Have you had any recent contact with your Dr. Silverstein?"

Fitzby looked back in wonder. "Are you out of your mind? Have I not told you, repeatedly, that Silverstein is the one fly in our ointment, the one person who could foil our project? Don't you ever listen to what I tell you?"

Ghali looked across at Fitzby thoughtfully. "If what you say is true, how is it Silverstein knew my name?"

Fitzby shot to his feet. "You met Silverstein? Did you kill him?" He hesitated as Ghali continued his stare. "Tell me, goddamn it, is Silverstein dead?"

Ghali scowled in his reply. "No, he's not. I'm sorry to say he got away."

Fitzby slammed his fist down on the desk and almost winced from the pain before he caught himself. "Fuck!" He then lifted his head and looked at Ghali. "What do you mean he knew your name?"

"Exactly as I said. He called me out by name. How would he know that, Mr. Fitzby?"

Fitzby sat back down, held his head in his hands, and pondered the significance of what he had just heard. Even if Silverstein had figured out that Fitzby lay behind this season's hurricane anomalies—which was likely indeed—how could he possibly know, or even recognize, Ghali?

Fitzby looked up sheepishly and responded honestly. "I have no idea."

Ghali's eyes continued to bore holes into Fitzby's. "I have just one more question."

Fitzby's mind, bathed in possibilities that could provide an explanation for Ghali's first bombshell, returned to the present. "Yes."

"Does the name Hector mean anything to you?"

Fitzby tried hard to keep his face unshaken and devoid of further emotion. *Hector Lopez.* "No, I'm sorry. That name means nothing to me."

*   *   *   *

Ghali rose and left the room, leaving the visibly shaken Fitzby to his own devices. He would have to keep a close eye on this one. Obvious contempt lingered in those eyes.

And right at the end, Ghali had the sensation, albeit nearly nonexistent, that Fitzby had reacted to the name Hector—which meant he had lied. What had it been: a sudden change in Fitzby's coloring, a nearly imperceptible movement of his head, a noticeable pulse in a vein, or a twitch of the eye? There was no way to return to that moment, to isolate what Ghali had noticed. But there was no doubt in Ghali's mind that Fitzby had reacted in some way.

Under other circumstances, Ghali would just as easily have dispatched from this world this miserable miscreant of a human being. But that wasn't possible just yet. There would be time enough for that later.

Ghali walked from the bunkered building, past the guard, and toward his car. Ghali breathed deeply. Outside, away from the chilled environment necessary to keep various equipment functioning properly, Bermuda temperatures suited Ghali just fine—closer to those in Cairo this time of year. Istanbul and Washington both cooled off too quickly as fall approached.

Ghali got behind the wheel of his car and paused to reflect on the inconsistencies facing him—and the events of the past two weeks. He had been lucky indeed to escape the United States. After leaving Fort Collins early on Thursday morning, he had hidden out for the night on a side road outside town. Knowing that Mexican government personnel could be easily bribed if need be, both at the border and later at airports, Ghali made his way south. He stayed on secondary roads and was close to physical collapse by Thursday dusk, well shy of the Oklahoma border.

Luck was with him when a farmer, whose pickup had overturned in the road near his farm, became his unintended victim. Ghali took advantage of the man's unknowing hospitality by staying the night and eating his food. He had been exhausted and could scarcely recall the details. The killing had been necessary and he would have done more had it been required. Nonetheless, he thanked the fates that this man lived alone.

Although he was not a religious man, Ghali abhorred the thought of taking human life needlessly. There had to be a good reason. He had had many philosophical discussions concerning that very point with his comrades in the Blade. Ghali took some pride in the fact that his organization had never performed a direct terrorist act. He wondered how the Blade would make use of Fitzby's technology. Would it be blackmail? Would the Blade purposely target a hurricane into an unpopulated area to make a point? No! That was impossible. The Blade's methods had always been more intellectual than physical. Ghali recalled previous research projects and their objectives, searching for similarities that might indicate how the Blade would make use of Fitzby's hurricane targeting technology.

Friday, the day following his night at the farm, Ghali left the Avis rental in the barn and drove the rest of the way to Mexico in the farmer's Honda Accord.

Ghali had to hand it to Silverstein's assistant. She had been one spunky female. And, those eyes! A man could get lost in those in no time. Ghali smiled to himself. His surprise at the slimy seat he jumped into when leaving the hotel would be one incident in his life he would *never* forget. Why she had done that puzzled Ghali. Other than the injections, he hadn't mistreated her. It made no sense.

Ghali had never married but, if he had, he always imagined someone of Kipling's breed: beautiful, strong, and brave beyond measure. She had attacked him with nothing more than her body as a weapon. A troubling thought now entered Ghali's brain. If he had successfully terminated Silverstein, could he have eliminated Kipling as well? *Damn!*

But what of the situation now? It was likely that Fitzby told the truth, that he had not communicated with Silverstein. Supporting that assertion, Ghali had never mentioned to Fitzby his original family name, Hamasay. So where did Silverstein get that information, and on such short notice? They had locked eyes on that United flight only hours before their encounter at the Mountain High Inn!

The only answer that made any sense had come from Warner. Once arriving in Mexico, Ghali contacted him. Warner did not react well to this new information. For two reasons. First, he said, it suggested that the US government had a file on Ghali, albeit with his original family name. Second, and more important to Warner, it also meant that his own position might be in jeopardy. Even on the telephone, Ghali could sense Warner's concern.

Ghali's mind focused on the present. He stretched his hand forward to turn the ignition key. He stopped. It was normal quitting time and employees were walking to their motor scooters and cars to go home.

Ghali scanned the faces coming toward him. He knew them all. Other than the Russians, Ghali had scrutinized the resumes of all the technical personnel Fitzby had hired. Although most had been local, hired off the island, several employees had relocated from the states. Could there be a spy among them? Ghali considered this possibility unlikely. On the other hand, he would have considered it close to impossible to be identified by name inside an American hotel in the heart of America. Ghali made a mental note to revisit the files of the Americans Fitzby had hired.

At last, Fitzby strode from the door. What had Silverstein said? "His character is severely flawed, Mr. Hamasay. Has he explained to you why he wants me dead? I suspect he has not." Ghali had deduced all along that there was more to Fitzby's request to kill Silverstein than just the success of this project. Silverstein's comment added confirmation.

Ghali watched as Fitzby walked across the lot, entered his small Toyota Corolla, and drove off. He had been so angry at Fitzby for violating his instructions that he decided, on the spot, to withhold information that would have given Fitzby an emotional high.

Following a week that had seen its share of disappointment and near disaster for Ghali, a call from Warner yesterday provided him a much-needed lift. Barbara Lopez had completed and tested the tracking software. Warner would accept delivery soon.

CHAPTER 24

▼

VEXATION

Naval Research Laboratory, Monterey, California, USA:
36° 35'N Latitude, 121° 51'W Longitude
Thursday morning, 0930, August 30, 2007

Since their return from Colorado, Silverstein had mulled over both the merits and downsides of eternity. For the second time within a week, he had faced death. To make matters worse, from the male point of view, in this latest escapade he had hardly been the hero.

After staying until Saturday in Fort Collins, he and Kipling flew home that afternoon. Neither had stayed overnight at the hospital during the early morning hours of the previous Thursday, although Silverstein thought Kipling should have. They had returned to the Mountain High Inn instead.

With a new desk clerk behind the counter, they pretended as if they had just arrived. As they walked forward to register, two men were removing the bullet-ridden sofa that Silverstein thought had done a commendable job of protecting him. Kipling stirred the pot when she turned to the desk clerk and asked innocently, in a perfect southern accent, "Did y'all have some problems here?" Silverstein turned quickly to stifle his laugh.

Without drama, the emergency room surgeon had removed the bullet in Silverstein's thigh. The discomfort was manageable and there had been no serious damage to either muscle or bone. In the aftermath, Kipling's injury proved the more serious—a dislocated shoulder. Against Kipling's objections, the emergency room doctor used an anesthetic to reset the shoulder, or do a *reduction*, a term new to Silverstein. Unless he performed this procedure carefully, the doctor emphasized, it would be easy to cause further damage. The reset shoulder, in addition to some torn cartilage, would cause her pain for some weeks. The doctor gave them appropriate medications and ordered rest.

Silverstein worried over Kipling's condition. Eventually, she politely asked him to stop calling her room, convincing him that she would live to see another day.

Although looking very much like the walking wounded—Silverstein with his limp and Kipling in her sling—neither wanted to stay home from work on Monday. Telling colleagues and bosses what had happened was not pleasant—because it was a lie. They explained their injuries resulted from a traffic accident that, in Silverstein's case, had given him a severe bruise to the thigh. This fabrication explained their missing the Boulder meeting.

Because their adventure had occurred in distant Fort Collins, word of what actually happened had not leaked outside that area. Moreover, other than Lopez, they hadn't run into anyone they knew. On Friday, the local paper did cover the gunplay in the Mountain High Inn, but the article was short on details. Silverstein figured Lopez might have had a hand in that.

There were two reasons for avoiding the truth with co-workers. First, the drama of what had occurred would bring them unwanted attention; the ongoing mystery involving Fitzby and Hamasay required Silverstein's complete concentration. More significantly, Lopez had asked that they keep this incident secret.

Beyond the obvious, what irritated Silverstein was something he had least anticipated. He had fully expected his old friend to be completely forthcoming with him regarding Hamasay: Who he was, where he came from, for whom he worked, and the like. He hadn't! To make matters more confusing, Silverstein had caught Lopez and his associate Miller arguing heatedly. Dissension in the ranks? By the time Silverstein and Kipling left the hospital, both men had disappeared.

Ironically, Silverstein had persuaded himself that now *was* the time to go public with Fitzby's hurricane manipulations, to alert scientific colleagues. Why Lopez would suggest otherwise seemed incomprehensible. When he asked why, Lopez said he could not say. In fact, Silverstein learned little more than what Lopez had told him on the telephone outside of Fort Collins. *I'd like to say more, but you're still on an unsecured line. Bullshit!* Considering the nature of their previous relationship—and that Hamasay had nearly killed him in Fort Collins—Silverstein felt slighted.

A knock at the door brought Silverstein back from his previous irritation with Lopez to another source of frustration. "Come...oh, it's you."

Silverstein grinned at the appearance of Kipling in her red sling. The color of the fabric had changed daily. "How's the shoulder coming along?"

Kipling grimaced. "I'll live. How's the leg?"

"Same."

Although they had talked off and on since their return, Silverstein felt distant and recognized he had not been treating Kipling fairly.

Kipling sat down slowly, holding her left arm steady with her right hand. "At least I had the good sense to fall on my left side."

She smiled weakly. Her voice then turned patient and understanding. "What's wrong, Victor? You've been acting strangely toward me all week. Did I do something to offend you?"

Silverstein decided to come clean. He was making miserable the one person who had no doubt saved his life—as if *she* had done something wrong. "I'm sorry, Linda. I'm embarrassed."

The skin in Kipling's forehead wrinkled together. Her voice became less patient and understanding. "Embarrassed? What the hell are *you* embarrassed about? I'm the one who got herself kidnapped. If there's any embarrassment in this room, it's sitting right here."

Silverstein responded with a smile, but it was short-lived. His facial features tightened. "I nearly got you killed, and then..." He stopped and stared down at his desk.

Kipling looked back in anticipation. "And then *what?*"

"Instead of me saving you from Hamasay, you saved me. That's not right."

Kipling hesitated before reacting, as if she required a second take on his words. Silverstein watched as her face changed slowly to the color of her sling. She then shot from her chair like a rocket, wincing in pain from the sudden ascent.

Kipling tramped to the door and stopped. He could see her taking deep breaths. Finally, she turned and faced him, a mixture of anger and surprise in her face. The quiet, consoling voice Silverstein had responded to just moments earlier was not at all evident.

"You know, Victor, you've got a lot of problems, most of which you, and I, know about. But never in all the time I've known you did I suspect you were a goddamn male chauvinist pig!"

Kipling spun back to the door, exited, and with her good arm grabbed and slammed it against the jamb.

Silverstein sat confounded, open-mouthed.

CHAPTER 25

▼

WOODEN STALLION

Naval Research Laboratory, Washington, DC: 38° 49'N Latitude,
77° 1'W Longitude
Friday morning, 0830, August 31, 2007

"It'll be ready in a week." That was the message Barbara Lopez had left on Clement Warner's voice mail the previous Monday. Perhaps as a reward for her considerable angst, she'd make the one-month deadline.

After working ungodly hours over past weeks, Lopez completed and tested that portion of her program that had been giving her fits—the software that linked the expert system to the hurricane model. That module took the inputs to the fuzzy expert system—inputs that were nothing more than the coordinates of the intended direction of movement—and processed them in an iterative fashion back and forth with the dynamic hurricane model. The result was a pattern of ocean temperatures that would steer the hurricane in the direction desired.

Lopez could likewise run her program backward. By specifying a pattern of heating, one could study the hurricane's reaction. To her, this latter option was the obvious strength of the software. While it might be fun to pretend to be God and decree where a hurricane should go, that was obviously impossible. If Warner hadn't insisted that the targeting option be a part of the program, Lopez could have finished her assignment much earlier.

When Warner had handed her this new assignment the previous November (cutting short her previous work, no small irritation), Lopez presumed this project had its roots in academia, perhaps at the Naval Postgraduate School (NPS) in Monterey. Another possibility was NRL's own Marine Meteorology Division, located a couple of stones' throw from NPS.

Both organizations possessed in-house expertise in tropical cyclones. The NPS meteorology department had made its mark on many an *1800*, the navy officer designation for oceanography, the big "O" that included the field of meteorology. This institution of higher learning had been in existence since its association with the Naval Academy back in the 1940s. Lopez knew that navy meteorologists would want a tool like hers to conduct theoretical "what-if" experiments to understand better why and how pools of warm water alter the strength and movement of hurricanes.

Although Lopez had no formal training in the atmospheric sciences, she had conducted enough preliminary research—as she always did when starting a new project—to know that scientists had learned as much or more about hurricanes from computer simulations as they had from expensive field studies or pure mathematical analysis. Predicting how hurricanes react and move in response to ocean temperatures had obvious practical implications for forecasting. For this reason alone, this project gave Lopez a feeling of satisfaction, that she was contributing to society. The same couldn't be said of the earlier tasks dispensed by Warner. That no journal article would be in the offing added to her frustration.

One contradiction puzzled Lopez. Why would this research be categorized *Top Secret*? In the three years she had worked for Warner, her projects had always focused on subjects one could assume would be highly classified. The incremental explosive power of different, known chemical agents; the theoretical extrapolation of the spread of biological diseases such as smallpox; varying hull strength across the navy's fleet of ships (although this topic hardly required much of her talent; she simply compiled a summary)—sensitive, clandestine topics one could imagine being examined in dusty, cipher-locked offices of researchers funded by the Office of Naval Research.

Lopez pulled out her notes and reviewed the government's definition for Top Secret: *That unauthorized disclosure of such information could reasonably be expected to cause exceptionally grave damage to the national security.* But hurricane research? Such information hardly seemed worthy of safeguarding for purposes of natural security.

Meteorologists, like scientists the world over, avoided having any aspect of their work classified, thinking (justifiably) that their science should remain unfettered, open to public scrutiny and further progress, whether here or abroad. Science was supposed to operate this way. Unfortunately, Lopez knew, the military-industrial complex often trumped that idealistic notion.

Classification served the government in two ways. Importantly, it allowed information to remain hidden, available only to those with a *need to know*. After all, the control of knowledge and ideas was the foundation of world interaction—and dominance, be it peaceful or destructive. But significantly—and in some ways contrary to the principles of a democratic society—such control also restricted scrutiny from those who might question the need or validity of such information.

How could this research possibly fall under those auspices? Alternatively, might the navy have a project to control hurricanes? That would explain why Warner had been adamant regarding the targeting option. Lopez admitted that she hadn't considered that possibility. *But how could you possibly heat water in such large areas around tropical cyclones?*

Lopez heard a knock and rotated to face the door. It was Warner. She hadn't expected him to drop by until Monday, figuring her phone call sufficient.

After a perfunctory greeting, Warner drew up a chair and faced Lopez. "Dr. Lopez, I received your message. I came by to congratulate you personally."

Lopez looked across the table and sensed the verbal offer to be sincere, although hard to tell through all the hair.

"Thank you."

Warner abruptly turned serious, obvious only from the narrowing of his eyes and the slowing of his words. "Dr. Lopez, I have to ask you something that is somewhat sensitive." Warner stood and shut the door behind him.

"Oh!" *What's this all about?*

Warner returned to his seat and grasped the sides with his hands. "As you are well aware, your work is conducted at the highest levels of classification. My superiors have approved of our arrangement and it has worked well for both of us."

Warner paused for emphasis and then raised his right hand to his forehead. "Recently, I've been contacted by those who worry about our government's secrets."

Lopez listened intently, concerned. What was he saying? That someone suspected she was on the take, that she had sold out her country for a few pieces of silver? No, he hadn't said that. *Calm down.*

"What did they say?"

"They said, and I tell you honestly that I have no idea what brought this on, that our association may be compromised."

Lopez's face flushed. "What do you mean *compromised*?" Her voice rose. "Are you questioning my loyalty, Dr. Warner?"

Lopez stared directly into the two dark spots between the hair.

Warner raised his arms in capitulation, his palms facing Lopez. "Dr. Lopez, believe me, I am the last person who would question your devotion. Please! Hear me out."

Lopez calmed down enough to listen further, at the same time pushing her chair back against the wall, as if distancing herself from Warner would make this unpleasant problem go away. If Warner didn't question her loyalty, why did he bring it up in the first place?

"I have to ask you this." Warner cleared his throat. "Has anyone questioned you about either our relationship or our projects? And, in particular, this one?"

Lopez leaned forward in her chair, her eyes never leaving their target. "No, goddamn it! You can take that back to your spooks and quote me verbatim."

Although she would be hard pressed to say why, Lopez still sensed concern in Warner's eyes. His immediate words in reply said the opposite. "I've known that all along and that's what I told them."

Warner stood and then spoke in a manner and with words that obviated the serious conversation that had just transpired.

"Please don't give it another thought." He turned toward the door, but looked back at Lopez. "I apologize for bringing this up. You can be sure you'll hear nothing more of it."

Lopez watched in mild shock at the quick conclusion to this disturbing conversation. Warner tipped his head and pursed his lips, as an indication of respect. Before departing, he made one more comment.

"See you Monday morning. Please burn me two CD's, would you?"

Lopez stood, tramped to the door, closed it behind her, leaned backward against it, and faced her office. *What the hell was that all about? Who were the "those who worry about our government's secrets" people Warner had referred to?*

Lopez immediately considered calling her husband, to get his advice. Her hand stopped short of the phone when she thought the better of it. *I can't do this to Hector!* He would naturally do all he could to help, but there were serious downsides. At the least, he might inquire into areas he had no business looking into. And should he discover something, what was he to do then? Confide to her in secret? No! Asking Hector for information would be unethical, and illegal.

The thought of her husband brought to the fore the images she had seen in his notebook. Lopez had felt so guilty afterward that she had recessed that information to the back of her mind. But now, the word *hurricane* stood out from those two pages, drawing her attention as if it were highlighted and blinking. Simultaneously, the names scribbled there came into focus.

Lopez returned to her chair, perplexed and frustrated. Contrary to her usual patient reaction when a situation like this confronted her, Lopez chose an immediate, direct course of action. Although devious and with some risk, it might confirm the existence, and legitimacy, of Warner's client—something that seemed important just now.

Lopez placed her fingers on the keyboard and started typing, ever faster. She brought up NRL's home page, *www.nrl.navy.mil,* clicked on *Field Sites,* then on *Monterey,* and then finally on the direct connection to Monterey, *www.nrlmry.navy.mil.* A few more clicks produced a telephone number. Lopez removed her cell phone from her purse and dialed.

"Hello. Dr. Victor Silverstein, please…thanks."

To obtain the information Lopez wanted, her words had to be credible. Lopez breathed slowly in and out to control her nervousness.

"Dr. Silverstein, this is Cynthia Morgan, Code 1030, from the public affairs office in Washington. How are you this morning?"

Lopez bantered with a few further pleasantries. She continued. "Hey, listen. The reason I'm calling is to update our records on the research going on in Monterey. As you probably know, our job here is to keep current on what's going on throughout NRL, so we can provide up-to-date PR for all of our divisions. Recently, we've gotten word that the navy's now involved in weather modification…yes, weather modification. In particular, we're hearing there's some research going on to maneuver hurricanes away from coastal areas. Are you folks in Monterey playing a role in that work and, if not, do you have any idea where that might be going on?"

Lopez listened intently to Silverstein's detailed response. "Well, thank you anyway. Goodbye."

Damn! Lopez pressed the disconnect button on her cell and leaned back, reeling against the directness of Silverstein's reply. She forced herself to take a breath. Following Lopez's question, Silverstein had paused for a palpable moment. Then came words that forced Lopez to cut the conversation short.

"Ms. Morgan…if you are calling from NRL DC, as you say, I'd see your number show up on my caller ID. I don't! That means one of two things. Either you do not work there, or you have chosen to hide your identity. It's probably the latter since a quick scan of the NRL DC personnel roster shows me there is no Cynthia Morgan employed at NRL. Either way, that means you are lying. Because you knew the correct NRL code for public affairs, I will assume you do work for NRL. Even though I don't know who you are, I'll cut you a deal." He hesitated for a beat, as if giving his caller time to think. "I'll give *you* a truthful answer to your questions, if you'll answer just one for me. The answer is no, on both counts. Now, it's your turn. Why do you ask?"

Lopez shuddered. She had learned two things from this call. Silverstein was every bit as smart as rumors suggested. More importantly, he had just informed her that he knew of no such research in the navy. If anyone knew, he would. He could be lying of course, but judging from the tone of his expression, and from his request to *cut you a deal*, that seemed unlikely. If so, then to whom would Warner deliver her software?

With that question now at the root of Lopez's concern, she turned again to her computer monitor linked to the Silicon Graphics workstation that held all her classified software development. She had never tried this sort of thing before and it would probably take her most of the weekend to complete and test.

Normally, only hackers and those up to no good would purposely do what she planned. But, Lopez concluded, this was an extraordinary situation that demanded like action.

Lopez decided to add a few extra, unique lines of code to the software interface—code which happened to be an integrated portion of the model itself. No one would ever deduce that code's existence because she would hide it in undecipherable machine language.

Anyone who used the targeting software had to connect to the Internet to download wind and temperature fields that fed into the hurricane model. During that linkup, Lopez's invisible module would transmit back (to Lopez), over the Internet, the specifics entered into the system by the user.

Medical books suggest you can't detect your own blood pressure. At that instant, however, Lopez concluded hers was on the rise. Her fingers typed slowly at first and then gained momentum. She marveled at the thought of having an invisible, ringside seat into the mind of the user of her software.

A layperson might not understand such deception, but might consider the result a feat of magic. Those within the software community had a name for the computer program that produced such legerdemain. They called it a *Trojan Horse*.

CHAPTER 26

▼

SURVEILLANCE

George Bush Center for Intelligence, McLean, Virginia: 38° 56'N
Latitude, 77° 8'W Longitude
Friday afternoon, 1530, August 31, 2007

"I still feel like shit, the way I treated Victor." Hector Lopez pounded his fist on the desk. His face registered pain and he could see Miller's reaction. "An international assassin almost killed him and his friend...and I couldn't tell him a damn thing about it."

It had been over a week since the incident in Colorado. Silverstein and Lopez hadn't spoken since. Although Lopez couldn't tell him anything more—even now—he still wished his old friend would call.

Miller stood and avoided eye contact, obviously embarrassed by this confession of feelings. "You had no choice...*but*, you're forgetting one thing."

Lopez wondered what it was he had forgotten.

"This Fitzby/Hamasay affair won't last forever. When it's over, you can tell him everything."

"Thanks, Marc. I needed that." Lopez sighed and then broke out laughing. "Hell! I can't wait to tell him the shenanigans we pulled off after Fort Collins. He'll die laughing."

Lopez's phone rang. He answered, listened briefly, and gestured Miller back to his chair.

Lopez scratched his head and looked up. "You don't say. Hot damn!" He wrote something on his desk pad. "You're doing a helluva job, Tom. Watch your ass, okay?"

Their chat proved shorter than the last. Tom O'Toole, a.k.a. Barry Emerson, had just called in from Bermuda. Lopez dropped the cradled phone into his hand and stared across his desk at Miller.

"Significant news! What we've suspected since Colorado is true. Hamasay *is* Fitzby's superior in Bermuda. He's only been in Bermuda a couple of times, but Tom recognized him from our photographs. But guess what?" Lopez looked down at his words. "He goes by the name of Ghali, G-H-A-L-I, now."

Miller's head jerked and he closed his eyes. "Son of a bitch! I don't think that leaves much doubt that he's the link to Fitzby's funding."

"Tom said something else. He still has no idea what their endgame is, but Fitzby's started dicking around again with the weather coming off Africa. But with no obvious method or madness. They're still waiting on the targeting software."

Miller looked up and seemed to mull over Lopez's words before he spoke. "O'Toole mentioned that software weeks ago and it's interesting they still don't have it. Where'd you suppose it's coming from?"

"Your guess is as good as mine. I'm more concerned with what Hamasay...Ghali...and Fitzby have up their sleeves once they get it. I've got a feeling that after that we'll know their intentions pretty damn quick. They don't have much time. Silverstein told me they have only a month or two before the hurricane season will be too far gone."

Miller stirred in his seat. "I sure hope you made the right call, Hector. We're way the hell out on a limb here. If Hamasay...I guess we should call him Ghali now, suspects anything, we're screwed." Miller held his fist out, extended the thumb, and rotated it to the floor. "All of our work will be lost."

Lopez nodded and smiled in a smug way. "So far, so good."

Miller laughed. "Yeah, that's what Moms Mabley said too when she proclaimed she planned to live forever. The good news is that *I'm* still alive. I swear I nearly had a heart attack when that car turned up the road." He pointed his finger at Lopez. "Next time we flip a coin!"

Lopez wadded up a piece of paper and threw it across the desk. "If memory serves me correctly, you volunteered, my friend."

Lopez had made a momentous decision back in Fort Collins. They could have apprehended Ghali within hours of his leaving town. Once Kipling told them Ghali's rental had the OnStar system, it proved to be a simple matter to follow him via satellite—once they acquired the vehicle PIN from Avis (fortunately, Kipling had been conscious during that phase of her adventure and remembered the car company, no small detail). They then tracked the vehicle as if a thief had stolen it. Because Ghali did not ditch his car earlier than he did meant he had no understanding of the OnStar's GPS capabilities.

Apprehending Ghali had not been the issue. Both Lopez and Miller *wanted* him to escape. Paradoxically, it would have been a setback if Silverstein or Kipling had, in fact, taken Ghali down at the Mountain High Inn.

On the telephone with Silverstein back in Alexandria was the first time in months that Lopez had reason to reflect on the name Hamasay (a.k.a. Ghali). Silverstein's physical description alerted him immediately. Years earlier, the agency had discovered an electronic tie-in with Sidki. That distinction earned Ghali a spot in the agency's database. Agency personnel responsible for such information then developed a file that included photographs and other available historical information. Still, Ghali had never been associated with a specific terrorist event. For these reasons, Lopez and Miller's early discussion on the flight to Colorado had revolved around Ghali's connection to Silverstein.

The question Lopez and Miller had to address after Ghali's escape from the hotel was whether they should take advantage of the serendipitous situation that had presented itself. (Had they wanted to capture him, it would have been easy—he had parked outside town, well into the morning.) Lopez and Miller had argued vociferously. Lopez wanted to go ahead with the plan; Miller wanted to play it safe, not risk anything more. Since Lopez held seniority over Miller, he made the decision.

Two members from the Mensa side of the house and two other agents departed Washington within six hours of that disagreement and crossed into Kansas airspace by noon. In the meantime, Lopez's friends in the bureau provided a helicopter. He and Miller raced to get ahead of Ghali's rental. Using GPS, the FBI had kept them informed of Ghali's movement.

Initially, Ghali headed east and made it as far as southwestern Nebraska, limiting himself to secondary roads. He then turned south, likely headed for Mexico. Based on this new trajectory, Lopez checked his map and redirected the CIA aircraft to Garden City, Kansas. In the meantime, they refueled the helicopter.

The chopper and jet met in Garden City. Lopez and Miller picked up Dr. Cynthia Reston, CIA agent and physician, as well as Chris Cooper, an Image Transformation Expert (ITE)—or in more vernacular terms, a makeup artist. Coincidentally, both Reston and Cooper hailed from the Mensa team. They returned to the air to locate Ghali's vehicle visually. It was mid-afternoon.

The other two agents, Averill Hansley and John Winston, rented and transferred their equipment to two vehicles, one a Nissan pickup truck and the second the largest SUV they could find in the rental lot. Lopez directed them to drive due west, intersect Kansas Highway 27 at the town of Syracuse, and wait. Ghali was driving south on 27. Unless he chose an erratic detour, it made sense for him to continue on that highway, which would lead him to Oklahoma. From there, he could make his way down through Texas and across the border into Mexico.

Once Lopez spotted and identified Ghali's car, they flew on ahead, south on 27, to locate an appropriate spot for their plan to unfold. They found it on a desolate section of highway not far north of Syracuse. The helicopter arrived first and the two vehicles later. The helicopter dropped off its passengers. Hansley and the pilot took off north to monitor Ghali's drive south.

Lopez estimated they now had no more than forty minutes to prepare.

Although Miller had made an impassioned plea to Lopez not to go forward with his plan, after the decision was made, he accepted its inevitability and volunteered for the crucial role. He made the valid point that he could pass for a Kansas farmer much easier than could Lopez. Lopez conceded the point.

Earlier, when they had taken to the air out of Garden City, Cooper set about to do his work. Miller changed quickly into a red plaid shirt, dirty work coveralls, and farm boots. Cooper then proceeded to add the farmer's tan to Miller's arms and face, as well as an appropriate amount of grime. Scratches and blood oozing from his arms and face came last.

The pickup truck that Hansley and Winston rented had been their second choice. They would have preferred a farm tractor, but there had been no time to locate one. On arrival at the planned site, they scooped roadside dust on the vehicle to give it a less than new appearance. Rolling it over onto its driver's side, wheels facing south in the middle of the highway, completed its transformation.

While this preparation continued, Reston, the physician developer and leading proponent for the use of her quick acting amnesia-inducing drug, gave Miller a quick course on its administration. Housed within a pressurized can the size of a man's travel shaving cream, it was only a matter of spraying the aerosol into the victim's face. Sedation occurred within seconds, she promised.

The plan seemed simple. As Ghali's car approached, Miller would climb out of the truck and flag him down. He would limp to Ghali's window, start to explain what had happened, and spray Ghali in the face. What could go wrong?

While Cooper and Winston drove south in the SUV to control traffic from that direction, Lopez directed Hansley and the helicopter to set down on the highway behind Ghali's vehicle to do likewise from the north. Lopez and Reston hid to the rear of the truck, weapons ready, to intercede should their strategy run awry. Miller climbed into the pickup cab through the top door and waited.

Only minutes had passed when Lopez yelled to Miller that he could see Ghali's vehicle coming, Lopez's signal that he should start climbing from the cab.

Miller timed his exit to coincide with Ghali's arrival. He waved his arms and limped toward the vehicle. To Lopez's immense relief, Ghali's car slowed and came to a stop. Ghali opened his window and Miller bent down to speak to the driver.

The milliseconds that elapsed turned into full seconds—too many of them, by Lopez's count. But then, Miller, his body angled to the right to shield his right hand's movement from the driver, reached for the spray can in his right pocket. Miller smoothly lifted his right arm, initiating the aerosol spray as Reston had instructed. As the aerosol can came flush with the open window, Miller backed away.

Lopez held his breath. If Reston's drug worked as advertised, Ghali should now be unconscious. Miller held the can in the window for a good two seconds before retreating. Reston had cautioned him that if he caught a whiff, he would fall unconscious as well. As luck would have it, the afternoon breeze blew from the east.

Miller backed away a considerable distance to avoid any possibility of contamination. Lopez and Reston stood and peered over the side of the pickup truck. Miller signaled them forward. Reston's spray had done its job and the tension in the air temporarily subsided. Using his cell phone, Lopez called back the agents in the SUV. He also directed the pilot of the helicopter to drop off Hansley.

Although Phase 1 had succeeded, the next part of their plan required considerably more preparation. First, they needed to attend to Ghali, to make sure he remained unconscious. Reston measured and injected a syringe of drugs she insisted would keep him that way for twelve hours— or until she injected a neutralizer. Hansley and Winston loaded Ghali into the back seat of the Ford Expedition. A big guy—and smelly, noted Lopez.

Lopez's next task was to locate an isolated house they could rent for the night. The large sum of cash offered to the older couple who lived in the small, two-bedroom farmhouse—not even a mile south of their starting point—solved Lopez's problem. Lopez promised the owners they could return to their home by noon the following day.

Although Lopez had been anxious about the moment when Miller would spray the aerosol, the planned end to Phase 2, just before daylight, would present an even tenser situation.

The CIA team spent the remainder of the day, into the early morning hours, preparing the farmhouse for Ghali's departure. From the SUV, Hansley and Winston carried Ghali to the bedroom and laid him on the bed. He would remain there until Reston injected the drug that would counteract the tranquilizer. Hansley and Winston departed to drive into Garden City to purchase a used car.

The agents who remained at the farmhouse had a critical job. To make it look like Ghali had hidden there, taken advantage of what was available in the refrigerator, and fallen asleep on the bed. If one believed the results of Dr. Reston's laboratory tests, Ghali would remember nothing from the immediate seconds prior to going unconscious—those crucial seconds when Miller administered the drug. Dr. Reston said he *would* recall Miller's overturned vehicle, his limping toward his car, and their discussion. *She damned well better be right!*

Following the apprehension, Lopez and Miller had pushed Ghali's car off the side of the road. Later, on purpose, knowing that the job would not be a pleasant one, Lopez asked Cooper to retrieve the Cadillac and drive it into the shed where the couple's Taurus had parked earlier.

"What the hell happened in that car?" was Cooper's annoyed reaction when he returned. Lopez and Miller howled in response. It took a good five minutes to give him the unabridged story of Kipling's escape from the Cadillac.

Lopez returned the Cadillac's keys to Ghali's pocket. He made a calculated guess. But from Silverstein's testimony of Ghali firing his weapon with his right hand, and from the three male agents' (all were right-handed) tally of which pocket they used for their keys (all agreed), Cooper inserted them into Ghali's right side pocket.

Hansley and Winston, in the meantime, returned with an older model Honda Accord, its tank filled, and parked it directly outside the front door. Hansley positioned the key, with its conspicuous Honda emblem, on a nail next to the kitchen door, along with other keys from the home-owners.

Lopez made a final inspection of the house, the driveway, the shed, and the Honda. All appeared to be in readiness. He hoped Ghali would not wait around long enough to note any overlooked inconsistencies. By then, midnight had come and long gone; the living room cuckoo clock sang its two-note cry four times. Most of what needed to be done was done. Time to spring the conclusion to this charade.

Lopez removed Ghali's pistol from his belt, took it outside, and fired it into the ground. In the meantime, Miller sat in the kitchen undergoing Cooper's makeover for his final curtain call.

Cooper removed the original makeup and started from scratch. In place of the farmer's tan, Cooper used a white undercoat that he manipulated with artistry-like care. The bullet hole in the center of the chest took more skill, and time. But by the end of it, everyone complimented Cooper that Miller did look like death itself. Miller thanked his co-workers for their honesty.

Before they left the house for the last time, Lopez turned on all available lights in the kitchen. Agents Hansley and Winston departed first, heading south in the Ford SUV and the Nissan truck. With all details seemingly handled, Lopez's mental clock started ticking the instant Reston injected the neutralizer into Ghali's veins. They had ten minutes.

Miller lay down just outside the door on the front porch, away from the light, but where he would be readily visible when Ghali exited the front door. Attending to careful positioning to make sure all looked natural from someone falling after a gunshot, Cooper nodded to Lopez and Reston.

All three took off running toward the grassy field adjacent the house. Two hundred feet later, they stopped and knelt down on the now wet grass. Although all agents trained in the use of firearms, Lopez knew Cooper had the best aim of the trio; he had lost several friendly bets establishing Cooper's credentials.

Cooper removed his rifle from its custom case, careful to disengage the thermite self-destruction anti-theft system. More than one agent over the years had faced severe embarrassment by inadvertently destroying this thirty thousand dollar weapon. He assembled the components quickly, choosing to fire from a tripod to increase accuracy, and with an infrared night sight.

Although the user could fire the weapon either with or without a silencer, Cooper chose the former. He lay in position and sighted in on the porch. If for some reason Ghali concluded Miller wasn't dead and made a threatening movement, Cooper would have no choice but to take Ghali out. The hollow point bullet from this precision weapon would make quick destruction of Ghali's cranium. Lopez counted on that not being necessary.

Lopez had briefly considered replacing Ghali's bullets with blanks. Because Ghali could later discover the switch, he quickly discarded that thought as a foolish one.

Lopez checked his watch. Six minutes had passed when Lopez's heart nearly stopped beating. Into the quarter mile dirt road that fronted the property from the highway turned a vehicle, its headlights trained up the drive to the house. True to his training, Miller remained motionless. *Shit! Of all times, not now!* The three of them exhaled a palpable sign of relief when the vehicle backed up and sped off in the direction it had come. Obviously, the car was only turning around. Fortunately, the car's headlights shone to the side of the house and not on the porch to reveal Miller.

Less than a minute later, Lopez observed motion in the bright lights of the kitchen. "This is it, folks," he whispered.

The figure moved back and forth and then was gone.

Reston spoke softly. "He's probably gone back to the head. I was surprised he hadn't peed himself in the bed before we left."

Lopez caught the glint off his watch's second hand. Sixty, seventy more seconds elapsed. Finally, Ghali opened the front door and exited to the porch, his pistol breaking the air in front of him. He scanned the night air to the left, straight ahead, and then to the right. It took several seconds before he noticed the body.

"Do you have him, Chris?" Lopez whispered.

"I have him," Cooper came back.

It was a sign of immense relief when Ghali's hand with the gun fell to his right side. He walked over and stared at the body in the dim light. He then lifted his gun, but at the same time walked to the left, directly underneath the porch light. He removed the clip, inspected it, replaced it, and looked back again at Miller.

In the following instant, Ghali's pace quickened. He reached with his right hand into his right pocket and removed his keys. At the same time, he looked to the left where the Cadillac sat readily visible in the shed. He stared at the keys again, and then at the Honda sitting in front of him.

"Go look for the keys, you son of a bitch!" Lopez mouthed, but with no sound.

Lopez, Cooper, and Reston again let out their breaths in unison as Ghali rotated and walked back inside. The shadow moved back and forth and then finally exited into full form. Once again, he paused to look down at Miller. At that instant, he placed his pistol inside his belt and walked to the driver's side of the Honda.

Again, Ghali hesitated. He looked around the farm, held up his watch to catch light from the porch, and finally got in. The engine started and the lights came on. After another few seconds of seeming indecision, the trio heard the car shift into gear and watched as it moved slowly down the dirt road to the highway. There the vehicle stopped.

Lopez realized that Ghali now had a problem. "He doesn't know which way to turn."

Seconds passed. Before long, the Honda accelerated, correctly, to the right. The hint of twilight straight ahead had signaled Ghali that south lay to the right.

Lopez lifted his two-way and pressed the transmit button. "Hansley, he's on his way. Monitor his passage but stay in position. I can't take any more surprises for one day."

"Roger; will do."

Lopez, Cooper, and Reston remained in place, afraid that even a single muscle's movement might somehow jeopardize all that had transpired.

Lopez knew that Miller wondered why they hadn't yet returned to the house.

Finally, two minutes later, came the all clear. "Hector, the Honda just passed and he's hauling ass."

The phone rang a second time and Lopez answered. "You don't say? Cairo, huh?" Lopez set the phone down and looked across at Miller. "Ghali's blown Bermuda and showed up yesterday in Egypt."

Miller's brow furrowed and his eyes closed. "This is the first time we've pinpointed him outside of Bermuda."

Miller opened his eyes, leaned across the desk, and extended his hand to Lopez. "I've got to hand it to you, you pulled it off."

Lopez accepted the handshake, but was quick to reply. "*We* pulled it off, Marc…especially you and Reston. Thanks for being her assistant during the surgery. The transmitter appears to be working just fine."

CHAPTER 27

▼

REDIAL

Naval Research Laboratory, Monterey, California, USA:
36°35'N Latitude, 121°51'W Longitude
Friday morning, 0830, September 7, 2007

"I've been thinking."

"Victor, how many times have I reminded you that's when you get into trouble?" Kipling's eyes squinted with telltale mischievousness.

Silverstein grimaced in reply. It had taken him a week, but he had finally gotten back on the good side of Kipling. Not that it had come cheap—three separate deliveries of two dozen, long-stemmed roses, each matching the color of her shoulder sling for that day. He hoped she had noticed the color connection, although she hadn't mentioned it. She probably had, but didn't want to give any more positive feedback to him than necessary. He had sent them to Kipling's apartment because, had he not, tongues would have wagged in both Building 704 and across the street in 702. No point in fueling rumors any more than necessary.

"Speaking of which…" Silverstein had a habit of changing the topic to fit his own agenda, as if it were somehow a continuation of the previous subject. "How soon will your wing be fixed? If I'm in any more physical danger, I want to be sure I can count on you."

Silverstein grinned. It had taken not only flowers, but some serious words of contrition to offset his faux pas. *Male chauvinist pig indeed!* Kipling had merely confused a male's need to protect those around him, particularly those of the female persuasion, with her own sense of personal worth. Even so, he admitted to himself, he could have avoided a lot of needless pain if he had thought that one through a little more.

"I'm healing fast, my doctor says. She wants me to start some light exercises in about a week. There really isn't any more pain to speak of."

Kipling paused. "Okay, I bite. What were you thinking?"

"I'm still trying to make sense of that phone call. It's possible, I suppose, that the whole thing could have been innocent. But then, why did she hang up on me if it were a legitimate call? What do you think?"

Kipling hesitated and then responded. "Let's reexamine the facts. One, she pretends to be from NRL Public Affairs and you confirm there is no Cynthia Morgan in that department. Two, she asks you if you are involved in, or know of, any hurricane modification work ongoing. You reply *no*, but then she hangs up on you."

"Nice recap, Linda, but tell me something I don't know."

"Okay! Here's what you do know. First, she both lied to you and, when faced with explaining why she had called, she didn't want to say and hung up. What does that tell you, oh brilliant one?"

"It tells me she's protecting something or someone."

"Yeah, and what else?"

"That she's afraid to say anything more?"

"Good. You're getting close. And, what else?"

Silverstein feigned exasperation. "Since she knew the code for NRL Public Affairs, she works for NRL!"

Kipling sneered in reply. "That's a given. We've already decided that. What more? Put the two together."

"I'm all thought out. Tell me."

"It means…it might mean she herself is somehow connected to the project…and, she's afraid."

Silverstein's face contorted, as if he had just taken a bite from a lemon. "How the hell did you come up with that one?"

Kipling stared back and held up the index finger of her right hand. "Remember her specific words. She asked if you knew anything about 'maneuvering hurricanes away from coastlines?' You and I have both been searching the papers to see if the media has picked up on any of this. There's been no mention of weather modification, and least of all about maneuvering hurricanes."

Silverstein placed his hands flat on the desk and stared back. "If she's already involved, what point would there be in asking me? She already knows the answer."

"That's what I wondered too." Kipling's eyes drifted away. "There's only one reason that would explain that inconsistency."

"Yeah? And what would that be?"

"That she is only one piece of what's going on. She's fishing for the other pieces. She's in the dark as much as we are. She's never heard of Fitzby, or his twenty-five year old research. And, somehow she got hold of your name."

Silverstein stood and looked down at Kipling. He then threw up his hands in frustration and faced the window. After a second, he turned back. "That's a stretch, Linda."

Kipling sighed and returned a look of capitulation. "You're probably right." Her attention then piqued. "So, what was it you were thinking about earlier? You never really said."

Silverstein sat back down. "Actually, it does piggyback on something you said. Ms. Morgan was being very specific when she used the term *maneuver*. It got me to thinking. Like you said, there's nothing the average citizen would suspect. Outside of Lopez, I've made no mention of this to anyone. Not even here at work."

Kipling held her hands face up in front of her. "You think that woman is linked to Hector, your friend? Now *you're* making no sense. If Hector wanted something from you, he would call. He was the one who stiffed you! Remember? Everything was so hush-hush with him."

"You're right. I think we're both way out on a limb." Silverstein pursed his lips and stuffed his hands in his pockets. "Tonight I'm going home and drinking a whole bottle of wine by myself."

Kipling stood, ignoring Silverstein's remark. "You know what I think? I think it's time we call back that friend of yours who's so curious about maneuvering hurricanes."

Silverstein let loose a sarcastic laugh. "Great idea, Kipling! And how do you suppose we do that? The number never came through on my caller ID."

Kipling marched to the door and looked back. "I've decided to act on something I thought of yesterday. Thank God, I can still type with both hands. By Monday morning, I think I can have a working version. One that will operate from our digital phone system. Don't plan anything for Monday, okay? I figure, if we divide things up, it'll take about four hours."

Silverstein stared back, confused. "What is it you're going to code up, my esteemed colleague? Anything I can help with?"

"You're a smart person; figure it out. Here's your clue: One summer, during graduate school, I designed code for a telemarketer."

A knowing beam of white teeth accompanied Silverstein's reply. "I'll be all yours come Monday morning."

CHAPTER 28

▼

PLAN REVEALED

*Anselina Corporation, Hamilton, Bermuda: 32° 18'20"N
Latitude, 64° 47'20"W Longitude
Friday afternoon, 1400, September 7, 2007*

"What the hell! You want me to do what?" Fitzby rocketed from his chair and began pacing the room. He couldn't believe what he had just heard. He pulled up and glared back at Ghali. "You're out of your fucking mind."

Fitzby cast his eyes to the ceiling and then back to Ghali. "Let me see if I can recall your exact words when we first met in Istanbul."

Fitzby stood tall, took on the air of Ghali, and mocked his words. "We don't go around with plastic explosives wrapped around our bodies, blowing ourselves up." He gestured with his hands. "Our methods are more sophisticated, but motivated for a common good. I suppose *you* think sending a Category 5 hurricane up the Chesapeake toward Washington, DC is sophisticated. Flooding the Potomac River basin benefits a common good, does it?"

Fitzby threw himself back into his chair, looked up at Ghali, and waited for a reply that would make some sense.

Ghali sighed in deference. "You are correct. What I'm suggesting is different from what I said last year."

Fitzby nodded his head, returning a look of incredulity.

Ghali held up his right hand. "But…the situation has changed, and so have our plans. Unfortunately, I have no control over the decisions of my superiors."

Ghali sat down slowly in the chair opposite Fitzby and stared back, his face rendering no change in expression. Fitzby could read nothing from the blank face in front of him. Ghali wasn't joking.

Fitzby commanded himself to calm down and consider the implications of all he had just heard. Although Fitzby had always figured Ghali was up to no good, he had no idea Ghali's plan would be purposely malicious. Now Ghali had just said, with no hesitation, that he wanted Fitzby to assist in an act of terrorism—maybe not as spectacular as the planes used on 9/11 or with the same degree of surprise, but not far behind in concept.

Fitzby tried to remember the cost in dollars of the more famous hurricanes of the past century. Those that streamed through Florida in 2004 had been devastating, but not as damaging as Florida's Andrew in 1992. *What was it, $38 billion or so for Andrew?* In terms of financial losses, the Galveston hurricane of 1900 wasn't far behind, but it had also claimed six to seven thousand victims from storm surge-induced flooding. Considerably more than the three thousand lives lost to terrorism on 9/11, Fitzby reflected.

Although the notion of such devastation initially struck Fitzby as abhorrent, the idea of a hurricane taking direct aim at the Office of Naval Research or the National Science Foundation seemed not an altogether unpleasant thought. Both agencies had rejected his request for funding. That both government facilities operated out of Arlington would make the targeting easier.

Fitzby turned to Ghali, a question now stirring in his mind and awaiting formulation into words. *Always look out for yourself first*, his mother had cautioned. *You can be sure no one else will.*

"Except for the pride of working for as respected an organization as the Blade," Fitzby responded sarcastically, "what's in it for me?"

Ghali exhibited no surprise at Fitzby's forthrightness. "I told my superiors you would react this way. They have authorized me to place one million American dollars in a Swiss bank account in your name. And, once the job is done, I will provide safe passage to a location of your choice."

Fitzby felt confident that his facial expression didn't betray him. *One million dollars!* A sizable sum, to be sure—but was it enough? No, it was not. *Your adversary will always underestimate your worth by at least a factor of two.* "Make it two and you've got yourself a deal."

Ghali groaned. "I have no authority to grant such an increase, but I will contact my superiors. Except for the size of your fee, may I reassure them you will see our goal through to the end?"

Fitzby knew he was in the driver's seat and Ghali understood that as well. "Tell your superiors they have my commitment...*if* I am properly compensated."

Ghali stretched his right hand across the desk. "It's agreed."

They shook hands. Ghali rose, walked to the door, and then turned back. "How important is Emerson to you just now?"

Fitzby hadn't expected the question and answered honestly. "Not very anymore; he's just babysitting the code." *What was this all about?*

Ghali left the room. Fitzby stared after the departing figure and reflected on what he had just done. Had he duplicated Judas' treachery when he sold his soul for thirty pieces of silver? Was he betraying his country? Maybe, thought Fitzby. But then, he would have his revenge! And revenge was sweet, wasn't it? Particularly against the Professor Blackbeards of the world—all those small-minded people who couldn't see beyond the ends of their noses and who had tossed him and his research aside. Fitzby smiled inwardly as he tried to imagine Silverstein's reaction afterward, when he grasped the totality of what had occurred.

But there was more, thought Fitzby. If he pulled this off, he would have the respect he so deserved. That was all he had ever wanted. To be sure, he would be loathed initially. But fifty or one hundred years from now, it would be Fitzby whose name would adorn meteorological textbooks as the one who had spared future generations the wind and water destruction from hurricanes and typhoons. Fitzby imagined a constellation of laser satellites on the ready to steer storms away from coastal areas.

Now, there was no reason why this dream wouldn't occur. All would soon be in place. Just twenty minutes earlier, Ghali had handed him a compact disk that contained the final element needed to accomplish his technological miracle.

Fitzby grabbed the CD and headed toward his command center to load the software. His thoughts returned to the most damaging hurricanes to strike the US in the previous century. He considered it interesting that the famous ones attained only a Category 4 rating, with maximum sustained winds that never exceeded one hundred and fifty-five miles per hour. Category 5 hurricanes were the ultimate.

With this thought surging through his mind like a chemical stimulant, Fitzby's steps quickened. There were tropical waves sloughing off Africa that awaited his magic.

Ghali couldn't wait to leave the building and fill his lungs with fresh air. He turned the corner down the hall, exited through security, entered his car, and twenty minutes later walked into his apartment. He poured himself half a glass of Puerto Rican dark rum, added two ice cubes, and settled onto the sofa.

All that had happened in the past week was a jumble, a whirl of events both rushing together and flying apart. On the one hand, he experienced immense relief when Warner's software arrived; nothing could stop his team from executing the technical aspects of their plan. Ghali had seen enough of what Fitzby could do with hurricanes to recognize that he could grow and target a hurricane at will. There was no question that Fitzby possessed a genius mentality.

On the other hand, he had received a blow to his psyche every bit as strong as those to his body during the battles of 1967 and 1973. The meeting in Cairo had not gone well. For most of his adult years, he had made the goals of the Blade his life's work and devotion. Until now, the results of research funded by their organization benefited the Blade directly, or affected policy—or at least that was what Ghali understood. In Istanbul, Ghali had believed in his heart the words he had spoken to Fitzby—*Herkesin yararına,* a common good.

The Blade had ordered Ghali to execute a terrorist act thousands of times worse than anything Hamas had ever done with their homemade, strapped-on bombs. He had not seen it coming. He had never considered himself a terrorist. But if he proceeded with what the Blade had ordered, his name would be right up there with Khalid Sheikh Mohammed, the mastermind behind the Osama bin Laden 9/11 attack—who had been so ignominiously dragged out of bed in Pakistan and captured back in 2003. Is that how Ghali would wind up, with the world savoring his arrest?

Ghali stirred on the sofa, recalling Fitzby's reaction to the Blade's specific order. Although it would have fueled additional complications—because he would then have had to resort to threats—Ghali would have felt better if Fitzby had refused the order, if he had stated he could not in moral consciousness carry out such a despicable act. Ghali could have respected that. But, he had not! His initial words suggested a moral concern, but it didn't take long before he wanted to know what was in it for himself. Silverstein had warned him: *His character is severely flawed, Mr. Hamasay.*

Now, here he was. There would be no turning back. Ghali had given his life to an organization he trusted and in which he still believed. Their goals were honorable, were they not? Who was he to question the wisdom of his superiors? They obviously had a better grasp of what would benefit the objectives of the Blade. *Didn't they?* He would proceed as ordered and execute the plan.

And on top of everything else, another detail required his attention just now. Upon checking Barry Emerson's references, Ghali discovered that his credentials proved less than consistent. Telephone calls led to individuals currently unavailable, or nonexistent—strange indeed for an organization where Emerson had worked not that long ago. Emerson's personnel file indicated that these same telephone numbers months earlier had produced valid references.

These discrepancies pointed to Emerson as an outside plant—not a particularly encouraging thought at this stage of the operation, thought Ghali. Because nothing detrimental had happened thus far, meant that Emerson's employer awaited further feedback. Ghali would have to remove Emerson. Timing proved critical—not so soon as to alarm Emerson's handler, but prior to his discovery of the project's ultimate objective.

Ghali sat, exhausted. He staggered to his feet, filled his glass three quarters of the way this time, downed it in four swallows, padded into the bedroom, and fell into bed. The demons he had faced so many times in his dreams would be returning full force tonight. The alcohol would keep them at bay for a few hours.

CHAPTER 29

▼

SNARE

George Bush Center for Intelligence, McLean, Virginia: 38° 56'N Latitude, 77° 8'W Longitude
Monday, noon, September 10, 2007

"Should we put a tail on him?" Miller spoke softly across his salad in the CIA cafeteria.

Lopez picked at the beef stroganoff, the special for the day. When its rotation came up on the menu, about every three weeks, Lopez never failed to look forward to lunchtime, hoping the dish would someday be as good as his wife's creation. He always came away disappointed. Lopez had even considered offering Barbara's recipe to the cooking staff.

Miller's comment directed his thoughts away from the food. "What's the point? It's not like we're going to lose him."

Miller finished his salad and returned his fork to the plate. "I keep thinking he'll either discover the implant or it'll fail. Ghali will then disappear into the ether and our hard-earned link to the chain will be lost."

Lopez gave up on the stroganoff and reached for the chocolate cake. Unlike Miller, he had the metabolism to dissipate the calories.

"First of all, Marc, you worry too much." Lopez ran his fork along the side of the cake where an invitingly thick layer of icing lay. "Second, if Ghali hasn't noticed the implant by now, he's not going to. At least that's what Reston tells me. She also says that this unit is very reliable. And third, you forget he keeps coming back to Bermuda; O'Toole will keep us up to date on what's happening there."

Lopez forked the coveted section of cake, lifted it to his mouth, and savored the flavor. *At least the chocolate cake makes the trip to the cafeteria worthwhile.*

Lopez and Miller had discussed at length Ghali's recent travel schedule. He had spent six days in Cairo. Next, he flew directly back to Bermuda. Four days later, on Sunday evening, he was back in the air to Gatwick; from there he shuttled to Heathrow and flew home to Istanbul. He arrived there just today, on Monday afternoon, Istanbul time.

O'Toole's Saturday telephone report suggested something was up. He reported that Fitzby had another of his shouting matches with Ghali. As before, O'Toole could not decipher the nature of their dispute through the thick walls. (Lopez had earlier suggested that O'Toole bug Fitzby's office. That plan was quickly nixed when Fitzby casually mentioned to O'Toole that Ghali was paranoid, that he scanned their offices for bugs each time he came to visit.) Following this row, O'Toole reported that Fitzby's pace had become even more frenzied than usual. When O'Toole asked what was going on, Fitzby stalled. This change in attitude was unusual—Fitzby had always been quite open with him.

Miller pushed his tray to the side. "What if he never returns to Bermuda? He's got to be worried someone might be on to him."

Lopez forked a second piece heavy with chocolate icing. "He will! Ghali's sunk a lot of cash into this operation and it's obviously important. And from the way Silverstein described Fitzby, I think Ghali would want to keep him on a short leash." Lopez pointed his fork at Miller. "By the way…remember, there's some risk in using a tail in the Middle East. Baxter's as good as they come; he looks the part and speaks fluent Arabic. But remember that Ghali is a professional too. If he were to pick up on Baxter's tail, it could be worse for us than if he discovered the transmitter."

Miller nodded. "Okay, I'll concede that point to you. But I've been thinking and I have a new idea. Want to hear it?"

Lopez scraped the last of the cake from his plate. "Shoot." He pushed himself back from the table and folded his hands in front of him.

"Have you ever considered that the mole we've been chasing may be passing information to Ghali?"

Lopez raised his eyebrows. "No, I haven't! How could you possibly think there's a connection?"

"Did it never concern you how Ghali identified Silverstein so quickly in Monterey?"

Lopez held both hands out, palms up. "There's nothing to understand. Silverstein's been working in Monterey forever and Fitzby knows that."

"That's right, but Silverstein told us he hadn't seen Fitzby in twenty-five years. We can assume that the reverse is true. People age in that time, Hector. Didn't you say it had been ten years since you last saw Silverstein? I bet he changed some."

In addition to several other annoying characteristics, Miller tended to draw out an explanation, often so much that the recipient had forgotten the original point of the discussion. Although Lopez teased Miller that he would do better for himself writing fiction, this characteristic annoyed the hell out of him.

"Let's cut to the chase, Marc! What's your point?"

"What I'm getting at is this." Miller lowered his voice. "Silverstein told us Ghali had flown into Monterey just prior to his following him and Kipling all the way to Denver. How did he pick up on Silverstein so fast? In the airport for God's sakes!"

"In case you didn't notice..." Lopez recognized his voice was rising, stopped talking, and began again, this time in a near whisper. "In case you didn't notice, Silverstein is *black* and stands six foot three, at least."

"I'll give you that, but I'm saying it took more than that for Ghali to recognize him straight off. Silverstein reported Ghali looked tired and disheveled in Monterey, probably from a long day of traveling. Even so, Ghali was sure enough he had identified Silverstein that he turned right around, bought a ticket, and flew to Denver. What I am *suggesting*, Hector, is that our friend Ghali had more than a quarter century old description from Fitzby of what Silverstein looked like! Where would he have gotten that, Hector? I checked the obvious place, the NRL Monterey Web site, and his picture's not there. I spent two hours on the Web and couldn't find one photograph of Silverstein. I even checked the journals in which Silverstein usually publishes and they don't include photographs."

Lopez slid down in his chair, head back, and stared at the ceiling. "You make a good point. Black people are a minority in our population, but not that much of a minority. Ghali wouldn't have followed Silverstein unless he was positive it was him." Lopez paused. "Still, his mole might not be our mole."

Miller laughed aloud. "You're one encouraging son of a bitch. You know that? One infiltrator isn't enough for you? In my tiny, simplistic world, I have room for only one mole. Okay?"

Lopez smiled in return. "Okay, simplistic, but brilliant one, how do we go about using this information to our advantage?"

"That's where I was headed next." Miller laid his hands flat on the table. "Let's say that Ghali does have someone undercover here who's providing him information. We could take out the mole with no adverse influence on our show with Ghali. Right?"

Lopez replied sarcastically. "Yeah, that's right. You tell me where he is, and I'll bring him in myself this instant."

Miller smiled. "That's what we use Ghali for, to lead us to the mole."

Lopez's impatience returned. "And how do you propose we do *that*?"

Miller scooted his chair forward and sat close to the table. "We use to our advantage the one piece of information we have about Ghali. That piece of information is his whereabouts."

Lopez became exasperated. "Marc, you have a way of drawing things out that drives me up the wall. Quit stopping to dot all the i's and cross all the t's. Spit it out! *How* do we make Ghali lead us to the mole?"

"We use O'Toole."

Lopez finally lost his patience and shot to his feet. "Goddamn it, Miller. If you don't get to the point right now, I swear I'm going to take out my service revolver and blow you across the room."

Lopez quickly realized his display of emotion, though mostly feigned, attracted attention. Everyone in the room stared across at their table.

Lopez sat down meekly and tried to concentrate on Miller's reply. The conclusion to Miller's proposition had to be coming soon.

Miller went on as if he hadn't heard Lopez's outburst, his eyes shut tight. "We bluff Ghali. We assume his mole is here in Washington. O'Toole has told us Fitzby e-mails Ghali all the time in Istanbul, giving him reports of their progress. Here's what we do. We have O'Toole send Ghali an e-mail, one that can't be traced, that's sent from an anonymous server. With a short, specific message."

Lopez's interest had piqued. "Yes."

Miller opened his eyes and looked at Lopez. "We'd have to work on it, to make it as innocuous as possible. It would go something like this: Situation compromised…imperative we meet…usual location."

Lopez thought for a minute and then replied, this time remembering to keep his voice low. "That's brilliant, Einstein, but Ghali is only half the puzzle. How will the mole know to meet Ghali? And when?"

"Oh, I was just getting to that."

Lopez looked at the ceiling in disgust. He squeezed his nails hard into his palms to maintain his composure.

"There would be a few final words to the e-mail. They would say something like this: E-mail me *only* with date and time."

Miller pushed himself back from the table. "I know what your next question will be. When they do meet, they'll know something's up, that they've been tricked. That's okay! They'll leave separately and we'll nab the mole. Ghali will thank his lucky stars he got away and figure the mole made some stupid mistake. But…we'll have the mole! The Mensa team will have another entry to add to their yearly accomplishment record." Miller winked.

Lopez sensed his heart rate lowering and his optimism rising. He grinned. "Miller, you're a pain in the ass, but you're one smart cookie. I'm glad I didn't fire my weapon."

Miller returned Lopez's smile with a blank, confused look on his face. "Huh?"

CHAPTER 30

▼

RETURN TO SENDER

Naval Research Laboratory, Monterey, California, USA:
36°35'N Latitude, 121°51'W Longitude
Monday afternoon, 1230, September 10, 2007

"Hello. May I speak to Cynthia Morgan, please? No? I'm sorry, I must have misdialed."

Silverstein and Kipling had split the list of NRL DC phone numbers and Silverstein had just dialed number three hundred and twenty-six. Kipling had worked through the weekend writing code to cycle through the numbers without having to dial each manually. If no one answered a given number, her code automatically saved it for later redialing. Since most NRL employees were male, a non-female response led immediately to the last sentence of their script. They agreed that should either of them hit pay dirt, they would hang up to confer on their next course of action. It made some sense to investigate first the woman they had identified.

Silverstein had made the argument that he should make all the calls since he would recognize the voice from ten days earlier. Kipling pointed out that, although that was true, it was also a good assumption their mark would hesitate slightly upon hearing the name Cynthia Morgan. With both of them involved, they could complete the task quicker.

Kipling added one additional feature to the code. To keep their identity secret, she had disabled the caller ID function for NRL Monterey. Kipling had pretty much thought of everything.

"You can stop calling!" Kipling all but removed the door from its hinges with her right arm as she burst into Silverstein's office.

Silverstein clicked the cancel button on his monitor and set down his phone. He hadn't expected so quick a conclusion to her plan of action. Besides, he was disappointed he hadn't been the one to make the identification.

"You're sure?"

"I'm more than sure, Victor." Kipling walked in, took a seat, yellow notepad in her right hand. She inserted the pad into the left hand still confined by the sling and proceeded to write a word. When finished, she turned the pad around, held it up for Silverstein to see, and waited for his reaction.

"Lopez? What do you mean, Lopez?" Silverstein thought for a moment. "Why would Hector's name come up? He doesn't work at NRL."

She wrote again and pressed the pad to her chest. "Do you remember Hector's wife's name?"

"Of course; it's Barbara. We've never met but Hector's mentioned her."

Kipling slowly rotated the pad toward Silverstein. His mouth dropped open. She continued. "The person answering the phone said *Lopez*, which for an instant, threw me off course. I responded with our canned question. After the short pause that I predicted would occur, she asked a question: *Who's this?* I hung up. I did a crosscheck of that phone number to confirm it was Barbara Lopez. We've identified your caller."

Silverstein sat quietly, trying to comprehend the significance of this breakthrough and, at the same time, not wanting to believe it. "It's probably just a coincidence."

Kipling leaned back. "I think not. Where does Hector live?"

"In Alexandria, south of Washington."

Kipling responded with the kind of smile you make when you'd just as soon not smile. "Bingo! Lopez is three for three. She's got the first name, she did the pause, and she just happens to live in the same town as your friend. I think we have a winner, Victor."

Silverstein shot to his feet and faced the window. "What the hell!" Just as quickly, he turned and sat down. He rotated to his monitor and started typing.

Kipling responded curtly. "Don't even bother. That was the first thing I did. Ms…correction, *Dr.* Lopez works in Code 5510, NCARAI, the Navy Center for Applied Research in Artificial Intelligence. We've dealt with some of their people over the years."

Silverstein turned to face Kipling, his mouth still partially open. He began to gesture with his hands at the walls and ceiling. "What does all this mean? Is Barbara somehow working with Hector?" Silverstein stammered. "That…that…that makes absolutely no sense at all." Silverstein turned again to his monitor and started typing. "I wonder what kind of work she does."

Kipling replied nonchalantly. "I've already checked."

Silverstein whirled around and pretended to be angry. "Kipling! Are you a goddamn mind reader? Because if you are, you should have pointed this out to me a long time ago."

Kipling winked. "Until two years ago, Barbara Lopez was a star NRL scientist, in the very sense that we're judged as scientists. She averaged *three* journal articles a year."

Silverstein understood the significance of Kipling's statement. One of the criteria for evaluating an NRL scientist was his or her publication record. Compared to other traditional occupations, where production output or customer satisfaction made an easy task for a supervisor to rate an employee, the value of a scientist proved harder to measure.

For as long as Silverstein could recall, the number of journal articles a scientist had published in the preceding year predestined whether he or she received a bonus—or, sometimes, even remained employed. Silverstein and Kipling had done well in the publication department. In fact, they laid claim to the NRL Monterey record: nine between the two of them in one year. Nonetheless, an average of three for one person was outstanding. Silverstein supposed that most NRL scientists averaged between one and two. For those involved in 6.1 and 6.2 Research—Department of Defense (DoD) lingo for *Basic* and *Exploratory Development*—publication proved key to advancement.

Publication played a lesser role for those scientists whose accomplishments lay in *Advanced Development*, 6.4 Research. This form of research meant adapting existing technology to operational use—resulting in less opportunity for journal publications. To wit, Nobel Prizes usually resulted from basic research, and it was a source of some institutional pride that NRL had laid claim to one of those back in 1985. Jerome Karle and Herbert Hauptman both received the Nobel Prize for chemistry using x-ray diffraction analysis in the determination of crystal structures.

Silverstein rotated slowly toward his monitor. "I wonder what…" He quickly realized the senselessness of his action and turned back to Kipling. He looked at her inquiringly.

Kipling beamed. "Nothing related to meteorology *at all*, not in the ten years I checked. And considering where she works, it's not surprising that most of her publications revolve around artificial intelligence of one form or another. Considering how much AI we've adapted to meteorological applications, it's surprising neither of us has bumped into her. She's obviously very good at what she does. The abstracts I scanned often involved system integration."

Silverstein listened carefully. He then rewound in his head the tape of their preceding conversation. "Repeat the first part of what you said earlier, something about two years ago."

Kipling replied hastily. "That's right. Two years ago, Lopez's publication record came to a halt. Since then, there's been nothing, nada, zip."

Silverstein pushed himself back from his desk, his right fist closing against his mouth. "That's interesting, isn't it? Since it takes about a year from the time we submit an article until it's published means she hasn't sent anything in for at least three years."

Kipling slumped in her chair. "Makes sense. But, she's still gainfully employed. In fact, I dug out some older NRL directories. She's been in the same office for at least five years."

Silverstein thought for a few moments. "You don't remember Peter Duncan. He was before your time. He was going along merrily as a research scientist and then got involved in some black satellite project. He'd go over to the Naval Postgraduate School and work in the SKIF."

Kipling interrupted. "What's a SKIF?"

"I don't know what the acronym stands for, but it's a secure, locked room where you go to study classified material. It's not only locked but guarded, and unless you have special access, you don't get in."

Silverstein pointed at Kipling with his right index finger. "Take my advice! If you can help it, *never* work with classified data."

Kipling seemed satisfied and saluted with her right hand. "Aye, aye, sir."

Silverstein continued. "Anyway, Duncan got so involved in that research that, from then on, any publication with his name on it became classified. I never saw his name in the public literature again. That's one of the big downsides of black work. You might come up with the next best mousetrap, but you won't be able to tell a soul about it. From all you've told me about Barbara, and if she's as smart as you suggest, I'd say that the spooks have picked her up."

Kipling's eyebrows rose. "Hector's a spook."

Silverstein reflected on this obvious fact. "That's true, but I can't believe he's involved. Research money normally flows through research channels. And from what I know of Hector, he's a spook in the conventional sense. I'd bet a dollar to a doughnut, if Barbara's work is classified, he knows nothing about what she does."

Kipling sat straight in her chair and stared at Silverstein. "All of this is speculative, Victor. But we now know for sure it was *she* who called you. The relevant questions are why and what do we do now? Do you think you should call her back and ask what gives?"

Silverstein pressed his fingers together in front of him as if he were praying. "That's sure tempting, Linda, but I think we need to think this through some more. If I call her, she may panic. She's obviously hiding something and we have no idea how she'll react." He pointed to the ceiling. "If she denies everything, we'll have blown our chance." Silverstein paused. "And I'm beginning to get worried."

Kipling peered back, concerned. "What do you mean?"

"Remember what we talked about earlier? I don't think it's a coincidence Barbara Lopez wanted to know whether we were doing anything in hurricane targeting. Somehow, I'm afraid she's involved with Fitzby. I keep coming back to our conversation when I told her I would answer her question if she answered mine. She hung up when it was her turn."

"What about calling Hector?"

Silverstein shook his head. "That's even more delicate than calling Barbara. We then involve two people. Barbara, who might be protecting secrets and Hector, who would first question me, and then Barbara about why she called me. That wouldn't be fair to either of them."

What to do? In situations like this, Silverstein often reverted to a technique he found profoundly useful. Recalling similar situations in his past life, remembering how he had responded to the problem, and evaluating later whether that approach had been successful. Why develop a new solution when a perfectly satisfactory one lay somewhere in the past, ready for the taking? In modern science, they had a name for this process—analog pattern recognition—looking for historical patterns that matched the present in order to predict the future.

The analogy that popped up in Silverstein's mind came from long ago, during his senior year in high school. The memory still gave Silverstein an intense feeling of satisfaction. At that time, in Atlanta, his father represented the stereotypical general practitioner physician who practiced out of his house, quite common before the 1970s. He had nearly as many black patients as white. Dr. Silverstein made no color distinction in his patients, much to the consternation of their white neighbors, his black son Victor notwithstanding.

Young Victor could count on one hand the number of black students in his high school. One of them, Simon Carver, was one of his friends. Simon's parents, of modest means, had scraped and saved to send him to private school. One day, Simon told Victor that his sister had confided in him that she was pregnant and didn't know what to do. He said she was beside herself with fear. Simon feared she would run away or do something worse.

It was then that Victor hatched a plan to help. He took a piece of his father's office stationery and wrote a letter to the girl in the guise of his father. Forging his father's nearly indecipherable handwriting had not been difficult. In the letter, his father unknowingly stated that, although he would not say how he knew, he had become aware of Charlotte's difficulty and offered to be of assistance. He suggested she come pay him a visit, to talk, and that he wouldn't charge her a dime. Whether she came or not, Dr. Silverstein would tell no one.

Shortly after mailing the letter, Victor went to his father and explained the situation involving Simon's sister. He asked him if he would help if she asked—although it was a foregone certainty that he would. More importantly, Victor knew his father had that special combination of sympathy, kindness, and intelligence necessary to address this sensitive situation.

Victor's plan worked as he hoped. Dr. Silverstein counseled Charlotte concerning her options; she chose not to end the pregnancy. Seven months later, she delivered a girl and placed her up for adoption. Afterward, Simon asked Victor if he knew how his father had learned of the pregnancy. Silverstein remembered his reply as being one of the few, and proudest, lies he had ever told.

Silverstein's eyes rose to catch Kipling's. "I think honesty may be the best policy here. But a telephone call would be too blunt an instrument. We're going to lay it all out in a letter to Barbara. Contrary to what Hector would say or do, *we* have no secrets to hide. If Barbara needs someone to confide in, we're here to assist."

Kipling nodded. "Sounds like a plan. Do you want me to help?"

Silverstein felt confident. "You bet! The words have to be crafted carefully. Let's draft it tonight and you can sign it first thing tomorrow morning. If we overnight it, it'll be there first thing Wednesday."

Kipling's eyes squinted in puzzlement. "I'm confused. Won't the letter be from you?"

"No…and yes. *You're* the one who talked to her today. *You're* the fellow female scientist. For us to draw her out, to trust us, it's important she not feel threatened."

Silverstein reminisced, a warm smile coming to his face. "I learned a long time ago that a little deception can sometimes do a world of good."

CHAPTER 31

▼

APPOINTMENT WITH
DESTINY

Bermuda Weather Service, Bermuda International Airport,
Bermuda: 32° 22'02"N Latitude, 64° 40'39"W Longitude
Wednesday afternoon, 1345, September 12, 2007

Jim Avery's eyes burned and his head ached from watching repeatedly the video loop of Meteosat images from the past two days. "Here we go again! And this one here is moving straight as an arrow. Most unusual." He pointed to the screen.

Kendall responded, annoyed. "You didn't hear me, did you? Barry's disappeared."

Avery drained his coffee cup and turned back toward Kendall. "What do you mean, he's disappeared?"

The intensifying tropical cyclone one thousand miles to the east suddenly held less interest than did Kendall's words. That Emerson hadn't shown up on Sunday was surprising, particularly since they had rescheduled, at his request, from the dinner planned a week earlier. Avery, his wife Jennie, and Kendall enjoyed a fine evening by themselves. Their plan had backfired; the whole purpose of the get-together had been to pump Emerson for information.

Kendall thrust her hands into the air. "What I'm *saying* is that he's disappeared from the face of the earth. You know he's been staying in an apartment in Hamilton. I called his landlord. She said she saw him last Wednesday and everything seemed fine. This past Monday, when a plumber dropped by his apartment, he was gone." Kendall looked to make sure she had Avery's attention. "Not just gone in the sense that he wasn't there, but gone in that his clothes and things had vanished as well. She said he had paid his rent on the first and hadn't said anything about leaving."

Avery stood and walked slowly toward the coffee machine. "Have you tried calling him at work?"

Kendall responded forcefully and started pacing. "I did better than that! Yesterday was my day off and I went down to Hamilton. The number eleven bus goes within a block of Anselina. I couldn't get beyond the guard at the gate, but they did patch me through to personnel. The man I spoke to told me Barry had a family emergency and quit. He said they were sorry to see him go, that he was a good employee."

Kendall stopped moving long enough to join Avery. She filled both their cups and looked him in the eye. "I was starting to get attached to him, you know."

Avery empathized with the pain he saw in Kendall's eyes. *Oh, the heartache that accompanies young love.* As he proceeded to his desk, he turned and looked back. "If it makes you feel any better, from everything you've told me, his leaving has nothing to do with you." Avery thought for a moment. "Was there nothing from the last time you saw him to suggest something was up?"

Kendall caught Avery's eyes again. "No, nothing! If there had been some family emergency, he would have told me." She lifted her cup and took a sip. "And, think about it, Jim, if you had a family emergency, would you quit your job, check out of your apartment, and leave town? Come on!"

"Can you call his family?"

"That's the hell of it. I know a lot of general stuff about him, his family, and so on, but nothing specific. He said his parents and two younger sisters live in Pennsylvania and that he graduated from the University of

Maryland. That's about all I know. He had a way of deflecting questions if I got too specific. I never thought about it until now."

Avery tried to help. "Think back to the last time you saw him. Was anything wrong? Did he complain about anything? Was he sick?"

"Nothing I can think of…oh…there was one thing, but it was trivial."

Avery's attention spiked. "Yeah, what was that?"

"Barry said that something was up at work, that his boss Fitzby had turned into a maniac. Some software he had been waiting for had finally arrived."

Abruptly, Avery's face flushed with blood and his head jerked to the left toward Kendall. "What did you just say?"

Kendall looked over, puzzled, at Avery's unexpected reaction. "I said that something came up at work."

"No, after that!"

Kendall obliged. "That his boss Fitzby had turned into a maniac, that he received some important software. Why?"

Avery stood and looked around the room, oblivious to his surroundings.

Kendall walked over. "Jim, what's wrong? Are you okay?"

Avery refocused his thoughts, realizing that Kendall had placed her hands on his shoulders. He looked her in the eye. "Did Barry ever mention Fitzby's first name?"

Kendall released Avery and backed away. "Uh, yeah…let me think…*Cameron*."

Avery raised both arms and placed them on the sides of his head. "Son of a bitch!"

Kendall's face took on the look of surprise and she grinned. "In all the time we've worked together, I've never once heard you swear. Son of a bitch what?"

Avery blushed, this time in embarrassment, and knew that Kendall noticed. He calmed down and responded. "Cameron Fitzby was a graduate student in meteorology when the air force sent me to Penn State in 1980." Avery cupped his face in both hands and tried to remember the details. "I had completely forgotten that name until you mentioned it just now."

He sat down, gathered his thoughts, and looked up. "I told you I was in the air force for ten years, right?"

"Yeah, I remember."

"Well, back then, Penn State was one of the schools the air force sent its meteorologists to for advanced degrees. That's how I got my Masters. While I was there, there were two genius graduate students in the department, Cameron Fitzby and Silver…Silver…Silverstein…Victor, I remember now. They were both heads above me in IQ and weren't part of my clique of friends. Silverstein was black, by the way."

Kendall held her cup in two hands, eyes wide. "Go on."

Memories from nearly a quarter century earlier streamed back in waves. Avery started slowly, but picked up speed. "Fitzby and Silverstein were roommates. Everyone knew that. Silverstein aced all of his classes and finished his PhD in record time. Fitzby had a rougher time of it. He was arrogant and unfriendly, not someone you'd want to pal around with."

Avery paused and held up his right hand, his index finger extended. "Here's the thing. I can't believe I'd forgotten all of this until just now. Fitzby's dissertation, or his proposal for one, concerned the artificial growth of hurricanes, using a laser from space. I remember his theories were so incredible…I guess that's the right word…that everyone in the department knew about Fitzby and his wild ideas."

Kendall stared intensely at Avery. "That would explain why Barry kept asking me questions about hurricanes. You don't think Fitzby…"

Avery slid forward in his chair, hands folded, and stared at the floor. "I don't know, but a lot of things that haven't made much sense are taking on new meaning."

Except for the sound of the reverse thrusters of a plane landing outside their window, the room turned quiet as both forecasters pondered this new information. Finally, Kendall broke the silence. "What do you think we should do?"

Avery looked up. "Silverstein went to California to work as a research scientist for the navy; I remember that. If anyone would know what happened to Fitzby or his research, he would. I've got to talk to him."

Avery swiveled around to his computer, brought up Internet Explorer, the search engine Yahoo, and did a search with *Navy, Monterey,* and *research* as key words. One of the first hits to appear, *www.nrlmry.navy.mil/ sat_products.html,* combined with several more key clicks, yielded a phone number.

Avery checked the wall clock. He noticed Kendall staring over his shoulder. "It's two o'clock here, which means it's ten in the morning on the west coast. I'm calling him."

Kendall moved around to sit on the edge of Avery's desk. "What makes you think Silverstein still works in Monterey? That was a long time ago."

Avery stopped his dialing and replied. "You may be right, but it's a place to start."

Kendall held her hands up for Avery to see, index and middle fingers crossed on both hands.

Avery finished dialing, waited through the usual delay, and heard the connection. Two rings later, he responded to the secretary's greeting. "Hello, this is Jim Avery from the Bermuda Weather Service. Can you tell me if Dr. Victor Silverstein still works for your facility…Yes? Is he in today, please?"

Avery shielded the mouthpiece and smiled up at Kendall. "Hallelujah."

"Hello, Dr. Silverstein, this is Jim Avery from the Bermuda Weather Service. I was a graduate student at Penn State in the early eighties. You won't remember me…"

Avery paused to listen and looked up at Kendall, his eyes wide open and his lips pursed downward. "Why, yes…that was the title for my Master's thesis. I find it hard to believe you remember that."

*   *   *   *

Anselina Corporation, Hamilton, Bermuda: 32° 18'20"N Latitude, 64° 47'20"W Longitude
Wednesday afternoon, 1500, September 12, 2007

Cameron Fitzby sat at the computer console that controlled the satellite laser, his head buzzing, and his fingers twitching. He hadn't slept for over thirty hours. The coordinating software provided by Ghali functioned precisely as it should—further proof of Fitzby's inherent genius. What before had been a medley of software pieces that could scarcely function together—*loosely coupled* in scientific lingo—were now tightly linked components that functioned in harmony. Since receiving the software five days previous, Fitzby had proved to himself he could grow and, simultaneously, nudge a tropical cyclone smoothly in the direction he wanted. In one instance, he purposely stalled a tropical storm and then reversed its direction.

Fitzby's lack of sleep resulted from something other than the excitement of his complete, now functional system. It had come from yesterday's phone conversation with Ghali. Before Ghali departed, Fitzby had recommended they move quickly. That Silverstein hadn't blown the whistle already was a miracle and one Fitzby couldn't understand. From Istanbul, Fitzby received the go-ahead to their agreed-upon strategy. Of course, this dialogue segued from Fitzby's not too subtle inquiry, and Ghali's subsequent confirmation that his superiors had approved Fitzby's request for a salary increase. Fitzby insisted on a numbered Swiss bank account that he could check before Ghali returned.

Prior to Ghali leaving Bermuda, they had devised a course of action. Washington, DC by way of the Chesapeake Bay, became the intended target. Ghali's simplistic thinking recommended one humongous hurricane driving up the Chesapeake, to achieve as much damage as possible in one shot—to do in a more efficient, controlled fashion what Hurricane Isabel had accomplished in 2003. Fitzby told Ghali that if maximum destruction and loss of life were the intended results, he had a better plan.

He patiently tutored Ghali on the finer points regarding hurricane landfall; that, although the incipient rainfall and wind would do their share of mayhem, truly horrendous damage came from flooding. Fitzby explained that the thousands of lives lost in Galveston in 1900 didn't come from wind or rain, but from storm surge—the raised levels of water caused mostly by the *push broom* effect of the winds (and partially by lower atmospheric pressure) on the ocean that then builds in height as swirling waters touch bottom near the shore.

Washington, DC would be a good choice in that regard; Fitzby complimented Ghali on his selection. As the hurricane wound its way up the progressively narrowing Chesapeake, storm surge would force the water level higher and higher. Although storm surge and rainfall would occur in any event, Fitzby stressed that there was one way to amplify their effects. River levels should be up and the soil along the Chesapeake as waterlogged as possible.

For that reason, Fitzby recommended, prior to the arrival of their hurricane, that they send ahead a small, innocuous tropical cyclone. Winds would be relatively light and spark little concern. However, the attendant rainfall would saturate the soil and raise river levels, preferably to flood stage. Excess water resulting from storm surge and rainfall from the second storm would have nowhere to go. An environmental disaster would be at the ready.

Ghali seemed to appreciate the sound scientific logic behind Fitzby's recommendation and thanked him for his forward thinking. For this reason, Fitzby now focused attention on the first of the trio of hurricanes that would soon do his bidding.

Because events would be taking place rather quickly now, Ghali informed Fitzby he would return to Bermuda immediately. However, for a reason not shared with Fitzby, Ghali had to make an intermediate stopover in Washington, DC. Fitzby accepted the fact that Ghali withheld information from him. He had learned that the hard way.

For parallel reasons, Fitzby thought it appropriate he not share everything with Ghali either. First, so nothing would be lost in the pandemonium sure to follow in the wake of their actions, Fitzby had copied the entire software system, from soup to nuts. He had already mailed the ten CDs to a secure site in London, set up on one of his earlier trips to Istanbul. Once the scientific community recognized the greatness of the act he had orchestrated, he would naturally want to share his expertise with the world community. Certainly, his peers would understand he had no choice but to respond to the threats of a maniac. The more Fitzby thought about it, the less likely it seemed he would have to go into hiding at all.

Second, Fitzby understood the necessity of providing an out for himself. It didn't take a genius meteorologist to predict that, once he had fulfilled his duties, Ghali would have no further use for him. It was a naïve thought that Ghali would simply congratulate him on a job well done, shake hands, and say goodbye. Fitzby had taken notice that Barry Emerson no longer worked for Anselina. Ghali's earlier query as to Emerson's present usefulness reverberated in Fitzby's brain.

It was for these reasons that Fitzby did not intend to inhabit the same building with Ghali during the final days and hours of their operation. Fitzby had chosen this alternate course of action just recently and had quietly tested both landline and digital cell phone connections to allow him to control all central-site operations from his own laptop divorced from the Anselina Building. He had secretly rented an alternate apartment in Hamilton from which he would control the entire computer operation. Near the end of their operation, Ghali would find a letter in his office detailing how the final steps to their enterprise would proceed. Fitzby decided he had no need for Ghali's offer for refuge. He would hide on the island until he felt it safe to emerge.

Finally, as a *coup de grâce*, Fitzby had devised a strategy that would not only complement his hiding during those crucial final hours, but also guarantee that Ghali's goal (and Fitzby's brilliant operation) culminated as planned. To mitigate any final effort by Silverstein or others to stop him, Fitzby planned for a third tropical cyclone to play a role in this unprecedented display of Fitzby's genius.

That third cyclone would ensure no one interfered with Fitzby's historic rendezvous with destiny. It would isolate Bermuda from the rest of the world, from both ship and air. That hurricane would stall on Bermuda itself.

CHAPTER 32

▼

APPREHENSION

The Asylum Tavern, Washington, DC: 38° 55'02"N Latitude, 77° 01'51"W Longitude
Thursday evening, 2015, September 13, 2007

Two males, stooped and with threadbare clothing, took their place at the bar. They had walked in slowly and deliberately like the old men they appeared to be. Lopez and Miller ordered beers, laid money on the counter, and began conversing as regular patrons would.

Chris Cooper had done his usual outstanding job of disguising his charges. Although Ghali had fled down the hallway at the Fort Collins Mountain High Inn before they arrived on the scene, it made sense for the two agents to appear as harmless and innocuous as possible.

From the corners of his eyes, Lopez located Ghali sitting in a corner booth. He appeared to be alone. Tracking him here had been a coordinated effort. Once Ghali's transmitter placed him at the Istanbul airport, Lopez concluded he was on his way to the United States. Ten hours later, his electronic signal reappeared outside JFK airport in New York. Although Ghali could have flown anywhere from there—and they would not know where until he landed because the weak signal from the embedded transmitter could not penetrate the aircraft's skin—Lopez concluded that Ghali's destination would be Reagan National Airport. Lopez's belief held sway.

Hansley and Winston, armed with photos updated from Kipling's description, easily identified Ghali after he deplaned. They then tailed him to the Asylum, notifying Lopez and Miller as to their direction of travel.

As decided beforehand, Hansley and Winston waited outside, wireless receivers and microphones at the ready to receive instructions from inside—and in different disguises from those at the airport. Both agents wore Chris Cooper's most popular invention. Outerwear that, given fifteen seconds and a few zips and pulls, changed the complete external appearance of an agent. Known affectionately as the *Cooper*, the ingenious outerwear permitted the user to have three different changes of clothing (from the viewpoint of an observer) available nearly instantaneously, and to change back and forth at will. Cooper had been a professional magician (as had, coincidentally, several other Mensa team members) prior to joining the agency. Knowledge from this line of work no doubt played a part in his cunning design.

Not knowing where Ghali sat when they entered the bar, Lopez and Miller chose stool seats that permitted, between the two of them, maximal view of the bar's interior. Ghali would have chosen a position to afford him a clear view of those entering the establishment. That meant the mole—the reason Lopez and Miller had invented this rendezvous—would sit hidden from their view. After all, it wasn't Ghali's face they had come to see.

"I've got him. Ghali just ordered from the waiter." Lopez pretended to look downward but, in fact, had his eyes trained on the booth.

Both Lopez and Miller only pretended to drink their beers. Not only were they on duty, but this assignment had momentous implications. Neither agent wanted to risk the day's hoped-for conclusion.

Although Lopez could see the booth, at least one side of it, Miller's angle permitted him a clear view of the single door that served as the bar's entrance. "Several new potentials coming in, Dennis."

Lopez chuckled to himself, recalling the alias Miller had given him on an earlier assignment. Despite his young age, Miller had been a fan of the

1960s comedian, Bill Dana and his alter ego, José Jiménez. Lopez's pseudonym had arisen from Dana's famous line: "*My name…José Jiménez; my brother, Dennis…Dennis Jiménez*"—referring, of course, to Hank Ketchum's comic strip character, Dennis the Menace.

Lopez gestured indiscriminately. "What? You don't think you'll be able to pick him out firsthand?"

Miller returned a smile. "No, but I do trust you with that heavy responsibility."

Lopez glanced at this watch. He and Miller had entered the bar a little after seven-thirty. It was now eight-twenty. Those minutes allowed Lopez time to reflect on their plan, which not unlike several previous decisions, had evolved from a fierce argument. Each agent had made a potent defense for his proposal. Unlike the situation when Lopez's seniority had allowed him to veto Miller's arguments in Colorado, Lopez concluded Miller had the best instincts this time around.

Ghali felt uncomfortable, considering the circumstances—a situation where he did not possess complete control. He had responded to Warner's e-mail as requested, passing along only the date and time for Warner's proposed meeting. Warner had never before made such an unusual request.

Moreover, Warner was late. The terseness of his message meant trouble. Ghali had noted Warner's seeming discomfort when Ghali had made contact from Mexico City. Had Warner's cover been blown? Had he discovered it necessary to provide a revised version of the hurricane software? What information did he possess that was so sensitive that normal channels of communications wouldn't suffice? Irrespective of the reason Warner had called this meeting, Ghali had continuing concerns about Dr. Lopez, notwithstanding Warner's message twelve days earlier. Warner stated he had spoken to Lopez and convinced himself that she posed no risk. Ghali, ever the one to leave no stone unturned, ordered Warner to check further, perhaps on her computer.

It had been a year since Ghali began negotiations with the Russians for their satellite. He could see the light at the end of the tunnel and this thought brought him some comfort. This undertaking had been more unpleasant than previous assignments and the stakes significantly higher. Never before had he attempted as complex—and destructive—a mission as this one. His efforts would cause untold devastation and suffering, an outcome that weighed on Ghali's mind. Ghali had grown weary and was now anxious to rid the world of the arrogant, selfish, miscreant of a human being with whom he had shared the past ten months. He would enjoy completing the final directive handed down by the Blade.

Nonetheless, compared to previous missions, the death count thus far had been low, only three: the Russian, the Kansas farmer, and Emerson, the likely spy at Anselina. Of course, this list did not include the Ishmael twins who had served the Blade well and whose deaths proved to be an immense loss. Their demise was another reason to hate Fitzby. In the case of Emerson, Ghali admitted to himself he would never know if he had posed a threat in reality. However, at this phase of their operation, too much lay at stake to take a chance. Once Ghali had dispatched Emerson, he petitioned the Blade for an immediate go-ahead for *Category 5*, the code name for this operation.

Ghali sipped his beer, his eyes on the door to the front and, as was second nature to him, on the other patrons frequenting the bar at this early hour. Everything appeared normal. *Or did it?* No, something was wrong! What was it? Ghali's eyes scanned everything within his sight. There it was—the older fellow at the corner of the bar, sipping beer. *Orospu çocuğu! Son of a bitch! Why was his glass as full now as it had been ten minutes earlier?*

"One possible just came through the door…he's looking around…he's moving in Ghali's direction!" Miller raised his glass to take a sip.

"Can you see his face?" Lopez's heart rate elevated. This could be it!

"No. Five-ten, one seventy, one eighty. Lots of hair, gray-black. He's out of my sight line now."

"I've got him. I see the hair. He's headed for Ghali's booth. He's got to be the one. Five feet away now…shit!"

"What's wrong?" Miller turned his head slightly.

"Ghali's getting up! He's laying money on the table. What the fuck's wrong?" It was all Lopez could do to keep his face from revealing his emotions.

"Keep talking!" Miller's voice betrayed his tension.

Lopez knew something had spooked Ghali. "Ghali just walked past your guy as if he were invisible!"

Miller's head remained fixed toward the door. "Ghali just left."

Lopez remained in character and in position. "Wait! The guy stopped in his tracks. He's still facing the booth...and obviously thinking. He's turning slowly...slowly. Damn, he's turning away from me...still can't make out the face. He's now made a one-eighty and he's retracing his steps." Lopez depressed the transmit button inside his right pocket. "Hansley, in ten seconds, gray-black beard."

Miller lowered his glass to the bar. "He's in my view. He's going out the door."

Lopez relinquished his beer and both agents walked slowly to the door and stepped outside, continuing their elderly demeanor. They walked past Hansley and Winston and stopped, waiting for the words that signaled their success.

Winston obliged. "Ghali walked down the block to the left and is out of sight. The bearded one had a taxi waiting. You missed him by seconds. But not to worry. I got him on the way in *and* the way out. For good measure I tagged the taxi."

The two men straightened their posture. No point in continuing their charade. Lopez caught Miller's eye and they both sighed, recognizing they had made the correct decision some six hours earlier back at the farm.

Lopez gave the order. "You guys follow him and set up surveillance." Hansley and Winston took off running while he and Miller took in the night air.

The decision they fought over earlier in the day concerned whether they should take down the mole immediately or simply follow him after his meeting with Ghali. Miller made a rational argument, to the effect that one shouldn't burn bridges, that once they ID'd the son of a bitch, they might have more use for him by leaving him in his position—whatever that might be—rather than taking him out.

For that reason, Hansley and Winston had waited outside the Asylum. Not knowing what personage the mole would inhabit, they *tagged* all who entered.

Again, it was the Mensa team who received credit for the elegant, but simple, method for marking an object, whether biological or otherwise. In two side pockets, Winston carried two dart guns, fueled by CO_2 cartridges. The projectiles they fired housed radio transmitters (not unlike the one surgically implanted in Ghali's head) embedded in tiny streamlined shells with fins that retracted on impact.

The user needed two guns because two types of darts proved necessary. One kind with tiny claw-like needles at the front (again, inspired by the magicians in the Mensa group) to grasp securely any manmade or natural fiber; and a second type with a tiny suction cup for adhering to smooth surfaces such as a car's paint. The small gun fit compactly within a normal hand and was usually fired as the hand hung naturally below the waist. A small microcomputer, carried in the breast pocket of the agent firing the darts, kept track of signals from multiple darts, identified by Winston's voice through a hidden microphone.

Lopez knew the exact drill that Winston would now follow because he had personally used the dart system himself. Winston would plug his computer into the vehicle-installed satellite tracking system and program it to home on the dart attached to the taxi. At the same time, using the computer's voice activation software, he would deactivate reception of signals from unintended victims in the bar. If necessary, they would transfer tracking to the transmitter on the target's person. More likely, once their mark left the taxi, they would stalk him the old-fashioned way—visually, by sight.

Lopez leaned against the wall and took a deep breath. Low clouds, visible from the city lights, looked thick and threatening. Earlier, the radio had warned of heavy rain from a tropical storm headed their way.

Miller turned toward Lopez. "What do you think spooked him?"

"I have no idea."

Lopez thanked his lucky stars that, at least at this moment, all seemed right in his mysterious, treacherous world.

CHAPTER 33

▼

REVELATION

Naval Research Laboratory, Monterey, California, USA:
36° 35' N Latitude, 121° 51' W Longitude
Wednesday morning, 1045, September 19, 2007

Kipling marched into Silverstein's office and pulled up a chair, facing backward as usual. The need for an arm sling had run its course, much to Silverstein's relief. The multi-colored cloth straps now hung decoratively, like curtains, atop the window in Kipling's office. Kipling had earlier pronounced her shoulder and arm eighty-eight to eighty-nine percent of normal. Silverstein appreciated her precision.

"It's time you snapped out of it, Victor."

Silverstein, deep in thought, scarcely heard the voice intruding into his consciousness. Ever since the call from Jim Avery in Bermuda a week earlier, Silverstein had to face what he had been avoiding since the beginning of this mystery. That he would soon face Fitzby, his own exclusive version of Marcus Junius Brutus, one of Caesar's traitors. For days, he had sidestepped that thought by concentrating on Fitzby's motives rather than the man himself.

Jim Avery not only lent credence to what Silverstein and Kipling had suspected all along (although, even now, what they knew was circumstantial), but had *located* Cameron Fitzby in Bermuda, at a place called

Anselina Corporation. Silverstein thought to himself that this Avery must be one sharp cookie to have put together the various bits and pieces of information and then remember that Fitzby had once been Silverstein's roommate. Still, neither Silverstein nor Avery knew Fitzby's intentions. Silverstein, mindful of Lopez's admonition, had avoided any mention of Hamasay.

Silverstein did explain to Avery the basis of Fitzby's thesis; and if you could believe that Fitzby had somehow acquired a powerful enough laser and had it launched into space, the anomalous ocean temperatures observed earlier in the summer were the likely byproduct.

Silverstein had asked Avery to keep this information close for the moment. Silverstein wanted to think it through to decide on the appropriate next step. Should he and Kipling take the next plane to Bermuda and confront Fitzby? But why would they do that, having no notion of Fitzby's motivation? Moreover, such action could prove unpleasant indeed, considering Silverstein's earlier run-ins with Hamasay's henchmen, and then Hamasay himself.

Kipling became impatient. "Talk to me! Last month, I asked if we should go to the authorities and you said it was premature. It hardly seems premature anymore."

Kipling made a good point. Should they notify their navy superiors? Or was it time to swallow his pride and contact Lopez, even though he hadn't heard word one from the CIA operative since the Colorado debacle? Although Fitzby hadn't done anything criminal, his association with Hamasay, someone the CIA knew well, did not bode well. But then, Lopez had to know that too.

Silverstein looked up. "You're the more logical one between us. What do you think we should do?"

Kipling stood and started pacing. "Okay, here's what we know. First, we've finally located Fitzby in Bermuda. Assuming he's the one mucking around with Atlantic-based tropical cyclones using a laser satellite, I now understand why he picked this location. If the satellite sits over the tropical Atlantic, Bermuda makes perfect sense for a controlling station."

Silverstein leaned back, smiled internally, and took in Kipling's neat dissection of their situation.

Kipling continued. "Second, based on our memorable encounter with Hamasay in Colorado, we're certain that he and Fitzby are in cahoots. From my viewpoint, Hamasay's role in all of this is a huge concern, considering that your friend Lopez wanted you to keep things under wraps...which is what we have done faithfully, I might add. Assuming Lopez has a good reason for this subterfuge suggests you go back to him first. He obviously knows, or thinks he knows, more than we do."

Silverstein leaned forward, elbows on the desk, hands folded, thumbs pressing against his lips. "That's what I've been thinking too. I need to swallow my—"

The electronic twitter interrupted his concentration.

Silverstein turned and lifted the handset. "Silverstein." He could hear the connection, but nothing else. "Hello, this is Victor Silverstein," he repeated.

The voice left no doubt, even before she mentioned her name. "Hello, Dr. Silverstein. This is Barbara Lopez from NRL Washington. I received your letter."

Silverstein turned toward Kipling and pointed his finger to the telephone. "Thank you for calling. You know my colleague, Linda Kipling, of course. She's here in the office with me. Would you mind if I put you on speakerphone?"

Lopez's reply came back in the negative. No, she did not mind.

Finally, they might have a resolution to the puzzle that stemmed from the wife of Hector Lopez himself. Kipling pulled her chair within inches of the speakerphone.

Silverstein took a deep breath and commanded his voice to remain calm and reassuring. "How may we be of assistance, Dr. Lopez?"

Seconds passed before a reply. "I received your letter...and I need to talk to someone. Hector has spoken highly of you. I sense I can trust you and Dr. Kipling."

Silverstein leaned forward and spoke directly into the phone's microphone. "Does this in any way concern Cameron Fitzby?"

The voice in reply was soft, and concerned. "I honestly don't know, but it may. But…I'm terrified…I've set something in motion."

"Please, go on." Silverstein and Kipling inched closer to the speakerphone, even though their chairs now touched.

"I shouldn't talk over the phone…but I'm afraid this can't wait any longer." The strain in her voice was palpable.

Silverstein raised his hands to his face and replied. "I think I understand. Let me ask you several questions and all you have to do is answer yes or no. Does your work in any way involve the movement of tropical cyclones?"

A long pause. "Yes."

Silverstein stared at Kipling, her lips pursed together. "Do you have reason to believe your work is being used now by someone like Cameron Fitzby?"

"Yes."

Silverstein willed his speech to remain steady in preparation for his final query. He prayed for a reply in the negative, but was sure it would not come. "Is there urgency to your current situation?"

"Yes!"

Silverstein shot to his feet, dropped his arms to his sides, and balled his fists. Seconds expired. He relaxed his fingers and leaned down to the speakerphone. "We understand completely."

Silverstein sat down and looked at Kipling. Once again, as if she had intercepted his thoughts, she gave him the thumbs-up sign.

Silverstein continued. "This is Wednesday morning; it's eleven o'clock here. Can we meet you in your office first thing tomorrow morning?"

"Yes!" A sensation of relief permeated the resonance of that single word.

"Linda and I will take the redeye to Dulles tonight. We'll drive directly from the airport to your office. Do you agree that is what we should do?"

The reply was sudden. "No!"

Silverstein looked at Kipling, now afraid he had been too insistent.

Lopez continued. "I'm scared to death, Dr. Silverstein. We have so little time. Can you leave sooner?"

"We'll do what we can."

"We can save time if I pick you up. E-mail me your flight and arrival time. And, one more thing…you must understand Hector knows nothing of this."

Silverstein looked at Kipling, nodding his head. "We understand and have suspected as much. We'll get right on it."

The line went dead.

Silverstein and Kipling pushed back from the speakerphone, each pondering the significance of the preceding conversation. Silverstein reflected. "She's terrified."

Kipling nodded. "She's unwittingly involved in Fitzby's operation. And did you sense the pressure?" At once, Kipling's eyes opened wide. "Have you checked our tropical cyclone page recently?"

Silverstein whirled around to his monitor and brought up the NRL Monterey Tropical Cyclone home page. Over the years, this site had become one of the more popular Internet addresses for summarizing existing tropical cyclones. Combining various satellite imagery and data, the site provided both a space-based view of every tropical cyclone on the planet and a map of its geographic movement.

Three listings showed up for the Atlantic, the latter two being full-fledged hurricanes. The first, Tropical Storm Lorenzo, had relinquished its hurricane status days earlier, becoming a lesser tropical storm before it deluged the Washington, DC surrounds and caused minor flooding. It had made the news recently, but had diminished further into a tropical depression as it drove inland and no longer posed a threat. In fact, it provided much needed rainfall to northern Virginia and Pennsylvania. The public didn't always understand that tropical cyclones could provide benefit as well as disaster.

"Washington got soaked," was Silverstein's analysis.

Silverstein highlighted the second of the listed cyclones. Thus far this hurricane season, fourteen cyclones had achieved either storm or hurricane status (either class qualified them for an official name). They had used up two thirds of the twenty-one names allocated for 2007—and more than two months remained in the season! This one, Hurricane Melissa, lay two hundred miles southeast of Bermuda. Silverstein scrolled down and noted the cyclone's progress since it had spawned off western Africa. It had initially gained strength quickly but with a slow forward motion; it now held steady with moderate winds, a Category 2 hurricane. Based on its current progress, Melissa would strike Bermuda in another ten hours.

Kipling was the first to say it. "Look at Melissa's track! Straight as an arrow, aimed directly at Bermuda."

Silverstein clicked on the second hurricane, Noel. This one had spun up more gradually and had a more interesting itinerary. It had maintained a southern route across the entire Atlantic before traversing the Leeward Islands. Just prior to a seemingly near certain landfall with Jamaica, it recurved hard to the northeast, threading the needle between Cuba and Haiti through the Windward Passage. Noel then paralleled the east coast and now lay three hundred miles northwest of Bermuda.

"Victor, do you see how Noel stayed to the east and followed the Gulf Stream? That's where he's getting his energy. Lorenzo stuck to the west of the Gulf Stream and stayed small."

Kipling looked at Silverstein to gauge his reaction.

Silverstein remained silent as he studied the tracks in front of him. Kipling was correct. Contrary to Lorenzo, a tropical storm with winds now below hurricane strength, Noel had transitioned into a brute, a Category 4 hurricane, with maximum winds approaching one hundred and fifty miles per hour. Silverstein's attention had been so sidetracked this past week, he had ignored recent news discussions regarding the destructive potential of this powerful hurricane. As if Noel had suddenly picked up the scent of his weaker cousin Lorenzo, he turned hard to the west toward the Potomac. If Noel continued on his present course, the waterlogged areas surrounding the Potomac would suffer an environmental disaster, making Hurricane Isabel's trek and impact in 2003 seem like child's play.

Following their near-simultaneous, identical words, Silverstein remarked to himself that he and Kipling indeed represented two birds of a feather. The conversation with Barbara Lopez, together with what they could see on the monitor, caused their brains' synapses to draw the identical conclusion. What they saw in front of them was the work of man, not of nature.

Their words were simultaneous and not without drama. "Oh, my God!"

Both researchers sprinted out the door within seconds; Kipling to her office to arrange travel and Silverstein to his house to pack. Although Silverstein kept a packed suitcase ready for such emergencies, he concluded that he should add one item to its contents.

Silverstein would never admit it, but knew it was more than sentimentality that made him keep his father's .38 revolver and maintain its legal registration. He had told no one, not even Kipling, about his ever-recurring nightmares in which he confronted Fitzby. Over the years, beginning on that first night out of Penn State, that dream had taken many forms, but the result had always been the same.

Most passengers on commercial airlines don't realize that carrying a gun in checked baggage is legal, as long as the owner packs the firearm and ammunition separately, and he or she declares the weapon to the airline. For the first time in his life, Silverstein chose to take advantage of that prerogative.

CHAPTER 34

▼

BARBED JUSTICE

Naval Research Laboratory, Washington, DC: 38° 49'N Latitude,
77° 1'W Longitude
Thursday morning, 0230, September 20, 2007

The reaction of the person sitting in front of the computer monitor reminded Silverstein that he had seen an identical response once before, from his teenage years in Atlanta. That memory included his best friend Larry Janowski. He and Larry had stayed late after school one day, as happened frequently when Silverstein helped Larry with his mathematics homework.

Following this session in their homeroom, Larry remembered he had forgotten his lunch bag in the chemistry laboratory and they walked back to retrieve it. The look Silverstein recalled so vividly came from the face of a Mr. Samuel Edwards, their chemistry teacher. That Mr. Edwards revealed himself in a somewhat compromised position with Miss Sarah James, the new secretary to the principal, had everything to do with that expression. Backing out of the room and never telling anyone about the incident seemed to them both the proper response at the time. Naively, Larry never questioned that his A in chemistry ever came from other than hard work.

Even through all the facial hair of someone Silverstein had never before laid eyes on, the duplication of that stunned look came through conspicuously from the man seated in front of them.

"Dr. Warner, what are you doing here?" Lopez's exclamation upon entering her office at two-thirty on Thursday morning caught everyone by surprise, not least of all, Dr. Warner. Silverstein blinked at Lopez's words and stared. Dead tired after a long day's flight across the continent, Silverstein had to think twice to comprehend the significance of this situation—in the office of Dr. Barbara Ann Lopez, at the Naval Research Laboratory in Washington, DC.

Kipling had arranged their flights so quickly that the phone rang the moment Silverstein arrived home. They were to fly out of Monterey at two o'clock in the afternoon, switch planes in Los Angeles, and arrive at Dulles after midnight.

As promised, the wife of his friend Hector Lopez waited for them outside the secure area of the Dulles terminal. Barbara Lopez explained she had told her husband that a special project required her presence at the office.

Had it not been for Silverstein's checked bag, the three of them could have departed the airport a full twenty minutes earlier. Had they done so, the awkward encounter to occur in Lopez's office might not have happened. Warner would have seen a light and bypassed the office. Twenty minutes on the other side of that critical moment might also have altered the outcome. But as it was, their timing placed three surprised, confused individuals eight feet away from a startled, unsettled man.

Lacking any description, Silverstein had nonetheless identified the attractive female waiting for them at Dulles. The eyes, combining tension, concern, and fear all at the same time, gave her away. Introductions were brief.

Silverstein and Kipling listened to her story in earnest during the drive to NRL, where Lopez stated she would show them the evidence she had uncovered. Silverstein, sitting in the front seat, looked back and caught Kipling's eye. Silverstein noted that the speed of their automobile had increased steadily since they departed the airport, even as they drove in and out of rain showers, early signs of Noel.

Lopez detailed her latest project for a Dr. Clement Warner, her ONR sponsor. Within days after turning over the targeting software, the Trojan Horse she had installed began transmitting its data back to her on the Internet. At first, she said, she paid little attention, smug in the knowledge she had pulled one over on the user.

Lopez explained, however, that as the data streams continued, she took a closer look and began plotting the information. It wasn't long before she realized the coordinates matched exactly those of existing tropical cyclones. Soon, it became unavoidably clear to her that the user was manipulating tropical cyclones using her software. Lopez could not confide this information to Warner, obviously, and didn't have the nerve to tell her husband. Kipling's letter proved to be the lifeline she so desperately needed.

Back in Lopez's office, the atmosphere turned frigid; no one moved. From what Barbara Lopez had told them, together with what they already knew, Silverstein concluded that Warner knew Hamasay, and thus Fitzby. As the three of them stood together in that solitary moment of tension, Silverstein deduced that conclusion and assumed Kipling had done so as well. Lopez, meanwhile, likely knew nothing of Hamasay, thought Silverstein—although that begged the question of how she had known the name Fitzby, as implied during their phone conversation. All of this information now focused Silverstein's awareness on the male sitting in front of them.

Lopez, incredulous, repeated her words. "I said, what are you doing here?"

Warner's eyes caught Silverstein's. Warner turned and, surprising as it seemed at the time, reached over calmly to switch off the electrical strip that powered the computer and monitor. He then stood slowly and walked toward the door. Following his first step, he took off at full steam into the void between the obstructing parties, Lopez and Kipling holding the door to the left, and Silverstein standing alone to the right.

Startled by the sudden movement, Silverstein did not react quickly enough. Kipling, on the other hand, acted without hesitation. She slid to the floor parallel to the door, raised her right leg in a scissor-type action, and obstructed the pathway. Warner tried to jump to clear the out-stretched leg and boot, but chose that course of action much too late. Warner crashed face-first to the floor and slid headlong into the wall across the hall, his eyeglasses separating from his face.

By then, Silverstein's attentiveness matched that of Kipling. If there had been any doubt in Silverstein's mind that Warner's visit to Lopez's office may have been legitimate, his decision to run erased that thought.

No sooner had Silverstein stepped into the hallway than Warner jumped to his feet and started running. Silverstein gave chase. Warner blasted through the double doors at the end of the hall, into the lobby, and out the front door. Silverstein remained a consistent three paces behind. Kipling's cowboy boots proved to be a decided disadvantage and Silverstein could hear a diminishing clapping sound to the rear.

Once outside the building, a foot race ensued—in now blinding rain—and Silverstein fell behind. Warner's automobile, if he had one, sat outside the gated entrance to NRL. For an instant, Silverstein's peripheral vision caught a glimpse of a moving figure off to the right. Silverstein maintained his concentration on his quarry. Overhead lighting kept Warner in clear view. He had made the mistake of wearing a light-colored jacket.

Warner increased the separation between himself and Silverstein to more than thirty feet. Silverstein felt the strain in his lungs and the rain against his face as he tried to keep up. He understood that the fear in Warner could easily overcome any shortfall in physical conditioning. Silverstein knew that for a fact from his teenage days when he had to outrun street thugs determined to make an example of a black Jew.

Although fear can induce superhuman performance, Silverstein knew the downside could be utter recklessness. He reflected on that liability in the upcoming moments.

Rather than sprinting to the gate some hundred feet farther down the chain-link fence, Warner chose instead to climb the barrier and crawl over the three rows of sloping barbed wire at the top of the fence. As viewed from the inside, the barbed wire sloped outward, and up, to keep anyone from climbing in—not the other way around.

Warner's decision made sense, thought Silverstein—a quicker escape to his automobile—although climbing the fence and making one's way across the barbed wire required both strength and agility. As such, a problem arose in the execution. Under normal circumstances, a six-foot fall to the ground would produce minimal damage to the human body, perhaps a sprained ankle or a broken bone. However, if someone fell through rows of tightly strung barbed wire, the outcome would be altogether different.

Instead of trying to step, crouched, over the three strands, Warner stood tall, obviously to position himself on the last wire and, from there, jump to the ground. It was while he stepped to the third strand, over the first two, that he lost his footing—probably because of the rain and the loss of his eyeglasses, concluded Silverstein.

Unfortunately, for Warner, the weight of his entire body, with one leg on each side, came down squarely on the center strand of three parallel barbed wires. By this time, Silverstein had arrived at the fence and watched the horrifying spectacle play out.

Instead of breaking, the tightly strung wire acted as a bow or trampoline and tossed Warner back into the air. The scream that penetrated the quiet night air started well before his upward trajectory.

Once again, and turning in midair to face Silverstein, Warner initiated his downward path, this time leaning inward at a twenty-degree angle perpendicular to the wire. Both feet penetrated cleanly the gap between barbed wire number two and barbed wire number three. As Silverstein looked upward, he knew that Warner wished they had not.

In sequential order, Warner's legs, his middle torso, and then his chest fell against the searing spikes of barbed wire number two, ripping clothes and flesh during the downward descent. Because the distance between wires number two and three spanned less than a foot, barbed wire number three did comparable damage to Warner's backside. At last came Warner's face, not spared any of the preceding traumas. Arms and hands were the last to exit. Amazingly (a credit to the manufacturer, thought Silverstein), the barbed strands appeared none the worse for wear.

Silverstein watched as Warner's shredded body finally struck the ground below. At this point, Kipling and Lopez caught up and joined Silverstein to look at the horrendous sight just feet away on the opposite side of the fence. It took but seconds before Lopez turned, walked away, and threw up.

Silverstein knew the image in front of them would haunt their dreams for more than a single night. Facing them, curled almost into a ball lay a whimpering human being, his clothes ripped to shreds, blood streaming from multiple locations along the length of his body, both hands grabbing his groin. Warner's clothing, although torn, hid much of the damage from view. Such was not the case with his face; even the facial hair could not hide his injuries. One spike from the barbed wire had started its damage at the base of his chin, continuing through his right eye.

Silverstein prayed that shock and unconsciousness would relieve Warner of the pain he now experienced. Instead, Warner surprised them when he lifted his head and, with one good eye, stared at his witnesses. As he maintained eye contact, he slowly inched both hands to his face. What Silverstein witnessed in the next seconds seemed only the province of spy novels.

With his right hand, Warner fumbled with a ring on his left hand. Without losing eye contact with Silverstein, he removed what appeared to be a metal cap, turned the ring around on his finger, placed his open hand alongside the exposed surface of his neck, and pulled, seemingly until it caught. Warner winced as he gave the ring one final jerk.

Within a minute, the apparent poison accomplished its purpose. Warner convulsed twice and moved no more.

Silverstein and Kipling then duplicated Lopez's earlier reaction.

CHAPTER 35

▼

QUOD ERAT DEMONSTRAS (Q.E.D.)

George Bush Center for Intelligence, McLean, Virginia: 38° 56'N Latitude, 77° 8'W Longitude
Thursday morning, 0630, September 20, 2007

Hector Lopez glared across the office at Miller, shoved his hands in the air, and almost shouted his reply. "What do you mean, he's dead?"

Lopez stood straight and gestured as he made his point. "Let me see if I've got this right. We go to all the trouble of locating our mole, learn his name is Clement Warner, that he works for the Office of Naval Research, and then he kicks the bucket?" Lopez could scarcely control his emotions.

Miller pulled up a chair, sat down, stared at the floor, and started explaining matter-of-factly. "It was Hansley's turn at surveillance last night. Instead of going to bed, the way most normal people do, Warner chose an after-midnight outing. Hansley tailed him to the Naval Research Laboratory, on Overlook Avenue. You know the place."

Miller looked up, waiting for a response.

"Of course I know the place! Barbara works there. You *know* that."

Miller stared back at the floor. "Well, I *do* know that...which is why I wanted to make sure I had your attention."

Lopez walked to his desk, plopped himself down, and folded his hands in front of him. "I'm listening. Go on."

Miller straightened in his chair. "Warner leaves his residence at one-thirty this morning. Hansley tails him to NRL. Because NRL is a closed compound, Hansley stays in his car outside the gate at the end of the parking lot while Warner goes inside. Hansley figures he'll just wait until he returns. That's around two o'clock." Miller caught Lopez's eye. "Here's the part that'll blow you away. At two twenty-five, a blue Dodge Intrepid pulls into the lot. Three people, two women and a tall black man, get out and go inside."

Lopez's eyes opened wide and he rocketed to his feet. "Are you telling me that was Barbara? Last night she told me she had to go to work for a special project and would be out most of the night. Then, this morning, she left a message on our answering machine while I was in the shower, saying she'd get back to me later today."

Miller nodded. "Yes, but wait; it gets better." He took a breath. "At two thirty-five, Warner comes *flying* out of the building several steps ahead of the black man and the two women. Hansley gets out of his car and runs up the parking lot, hiding in the shadows."

Lopez held up two hands, straight fingers from the right touching perpendicularly the palm of the left, signaling time-out. "The person we've identified as Dr. Clement Warner is being chased out of the building by three people…one who's my *wife?*"

Miller stared back. "Affirmative."

Lopez, alarmed, blurted out his next question. "Jesus Christ! Is Barbara okay?"

Miller raised both hands, palms out, facing Lopez. "Don't worry, Hector. She's fine."

Realizing that Miller would have told him if something had happened to Barbara, Lopez inhaled deeply and commanded himself to calm down. "Okay, go on."

Miller continued. "Warner has a pretty good lead on the black guy and decides to climb over the fence. Okay?"

Miller paused and stood up. "Here's the part that wasn't any too pleasant. The fence has strands of barbed wire at the top. You've seen them, at an angle, to keep people from climbing in. To make a long story short, Warner managed to fall through the barbed wire."

Lopez grimaced at the thought. "Are you telling me Warner died from a few scratches inflicted by a barbed wire fence?" He shook his head back and forth, disbelieving.

Miller countered, annoyed. "It was more than a few scratches, Hector. He even lost an eye in the process. You weren't there. Hansley said it was horrible…but no, you're right. The black man and the second female, not Barbara, witnessed what happened next. He killed himself! He used the classic poison in the ring trick and died within a minute."

Lopez sat down, slumped back in his chair, and pondered the meaning of what he had just heard. Knowing he couldn't escape, Warner decided he had no further options. *A damn shame!* Although Lopez wouldn't mourn Warner's passing, the considerable downside was that the agency had lost its chance at learning what secrets Warner had given away over the years. Of course, Lopez consoled himself, if they had never identified Warner in the first place, he would still have suffered the same fate. At the least, they had the benefit of knowing their mole was now dead.

Miller interrupted Lopez's train of thought. "If you think what you've just heard is strange, get a grip as to what the clincher is!"

Lopez frowned, wondering what could be more improbable than what he had just heard.

"The black man was your friend! Victor Silverstein? You remember his colleague, Linda Kipling? The female who single-handedly almost took out Ghali in Fort Collins?"

Lopez stared back, incredulous. "Barbara's never met Silverstein! I know that for a fact. What the hell is going on here?"

Miller went on. "Following Warner's untimely end, Hansley impersonated an undercover cop who happened to be passing by and took a full report. It was lucky for us none of them had ever met Hansley. I've got to hand it to him. He realized there was more there than a simple burglary. He called in Clean-up. So, we have the body."

"Good idea."

"Chemistry did a preliminary on the poison. Looks like curare. He was gone in less than a minute. And, catch this." Miller bit his lip. "Warner's ring was one sophisticated piece of engineering. It had two separate bladders attached to a curved, mini-injector. Our people still haven't figured out what's in the second—"

Lopez, impatient, interrupted. "So what else did they tell Hansley? What's their connection with Warner, for God's sakes?"

"I was getting to that. Here's the part that ties the loose ends together. Your wife said Warner was her sponsor at the Office of Naval Research."

Lopez, unable to contain himself any longer, flew to his feet and screamed. "I can't fuckin' believe this! We've been after this goddamn mole for years, and now I learn *my wife* has been having a one-on-one relationship with him?"

Miller sighed. "She never knew he was a mole, Hector. She may not know it even now. Warner obviously fooled people considerably higher up the food chain than Barbara. Don't blame *her* for chrissake!"

Lopez capitulated. "You're right, Marc. It just blows me away this guy has been sitting practically under my nose for God knows how long."

Miller stood, walked to the desk, and sat on the edge. "Hector, we've got to concentrate on the here and now. And figure out what all this means."

Lopez touched the ends of his fingers together into the shape of an upside down V, rested his lips on the peak, looked across at Miller, and replied. "You're right. For a change, let me summarize what we know so far. Correct me when I get out of line."

"Okay."

"First, what you've just told me suggests that Warner used Barbara in some fashion. Barbara does research; that's what she does. That implies she was doing something for Warner without the knowledge there was anything illegal or untoward about it." Lopez paused and pointed his right index finger at Miller. "About a month ago Barbara told me she had a new project that had to be completed within weeks, that there was some urgency. She worked day and night."

Miller nodded, his eyes now closed tight.

"Second, Silverstein…" Lopez paused as he noted Miller's head suddenly jerk upward. "What?"

Miller's eyes opened and he slid off the side of the desk. "Don't you see?"

"See what?"

"Whatever Warner was involved in, it somehow relates to Silverstein. Did Barbara ever tell you what she was working on?"

"No. She's too cagey for me."

"Just look at the connections we now know. Hector, they're *not* coincidental! When we identified Warner, we established his link with Hamasay…Ghali. Right? Now, we find out that Barbara worked for Warner. Who shows up now? Silverstein! Who tried to kill Silverstein in Colorado? Ghali! Do you see the circle? Where is—"

Miller's cell phone interrupted his final sentence. He scanned the screen and looked up at Lopez. "It's Hansley." Miller pushed the receive button. "Yeah, Averill…yeah…yeah…you don't say…when? I'm here with Hector now…I'll tell him…bye."

Lopez studied Miller's reactions, his exasperation getting the better of him.

Miller pocketed the phone. "The last thing I was going to say before the phone rang was *Where is Ghali now?*"

Lopez responded tersely. "We know for a fact he's in Bermuda. The Mensa team's still crowing over their triumph with the embedded chip." (When the Mensa geniuses had a success, they weren't shy in letting everyone know about it.)

Miller continued. "When I told Hansley earlier that Barbara was your wife, he decided to keep an eye on her for a while. Figured you'd want that. An hour or so after the incident, they left NRL, the three of them together. Hansley tailed them all the way to Dulles."

Lopez's eyebrows rose at that statement.

"Thirty minutes ago, they flew out on a chartered jet." Miller's eyes bored in on Lopez. "I'll give you one guess where they're headed."

CHAPTER 36

▼

TURBULENCE

Chartered Cessna Citation, 560 miles southeast of Washington, DC.
Thursday morning, 0725 EDT, September 20, 2007

This time he found himself in a tall tree, of all places. "Get off me, Cameron. What are you doing?"

Silverstein struggled to free himself, but seemed powerless under Fitzby's mass astride his middle. Silverstein turned his head to look down, realizing that the slightest slip from their precarious perch would hurl them both headlong to death. Worse, the wind had come up and rocked the branch not only sideways, but up and down.

With all his strength, Silverstein swung his right hand around and caught Fitzby square on the side of his head. The force of the blow knocked him off balance and he lurched to the side. Rather than fall cleanly away, he held on to Silverstein's body as they rotated to the underside of the branch. Silverstein managed to wrap both arms around the bough, and now hung vertically, with Fitzby's arms hugging Silverstein's waist.

Fitzby looked up and offered encouragement. "Hold on. I'll climb up your body, crawl to the top the branch, and pull you up."

Slowly, Fitzby inched his way upward until he had a handhold, finally removing his weight from the dangling Silverstein. Fitzby climbed atop the branch and looked down. Silverstein, dangling from one hand, thrust out the other. Fitzby grabbed and pulled. With Silverstein halfway up, Fitzby hesitated.

Silverstein looked up. "Keep pulling, Cameron. I'm just about there."

As Fitzby's eyes telegraphed his intent, Silverstein remembered again, always too late, that he had trusted the wrong person.

Fitzby smiled as he said the words. "I think it's time you joined Sylvia."

With that statement, Fitzby released his grip. Silverstein fell into the abyss and screamed aloud.

"Wake up, Victor. Wake up!" Startled by a second voice to accompany his fall into the deep black hole, Silverstein opened his eyes and stared blankly at Kipling.

Startled by the outburst, Lopez lifted her head and looked across at Silverstein. Her seat, as well as Kipling's, faced the rear of the airplane, with Silverstein facing forward, directly in front of Kipling.

Kipling immediately unlashed her seat belt and knelt across the distance between the seats. She stared upward into the eyes of Silverstein, who was obviously embarrassed. "We'll get there in time. Hang in there."

Kipling returned to her seat.

Lopez watched this minor display of affection play itself out. Kipling obviously cared a great deal about her boss. And, based on her quick thinking back at the office, Lopez concluded that this was one female not to be messed with.

Soooo, Lopez thought to herself. Across from her sat the famous Dr. Victor Mark Silverstein, the person Hector said had saved his life. Although Silverstein wouldn't know it, Lopez had earlier memorized the features of this handsome stranger. She had developed that technique in college—to study someone's face without looking directly at them.

Stranger? Hardly! Although she had known him less than eight hours, what they had experienced together in so short a time made it seem much longer. Lopez knew that to be a natural response. Her grandfather, a

World War II veteran, had explained how spectacular, memory-searing events that occur over the space of mere hours can make permanent imprints on your brain.

Discovering Warner in her office at two-thirty in the morning, riffling through her computer, had been the first of two culminating shocks, adding to everything else that had happened the previous day. Silverstein's offer to fly to Washington had been a godsend. She now had two others with whom to share her burden. Warner's subsequent, horrible death would make Silverstein and Kipling lifetime partners, if in memory only.

Warner's actions and suicide, together with what Silverstein and Kipling told her, convinced Lopez that a terrorist attack on the east coast of the United States was underway. It didn't take much convincing on Silverstein's part for her to accompany them to Bermuda to locate Fitzby, and for Lopez to redirect Hurricane Noel before it was too late. Only she could pull that off. She had been the one to supply the software—and if things didn't go as hoped for, the one to blame.

Lopez looked across, straight into the eyes of Silverstein. She wanted to come right out and thank him for having saved her husband's life, but knew that now wasn't the moment. There would be time enough for that later.

Silverstein lowered his head and stared at his watch. In the last hour and a half, their flight had gone from smooth to bumpy. Repeatedly, the seat belt tugged at his waist.

"Try to get some shuteye, why don't ya?" he had articulated earlier to his two traveling companions. As if to demonstrate the soundness of his own advice, Silverstein had pushed back into the plush leather seat and closed his eyes, trying hard to appreciate the five thousand dollar per hour (double the normal rate because of the weather) it was costing him to rent this Citation Bravo. An aircraft that would cover the eight hundred plus miles to Bermuda in less than two hours. Silverstein knew he wouldn't be able to sleep. Even if he did, his dead-tired body convinced him he could avoid Fitzby this time around. He had been wrong on both counts.

Silverstein's first thought of flying to Bermuda commercially proved short-lived. All scheduled airlines had discontinued service as of last night. Hurricane Melissa's Category 2 winds were already lashing the island paradise. The only way he could convince the charter service to fly at all was to sign off on their conditions: "...safety is paramount, Mr. Silverstein...we'll try our best to land the plane, but you must understand that if we can't, we'll return...and because of Noel, probably not to Dulles."

Back at Barbara Lopez's office, Silverstein had briefly considered calling Hector Lopez and asking for assistance, to enlist the considerable resources of the CIA. It would have been a tough pill to swallow—and their *only* option had they not found a charter aircraft to get them to Bermuda. Hector Lopez had hardly been forthcoming in sharing information. But beyond that, Silverstein worried that he could not predict Lopez's reaction. This was not the time to go in with guns blazing. Silverstein knew their only hope at averting this disaster lay with him. With luck, they would get there in time to convince Fitzby to alter Noel's path.

When they left Lopez's office, Hurricane Noel lay one hundred twenty miles southeast of the Delmarva Peninsula and had grown even stronger, attaining the awesome and rare, Category 5 rating. Reconnaissance aircraft reported maximum winds approaching two hundred ten miles per hour, a veritable beast of a hurricane. Already, hurricane force winds lashed the southern tip of the peninsula. Aircraft reports from when Noel lay far from shore documented a pressure-induced storm surge of greater than two feet within the eye.

State governments in Delaware, Maryland, and Virginia readied their National Guard troops. Newspapers, television, and radio alike warned those living along the Delmarva Peninsula, the Chesapeake Bay, and the Potomac River to pack up and leave immediately. Experts warned that once the swirling waters beneath Noel touched bottom, the combined effects of wind and low pressure would force storm surge to attain heights of twenty feet or more in the shallows. The National Weather Service predicted flooding on a massive scale and catastrophic devastation.

Embarrassed, Silverstein avoided looking across at his traveling companions, both staring at him after his verbal outburst from the dream.

"I apologize. Please forgive me." Silverstein looked up, sheepishly, at Lopez.

For the first time during the flight, Lopez's face took on some expression. "Apologize? What for, for God's sake?"

Kipling placed her hands on her knees, straightened her back, and laughed. "You have to forgive Victor. He has difficulty expressing weakness in front of a female. Ignore him for a while and he'll get over it. I speak from experience."

Silverstein smiled back across the aisle, directly at Lopez. "Dr. Lopez, I should have warned you about my colleague, Dr. Kipling. She carries around, perpetually, a deep sense of the absurd, thinking that the female of our species can get along just fine without her counterpart. I assure you, it is *I* who speak from experience!"

Silverstein's commentary broke the tension. Everyone laughed.

Lopez's laughter turned into a grin that transitioned into a look of concern. "What do you think our chances are?"

Silverstein heaved a sigh. "Here's the way I'm hoping it'll play out."

Back in Lopez's office, once they all knew what was happening, Silverstein's rush to the telephone to locate a charter aircraft left no time for elucidation. "When I last checked, Noel lay one hundred and twenty miles southeast of the Chesapeake Bay. His speed has been steady, twenty-five miles per hour toward the northwest. Fortunately, for us, he's slowed some. But once he leaves the open ocean, we'll have no chance at turning him around. There'll be too little water on which to train the laser. That gives us a little under five hours." Silverstein checked his watch again. "Our northerly flight path to avoid Noel hasn't helped. We've already used up two hours and—"

The PA system crackled and the pilot spoke. "We're twenty minutes out and starting our descent. Unfortunately, we have to fly smack-dab through the middle of this bastard. Cinch in those seat belts, folks, and hold on. I gotta tell you…right now, it doesn't look good. Crosswinds on the runway are gusting to forty-five knots."

Turbulence had increased steadily the past half hour, although it had been minor at the thirty-seven thousand foot level during most of the flight. Things would get interesting once they started down through the core of the hurricane, Silverstein knew. He looked back and forth out each side of the plane: Mountains of clouds passed by; in and out of rain showers; an occasional cloud-to-cloud lightning strike; updrafts and downdrafts that pitched the plane about.

Silverstein considered it a downright miracle that the charter agency had any pilot who would agree to fly into Bermuda under these conditions. As it happened, Captain Raymond Winchester, from his earlier days as a navy pilot flying hurricane reconnaissance, had flown WC-121s into hurricanes for a living. To Silverstein's added surprise, he learned that Winchester had piloted the same prop-driven Super Constellations in the early days of Project Stormfury. The copilot, thirty-five years his junior, with the imprudence of youth, volunteered quickly.

Silverstein blessed the fact that charter pilots were not subject to the sixty-year-old retirement threshold that plagued airline pilots. When the Joint Typhoon Warning Center (JTWC) discontinued routine operational flights into Pacific typhoons back in 1987, a steady supply of pilots with that sort of flying experience diminished considerably—although Air Force Reserve and NOAA pilots continued to fly Atlantic hurricanes. In a typical year, far more typhoons developed over the Pacific than did hurricanes over the Atlantic.

Silverstein continued. "Anyway, our only hope is to hightail it to Fitzby's operations in the city of Hamilton. It's about thirty minutes west of the airport, according to Avery."

Following his earlier call to the charter service, Silverstein had phoned the Bermuda Weather Service. Luckily, Jim Avery was working the night shift. Silverstein explained the situation and that they were on their way. Avery said he and another forecaster, Marsha Kendall—who he said had a vested interest in the place where Fitzby worked—would be waiting at the airport. But, he also expressed concern. He explained that Bermuda's primary runway lay east southeast by west northwest. Melissa had transited slowly up the east side of Bermuda—which would place it in perfect position to generate crosswinds at the airport. Fitzby had thought of everything, Avery volunteered.

"What the hell was that?" The jet had dropped suddenly. Lopez's face turned ashen. "I've got to warn you; I don't do well in stormy weather."

Silverstein pulled tight on his seat belt. "Cinch your belts as tight as you can stand it. We'll be fine. Some years ago, I took flying lessons. I'll always remember what my flying instructor told me. *'Don't worry about the airplane,'* he said. *'She can take a lot more abuse than you can'.*"

Silverstein smiled but felt his stomach quiver. He could talk the talk, but he had never flown into anything like this either.

Again, the intercom. "Sorry about that, folks. But it may get worse. We're punching through twenty thousand now, seventy miles out. We've turned and are flying in from the southeast, to land on three zero. Get ready to see the view of a lifetime. The eye of Melissa is dead ahead."

Silverstein watched as the plane traversed in and out of the feeder bands that spiral out from a hurricane's center. Within another minute, it was as if someone had turned out the lights—they were in the soup. The low sun angle, together with layers of clouds, robbed the air of light. Turbulence increased. During the earlier descent from thirty-seven thousand feet, there had been a few large pockets of up and down air. Now, the plane rocked steadily, in all dimensions, some jolts sharp and some gradual. The stiff wings of the relatively small plane transmitted the shocks, undiminished, through to the passengers.

Based upon the last satellite images that he examined back in Lopez's office, Silverstein pictured in his mind's eye the plane's likely position relative to the hurricane. The good news, which Silverstein recalled from his training in Tropical Meteorology, was that they would be entering Melissa from the right rear quadrant (based on the directional movement of the hurricane). The two trailing quadrants were typically the least violent of the four hurricane divisions. The bad news, and which Silverstein thought it wise not to tell Lopez, was that their final descent to the runway, once they cleared the eye, would be through the eye wall once again in the opposite, stronger northwest sector of the storm—not as fierce as the right front quadrant, but strong nonetheless.

Suddenly, as if the plane had driven from a bumpy road onto a bed of cotton, all became smooth. The pilot's voice articulated the sense of the moment. "Ladies and gentlemen, take a gaze. None of us will likely have this opportunity again in our lifetimes."

Silverstein and Kipling undid their seat belts and knelt on the floor looking out the windows adjacent to Lopez on the starboard side of the plane.

To add to the majesty of the setting, the sky around the plane swelled with filtered light, although heavily muted this early in the morning. Their aircraft now flew within a cathedral of clouds that stretched high to the sky. Looking north, they saw the eye wall. Silverstein marveled over what appeared to be a reasonably defined eye. It was one thing to pore over satellite pictures, to study the eye and related storm structure from a photograph taken from space, and yet quite another to witness this awesome energy up close and personal.

Silverstein stepped across to the port side. From there he looked down on the low stratocumulus that hid much of the water from view. Hurricane eyes were rarely devoid of clouds. Looking south, the eye wall had a jagged appearance more befitting its violent nature. Looking ahead, Silverstein saw the beckoning wall of the eye to the west. His stomach tightened and his hands, earlier sweaty, now turned clammy. He turned to look at Kipling, still facing the window and appreciating the grandeur of one of God's most magnificent creations.

"Get back in your seats and hold on!" barked the pilot from the overhead speakers. Silverstein and Kipling fastened their seat belts mere seconds before the first litany of renewed abuse ensued. All three grabbed their belts and pulled. It was as if hell itself had unleashed its fury upon the tiny aircraft. The nose suddenly pulled upward, and then just as fast downward. The pilot was having a hard time controlling the aircraft.

The voice of the pilot returned, completely calm and controlled, but discontinuous—the way a child would talk when bounced on his or her father's knee. "We've picked...outer marker...fifty-five hundred feet...twenty-two miles out. If the plane holds together, we'll make it to the airport."

Silverstein looked across at his two companions. He pretended not to see Lopez's head shake sideways following the pilot's final statement. Silverstein was sure his own complexion had dropped a notch on the color scale; this was a terrifying experience. Kipling, ever the brave soul ready to handle anything, held her arms stiffly to the side, hands gripped to the underside of the seat, her face stoically glued to the window. Lopez revealed more concern. On the color scale, her face registered ghost white.

Aside from the cracking and moaning sounds emanating from the airframe itself, the fury of the storm added more. An occasional lightning bolt would light up the outside as if an old-fashioned flash bulb had exploded outside each of the jet's windows. Silverstein recalled the old rule of thumb: For every count to five between the lightning strike and thunder meant one mile of separation. Unfortunately, with the last strike, that separation had decreased to zero.

The ensuing detonation sounded as if they had ringside seats *inside* an exploding bomb. Simultaneously, Lopez screamed aloud, barely audible above the accompanying melee. Tears streamed down her face, even though her eyes closed tightly. Silverstein looked over and saw her lips forming words, probably a prayer.

Winds howled against the aircraft from the starboard side. The aircraft crabbed significantly into the wind; the pilot was skidding the plane sideways, doing his best to follow the electronic signal that would guide them to the end of the runway. To complement the wind and thunder, bullets of rain hammered against the aluminum skin.

Again, the speaker. "Eighteen hundred feet…five miles out…fifty knots crosswind, they're reporting. If it's…high, there's no way we can land."

Silverstein's body dripped with sweat. And this time, it was not from fear of dying. The true import of this flight seized Silverstein. Unless they landed, Fitzby and Hamasay would succeed. Hamasay would achieve his objective, for whomever he worked for, and Fitzby would have his vengeance on those who had questioned his brilliance.

Silverstein trained his eyes through his window and prayed for the ground to come into view. He had done a quick check of Bermuda's airport over the Internet before they left Lopez's office. Runway Three Zero was the precision approach runway. Had they been able to land visually, they could have flown in from the northwest and avoided most of the hurricane. Three Zero could handle only Instrument Landing System Category I landings—which meant the electronics were good enough to get them down to two hundred feet above the runway before the pilot had to call off a landing. Silverstein knew that the winds, more so than ceiling height, would likely dictate their chances of landing.

"I see water!" Kipling yelled above the wail of noise cascading around the interior of the jet.

Silverstein looked down at his watch and then out the window. Minimal light illuminated the sky outside the aircraft, even though it was now nine o'clock Bermuda time. Layer upon layer of clouds above the plane drained the sky of daylight.

Finally, Silverstein saw water too. They were less than five hundred feet above the surface, he estimated. He saw land ahead, and with turbulence less than before—a good sign. Unfortunately, with due respect to the rock singer Meatloaf's vocal entreaty, Silverstein knew that two out of three wasn't enough. Too much crosswind would make the landing difficult. The pilot had earlier informed him that thirty-five knots was the airport limit for crosswind landings. The airplane appeared to be crabbing about thirty degrees to the right, not an encouraging sign. Under these extreme winds, when a pilot would necessarily come in hot, the difficulty of a landing compounded.

At once, when Silverstein concluded they would make it, Silverstein felt the powerful thrust of the jet's engines; the aircraft angled up sharply. Over the intercom came the words, "We're going home!"

Silverstein yelled out an expletive and then a command. "Go around and try again!"

Above the roar of the engines, the howling wind, and the bullet-like crescendo of the rain came the reply over the intercom. "Crosswinds are running fifty-five knots. It would be suicide to touch down."

Silverstein released his seat belt and immediately felt himself thrown to the roof of the aircraft and then back to the floor. Wincing from the pain to his left knee and right arm, he dragged himself past the slack-jawed Kipling and the now immobile face of Lopez. He took a quick look to make sure the latter was still alive. The plane rocked back and forth as he pulled himself forward. Just before he reached the door to the cockpit, the jet's nose pitched up sharply. Silverstein felt himself thrown backward past both sets of seats to the rear of the aircraft. In the process, his body turned and his head struck the front panel of the lavatory. The blow proved painful, but Silverstein remained clear-headed. He instinctively reached to his face and his hand came away red.

Silverstein tried again. Thanks to a few seconds of relative calm, he made it to the cockpit door this time. He yelled at the top of his lungs. "Go back and try again!"

Both pilots turned as Silverstein hurled again to the ceiling and back to the floor. "What the hell are you doing? Get back to your seat! You'll get us killed."

Silverstein prayed for a few moments of calm. To his relief they came. He struggled to his feet and looked forward. He could see the altimeter rising fast. The Cessna, with its twin Pratt and Whitney's, had plenty of power to get out of trouble fast.

Silverstein, trying to ignore the pain in his knee, arm, and now head, said the first thing to come to his mind. "Have you heard of Hurricane Noel?" Once the words left his mouth, he realized he had to do better.

The pilot, more than annoyed, and fighting the plane at the same time, replied. "In case you've lost your bearing, we're trying to survive Hurricane Melissa here. I don't give a damn about Noel."

Silverstein scanned the sides of the plane looking for handholds and then focused all his energy into getting the words right this time. In light of the circumstances, Silverstein marveled at his polite elocution.

"Gentlemen, you must listen to me! My name is Dr. Victor Silverstein. My colleagues and I are scientists from the Naval Research Laboratory. Noel isn't an ordinary hurricane. Noel is a terrorist weapon controlled by a lunatic in Bermuda. Our only hope is to get to him before the hurricane achieves landfall. If we get there in time, we *might* be able to turn the storm around. If not, there'll be an environmental disaster comparable to 9/11. I beg you! You've got to try again."

Silverstein struggled to stay on his feet, one arm braced against the ceiling and the second gripped tightly to the doorway, with feet and knees clawing for a hold any way possible. The pilot looked over at the copilot and was the one to reply. "Are you *serious?*" Winchester turned to face Silverstein for an instant. "Are you telling me *that's* why you chartered this plane? You're the only ones who can stop it?"

"That's what I'm telling you."

Winchester shook his head in seeming disbelief. "Damn...I can try...but the chances are good we'll get blown off the runway and crash."

Silverstein responded with no hesitation. "Will we walk away from the wreckage?"

"Probably...but my career will be over and I'll lose everything. I can't do that to my wife."

Silverstein paused to contemplate his next action. He reached behind his back and pulled the weapon from his pants. To his relief, it was still there. Silverstein yelled again, to be heard above the rapid-fire rain pelting the windscreen.

"You have my word. No matter what happens, your career will be intact. You will tell the authorities I threatened you, that you had no choice. On my parents' honor, I will not contradict that statement."

Silverstein, his right hand now shaking uncontrollably, thrust the firearm between the two pilots. "This gun tells me, no matter what it takes, you will put this aircraft on the ground."

Startled, both pilots simultaneously turned to face Silverstein. By now, Silverstein's right eye blinked continuously. Blood flowed steadily down his forehead. In no more than an instant, Silverstein and Winchester exchanged a tacit understanding. Winchester ended the conversation. "Go back to your seat and look after that wound."

Silverstein crouched on the floor and crawled backward down the aisle. The thought of what he had just said made him sick to his stomach. Would his own career and life lie in shambles at the end of this day?

He looked down at the weapon still gripped tightly in his right hand. The fact that he had not yet had time to load any bullets into the gun's firing chamber was irrelevant.

CHAPTER 37

▼

BEST LAID PLANS

Unit 606, Atlantis, Hamilton, Bermuda: 32° 17'43"N Latitude, 64°46'54"W Longitude
Thursday morning, 0830, September 20, 2007

Cameron Fitzby peered out the window of his sixth floor apartment, the city of Hamilton bathed in darkness from a combination of the steady downpour and the early morning hour. A flicker of light from his computer screen drew his attention. He returned to his laptop and stared. He couldn't believe what just popped up on his screen. *What the hell's going on here? How did he do that?*

The past week had played out precisely as Fitzby had planned. From the day Ghali had given permission to proceed, Fitzby chose and nurtured three tropical cyclones in their movement across the Atlantic. Synchronization proved critical for cyclones two and three, requiring careful orchestration to position them where they needed to be, simultaneously.

Tropical Storm Lorenzo, number one, whose timing had been less significant, nonetheless held ultimate import in setting the stage for maximum devastation from number three, Hurricane Noel. Lorenzo saturated the banks and surrounds of the Chesapeake Bay and Potomac River. Ghali seemed impressed and, much to Fitzby's surprise, offered a compliment to Fitzby's forethought (since the beginning of their relationship, Fitzby counted only two times when Ghali had provided any positive feedback). Hurricane Melissa, number two, would stand as sentry to the island during the final decisive hours.

All had proceeded well. Noel moved steadily toward his destiny and Melissa lurked in position just east of Bermuda, guarding Fitzby's base of operations from any assault from the water or air. Since Ghali had failed to eliminate Silverstein, as Fitzby had demanded, it didn't hurt to play it safe. It was one thing to accept Ghali's ineptitude and quite another to tempt fate in case Silverstein decided to ride in on his white horse at the last minute. Fitzby's mother had always chided, *fate is what you make it.*

Melissa had earned her keep. All airlines had cancelled service to the island. Although Fitzby couldn't keep Melissa in place much longer (he had demonstrated earlier, both numerically and in practice, that it was much easier to control a moving cyclone), Melissa's protective shield wouldn't be needed much longer. Mere hours separated Fitzby from his vengeance on the Washington establishment that had ignored his brilliance for so long.

Fitzby pondered Ghali's unusual disposition these past days. He had been strangely quiet since returning to Bermuda, saying little, much to Fitzby's relief. Fitzby had mixed feelings about Ghali anyway and, at this critical stage, Fitzby required solitude. Besides, he wanted to relish in peace the final moments he had anticipated for so long.

Despite Ghali's more mannered, civilized demeanor, Fitzby concluded that his earlier planned precaution to operate separately from Ghali during the final hours of their operation was a prudent one. So, a month earlier, he had leased a one-bedroom apartment in a relatively new luxury complex in downtown Hamilton, only a mile from Anselina. Because of the frugal nature he had projected to his co-workers, Ghali would not expect him to rent such an upscale unit. Nonetheless, he had accomplished all the legwork on days off to minimize the chance of someone following him from work.

Fitzby had purposely chosen a location within walking distance of Anselina. Except for bringing in a few sticks of furniture, stocking some food, and testing his computer interface (and always late at night, to lessen the likelihood of a co-worker noticing him), he went there as little as possible to ensure his refuge remained secret. Three days ago, he had stashed his car in a rented garage.

It was yesterday afternoon, then, when Fitzby quietly walked away from the facility he had named, built, and nurtured. He had no desire to look back. His future, and preeminence in the scientific world, existed in the future. Leaving a note for Ghali explaining how he would control the final machinations of Melissa and Noel was a courtesy Ghali didn't deserve.

Fitzby stared again at the screen. He found the blinking message so unexpected that he caught his breath:

> *I need you HERE during these final critical hours! I've spent too much money and effort to have it all riding on a phone connection.*

Fitzby marveled to himself that Ghali had figured out how to send him a message. Well, no matter, thought Fitzby; he can send all the messages he wants. *That doesn't change the fact that I'm here, he's there, and that's the way it's going to stay. Besides, Ghali needn't be worried. Does he think I would risk anything going wrong?* Even if the electricity went out, Fitzby had batteries to power his end of the operation. He knew he could count on Ghali to fire up the Anselina generators.

Fitzby had tested repeatedly his digital cell phone connection and felt confident of its durability. If for some reason the wireless connection did fail, he could transfer to a landline. Fitzby had checked that latter mode of communication only once; he knew Ghali could trace such a call back to his apartment. Should the unlikeliest of scenarios befall, that both wireless and landline connections failed, he would simply walk back to Anselina. Ultimately, no amount of fear would keep Fitzby from his destiny.

The winds from Melissa shrieked outside Fitzby's window. That, together with Fitzby's concentration on the words in front of him, made him oblivious to the rapping sound in the background. Before long, the clamor grew louder and words accompanied the sounds.

"*Açın!* Open up!"

That Ghali was the voice behind those words brought a chill to Fitzby's very being.

CHAPTER 38

▼

CRASH LANDING

Five miles east of Bermuda International Airport
Thursday Morning, 0910, September 20, 2007

Kipling watched as Silverstein crawled back toward his seat—but not before another pocket of air hurled him halfway to the ceiling of the small aircraft and back to the floor again. His face contorted in pain as blood flowed down the right side of his head. Kipling released some tension in her seat belt, reached across, and held on to him as he climbed into his seat. He finally latched the seat belt and gave a strong tug.

Kipling caught Silverstein's eye and looked at a visibly shaken man. For the first time, she noticed he held a gun in his right hand. He proceeded to place it in his waistband. *Where the hell did that come from?* Kipling unzipped her fanny pack, removed a wad of tissues, and handed them across. He rewarded her with a feeble smile and a right-handed thumbs up.

Judging by the aircraft's turn and Silverstein's demeanor, Kipling concluded that he had talked the pilot into making another approach to the runway. Kipling knew why he had called off the landing. From her game warden days, flying into tiny airports deep within the Rockies, Kipling understood the inherent difficulty of landing in a crosswind.

Kipling settled back into her seat and prepared for the next iteration of turbulence, sure to match the first. She peeked to her left, to check on Lopez. Kipling had become increasingly concerned about her behavior. It wasn't clear at all whether Lopez would live through the landing, no matter if the plane survived intact or not. Her eyes darted continuously about the cabin, wild with fear. Kipling reached over and grabbed Lopez's shoulder, to offer some comfort. At once, Lopez reacted, but not in the way Kipling had hoped. Fortunately, Kipling recognized the signs and handed Lopez a barf bag. The only positive effect from the cacophony of sounds emanating through the airplane was that Lopez's retching appeared as a silent movie.

Kipling settled into her seat and did her best to control her own fear. They flew back out over the ocean and repeated their descent toward the runway. The pilot had been wrong; fate was giving them a second chance to marvel at nature's majestic creation. Turbulence during their second approach matched that of the first.

As they once again approached the runway, Kipling strained out her window to see the ground. Interestingly, there had been no pilot comments during this second try. *What had Victor said in the cockpit?* When darker shades of the ocean finally penetrated the overcast from below, because her seat faced backward in the plane, she turned her head to look forward. Good news, she thought. She could make out the runway lying straight ahead. What didn't make sense, at first, was why the pilot appeared to be flying toward the control tower. Abruptly, Kipling understood. They were flying sideways to counter the northerly crosswinds. To compound matters, the plane rocked back and forth, from one wing tip to the other. If that happened when they were near the ground and a wing tip caught, as Martha Stewart would probably agree, it would be a *bad* thing.

As Kipling had experienced hundreds of times in commercial airliners, she watched as the earth rose to greet them. Looking down, she knew they were coming in *hot*, standard procedure for erratic winds or when a sudden loss in wind speed could stall the aircraft.

Within ten feet of the runway, the jet suddenly rocked left and then right. Kipling could still see the tower. At the last instant, the pilot straightened the plane, aligning it with the runway. Simultaneously, the starboard wing dipped and Kipling prepared for the worst. At once, she felt the impact but held her breath when she realized they had touched down on one wheel only.

The jet rolled several hundred feet when two things happened in quick succession. The plane leaned left to catch the other rear wheel. An instant later, Kipling heard the thrust reversers kick in. The twin jet engines whined loudly in unison. In another second, the front of the plane lowered and Kipling could sense all three wheels on the runway.

Winds continued to buffet the jet. The run down the runway was a frightening one, with the pilot fighting to maintain control. The plane swerved left, then right, then left again. While the jet engines wailed into the thrust reversers, Kipling felt the brakes contributing to slow their velocity. At one point it became obvious that they were hydroplaning sideways; they would slide off the runway! She prayed the tires would reassert their grip, and they did. When they came close to a stop, the pilot quickly turned the plane into the wind and the plane vibrated to a halt. A moment of relative silence ensued.

Over the intercom came a relieved voice. "Ladies and gentleman, by all rights we shouldn't be sitting here…"

The pilot hesitated, listening to a transmission over the radio. Suddenly, he gunned the engines and pulled off the runway. He continued. "As I was saying, by all rights we should now be climbing out of a twisted tube of metal. If you're of the belief we're born with nine lives, you now have one less…and if that isn't enough to make my day, you wouldn't believe what the tower just told me. The idiot in the Lear Jet that's been following us all the way from Washington is on the approach right behind us."

CHAPTER 39

▼

CRESCENDO

Anselina Corporation, Hamilton, Bermuda: 32°18'20"N Latitude, 64°47'20"W Longitude
Thursday morning, 1015, September 20, 2007

Silverstein stared ahead at the windswept, rain-drenched street. Vegetation uprooted from the northerly winds lay strewn across the roadway, having made the drive from the airport one of avoiding obstacles. According to Avery, the Anselina building was ahead, to the right, on a slight slope that led to the ocean. Silverstein knew that Cameron Fitzby had to be inside. Would he be able to control his emotions and address the problem at hand? *Forget about Sylvia. Your anger is irrelevant. The fate of millions of people is at stake here. That's what's important. Stay focused!*

Silverstein removed his weapon from his jacket pocket and, for the second time since leaving the airport, checked to make sure it was loaded. Jim Avery, sitting to his right and driving the car, noticed and appeared worried.

"Hopefully, it'll never come to this," Silverstein reassured him, admitting a lie.

Kipling, sitting in the back seat between Lopez and Kendall, saw Silverstein's lips move but could hear nothing above the howl of the storm. She looked to her left at the partly comatose Barbara Lopez and to her right at Marsha Kendall, the second forecaster who had been waiting for them at the airport. It had taken two of them, Kipling and Silverstein, to walk Lopez from the airplane to the car.

The fury of the storm had prevented any meaningful conversation during the forty-minute drive from the airport to the city of Hamilton, where Avery said Fitzby worked. Their drive across the causeway from St. George's Parish brought back memories of Hurricane Fabian from 2003. Kipling recalled that four people had lost their lives when that hurricane blew their vehicles off the causeway. Water lashed at the rocks that bolstered the sides of the raised roadway, ahead of mountainous, white-capped waves. It took all of Avery's concentration to keep his small car pointed straight ahead. The Suzuki WagonR (a small car Kipling had never seen before), with its relatively tall stance, made an inviting target for the winds.

Kipling's mind snapped suddenly to attention. After weeks of deciphering strange SSTs and unusual hurricane activity in the Atlantic—and debating the sixty-four thousand dollar question of whether Cameron Fitzby was behind it all—they sat within a stone's throw of ground zero. *How would it all play out? Would they be too late?*

"Jim, park here on the street. No doubt they have surveillance cameras that would give us away."

Silverstein strained his eyes through the undergrowth that hid most of the building from view. Except for three cars in the parking lot, he saw no sign of activity around the medium-sized, concrete building. If windows existed, they were on the opposite, ocean side.

Silverstein looked in all directions and turned to face his passengers. "I have no idea what we're going to find here. My suggestion is that you all stay out here while I go investigate."

Jim Avery was the first to respond. "From what you've told me, they'll probably not even let you in the building. That building is a fortress. What are you going to do then?"

"Good question. I'll think of something."

Kipling spoke next. "You need me, Victor. I'm going with you."

Silverstein turned his head, understood, and nodded. He looked outside again through the windshield, willing the rain to moderate. It looked worse.

Silverstein, in the left seat of the right-drive car, turned himself completely around to face Lopez. "Barbara, you've got to pull yourself together! Once we get inside, you are our only hope at getting Noel turned around. You understand that, don't you?"

Although Lopez's face still registered fear, its intensity had ratcheted down two clicks. Silverstein looked into her eyes and was relieved to see again the soul of the woman he had met only hours earlier. Lopez nodded and blew her nose.

"Linda, let's walk ahead on the street and make our way in perpendicular to the side of the building. I don't see any fence. If there are cameras, they probably face the parking lot. Okay, let's go!"

Silverstein and Kipling opened their doors into the gusting wind. He estimated its force at about fifty miles per hour—bad, but not so severe they couldn't fight their way forward. They walked, crouched, some hundred feet to a break between the trees and then dashed the eighty feet to the side of the building. Silverstein sighed in relief when he saw no windows.

Cameron Fitzby stared at his computer monitor, scanning both the visible and infrared images from the GOES East geostationary weather satellite. Although it had been a shock for Ghali to show up at his apartment when he did, being back at Anselina and able to witness Noel's steadfast progression on a high-resolution monitor had its advantages.

Fitzby sensed Ghali's presence over his right shoulder and felt it was time to brag. "Take a look. You will never again see anything so beautiful—a Category 5 hurricane, as perfect as you can imagine. Look at its size, the perfection of the eye! That eye must be fifty miles across. That's bizarre! Usually, the bigger the storm, the smaller the eye."

Fitzby pointed to the screen. "There are very few clouds in the center. You can see right down to the ocean waves. Miami is reporting Noel's winds outside the eye in excess of two hundred miles per hour." Fitzby couldn't help but grin. He had done it!

Fitzby rotated his head briefly to observe Ghali's reaction. "In another two hours, she'll be entering Chesapeake Bay proper. You and your people will have your holocaust. I predict the damage will exceed that of 9/11."

Puzzled over Ghali's silence, Fitzby swiveled his chair to face him directly. Ghali's response proved far different from what he expected. His eyes lay deep and drawn, hair disheveled, expression numb. Confused, Fitzby searched for meaning in Ghali's eyes, but saw nothing.

Fitzby turned back to his screen. If Ghali didn't want to partake of the excitement and joy to follow, that was his choice, thought Fitzby.

Silverstein and Kipling stood flat against the southern masonry wall of the building, temporarily shielded from the rain that rode in on the back of the northerly winds. It hardly mattered; their clothes had few dry spots remaining. The mild temperatures together with their bodies' adrenaline kept them from shivering.

Kipling looked at Silverstein. "Any bright ideas?"

"Not really. How 'bout you?"

Kipling turned sideways and smiled. "I was hoping you'd ask. Here's the way I see it. Somehow, we've got to trick them into opening the door. We could approach from the front but there are cameras there and—"

Silverstein interrupted. "Wait a minute. Do you hear that?"

"Hear what?"

Silverstein cupped his hands to his ears. "Of course!" He stepped around Kipling and gestured that they should walk to the rear of the building. He turned to face Kipling. "Did you notice during our drive from the airport, most houses had some lights on?"

"Yeah, so what?"

"Did you also notice about a half mile back, the lights went out? I'll bet you Fitzby has a generator to provide backup power."

As they walked, the sound of a combustion engine became unmistakable. Silverstein peered around the corner. Attached to the building proper stood an enclosure surrounded by a chain-link fence open to the sky.

Inside the enclosure pulsed the methodical reverberation of a diesel engine.

Silverstein gave a thumbs-up sign. "That's all we have to do. Temporarily cut the power to the building. Someone will come out."

Kipling nodded.

Examining the building's eves to ensure no video cameras protected this area, they stooped and walked the perimeter of the enclosure, looking for an entry. Through the cracks between the wooden slats that created a visual barrier, Silverstein confirmed his suspicion—inside stood the electrical generator. On the opposite side, they found a gate, but with a padlock attached.

Silverstein linked his two hands together and gestured with his head. "We've got to go up and over. Here...I'll lift you up. Take a look, okay?"

Kipling lifted her right foot onto Silverstein's hands, balancing herself with her left hand against the fence and her right hand on his head. "Go."

Silverstein lifted Kipling three feet off the ground, enough for her head to peek over the eight-foot fence. Silverstein waited.

Kipling angled her head downward so she could be heard above the wind. "Looks good! There's a single door that opens outward. The coast is clear."

"Okay. Over you go." Silverstein lifted Kipling slowly, to the height of his shoulders. From there, she raised her left leg over the fence, grabbed tightly the smooth top of the fence with both hands, and then brought her right leg over as well. Silverstein peered through the fence to make sure nothing lay beneath her. Once over the side, she lowered herself down to the extent of her arms, paused briefly to look down, and dropped the remaining inches to the concrete surface.

Silverstein repositioned his handgun from his front to his back waistband, checking the safety as he did so. He leaped, grabbed the top of the fence with two hands, and struggled to get his left foot across the top. Once he did so, he raised himself farther with the muscles in his arms and shoulders and brought the other leg smoothly over the top. Before jumping to the concrete beneath him, he looked down. Kipling stood waiting.

Once inside the enclosure, Silverstein took stock of their situation. The enclosure revealed nothing more than what they thought it was, an addition to the building to house the generator. A single metal door led to the building. He now had to figure a way to temporarily stop the generator, but not do any permanent damage in the process. Once he and Kipling took control of the situation inside, they would need electrical power.

It soon became clear to Silverstein there was no on/off switch. The controls to the generator lay, protected, inside the building. The simplest idea would be to cut off the fuel. It would be a simple matter then to restart the fuel-starved engine later. He needed only to find a suitable connection along the fuel line where he could create a temporary break. He had had the good sense to bring along his Leatherman and proceeded to open the tool to expose the pliers. He was about to begin turning the hex nut at the end of the feed line when he saw Kipling waving her hands frantically.

Kipling placed one hand on the door handle and pointed to it with the other. "It's open," she mouthed.

Silverstein held both hands palms up, rolled his eyes and then closed the Leatherman. Incredulous, he walked over to confirm Kipling's diagnosis. Halfway there, he stopped and thought.

He walked the remaining distance between them, cupped his hands and spoke directly into her ear. "Fitzby isn't a fool. It could be a trap."

Kipling turned and put her mouth to his ear. "What difference does it make? We have no choice, do we?"

She waited to judge his reaction and when she saw none, she turned the doorknob and pulled.

CHAPTER 40

▼

ŞEREFLI BIR ADAM

*Anselina Corporation, Hamilton, Bermuda: 32° 18'20"N
Latitude, 64° 47'20"W Longitude
Thursday morning, 1025, September 20, 2007*

Fitzby, sensitive to such things, noticed the sudden change in air pressure immediately. Someone had opened either a window or an exterior door. He looked around quickly, alarmed to confirm that the remaining skeletal staff sat within eyesight. Ghali in his office straight ahead, and the two Russian technicians overseeing their equipment to the far right. Only two doors led to the outside, the main entrance and the single exit to the electrical generator. *Did someone go out to check the generator and forget to lock the door?*

As he scooted his chair back to look down the hallway toward that door, the words reached his ears before he saw the mouth that spoke them. "There's still time to redeem yourself, Cameron. Turn Noel around!"

Ahead of Silverstein sat Cameron Fitzby, looking toward the voice that had startled him. The open door hadn't been a trap. *They had simply forgotten to lock the back door!* Silverstein stood straight-legged, his arms parallel with the floor, his .38 Special pointed at Fitzby's chest, ten feet distant. His training at the firing range told him he was reasonably accurate at this range. Though his heart raced, his hands held steady. He reminded himself that he had unlocked the safety. Unfortunately, he had arrived at that moment in his nightmares when Fitzby would now talk his way out of the situation, get the upper hand, and condemn him to an eternity looking for Sylvia.

Fitzby leaned back in his chair and smirked.

That's it, thought Silverstein. The open door had been a trap. It had happened so many times before—this *was* all a dream. He shook his head to waken himself. Nothing changed. The figure seated in front of him spoke.

"You're too late, Victor. I've preprogrammed the software to take Noel exactly where I want. You've always underestimated me. Deep down, I knew you would come." Fitzby sighed. "Frankly, I'm disappointed though. I thought you'd get here sooner."

The adrenaline in Silverstein's body overcame the fog of fatigue and the disquieting sense that all would soon disintegrate into disaster. "It's not too late, Cameron. You've proven everything you said at school. Turn Noel around and take credit for your brilliance. I beg you, Cameron!"

Fitzby sat straight in his chair and replied, "I can't, Victor."

"Why can't you?" Silverstein stood firm.

"Look out!"

Silverstein heard the voice and at the same time sensed quick movement from his left. Kipling shoved him to the floor. A shot rang out and the glass from an office door exploded behind them. Silverstein and Kipling crawled quickly behind the bank of computers that lined the wall in front of Fitzby.

A loud voice punctuated the room. "The reason he can't, Dr. Silverstein, is that he works for *me!*"

The sensation of déjà vu was more than Silverstein could believe. "Is that you, Mr. Hamasay? Every time I run into you, it seems like I'm crawling around on the floor and you're standing there shooting at me. Maybe you and I could come to some kind of agreement this time. Despite our earlier encounter, I sense you are a man of honor. Is that not so?"

The voice replied, seemingly from the same position. "I *am* a man of honor, Dr. Silverstein."

"Then why do you want to kill thousands of people and cause untold damage to the United States? Is that the sort of behavior that comes from a man of honor?"

To Silverstein's surprise, Hamasay paused noticeably. He spoke in a restrained manner. "You do not understand, Dr. Silverstein. There are many forms of honor. My duty is to obey my superiors. There is no greater honor."

"I would disagree with you, Mr. Hamasay. There is an honor to your creator. And I must tell you! I have an obligation to my superiors as well. Lay down your gun and surrender. Otherwise, I will kill you."

Kipling looked over and seemed satisfied with Silverstein's choice of words. At the same time, she pointed to the other end of the three-foot gap behind the computers and the wall. There was an opening there and she crept in that direction. Silverstein grabbed at her pant leg. She looked back. Silverstein stretched out his hand and handed her his .38. Kipling understood in an instant and grabbed the firearm. She kept crawling.

Silverstein could hear Hamasay stepping closer. "I have the upper hand here, Dr. Silverstein. I am the aggressor; you are the hunted."

Silverstein turned his head to see that Kipling had reached the end of the crawlspace. She sat in a crouched position, gun in two hands. "You forget that this time, I have a firearm as well and I will use it."

"Dr. Silverstein, don't make me laugh. I carry a Colt .45 caliber. I noticed you have a .38. Do you think that little toy worries me?"

Silverstein searched for words that would give Kipling more time. "I'll grant that you have the bigger gun, but I have something much more powerful."

Hamasay's voice came closer still. Silverstein looked down toward Kipling and raised three fingers in the air. Kipling nodded. Silverstein raised one finger, and then two.

Hamasay retorted with a mocking reply. "And what would that be? Is your cavalry waiting outside, Dr. Silverstein?"

Silverstein raised three fingers.

Everything then seemed to happen at once.

Silverstein looked down to see Kipling leap sideways from behind the end of the computers and disappear from view. Silverstein knew he would remember the anger behind her words for some time to come. "No, it's me, you son of a bitch! This is for Colorado."

Three shots rang out in close succession.

Time to move; Hamasay was distracted. Silverstein crawled sideways, crouched, and leaped toward the last sound he heard from Hamasay. Fortunately, as Silverstein looked up, he found Hamasay where Silverstein thought he should be. And, unfortunately, still standing! To Silverstein's relief, Hamasay did not hear his rapid approach until the last instant. Hamasay had his right arm raised and pointed down toward Kipling.

Silverstein caught Hamasay's body full and pushed him back. His .45 roared and the shot flew wild. They crashed backward together, overturning a chair and a computer monitor before their bodies landed on the floor.

Silverstein considered the positives. Kipling *must* have hit Hamasay. Further, Silverstein would be coming down hard on top of him. Unfortunately, as they flew through the air, across the chair and the monitor, Silverstein became aware of one significant negative: Hamasay maintained a firm grip on the pistol in his right hand.

Kipling thought she was a goner when the huge caliber firearm came to bear in her direction. She had aimed for the head but, as she slid across the floor, all three shots hit low in the area of the shoulder. Although Hamasay flinched, her bullets had not had their desired effect. Luckily, he hadn't noticed Silverstein until it was too late.

Kipling stood quickly and took stock of the room. Silverstein and Hamasay hurtled together to the floor straight ahead. Two men were rushing out the front of the building to her right. Ahead, and to her left, sat Fitzby, seemingly in a trance. But not for long.

Fitzby jumped from his chair and ran down the hallway. Kipling wanted to shoot Fitzby and get it over with, but common sense prevailed.

Barbara Lopez came along as their insurance policy, but a weak one. They needed Fitzby to get Noel turned around.

With this thought in mind, Kipling lowered her weapon and took off after Fitzby. He had a head start and reached the rear door several steps ahead of her. She saw the door slam ahead. She thought quickly. He had no time to unlock the padlock and so, Kipling concluded, he would climb the fence.

Kipling opened the door, rushed out, and realized too late she had misjudged Fitzby's plan. The down-rushing rain temporarily blinded her to the steel pipe that came flying around the corner, catching her square on her upper body. The fact that her peripheral vision caught sight of movement an instant before contact spared her from a worse fate. She turned sideways. The force of the blow hit between her right back shoulder and her rib cage. The gun fell from her hand.

Kipling winced from the pain, but she had experienced worse. Luckily, she thought, there was only the pain—she hadn't lost her wind. Remembering experiences as a child on the soccer field, when she had the breath knocked out of her, Kipling knew that would have incapacitated her and she would have been ripe for the kill.

As it happened, the impact of the blow also forced her away from Fitzby by about a yard, giving her a precious second of time before the expected onslaught. She looked down to see her gun lying at Fitzby's feet. He detected the movement in Kipling's eyes and backed up a step. His decision to crouch down to retrieve the weapon gave Kipling the opportunity she needed.

Kipling lunged forward, both hands clawing for the pipe before Fitzby could initiate a backswing. She arrived at Fitzby's feet, flat on the rain-soaked concrete, but with her left hand firmly grasping the one-inch diameter weapon.

Fitzby proved no match for Kipling's fighting skills. At once, Kipling took her right hand, placed it behind Fitzby's left ankle, and yanked. Fitzby flailed with his free left arm, but to no avail. His back came crashing down on the hard concrete, his right foot still planted on the ground. She removed the pipe and threw it aside.

Pent-up anger that had lain dormant—since Mississippi, where she had learned of Sylvia's rape—exploded to the surface. Now enraged and wanting to inflict the maximum amount of pain, Kipling seized the gun by its barrel and came down with all her might on Fitzby's groin. "This one's for Sylvia."

Fitzby's body convulsed and he howled in pain. Within seconds, he turned himself onto his stomach and started vomiting. Kipling picked herself up and looked down at the pathetic human being lying in agony in front of her.

Her anger built further. Still holding the weapon by the barrel, Kipling leaned over and took a full swing, hitting a glancing blow off the side of Fitzby's right ear. "That one's for Victor."

Fitzby recoiled in pain, screamed, and retched again into his own vomit. Kipling pulled Fitzby's legs to the rear so he was lying straight and his back cleanly exposed. Kipling laid the gun to the side.

"And this one, Mr. Fitzby, is for me." Kipling stood to the side of Fitzby, looked down to make sure he wasn't going anywhere, jumped slightly into the air, and came down squarely with her butt in the middle of Fitzby's back. She felt his chest compress as the air whooshed from his lungs.

Kipling rolled off to the side and looked over. The unmistakable sound of someone who had just had the wind knocked out of him was the effect Kipling had aimed for. She reached over to retrieve the .38, crouched, and waited, rain pouring down steadily. Slowly, painfully, Fitzby began to breathe.

Kipling knelt, inched over to Fitzby's head, stuck the barrel of the gun sharply into his bloodied right ear, and placed her mouth up against his left.

"If it were up to me, I would kill you right now for what you did to Victor..."

*   *   *   *

Silverstein stood with his back toward Hamasay, waiting for Kipling to return. Their earlier fight, such as it was, hadn't lasted long. Although Silverstein had come down hard on top of him, Hamasay maintained control of his weapon. Silverstein had ended up directly facing its barrel.

Hamasay spoke hastily. "Dr. Silverstein, I do not wish to kill you. This time, my magazine is full."

Remembering the loss of another of his nine lives back in Fort Collins, when Hamasay emptied his ammunition clip prior to Silverstein's attack, Silverstein decided that prudence did have its virtues. He awkwardly rolled off Hamasay and acquiesced.

Silverstein got to his feet and looked around the medium-size room for signs of Fitzby and Kipling. He vaguely remembered hearing running footsteps and assumed Kipling had chased after Fitzby.

Silverstein looked back to see Hamasay stand up slowly, all the while his gun pointed toward Silverstein's backside. Blood streamed from Hamasay's left shoulder and that arm hung limply at his side. Putting aside the effects of the gunshots, he hardly looked the part of someone who stood at the doorstep of success for a critical mission.

Hamasay backed up a foot or two and then surprised Silverstein with his next comment. "In Fort Collins, you warned me that Mr. Fitzby's character was flawed. Please tell me, what did you mean?"

Silverstein turned and, for the first time, looked carefully into the face of the man responsible for the upcoming environmental disaster. What he saw was not what he expected. He didn't see hatred, only sadness. Silverstein gave Hamasay a brief summary of Fitzby's crime decades earlier.

Silverstein realized he had an entry now. "I have granted your request, Mr. Hamasay. Would you allow me the same privilege?"

Hamasay nodded.

"Why are you doing this?"

Hamasay's response was slow and labored. "When I started this assignment, I had no idea it would lead to this. Never in my life have I conducted a senseless killing. I abhor my compatriots who do so."

"Then why do it? You still have the power to turn this around."

Silverstein heard a sound behind him and turned toward the hallway. He felt Hamasay rest the muzzle of the pistol against his head. Silverstein looked ahead and saw Kipling walking behind Fitzby, her gun to *his* head.

Hamasay spoke first. "Drop your weapon, Dr. Kipling. Unless you do, your friend will exist no more."

Kipling looked ahead, around the room, her eyes finally settling on Silverstein. Her gun clanked to the floor.

Hamasay pushed Silverstein ahead and gestured for Kipling to join him. He then waved his weapon toward Fitzby, indicating he should sit at Silverstein's right. At the same time, he motioned for Silverstein and Kipling to sit as well.

Silverstein glanced at Fitzby as he walked by and shuddered at what he saw. He looked up and noticed a similar reaction from Hamasay. Doubled over, Fitzby jerked forward in short, painful steps, breathing in halting, noisy increments. Bright red blood oozed from his right ear down his neck. He held his chest tightly with both arms.

Silverstein turned and stared at Kipling inquiringly. She held out her hands, palms up, and shrugged. Silverstein grimaced in reply.

Silverstein and Kipling sat together in front of the bank of monitors facing Hamasay, who stood. Fitzby sat to Hamasay's left, bent over, head in his hands.

Hamasay addressed Fitzby directly. "Mr. Fitzby, please look at me. I need your undivided attention."

Fitzby raised himself slightly.

"I need to know if what you said earlier is correct. You said that you had preprogrammed your software and that nothing can interfere with Noel's movement. How confident are you that is correct?"

Fitzby lifted himself farther upright, with obvious pain, grabbing the right side of his rib cage. He turned toward Silverstein and Kipling, a feeble smile attempting to replace his pained expression.

Fitzby spoke slowly and with difficulty. "I assure you, even the great Dr. Victor Mark Silverstein can't change its course now." He turned back to Hamasay. "You needn't worry. If it makes you feel any better, the situation now is even beyond my control."

Following this last statement, Silverstein felt a chill and shuddered.

Hamasay stared straight into Fitzby's eyes. "Speaking on behalf of my people, I thank you for your contribution to our cause. You will be rewarded in the afterlife as our creator sees fit."

With that statement, Hamasay raised his .45, aimed it at a startled Fitzby, and fired. The explosion from the large caliber handgun reverberated inside the room. Silverstein and Kipling instinctively pushed back in their seats, their mouths agape with horror. The force of the large caliber slug hit the left side of Fitzby's chest, forcibly ramming him backward over the rear of the chair. Fitzby slid to the floor in a crumpled ball.

Silverstein turned to face Hamasay, who stood staring at Fitzby on the floor.

Hamasay recovered, looked up, and faced Silverstein. "A few minutes ago you asked me why I couldn't go back on my commitment to avert the disaster I have created. I know that what is happening is wrong. Beyond that, I must honor those with whom I have entrusted my loyalty. I have no choice in this matter, Dr. Silverstein."

Hamasay paused and drew a deep breath. "Dr. Silverstein, I have one further request. If anyone should ask, please tell them that an Egyptian who goes by the name of Ghali is, indeed, *şerefli bir adam*, a man of honor."

Silverstein saw it coming a full second before it happened but reacted too late. A quick shout was all he could offer. "Hamasay! No!"

With those two words, Hamasay turned his weapon around, placed it deep within his mouth, and fired. For the second time in as many minutes, the room shook from the detonation. Hamasay slumped to the floor.

Silverstein and Kipling sat speechless. Not wanting to breathe, Silverstein listened as the room turned silent—except for the rasping sound to their immediate right.

*   *   *   *

Fitzby opened his eyes and felt warmth and moisture both within and outside his body. He saw light in the distance. He sensed no pain. Beyond the light, his mother, Anselina, beckoned, wearing her negligee that was his favorite. But he didn't want to go—not just yet! He would attend to her needs soon enough.

"Cameron, can you hear me?" The voice sounded distant and close, both at the same time. A dark-colored face interrupted the halo of light. Fitzby felt a hand cradle his head.

For a few seconds, clarity replaced fuzziness and reality replaced a vision.

"Victor, I'm sorry for what I did to Sylvia."

The hatred that Fitzby remembered from their last meeting twenty-five years earlier evaporated from Silverstein's face. "I forgive you, Cameron."

Fuzziness returned. Fitzby looked past Silverstein into the light above. He would now go to his mother, the only woman he had ever loved. She had died before he started college, leaving him all alone to fend for himself. Other women were pale imitations compared to her, unworthy of respect.

"I'm coming, Momma. It's time I put you to bed."

A different female voice entered his consciousness before Fitzby closed his eyes for the last time. "What does he mean by that?"

A male voice replied, thoughtfully. "I have no idea."

Silverstein looked away as Fitzby took his last breath. The veil of hate that had held him captive for nearly a quarter of a century dispersed into the ether. If God should see fit to take Silverstein from this earth at this moment, he knew he was ready. He felt at peace with himself and the world. God had blessed him with the tranquility that came with forgiveness. None other than his creator could bestow such a precious gift—not, certainly, Victor Mark Silverstein.

Kipling, kneeling on the floor next to Silverstein, turned, grabbed him gently by the shoulders, pulled him to her, and held him close. She whispered. "That part of your life is over; it's time to move on."

A loud knocking from the front of the building broke the mood of the moment. Silverstein drew back and looked at Kipling. "We don't have much time. Get Lopez!"

Kipling and Silverstein leaped to their feet. Kipling rushed to the front of the building. Silverstein, in a final show of respect, knelt down, picked up Fitzby's shattered body, and carried it to one of the side offices. He then did the same for Hamasay.

Lopez, Avery, and Kendall rushed into the room. They stood temporarily in awe of the destruction and bloody mess that panned before their eyes.

Silverstein spoke first. "Barbara, it's show time." He paused, walked over, his eyes boring into hers. "Tell me you're back with us in one piece. It's now or never."

An exhausted face smiled weakly in reply. Silverstein breathed a sigh of relief at what he saw. Eyes that shone clear and focused.

"Let's do it!" she replied.

Not knowing where to start, Silverstein spoke to all four people now staring at him. "Let's all do what we can."

Immediately, Lopez drew up a chair, sat down, and began entering UNIX commands onto the keyboard facing one of the monitors. The other three grouped around Silverstein who had finally noticed that one of the screens in front of him carried the GOES visible image of hurricane Noel. He felt temporarily buoyed when he saw that the position of the hurricane had not changed much, sitting farther from the coast than he expected. That sense of relief evaporated when he realized the image was thirty minutes old. He refreshed the display and gasped.

"Noel's only thirty miles east of Virginia Beach. That means we have less than an hour. If Noel enters the Chesapeake Bay, we're screwed."

Silverstein realized he needed to take charge. "Jim, Marsha! I want you to monitor the storm. I want to know what it's doing every step of the way."

Avery responded. "We have two things going for us. Once Noel started up the coast, NOAA and air force planes began providing position reports twenty-four/seven. Then, three hours ago, NOAA decided to switch to a Super Rapid Scan mode for GOES. That means we'll have imagery every sixty seconds, compared to the usual thirty minutes."

This was the first good news Silverstein had heard. "That's a real break for us. When we start firing the laser, we'll need to get instant feedback from you two as to its effect." Silverstein paused and pointed at Avery. "Bring up the track on the monitor so we can visualize Noel's..." Silverstein paused and then continued. "The aircraft can do better. Get NHC on the phone. Tell them we need continuous position reports from the aircraft radar."

Silverstein halfway turned toward Kipling, but then rotated back. "One more thing! There were two guys here who spoke Russian, who left the room when things got exciting. Did you see them when you came in?"

Kendall responded. "They're sitting in their car. They rushed out of the building in an awful hurry."

Silverstein turned to Kipling. "Linda, go get them and find out what they do here. We may need them."

With everyone now having a job to do, Silverstein pulled up a seat next to Lopez. He sensed she now had total control of herself. Lines of code streamed down the screen.

Without diverting her gaze from the screen, Lopez spoke. "I've got to give this Fitzby guy some credit. He's actually made some changes to the code I wrote, not an easy thing to do. I see what he's done though. Nothing that affects the basic idea behind the software." Lopez hesitated. "Wait a second!"

"What?" Silverstein stared at the screen.

"He preprogrammed a geographic route for the storm, from the time it started up the coast from Florida."

"Where does he have it going from here?"

"West and then almost straight north, up the Chesapeake."

"That makes sense. Based on what we know about Hamasay, Washington was probably their target. There's so little water area in the Potomac.

The Chesapeake route gave them a much better chance of controlling Noel. Even so, all bets are off once he leaves the open ocean. I don't think there'll be much control then, in any event."

Silverstein looked to his left and saw Kipling escorting two men, and talking to them in what sounded like Russian. A moment later, Kipling relayed that they were in charge of the laser. Silverstein asked her to ask them if the laser was fully operational. Kipling gave Silverstein a thumbs-up sign.

"Houston, we have a problem." Lopez looked closer at the screen.

Silverstein turned back to Lopez, exasperated. "Now what?"

Lopez scanned a column of numbers before she spoke. She turned to Silverstein. "Except for Melissa, the last time the laser fired was over three hours ago!"

"That's impossible!"

Lopez continued. "I'm looking here at the code. The laser fires only if two conditions are satisfied. First, the user, through my software, decides when and where to fire the laser. But there is a second limitation." Lopez turned to face Silverstein. "An input from the laser satellite itself makes the final decision to fire."

Silverstein's mouth dropped open. "Check to see what the control is, but I think I know. Fitzby's original design utilized a cloud classifier built right into the satellite, to identify the clouds the laser would fire through. Fitzby knew that if the clouds were too thick, the laser beam wouldn't be strong enough to penetrate."

Silverstein stood, started pacing, and then suddenly stopped. "Oh, my God!" He understood what Fitzby meant earlier.

Avery and Kendall, alarmed at the outburst, turned. Silverstein rotated his body on one foot. "Jim, Marsha! I'm afraid to ask. What's the synoptic situation over the Chesapeake? Bring up the navy's Web page in Norfolk."

Avery replied, "I don't have to go there, Victor. We've been following this all day and it's not what you want to hear. There's an upper level trough over the Ohio Valley and a surface high sitting off the east coast."

Silverstein slammed his right fist against his open left hand. "I can't believe this! That son of a bitch thought of everything. He timed the arrival of Noel so that even if the laser couldn't operate because of clouds, the steering flow would carry it northward toward Washington."

Silverstein twisted back to look at Kipling. "That's what he meant when he said it was beyond his control."

Kipling responded, her eyes registering defeat. "Does that mean we can't do *anything?*"

Except for the wind outside, the room registered only silence. Silverstein paced the room, replaying his earlier conversations with Fitzby back in college. It took nearly a minute of walking back and forth before Silverstein recalled one tiny detail from twenty-five years earlier.

Silverstein rotated on his heels, everyone facing him with downcast faces. "There may be one loophole in Fitzby's plan."

Silverstein barked a command to Lopez. "Go through the code and see if, somewhere, there isn't one other rule that prevents the laser from firing."

Lopez replied. "Where would I look? The control code is thousands of lines long. It would take me hours."

Silverstein's response exposed his panic. "We don't have hours, goddamn it! Let me think!" Quarter century-old conversations streamed through his brain.

Silverstein closed his eyes. When he opened them again, he spoke to Lopez. "In the software you wrote, is there anything that refers to the hurricane's shape, eye, or anything like that?"

Lopez was quick to reply. "Yes! I used pattern matching and fuzzy logic to determine nearly every characteristic of the hurricane, from the size of its eye to the length of the feeder bands."

Silverstein brought his right hand to his head. "That's it! Do a search to see if there is any controlling statement that depends on the eye or its size."

Lopez turned back to her screen and started typing. Thirty seconds later came her answer. "You're right!" She took off her glasses and moved to within inches of the screen, as if being closer to the set of instructions would make them more comprehensible.

Lopez responded to Silverstein. "He added a line that says the laser will not fire anywhere within the hurricane's eye."

Silverstein let out a deep breath. "Listen up, everybody! Fitzby based his theory on controlling the storm by heating ocean water outside of the storm's path. I once asked him why he chose not to heat water within the eye itself. He said that the eye was usually too small and, besides, his calculations persuaded him he had more control if he heated the water away from the center."

Silverstein looked around the room, catching everyone's eye individually. "That's our only hope." He pointed toward the GOES image. "As you can see, the entire area is covered with clouds; only the eye is reasonably clear. I say we train the laser on the northeastern corner of the eye and blast the hell out of it. All we have to do is nudge it slightly, enough to turn it back out to sea."

Silverstein walked close to Lopez. "Barbara! First, stop the laser from firing at Melissa. Second, disable Fitzby's code for the eye and program the laser to address Noel."

He then turned to Avery. "Jim, Marsha! Load the latest image and give Barbara the coordinates for the northeast quadrant of Noel's eye."

Silverstein faced Kipling. "Get the Russians aboard. Tell them that if they don't keep the laser operating, I will personally telephone Vladimir Putin to complain."

Within a minute, Lopez turned to face Avery. "It's done. Give me the coordinates."

Silverstein noticed, for the first time since entering the room, that the ocean-side windows looked out onto a sea of water, churned up, but not too badly since Melissa lay to the east of Bermuda. He walked closer and looked down toward the water at what must have once been a boathouse. Old, rusty rails led to the sea. Something of importance from days long gone, thought Silverstein.

An arm reached around him and squeezed. He looked to his right and stared at Kipling who looked straight ahead at the magnificent ocean landscape. He had learned more about her in the past two months than he had in all the years they had worked together. He couldn't imagine ever again meeting someone as brave or as passionate.

"We're ready, Victor!" Lopez's voice echoed through the room.

Without moving a muscle, he gave the command. "Do it!"

Twenty seconds passed. Back came the reply. "Okay, it's working; we're hitting it with everything we've got."

In another instant, the quiet of the room erupted in sound. An explosion from the front of the building brought everyone to their feet. *A bomb? What now? Hamasay's friends?* Before Silverstein had the presence of mind to remember where he last saw his gun, two men exploded through the inner doorway, guns pointed forward, jerking side to side.

Silverstein's heart pounded hard, but for only an instant. "Hector, what took you so long?"

Lopez and Miller, still on guard, scanned the room for threats and when they saw none, lowered their weapons and stepped forward.

Lopez spoke. "We're lucky to be here at all. You should have stuck around for the show. I'm in hock to the agency for one Lear Jet."

Abruptly, two words filled the air simultaneously.

"Barbara!"

"Hector!"

One Lopez ran across the room and enveloped the second in a big hug. Silverstein smiled at the obvious display of affection.

There was nothing to do now but wait. While Kipling brought the new arrivals up to speed, Silverstein walked quietly past them to the far side of the room, to the office where he had placed Fitzby and Hamasay. Silverstein sat down and looked at their crumpled, bloody bodies.

Silverstein reflected on all that had happened. Fitzby had apologized for Sylvia. Whether his words were sincere or not, Silverstein forgave him. As Silverstein had concluded, when he left Penn State so many years earlier, God would have the final say on Fitzby.

As for Hamasay, Silverstein understood he knew little of the man, not even the name by which he wished to be remembered. Perhaps he was an evil human being, perhaps not. He certainly had loyalty to his superiors— and, in Hamasay's mind, that counted for everything. In the end, though, Hamasay knew his actions were evil. Would God treat Hamasay differently from Fitzby? One apologized for his actions, while the other stood firm in unwavering, steadfast conviction.

At once, the room behind him erupted in shouts and exclamations.

"It's turning!"

"We've done it!"

Silverstein turned briefly to appreciate the words he heard and nodded.

He stared down one last time at Fitzby. Twenty-five year old images rushed back in a torrent: Sylvia with her high-pitched laugh; her parents telling him about her suicide; the confrontation with Fitzby after Silverstein discovered the truth.

The emotion from those memories, and from the totality of this single moment in time, detonated in Silverstein's heart, his head, and in his eyes. He lowered his face into his hands and sobbed uncontrollably.

EPILOGUE

---▼---

From *The Royal Gazette*, Saturday, Sept. 22, 2007

Anselina Corp. vacates after employees involved in murder, suicide

By James Mayer
The Royal Gazette

HAMILTON, Bermuda—While Hurricane Melissa kept most residents indoors on Thursday, a murder and suicide played itself out in the island's capitol city. Details of the incident came to light Friday morning when police were called to the scene.

Two employees of Anselina Corp. were pronounced dead. Their names have not been released. Their bodies were discovered in the Winston Building, named after local entrepreneur, Sam Winston. This structure on Hamilton's north side had been vacant for more than a decade, until February of this year when Anselina signed a one-year lease.

Anselina Spokesperson Dennis Jiménez refused to provide any further information except to say that the deaths resulted from a long-standing dispute between the two individuals. Most of Anselina's employees came from outside the island. Those hired locally either said they did not know what transpired inside or declined to talk. Further efforts yesterday to discern additional facts concerning the organization and shootings proved fruitless.

A neighbor who wishes to remain anonymous concluded that, because of antennas installed atop the building, communications were important to the operation. Yesterday at 5 p.m., our reporter saw no antennas and, inside the building, found only office furniture.

Locals reported seeing men removing and loading equipment into trucks as early as 8 a.m. on Friday. Armed guards protected the site from onlookers, but would answer no questions from our reporter.

The vehicles, accompanied by the guards, drove to the airport late Friday morning. Airline grounds personnel said they observed the contents being loaded onto a C-130 cargo plane that had flown in following the airport's reopening on Thursday afternoon. The aircraft left immediately thereafter. Airport personnel said they had no information on the aircraft's payload or destination.

From *The New York Times*, Thursday, Sept. 27, 2007

Research finds no physical explanation for Hurricane Noel's sudden shift

By Herbert Longfellow
The New York Times

WASHINGTON, DC—While residents of the eastern shore are still cleaning up after Hurricane Noel's winds and rain, the threat of an environmental catastrophe a week ago has all but faded from the minds of the citizenry of the nation's capital.

Such was not the case last Thursday morning when Hurricane Noel was forecast to come ashore and wreak havoc on the waterlogged banks of the Potomac and Chesapeake. Although no fatalities have come to light, portions of the Delmarva Peninsula took the brunt of Noel's fury. Civil defense agencies reported significant coastal erosion there and some damage to homes and other structures.

Dr. Alfred Davis, a meteorologist from the National Hurricane Center in Miami, said the center's follow-up analysis found Hurricane Noel's movement unpredictable and "extremely puzzling." He said researchers could find no physical explanation why Hurricane Noel shifted direction so suddenly and turned back to sea. "All meteorological conditions were primed for the environmental disaster that was unfolding," he said. "It was as if God himself decided to intercede to spare the eastern seaboard from another tragedy."

Glossary

AI—Artificial Intelligence

a.k.a.—Another known alias or also known as

APB—All Points Bulletin

APSC—Asian Pacific Space Centre

Bathythermograph (BT)—an instrument that makes a record, as it falls through the water, of the temperature at various depths in the ocean

BWS—Bermuda Weather Service; operated on behalf of the government of Bermuda, by Serco Aviation Services, provides meteorological observations and forecasts as support for operations at the Bermuda International Airport, for the general use of the Bermuda public, for local marine interests, and yachtsmen voyaging to and from the US east coast, Caribbean and trans-Atlantic

Category 1—Saffir-Simpson classification for a hurricane with maximum sustained wind speeds from 74 to 95 MPH

Category 2—Saffir-Simpson classification for a hurricane with maximum sustained wind speeds from 96 to 110 MPH

Category 3—Saffir-Simpson classification for a hurricane with maximum sustained wind speeds from 111 to 130 MPH

Category 4—Saffir-Simpson classification for a hurricane with maximum sustained wind speeds from 131 to 155 MPH

Category 5—Saffir-Simpson classification for a hurricane with maximum sustained wind speeds of 156 MPH or greater

CIA—Central Intelligence Agency

Coriolis Force—a fictitious force that causes the apparent deflection of a body in motion with respect to the earth, as seen by an observer on the earth. In actuality, the movement is caused by the rotation of the earth and appears as a deflection to the right in the Northern Hemisphere and a deflection to the left in the Southern Hemisphere.

DoD—Department of Defense

Doppler Radar—a radar tracking system, now common in meteorology, in which wind speeds can be determined by measuring the Doppler shift of a radar signal reflected by objects (usually dust, bugs, or precipitation) in the air

DSL—Digital Subscriber Line

Easterly wave—atmospheric low-pressure system that forms over western Africa, north of the equator, and is often the precursor to tropical cyclones in the Atlantic (also known as a tropical wave)

ECMWF—European Centre for Medium-Range Weather Forecasts, located in Reading, England; an international organization supported by twenty-five European states

EDT—Eastern Daylight Time

Enhanced 911 (E911)—a cellular telephone service that locates callers for emergency dispatchers

EUMETSAT—Europe's Meteorological Satellite Organization; EUMET-SAT's primary objective is to establish, maintain, and exploit European systems of operational meteorological satellites

FBI—Federal Bureau of Investigation

FNMOC—Fleet Numerical Meteorology and Oceanography Center; the Department of Defense's (DoD) primary central production site for operational meteorological and oceanographic analysis and forecast products worldwide, Fleet Numerical is one of a half dozen internationally recognized operational weather centers and the world's leader in global oceanographic and coupled air-ocean forecasting

Geosynchronous Orbit—a satellite orbit above the equator (approximately 22,300 miles) in which the satellite's rotation rate around the earth matches the earth's speed of rotation, such that the satellite always sits above the same geographic location

GOES East—Geostationary Operational Earth Satellite, East; NOAA geostationary satellite assigned to monitor the eastern half of the United States and the western Atlantic Ocean

GPS—Global Positioning System; GPS is a series of satellites positioned in earth orbit. Developed by the US Department of Defense, this system allows users to determine their position anywhere in the world. Anyone can make use of this system, although location information for civilians is not as accurate as that for the military

Hurricane—a tropical cyclone located in the central or eastern Pacific, or the Atlantic, in which the maximum sustained winds are 74 MPH or greater

Hurricane names for 2007: Andrea, Barry, Chantal, Dean, Erin, Felix, Gabrielle, Humberto, Ingrid, Jerry, Karen, Lorenzo, Melissa, Noel, Olga, Pablo, Rebekah, Sebastien, Tanya, Van, Wendy

IR—Infrared

ITE—Image Transformation Expert; a makeup artist

JTWC—Joint Typhoon Warning Center; located at Naval Base Pearl Harbor, Hawaii, JTWC is the US Department of Defense agency responsible for issuing tropical cyclone warnings for the Pacific and Indian Oceans

Laser—an acronym for Light Amplification by Stimulated Emission of Radiation

LCD—liquid-crystal display; a method of displaying readings continuously, as on digital watches, portable computers, and calculators, using a liquid-crystal film, sealed between glass plates, that changes its optical properties when a voltage is applied

Meteosat—EUMETSAT's geostationary meteorological satellite program

MDT—Mountain Daylight Time

NCAR—National Center for Atmospheric Research; a federally-funded research and development center; together with their partners at universities and research centers, they are dedicated to exploring and understanding the atmosphere and its interactions with the sun, the oceans, the biosphere, and human society

NCARAI—Navy Center for Applied Research in Artificial Intelligence; part of the Information Technology Division within NRL; engaged in research and development efforts designed to address the application of artificial intelligence technology and techniques to critical navy and national problems

NHC—National Hurricane Center, located in Miami, Florida; one of three branches of NOAA's Tropical Prediction Center, NHC maintains a continuous watch on tropical cyclones from 15 May in the eastern Pacific and 1 June in the Atlantic through 30 November

NOAA—National Oceanic and Atmospheric Administration; conducts research and gathers data about the global oceans, atmosphere, space and sun, and applies this knowledge to science and service that touch the lives of all Americans

NPS—Naval Postgraduate School; an academic institution whose emphasis is on study and research programs relevant to the navy's interests, as well as to the interests of other arms of the Department of Defense; the programs are designed to accommodate the unique requirements of the military

NRL—Naval Research Laboratory; NRL is the corporate research laboratory for the United States Navy and Marine Corps and conducts a broad program of scientific research, technology and advanced development; headquarters and primary campus for NRL are located in Washington, DC.

NRL Monterey—Marine Meteorology Division of NRL, located in Monterey, California. Conducts a research and development program designed to improve the basic understanding of atmospheric processes and the atmosphere's interaction with the ocean, land, and cryosphere; to develop and implement automated analysis, prediction, and weather interpretation systems for Department of Defense users; and to study the effect of the atmosphere on Naval Weapons Systems

NRL Stennis—primarily, the Oceanography and Marine Geosciences Divisions of NRL, located at NASA's Stennis Space Center in Mississippi

ONR—Office of Naval Research; coordinates, executes, and promotes the science and technology programs of the United States Navy and Marine Corps through schools, universities, government laboratories, and nonprofit and for-profit organizations

OnStar—General Motors communications system

PIN—Personal Identification Number

Project Stormfury—a hurricane research project funded by the Department of Commerce in the 1960s. The project's goal was to determine if seeding a hurricane with silver iodide in the clouds outside the eyewall might reduce wind speeds by making the hurricane less wound up; the results were ambiguous

RPM—Revolutions Per Minute

SAM—Surface to Air Missile

SKIF—a secure space used for handling classified information and documents

SST—Sea Surface Temperature

SUV—Sport Utility Vehicle

Tropical Cyclone—a cyclone that originates over a tropical ocean area and can develop into the destructive storm known in the United States as a hurricane, in the western Pacific region as a typhoon, and elsewhere by other names

Tropical Depression—an organized system of clouds and showers/thunderstorms with a defined surface circulation and maximum sustained winds of 38 MPH or less

Tropical Storm—an organized system of strong thunderstorms with a defined surface circulation and maximum sustained winds of 39 to 73 MPH

Tropical Wave—an area of low air pressure embedded within the tropical easterlies (also known as an easterly wave)

Typhoon—the usual name for a hurricane in the western Pacific

UNIX—a computer operating system

UTC—Universal Time Coordinated, also known as Greenwich Mean Time (GMT), refers to time kept on the Greenwich meridian (longitude zero); times given at UTC are invariably given in terms of a twenty-four hour clock. UTC is five hours ahead of Eastern Standard Time

Cast of Characters

Avery, Jim: senior weather forecaster for the Bermuda Weather Service

Baxter, Bill: CIA agent who reports to Hector Lopez

Cooper, Chris: CIA agent and Image Transformation Expert (member of the Mensa team); invented the Cooper

Davis, Dr. Alfred: Jim Avery's contact at the National Hurricane Center

Fitzby, Cameron: principal antagonist, genius; Silverstein's college roommate who proposed a method to grow and steer hurricanes using a laser from space

Ghali (a.k.a. Ahmed Abu Hamasay): Blade of the Sinai agent; Fitzby's Turkish contact

Gulyanov, Colonel Alekseyev: former head of secret Soviet research facility; sells laser to Ghali

Hamasay, Mohammed: Ghali's brother who died during the 1967 Arab-Israeli War

Hansley, Averill: CIA agent who reports to Hector Lopez

Ishmael Twins: hit men who work for the Blade

Kendall, Marsha: junior weather forecaster for the Bermuda Weather Service; works with Jim Avery

Kenworth, Dr. Mary: associate superintendent at the Naval Research Laboratory in Monterey, California

Kipling, Dr. Linda: Silverstein's assistant at the Naval Research Laboratory in Monterey, California

Lopez, Dr. Barbara Ann: NRL expert in artificial intelligence; works for Clement Warner; wife to Hector Lopez

Lopez, Jr., Hector Rodriguez: CIA agent specializing in Counter Intelligence, husband to Barbara Lopez

Mercer, Dr. Anthony: Silverstein's oceanographic contact at the Naval Research Laboratory at the Stennis Space Center in Mississippi

Miller, Marc: CIA agent who works for Hector Lopez

O'Toole, Tom (a.k.a. Barry Emerson): CIA agent who infiltrates Anselina Corporation

Reston, Dr. Cynthia: CIA agent and physician (member of the Mensa team)

Sidki, Ali: Blade employee; gofer

Silverstein, Dr. Victor Mark: principal protagonist; preeminent navy scientist, former roommate to Cameron Fitzby

Warner, Dr. Clement: a mole of the Blade who has infiltrated the Office of Naval Research; reports to Ghali

Winston, John: CIA agent who reports to Hector Lopez